THE
OTHER
ME

THE
OTHER
ME

Sarah Zachrich Jeng

WITHDRAWN

BERKLEY
NEW YORK

BERKLEY
An imprint of Penguin Random House LLC
penguinrandomhouse.com

Copyright © 2021 by Sarah Zachrich Jeng
Penguin Random House supports copyright. Copyright fuels creativity,
encourages diverse voices, promotes free speech, and creates a vibrant culture.
Thank you for buying an authorized edition of this book and for complying
with copyright laws by not reproducing, scanning, or distributing any part
of it in any form without permission. You are supporting writers and allowing
Penguin Random House to continue to publish books for every reader.

BERKLEY and the BERKLEY & B colophon
are registered trademarks of Penguin Random House LLC.

Library of Congress Cataloging-in-Publication Data

Names: Jeng, Sarah Zachrich, author.
Title: The other me / Sarah Zachrich Jeng.
Description: New York : Berkley, [2021]
Identifiers: LCCN 2020054295 (print) | LCCN 2020054296 (ebook) |
ISBN 9780593334485 (hardcover) | ISBN 9780593334508 (ebook)
Subjects: GSAFD: Suspense fiction.
Classification: LCC PS3610.E5235 O84 2021 (print) | LCC PS3610.E5235
(ebook) | DDC 813/.6--dc23
LC record available at https://lccn.loc.gov/2020054295
LC ebook record available at https://lccn.loc.gov/2020054296

Printed in the United States of America
1st Printing

Book design by Ashley Tucker

For my family
I'd choose you every time.

Man defines woman, not in herself, but in relation to himself;
she is not considered an autonomous being . . . He is the
Subject; he is the Absolute. She is the Other.

—Simone de Beauvoir, The Second Sex

And choice, of course, the devil only knows what choice.

—Fyodor Dostoyevsky, Notes from the Underground

THE
OTHER
ME

1

Day One

IT'S MY BIRTHDAY, BUT IT ISN'T MY NIGHT.

I arrive at the gallery and the crowd swallows me, a forest of elbows and shoulders and plastic cups of cheap wine. Even in heels I can't see more than a few feet around me, but I can visualize the pigeon's-eye view. My best friend Linnea's paintings pinned to the walls by spotlight beams; the gallery floor a seething mandala of humanity bunching, circling, coming together, and separating.

I slip between the bodies, giving out smiles and one-armed hugs. A while back I dated a guy who liked to say he didn't know why people even celebrated birthdays. So you'd made it through another year—big deal. It wasn't as if it was an accomplishment. He was one of those people who are always trying to prove how little they care about things, and I, dazzled by good hair and carefully cultivated body funk, took way too long to pick up on it. Tonight, though, I almost agree with him. People wish me *Happy birthday* and it's all I can do not to reply, *So what?*

Sour grapes isn't a good look. It's natural to be envious of your best friend—particularly when she has a solo exhibition while you, at freshly turned twenty-nine, have yet to get your paintings into a real gallery—but it's not constructive. Linnea would be happy for me if our positions were reversed. I've come to her opening to support her, and I keep a smile on my face, but my heart's not in it. Ordinarily I'd be happy to soak up the class-reunion atmosphere: I keep running into people I haven't seen in forever. Everyone we went to art school with loved Linnea. Most of them loved me too—in the shallow and intense way you love like-minded people with whom you share a rite of passage—but in the past couple of years a lot of us have fallen out of touch, our interactions limited to liking one another's posts on social media. It's taken Linnea's getting gallery representation to draw us all to the same place. Success is more of a magnet than sentiment. People hope it'll rub off.

I wasn't always so cynical.

It's good that so many people came tonight. That means reviews, which means visitors, which means collectors. Which means money, not that Linnea needs it. Everyone asks whether I'm showing anywhere, and they don't seem surprised when I say I'm not. I choose not to feel insulted, the same way I choose not to get upset when people think it's their business that I'm still single. In my view, being unattached makes having a career easier, though I'm further away from a meaningful career than I was when I graduated from art school.

I finish my plastic cup of chardonnay and make my way to the bar for another. I'm usually more of a microbrews-and-craft-cocktails kind of girl, but I take what I can get for free. "Kelly!" I hear as I'm turning back toward the room, wine in hand, and here's Linnea, tall and goddess-like, the crowd parting for her the way it never does for me. She gives me a hug, then tugs me by the wrist to talk to a woman with the sleek, pinched look of an aging trophy wife. A collector. "This is the artist I was telling you about," Linnea says to her, and the woman smiles and extends a bejeweled hand. Linnea comes from a wealthy family, part of Chicago's Black elite, which affords her connections as well as the time and space to make work full-time. I try as hard as I can not to resent this.

The collector asks a few polite questions about my work and excuses herself, depositing my card in a snakeskin clutch that probably cost more than a month's rent on my apartment. Linnea stands off to the side in consultation with a slender man wearing a mustard yellow waistcoat and a well-tended mustache, someone who works for the gallery. I scan the crowd for people I haven't talked to yet, wondering idly what my life would look like if I quit. Stopped making the scene, stopped schmoozing people who might buy my work or put it in a gallery. Moved out to the country and rented a romantic tumbledown cabin where I could pile up unsold paintings undisturbed. It's the kind of dream only someone with money could realize, the same as the urban artist's life I'm striving for now. After I came to Chicago it didn't take me long to learn, contrary to any ideas I might have developed growing up in small-town Michigan, that there was nothing special about me. Nobody would catch sight of me lying on the sidewalk and see my sparkle and pick me up; I had to hustle like everyone else.

If I let go of expectations—my own and the ones I imagine others have for me—would I still paint? Maybe my fear of being seen as a failure, of being *ordinary*, is the only thing that keeps me going. But I've chosen this path, and I need to see it through until I can't anymore. And all things considered, I like my life. It's not perfect, but it's mine. I can look back and see the result of every choice I've made—not all of them good—leading me to this point.

Someone calls my name. Very distinctly, first and last: *Kelly Holter.* I look around, but no one seems to be searching for me. I see Bobby, Linnea's boyfriend, towering above the crowd, and start to make my way toward him.

All of a sudden, I'm not feeling well. If this were anyone else's opening but Linnea's, I would leave.

The warmth of the packed gallery, pleasant at first after the nip of the April evening, is stifling. The hard surfaces break the voices and music into a vicious babble. Dizziness washes over me. I feel a heave of nausea and change course toward the bathroom, jettisoning my wine on one of the linen-wrapped cocktail tables. Outside the bathroom door I run into a trio of art school classmates. "Kelly! Happy Saturn return!" one of them cries. I flap a hand in greeting but don't break stride. I need the church-like echoes of white tile; I need to pat cool water onto my temples. Blood pounds in my head, shadows encroaching on the edges of my vision like mold growth in a time-lapse video, covering my eyes as I run the last few steps to the door.

I open it into another life.

2

EVERYTHING IS BLACK AND THROBBING. A RISING OSCILLATION fills my head, like the time I inhaled the gas from a whipped cream canister at a particularly dismal after-party. Chartreuse flares pop before my eyes. I lurch forward, trying to keep my feet under me.

The *wah-wah-wah* in my ears resolves into voices. Not the decorous dull roar of a gallery on opening night. A shout.

"Surprise!"

3

FOR A BAFFLED COUPLE OF SECONDS I THINK LINNEA MUST have engineered this somehow, gotten everyone ready to surprise me when I came out of the bathroom. It's the kind of thing she would do. Except I was heading *into* the bathroom, not out of it, and where I am feels bigger than even the most spacious ladies' room.

I pull in a breath. Instead of perfume and air freshener, the air smells like garlic. I read somewhere that a strong, out-of-context odor can herald a seizure. Is that what's happening? Am I having a fucking *stroke*?

My hand flails out and finds the back of a chair. I close my eyes until the dizziness passes. When I open them I see my hand gripping the chair, one of those upholstered metal-framed ones you see in unfashionable restaurants. I lift my head to take in a dim room with a dropped ceiling, a long white-covered table with candles in red glass jars, a blur of faces. I can't focus on any of it beyond the flash of impossible realization.

I'm not in the gallery anymore.

"Looks like she's surprised!" someone quips, and laughter breaks gently through the room. In its wake comes a congenial wash of voices, and I feel some of the attention disengage from me. One of the faces separates from the group and approaches. He's stocky, middle-aged, grinning; he's—

Dad?

My fear subsides a little. Even as a grown-ass woman, I maintain the instinctive, ironclad belief that nothing too awful can happen to me with my father around.

Except my dad is in Michigan. I talked to him on the phone not two hours ago.

(*I didn't want to ruin your birthday, Bug.*)

(*No, no. No need for you to come home yet.*)

"Happy birthday, Bug!" Dad's being here, using my old nickname, brings on a rush of disorientation. He holds out a glass of red wine, winking ruby in the warm light from the wall sconces. "You look like you could use a drink!"

"Dad, where—" But everything indicates I should already know where we are. I glance behind me, where a glass-paned door leads to the main dining room of a restaurant.

Luigi's. It's my favorite. They make great chicken Marsala.

The thought comes in my voice, but it's not mine. Or not that of any version of myself I recognize. Dizziness surges over me again. "You okay?" someone says. "Here, sit down." A hand brushes the small of my back, slips around my waist—unhesitating, intimate—and my heart bursts into panicked flight.

I twist away and out the door through which I presumably entered, muttering, "Be right back." I don't really see the man who touched me—I have an impression of compactness, broad shoulders, dark eyes wide in inquiry—but he seems familiar. As though I'll remember how I know him if I think about it for a minute.

"I'll be right back," I repeat, to keep him from following me.

Ahead is the dining room of Luigi's, which apparently makes great chicken Marsala. I don't eat chicken. I don't eat meat at all. But the memory—it's not just my voice telling me this is my favorite restaurant. I can *taste* that chicken Marsala.

I hurry down a short hallway to my right, which leads to the restrooms and, beyond them, a back exit. I've formed a nebulous idea of escape, but two steps from the door to the outside I stop, indecisive. If I've been kidnapped, my best bet is to run into the dining room, which is Friday-night crowded, and yell for help. But a kidnapper wouldn't be throwing me a surprise party to which he'd invited my father. I hope none of my friends would pull this shitty of a prank on me. Maybe someone put something in my wine. But I don't feel drugged, and I have no sense of any time missing. The transition from the gallery was instantaneous, literally like stepping from one room into another.

I fumble in my back pocket for my phone, not finding it, and that's when I realize two things: I'm wearing different pants, and I'm carrying a purse. I usually don't, not if I can help it. "What the fuck?" I whisper, looking down at myself and seeing jeans, a maroon sweater, ballet flats, nothing familiar. I pat my legs as though they might belong to someone else. Reaching into the hideous nylon crossbody slung around me, I find a phone: not my phone, but there's no prompt for a passcode when I wake it up. I'm in the phone app's keypad before it occurs to me that I don't have anyone's number memorized, not even Linnea's. I could call 911, but what would I say?

I've just started scrolling through recents (two missed calls and a voicemail from "Mom," which tells me nothing) when the banquet room door opens. I tense, ready to dive into the ladies' room or through the exit, but it's only a little boy, five or six years old. He looks around, sees me, and comes down the hall. "Hey, Aunt Kelly." He pronounces "aunt" like *ohnt*. I've never seen him before in my life.

He has curly hair and light brown skin, rose-petal flawless the way little kids' skin is, and arresting hazel eyes that pluck at something in my brain. "Have you seen my daddy?" He barely comes up to my waist: a peanut, like I was.

Kid, I don't know who your daddy is. Except I do. I can feel the knowledge waiting to be dislodged, like the last bit of something shaken loose from its container.

"He's not in the banquet room?" I hazard, and the boy shakes his head. I can see the wobble starting up in his eyes. He's being brave, but the tears aren't far off. I drop the phone (mine?) back in the purse. "It's okay, sweetie, we'll find him."

He puts his hand trustingly in mine, but I have no idea where to lead him. I'm turning toward the dining room when the back door opens.

My first year in art school, I spent spring break with Linnea and her family at their beach house in the Outer Banks. I'd never swum in the ocean before, just the small lakes within an hour's drive of my hometown and, one summer, Lake Michigan. My first day in North Carolina I waded in, unprepared for the raw power of the Atlantic, and a wave spun me off my feet and plowed me under.

What happens as soon as the door opens is like that. The same feeling of being caught off guard, the same battle between control and terror, only instead of my nose and mouth filling with water it's my brain filling with memories. It's too much to make sense of: images, snatches of music, names; swells of emotion disconnected from anything I recognize.

The boy's hand squirms in mine. I'm squeezing it too hard. I ease up and focus on his face. *Malik, his name is Malik. He's Nick's son—*

And here's my middle brother himself, coming in from outside smelling of night air and cigarette smoke. Seeing him in this unknown space comforts me. I get a flash of us at some high school party, sitting on somebody's back deck sharing a pint of vodka while he slurringly justifies his failure to live up to the expectations of yet another freshly dumped girlfriend. *That* memory feels like mine.

"Daddy!" Malik drops my hand, runs to him, and throws his arms around his hips. "I couldn't find you." Now I know why Malik's eyes look so familiar: they're my brother's, and mine.

"Sorry, buddy." Nick ruffles Malik's stiff bronze curls and gives me a vaguely apologetic smile. "Thanks for taking care of him. Sorry I missed your big entrance. Were you surprised?"

An acidic laugh bubbles out of me. "Oh yeah."

Nick, with a son. Except Nick doesn't have a son. "When did this happen?" I blurt, gesturing at Malik, and their faces crinkle in identical expressions of confusion.

"What do you mean?" Nick says.

Malik's watching me, wide-eyed. "Nothing. I mean, when did you guys have time to plan all this?"

Nick shrugs. "Ask Mom, she's the mastermind." Trust Nick to avoid all planning responsibilities, but show up for the free food.

Malik takes my hand again, his small, slightly sticky fingers pressing mine. He shouldn't exist. Nick never moved out of our parents' basement. Everyone pretended he'd stayed to look after them, but we all knew he was just riding the no-rent-and-free-meals train as long as he could. Jeff, our older brother, gave him shit about it every time we got together, which wasn't often. Nick would never be responsible enough to behave like an actual parent even if he had fathered a child. He delivers pizza . . .

No. He's a sous chef at a restaurant in Royal Oak. That's where he met Tamyra.

Tamyra, Malik's mother. Who dumped Nick when, at seven months pregnant, she discovered incriminating text messages between him and a hostess at their restaurant. The memory comes from my new stock, the flood that inundated me when Nick came in, but it's reassuring because it tracks with the lovable dirtbag I remember. Unlike the brother beside me now, who holds Malik's other hand, talking to him with a gentle smile on his face, as he steers us toward the banquet room.

A superstitious hope wells up that whatever happened to me will work in reverse. That when I open the door, I'll find myself back in Chicago.

Then the door flies open, and I have to jump back so it won't hit me in the face. A man steps out: the one who was next to me when I first came in, the handsy one. I want to hide, or run back down the hall and out the exit, but it's too late. His gaze settles on me.

"I was just coming out to check on you," he says with a shade of reproach. Nick and Malik slip past him into the banquet room. He leans in to kiss my cheek, and the realization of who he is feels less like a deluge than like a tide going out, laying bare the truth.

He's Eric, my husband.

4

THE DOUBLING SENSATION SHIVERS THROUGH ME AGAIN. HALF of me knows the man in front of me is my husband the same way I know my own name. The other half, the part that was in the gallery ten minutes ago, has to put effort into recognizing him.

Oh, Eric Hyde. From high school.

We shared a few classes. He'd moved from Dearborn to Andromeda Creek in seventh grade, and I'd been nice to him because I tried to be nice to everyone, plus I figured it wasn't easy to be the new kid in a district where everyone had known one another since kindergarten. We'd gotten into the habit of sitting together, a carryover from being seated alphabetically in middle school. Nice guy, quiet, though his reserve could have been a defense mechanism. At our school, people who didn't blend in or keep their heads down tended to get picked on, and he didn't fit into any one group: not the ostentatiously smart kids, not the geek-culture enthusiasts, definitely not the jocks. We did a project together in American history class, bonding over our utter lack of interest in the Revolutionary War. I remember thinking he'd be cute if he weren't so skinny.

He's not skinny now. He fills out his black Henley nicely. I remember buying him that shirt. And I remember when he started lifting weights in college, saying it was to keep me from getting snapped up by some frat boy. The memory of him telling me this—the joking-but-not-really lilt in his voice—darts up in my mind like a little silver fish swimming through murky water to the surface.

More memory-fish swim up to join it. We started going out at the end of eleventh grade. We went to Michigan State and got married a couple of years after graduation. We moved from East Lansing to Davis City three years ago, after Eric got a job offer from the community college. Both our parents were pleased we'd settled down so close, less than half an hour's drive from where they lived in Andromeda Creek.

All of this stands in direct opposition to the memories telling me that Eric Hyde and I have never been more than friendly acquaintances. At the end of senior year we signed each other's yearbook (*UR THE BEST!!! Thanks for saving my ass with that history presentation. Keep in touch!! XXOO Kelly Holter*), after which I merrily forgot his existence and went off to Chicago on an art school scholarship.

He pulls back and gives me a doubtful look. He's kind of a worrier, my husband. *My husband.*

"You okay? You still look a little off."

"I'm fine!" I smile to show him how fine I am. "I just needed some fresh air." Laughter floats through the banquet room door, the happy burble of people at a party. Now I remember the commercials for this restaurant, which were home-video quality and starred a paunchy, middle-aged, very much not Italian-American man wearing a fake mustache and singing a bastardized version of "That's Amore." *When you're craving a dish veramente delish—that's Luigi's!* Thinking of those ads gives me a strange sensation, as though two versions of me exist: one Kelly who's never seen them, and another who can sing every note from memory.

Eric doesn't point out that we've presumably just come in from outside. He just watches me, his expression blank.

"You guys didn't have to do all this," I say.

"You said you'd been feeling lonely."

I think of my life in Chicago, the continual dash between work and studio and dive bars and shows and occasionally even my apartment, where I have two roommates and a cat. There, I'm never alone.

"Ready to go back in?" Eric says. He still hasn't taken his eyes off me.

No. "Sure!"

"Good, I'm starving." He slips his arm around my waist again in that proprietary way, but this time I'm prepared, so it's not as startling. He's only a few inches taller than me, when usually I go for men who are big enough to make me feel tiny in comparison, but being near him feels familiar: his scent, the way he leans close and kisses my temple. "Love you," he murmurs absently, and the feeling of dissociation wells up in me again.

As we go in I glance around the banquet room, which contains a mix of my family and people I half recognize as Eric's. My dad holds court at one end of the long table with two couples around his age; at the other end a cluster of kids, including Jeff's two daughters and Malik, bicker over a tablet. No one's looking at the door. I step sideways, away from Eric, and bump into someone.

"Oh, Kelly!"

Mom. I'd know that note of castigation in her voice anywhere.

I whip around and there she is, dabbing red wine off the front of her blouse with a napkin. "I'm gonna need some club soda for this," she says.

"I'll get it." Eric disappears into the main dining room.

"Here, take this," she says, handing me a still-half-full glass of wine. "Dad got it for you."

My emotions are a complicated stew: confusion, longing, a dash of the old resentment. We're not close, my mother and I, in my Chicago life.

(*No need for you to come home yet.*)

I push the thought away. "Sorry."

"Oh, don't worry about it, it's just a top." She looks up from her dabbing. "Happy birthday, Bug."

"Thanks. Nick said you planned the party."

"Amalia did most of it." *Eric's mother,* my brain supplies. I'll have to take my brain's word for it. "All I did was make the reservation and order the cake. And pick it up. I'm sure Amalia's just forgotten to give me the money for it. I guess it's easy for some people not to think about things like that."

"Mm." I look away. I've had plenty of practice ignoring her little passive aggressions over the years.

"It was Eric's idea. He said you'd been feeling isolated . . ."

"Here you go, Mom," Eric says, back with the club soda and a cloth napkin. I flash on the two of us sitting on our couch in our college apartment in East Lansing, me making fun of him for calling my parents *Mr. and Mrs. Holter.*

I think by now you can call them Jake and Vicky.

I can't do that. It's disrespectful.

What? No, it's not.

It is according to my parents.

So I shouldn't try calling them Amalia and Tony? The look of horror on his face made me laugh, which made him frown at me. *Okay, okay, I'll try to avoid calling them anything at all,* I said, and that got a laugh out of him. I'd had my feet in his lap. The memory feels like a scene from a show I watched a long time ago.

"Oh, you're the best," my mom gushes. If the items had come from me, she'd have been sure to find something wrong with them. Not enough bubbles in the soda, the napkin not absorbent enough. But she looks at Eric like he's a Disney prince. I guess I've made good, in her eyes.

I take a fortifying gulp of wine, and she directs a laser gaze at me. "So you are drinking. I wondered, after that little fainting spell—"

"It was hardly a fainting spell."

"—if you two had something to tell us."

I have no idea what she's talking about, but Eric rears back like she's slapped him. "Oh! No. Not yet."

"Not yet what?" I ask.

"Oh, you know." Mom raises her eyebrows, purses her lips, and—when I still don't get it—pats my stomach.

Oh.

"Not *yet*. So you're trying?"

Eric's mouth hangs slightly open, as though he's stupefied by her sheer disregard for boundaries. I step in to save him. "Mom, believe me, if there were any news, you'd be the first to know." There'd be no keeping it from her.

"Fine, I was just asking. It's not like you're getting any younger." My mother taps her wrist like a watch, though she isn't wearing one.

"Jesus Christ, Mom."

"You don't have to swear at me."

"I'm not . . ." My family, though nominally Christian, is not and has never been religious. "Sorry," I say, to cut the argument off at the root. Maybe in this life I'm more willing to put up with her shit. Maybe that's the reason we talk to each other more than once a month.

"Excuse me," says a server, coming up behind us with a tray of drinks.

"Could I have a double vodka soda, please? With a twist?" I ask, before draining the last of my wine. The server gives me the exact same look I would give someone who asked me for something while I was holding a loaded tray, but this is an emergency.

"I'm sure this young lady would like to take our order," Mom says. "Eric, hon, could you get everyone sitting down?"

"Sure, Mom." He guides me to the table and pulls out my chair for me. The dutiful son-in-law: Mom must love that. Knowledge advances when I focus my mind on a subject, like moths fluttering toward light, and I remember she was worried when Eric and I got serious. She didn't want me to settle down too young. But she came around, especially after I opted to attend a state university instead of art school, and now she adores Eric. She's ecstatic that we live so close. Can't wait for us to have gorgeous little babies. By marrying myself off, I've managed what I never did in my other life: I've pleased her.

I fish out my phone—it *is* my phone, apparently—and hang my ugly purse over the back of my chair. The first thing I look at is the contacts list, which contains the usual assortment of names and monikers, some familiar, some not. Mom and Dad, of course. Names that make faint images pop up in my mind. Functional designations: *doctor, dentist, pharmacy.* Eric is near the top. He's listed as *Eric,* without nickname or endearment, in stark contrast to the various handles I've assigned to crushes on my other phone over the years.

What happened to that phone? Where did it go, when I stepped through a door and ended up here?

I don't have any more time to ponder the nature of whatever the hell's happened to me—dream or delusion or capricious aliens dropping me in this life like a doll into a new dollhouse— because a woman with a long brown ponytail plops down in the chair next to mine. "Oh, the drama," she says, rolling her eyes. She has an aura of warmth that makes me relax immediately. I can tell we're friends. She's Eric's . . .

Cousin. His cousin Ruby.

Despite her youthful appearance and the eye roll, she's only two years younger than me and has a degree in computer science. "What's going on?" I ask.

She flicks a hand. "Nothing important. My mom and Aunt Amalia are just bent out of shape because they're not running the show. Apparently your mom messaged, like, two days ago and told them where and when."

Vicky Holter, the original bull in the china shop. I'm not prepared to referee a battle between her and my mother-in-law.

"You need a refill?" Ruby nods at my empty wineglass.

"I ordered one." I toy with the idea of suggesting shots and decide against. If I get wasted right now, I'll say something that'll put me in a psychiatric unit.

"Well . . . fair warning, next weekend you'd better be ready for a party. They've got something to prove now."

"Next weekend?"

"Yeah, Sunday dinner? Except next week it's Saturday because Christine's going to be in town." She's looking at me like I should know this. And I do: Eric (*my husband!*) and I have dinner at his parents' every other Sunday, alternating weeks with my parents. How cozy.

"Oh yeah, I forgot," I say vaguely, and Ruby goes on about Eric's older sister, who will be visiting from California, and her new girlfriend. Ruby's not sure if the girlfriend will make it. "Apparently she's in the middle of trying to get another round of funding. She has a company that does . . . I wanna say face-recognition blocking? Oh, hi, baby." Ruby's husband, Glenn, a lanky, balding white guy who puts me in mind of a giraffe, has come over to say hello. He leans down to drop a kiss on Ruby's upturned forehead. "Do you remember what Christine's girlfriend's company makes?"

"Some kind of wearable. Privacy enhancement, it blocks signals . . ."

"Eric'll probably hit up Christine for a test model," Ruby says, nudging me. "He's so into gadgets. I don't know why he's not a developer."

"Not everyone's cut out for it," Glenn says.

"But he's obviously got *aptitude*. He's an instructional *designer*. If he wasn't so concerned about stability he could be making a lot more money, not to mention cool shit. I mean, I know you're a creative and money means nothing to you"—Ruby smiles at me, fluttering her fingers in the air—"but he'd totally change careers if you lit a fire under his ass. He'd do anything you wanted."

"Maybe Kelly doesn't want her husband in the office eighty hours a week," Glenn says mildly. "Not everyone gets to work with their partner." Like Ruby, he's a software engineer. They met working at the same startup in the "innovation district" nearby, a tech hub established with all kinds of government subsidies to help the region recover from the auto industry's slow-motion collapse.

"But doesn't one of Eric's friends work at that new company? New*ish*? The one with the AI assistant?" Ruby asks me. I shrug; I have no idea what she's talking about.

"I don't know anyone who's gotten past the first interview there," Glenn says.

Ruby snaps her fingers. "Peter! That's his name. He could totally get Eric a job. At least get him in as an intern—"

"They don't even *have* interns," Glenn says as the server brings my drink.

"How do they not have interns? Everyone has interns."

I take a grateful swig of vodka soda while the two of them continue to banter about my husband's career. I can already feel the alcohol relaxing me, though not enough to stop me from ruminating on how weird it is that I know all these things, when an hour ago I had no idea who Ruby and Glenn were and only a vague notion that a bunch of tech companies had opened up near my hometown.

"So, how's it feel to be thirty, Kelly?" Glenn asks.

Ruby swats him. "She's twenty-nine!" *(Kelly! Happy Saturn return!)* "Don't make her older than she is."

Glenn gets flustered, as though he's insulted me. "Oh, I didn't mean . . . You don't *look* like you're in your thirties."

I smile, feeling my cheeks stretch. "It's fine." When I was younger, I never understood why people panicked about aging, but lately I've been more conscious of the time ticking down. Not just time before I die, but time left to accomplish the things

I want to, or at least set myself up for it. In the art world, people talk as if there's some arbitrary deadline beyond which you'll never make anything worth looking at. There are old artists, just not old emerging artists.

Jeff's daughters sidle up to my chair. Their names are Ashleigh and Kaleigh, and they look exactly alike—little blond, blue-eyed girls—except one's two years older, and for the life of me I can never remember which one's which. That hasn't changed in whatever shift brought me into this life. The smaller one thrusts a folded sheet of construction paper into my lap and mumbles something I can't make out over the buzz of conversation.

I lean closer. "Can you say that again, sweetie?"

She twirls her upper body back and forth and mumbles again, just as incomprehensibly. Her older sister rolls her eyes, which makes her look like a teenager in the body of a five-year-old, and says with near perfect enunciation, "She says, our mommy said to make you a birfday card."

"Oh! Thanks, guys." The gesture charms me, coerced as it was.

"Aren't you gonna read it?" Ashleigh-or-Kaleigh's big blue eyes zero in on me, and she presses her lips together. She definitely inherited her mother's expressions.

Andrea, my brother's wife, comes up as I'm exclaiming over her daughters' crayon scrawls. "Did you give your card to Aunt Kelly?" she asks, unnecessarily, in a big cheerful voice.

"They did." I hold it up. The girls look like they want to escape to wherever the tablet is, but their mother has a restraining hand on each of their heads.

"I thought it'd be a nice little project for them." Andrea's very much in the supermom mold, stuffing her daughters' days

21

with crafts and activities about which she posts regularly on social media. She and Jeff got married young, a couple of years
after they graduated high school, and she used to work as some
kind of medical technician, but that stopped as soon as she had
her first baby.

A comment on the card seems called for, so I say, "It's . . .
very artistic."

"That's right, girls, Aunt Kelly is an artist!" Andrea's big
cheerful voice is back. It must get exhausting to use it all the time.
"We could have her come over for an art studio day!"

I smile as though that doesn't sound absolutely hellish. At
least Andrea remembers I'm a painter, though I have no idea, in
this life, how long it's been since I picked up a brush. "Maybe
when they're a little older—"

"Your kids are going to be so lucky to have such a creative
mom," Andrea interrupts. "You and Eric are waiting a while,
huh? Sowing those wild oats! I remember those days. We've all
got to settle down sometime, though, right?"

"I guess." I glance past her to Jeff, who's talking animatedly
with Eric's cousin Edgar and couldn't look more uninvolved in
this. He's wearing a clean button-down shirt but still has his
work boots on.

"Well, happy birthday." Andrea leans down to give me a hug,
then hustles the girls to a spot at the table where she's got a pre-
school classroom's worth of art supplies set up.

So, apparently I'm not worried about getting a break in the
art world anymore. In this life, I guess I'm supposed to worry
only about my eggs shriveling up.

I look around the room. Beside me, Glenn and Ruby comb the
menu for items that won't trigger Glenn's tomato allergy. Jeff and

Edgar expound on the various ways in which the Lions screwed the pooch last season, a conversation as mundane as the weather. Neither of them seems to be listening to the other as they make their points in progressively louder voices. Edgar is oblivious as his wife, Daisy, tries to soothe their baby while breaking up a tablet-related brawl between their toddler and preschooler. Across the table, Nick's given Malik his phone and is poking glumly at the ice in his drink with a straw. He has a tall glass, the kind the restaurant serves pop in rather than mixed drinks, because Nick doesn't drink on the days he has Malik (although he more than makes up for it when he doesn't). Everybody looks like they'd rather be somewhere else except for the older generation: my parents and Eric's, his aunt and uncle. Their hardest work is behind them and now they get to enjoy the fruits of their labor. Or not: they're coming up on old age, not enough savings to retire, maybe, deteriorating bodies forced to work beyond endurance.

I don't want to become any of these people. That's why I left. *Did you?*

A sly murmur in my own internal voice. It makes me question everything I know, not only this night but my whole life. *Did* I move to Chicago? Leave my family behind, my home? If that's the truth, then it also has to be the truth that earlier tonight I stepped through some kind of magical portal to end up back in Michigan. Put that way, it sounds outlandish. Impossible. But then my other life, all my memories of being an artist, would be impossible too.

I feel the weight of someone's attention and shift my gaze to find Eric standing by Jeff and Edgar, watching me. When I meet his eye he blinks, his expression relaxing into a half smile. I smile back reflexively, then look away.

Mom said she wanted to order food, but the waitress is nowhere to be seen, so I take a sip of my drink and get to my feet. It's time I joined my party.

SOMEHOW I MAKE it through. I manage to talk to everyone like a normal person. I greet my mother-in-law, who makes me want to both shrink into obscurity and stand up straighter, and my father-in-law, who gives a toast at dinner that includes the words *the light of my son's life* and gets everyone dabbing at their eyes. With the support of another vodka soda and a second glass of wine at dinner, I chatter. I laugh. I am convincingly charming.

It helps that my tolerance is almost nil. A single drink affects me as much as three would at home. Soon I find myself in an alcoholic fog, which—if not altogether pleasant—attenuates the panic that flares up every time I think too hard about my situation.

Eric and I don't seem to have any friends, or at least there aren't any at the party. People are busy with their own lives, their own families, and friends fall away so easily at our age. Or maybe my mother, conscious that she and my dad were paying the bill, limited the guest list to family. Ours is totally different from the family of choice I've assembled in Chicago, but valuable all the same. Even in my state, I can see that. As the drinks flow and the food arrives, the earlier pall I imagined over the room seems to lift.

After dinner, the kids are all occupied enough to give their parents a break, and people divide into conversational groups again. I hold down a corner of the table with my brothers and we talk about what everyone else who stayed in town is up to; we're all close enough in age that we know a lot of the same people. It's like old times, when I'd come home from Chicago for my infrequent visits, except there's less antagonism between us than I remember. In my other life, Nick and Jeff needled each other mercilessly: Jeff would tell Nick he needed to get a real job, Nick would fire back that Jeff was turning into our dad, and they both used to patronize the hell out of me. Now it's almost like we're adults who respect one another.

Everyone looks replete and content, comfortable. My party isn't exactly a rager, but everybody's having a good time. Eric sits next to his aunt Dora, listening to his uncle Wayne tell a story. As I watch him he glances at me, giving me a small smile. Since our conversation with my mom, he seems to be keeping his distance, giving me space to be with my family while he takes time with his own. Or has he noticed something's off?

We're finishing up with the cake—the singing, the obligatory jokes about all the candles melting the frosting, the sickly glaze of sugar coating the back of my tongue—when Daisy and Edgar's baby wakes up and starts to wail. This sets off a cascade of departures, and soon Eric and I are standing in the parking lot saying our good nights. I feel a prick of guilt at how little I thought of my parents when I lived in Chicago. Since high school it's been yearly visits and monthly phone calls, if that. When my mother hugs me, it feels like a reconciliation. I pull away with dampened eyes.

Then I'm in the dark car, alone with my husband.

5

"SO . . . NO CHICKEN MARSALA TONIGHT."

I jump, inside myself. "Sorry?"

"You usually get chicken Marsala when we go to Luigi's."

I ordered the eggplant parmigiana, which I barely remember consuming. I hug myself, feeling a sudden urge to tug my sleeve up and check for the watercolor tattoos I've been getting as I can afford them over the years. The same tattoos that were on my arms when I left my apartment in Chicago. My unease had receded—a little—but now it returns in a cold wave.

"What, I can't try something different?" I mean it to sound light, ironic. It comes out defensive.

"Sure. I was just . . . You always get the chicken Marsala. It's your favorite." Do I hear strain in his voice? Is Eric upset that I changed my freaking dinner order?

I put the window down and chilly wind sweeps in, whipping my hair into a flag. The hair I'm used to having is too short for that. I sawed it off one night in a half-drunk fit of audacity during my second year in art school, Linnea cackling as I wielded the scissors. The next day I got a friend of a friend who was in cosmetology school to fix it, but I liked the look and have never grown it out.

I hold my hair out of my face and take deep breaths of cool

air, staring out at blank fields and black sky, the occasional farm-house circled in cold floodlight. *Stop freaking out,* I order myself, but it's useless when I know, without having to look, that my arms are bare of ink under my sweater.

"How about my dad's toast, huh?"

Since Eric's making the effort to break the tension, I'll meet him halfway. "It was touching. You'll have to thank him for me." Tony talked about the night of junior prom, quipping that it had been hard for him and Amalia to believe Eric and I were actually dating at first. Eric, Tony said, hadn't been such a la-dies' man back then.

The line got its expected laugh, and then Tony went on to say he'd had a feeling I was special, that I was going to make his son happy, and he'd been right. He meant it as a compliment, but in my state of mind it worried me. What if I hadn't been there? What then?

"You could have thanked him yourself, earlier," Eric says. "He really loves you, you know."

There's no judgment in his tone, but the comment galls me anyway, my irritation sharper for knowing he's right. "I'll say something next time I see him. It's been a long night."

"Everything okay?" He puts a hand on my leg, and I fight the urge to brush it away.

"Yeah . . . I'm just tired."

I remember junior prom with Eric. It was our third date, and though I'd met his parents before, it had been as his classmate. I remember babbling, knocking over a picture frame on their mantel when we stood in front of the fireplace for a picture. They proba-bly weren't as impressed with me as Tony made out in his toast.

Up until then I hadn't been nervous about anything in con-nection with Eric. We were friendly but moved in different circles, intersecting only briefly, until one day in junior year—my seventeenth birthday, as it happened—he'd asked me out. Before then, it hadn't even occurred to me to think of him in a romantic way, and once we were dating he made me feel like he would worship me no matter what I did. No one had ever looked at me the way he did, like I was something marvelous.

His regard made me feel powerful, but it also inspired a sense of responsibility. He made me want to live up to his vision of me.

I also remember another prom night, when I went to the dance with my three best friends and we ended up at a party the next town over, Katie Spence casually puking over the porch railing. Nicole Petersson and I had to rescue Alicia Kang from being hit on by a guy in his late twenties who worked at the local burger chain. We wound up the night at Denny's, slumped in a booth in our sequined gowns, shoveling in waffles and bacon and drinking hot, strong coffee.

Eric and I are almost home.

The streets in our subdivision are named after Revolutionary War battles. When we first bought our house, Eric and I laughed at the serendipity of it: the universe was determined to make us appreciate American history.

Eric eases the car down Oriskany Way and pulls up next to a blue Malibu in our garage. The last time I left home it was from my apartment in Chicago. I'd filled food and water dishes for my cat, Sergeant Meeky, and called, *Don't wait up, Meeks!* as I wrestled the sticky dead bolt into the locked position. My roommates were both out working their restaurant jobs. I'd decided not to drive to the gallery, since parking would be iffy and I'd be drinking, and a semblance of spring had finally arrived and it was so nice out that I didn't mind the wait for the bus.

This house, a modest split-level, is ours. Mine and Eric's. That Chevy is mine. I remember buying it, new, to celebrate getting my first "real" job after graduating from MSU.

After he shuts off the car, he says, "Oh, I almost forgot," and it's not the forced casualness in his voice that gives him away, because Eric never *oh, almost forgets* anything. He reaches behind my seat and retrieves a small bag. "I never gave you your present."

My present. It's still my birthday. My throat closes up as I remember the paints that appeared a couple of days ago, as if by magic, in my area of the studio Linnea and I share. She didn't even leave a note: she knew I'd know they were from her. Most of my other friends are the type who'll just stand me a few rounds at the bar, and I'd been looking forward to a raucous weekend.

Inside the bag sits a jewelry case. In the case lies a delicate white-gold chain that holds a small round pendant encrusted with tiny diamonds. "Wow," I say.

"You like it?" Eric wears a small, hopeful smile.

"It's beautiful." It looks like an itty-bitty luggage tag.

"Let's see it on you." He reaches for the box, and I let him take it. We shift around, awkward in the small space, so he can clasp the chain around my neck. He surveys me, then nods as if satisfied.

"I don't know if this is the right outfit for it." I take the pendant between my fingers. It's rough on the front and smooth on the back, already warm from my skin.

"It looks fine. I tried to pick something that would go with everything, be good for every day . . . I know you don't dress up that often." For some reason he looks sheepish, as though it's his fault for not taking me anywhere.

"It's beautiful," I say again, nothing else occurring to me. Then something does. "Thank you."

"You're welcome," he returns, oddly formal.

He looks at me. I look at him. I realize he's waiting for me to do something, probably the normal thing a wife would do when her husband presents her with an expensive gift. But I can't bring myself to touch him.

A line appears between his eyebrows. "Is there—" His voice catches, and he clears his throat. "Is there something wrong?"

I could lay it all out for him. How I stepped from the gallery into the restaurant, the double memories, Chicago. He probably wouldn't understand—scratch that, he definitely wouldn't understand—but he's a problem solver. For him everything is concrete, has a cause and effect. He looks at the factors in front of him and sees patterns other people don't. He could help me see through the madness to what's real.

Except I'm not sure I can accept the reality. I love Eric—at least I *remember* I love Eric—but if I tell him about my life in Chicago, that life will become irrevocably not real. The possibility of my entire history ceasing to exist, of it never having existed, induces a dreamlike horror that stops up my throat. I can't speak; all I can do is shake my head.

Eric must sense some part of what I'm feeling. He leans in and kisses me on the cheek, caressing my other cheek with his hand, lips and fingers lingering on my skin. I almost flinch, but once the touch is happening it feels familiar, normal. Comforting.

"I love you," he says. His hand moves around to the back of my neck. He kisses my closed lips once, twice. The intimacy of his touch still unsettles me, but I'm drawn in to him, his contours matching mine. I feel another, powerful urge to tell him what's going on. It would be so easy to let the words float out and away, not my problem anymore.

Instead I kiss him back, a small one. Easy enough. "Happy anniversary," he says. His lips brush my cheek one more time; then he pulls away, his hand warm on the back of my neck. I could draw his face from memory. "Though I guess it's not, really, since we didn't actually go on our first date until after your birthday."

"Close enough."

"Ah-ah-ah." He shakes his head, smiling. "That's the kind of thinking that gets astronauts killed." He says that a lot. It's kind of a running joke with us, how he's the planner and I'm the one willing to let things slide. One of those inside jokes that flourish in a marriage.

A shiver passes through me.

"You sure you're okay?" he asks.

"Yeah, I just need a minute. I had a little too much to drink."

His smile grows indulgent. "You're not in your early twenties anymore. You should take some Tylenol before you go to bed."

Aleve, I almost correct him. Naproxen sodium is a far better hangover preventative, as I've learned from many a long night.

He kisses my forehead, then goes into the house while I remain in the car, hugging my elbows and feeling a chill my sweater can't touch. I think of my apartment, my cat, and wonder if Meeks exists. If she's curled up on the foot of my bed, waiting for me.

That's my life, I think. *That's the truth.*

I just need to find a way back home.

6

WHEN I GO INSIDE, I CAN HEAR THE SHOWER HISSING THROUGH the walls.

The door opens on our eat-in kitchen, the dining and cooking areas separated by a spur of countertop. Beyond the dining table, a sliding glass door gives onto the backyard. The lights switch on automatically in response to my movements, turning the slider into a dark mirror. Even though we don't have any neighbors behind us—just some woods between our subdivision and the next one over—the black expanse makes me feel watched. I close the blinds.

I fetch a glass and fill it from the water dispenser in the door of the refrigerator, which chimes an indication that the filter needs changing. "Would you like me to order a replacement?" asks the fridge in a soothing female voice, repeating the question until I say, "No."

The fridge is new, but the rest of the kitchen is from the 2000s, with pitted granite countertops and dark wood cabinets. The house itself was built in the 1970s, with a patchwork of renovations done through the years, and Eric's dream is to overhaul it completely. Smart heating and cooling, water recycling, biometric locks. Lights that sense when we're in the room without our having to wave at them every couple of minutes. The tech you never think you'd miss until you have it. To him it's not important how things look; it's what they can do.

How do I know what he wants? How do I remember the conversations in which he told me?

Toenails click on the tile behind me, a dog collar jingles, and Bear, our rottweiler-Lab mix, presses his warm bulk against my hip. I scratch him between the ears. I don't have to reach down very far. He's huge, and as dumb and sweet as a dog can be. Between me and Eric, Eric's his favorite. I stroke his silky head and try to think of nothing.

The shower shuts off, a sudden absence of noise that doesn't help the buzzing in my head, and Bear heads upstairs. The bathroom has a door that leads to our bedroom and another to the hall, the layout as clear in my mind as if I've spent years moving between those rooms. I hear the hall door open, then a waiting silence.

I keep still, barely breathing. After a time—long enough for the kitchen lights to switch off—the floor creaks with Eric's steps into our room.

I creep through the foyer, automatically avoiding the table where we drop the mail on the rare occasions we enter by the front door, and into the living room. The lights come on automatically in here too, recessed fixtures that aspire to a gallery aesthetic, though that's the limit of any sophistication in the decor. The furniture, overstuffed leather and heavy oak handed down from Eric's parents, stands at right angles on thick cream-colored carpet. The memory comes to me that when we bought this house I wanted to rip up that carpet and make the living room my studio, but Eric argued against it. He didn't want a mess to be the first thing people saw when they walked into our home.

A mess, that's what he called my work. A hobby, at other times. Which, to be fair, it was. This version of me never went to art school.

We went back and forth about the living room / studio issue for days, but in the end Eric got his way. I ended up with one of the small-windowed bedrooms upstairs, an elm tree blocking most of its light.

The curtains hang open, as they usually do, even when we're home for the night. We hardly use this room. Outside, the streetlamp makes a dramatic spotlight for the deserted street. Nothing moves. It looks fake, like a diorama. My shoulders ache and my eyes feel tight and itchy with fatigue, but I stand by the window for a long time, long past when the lights switch off, until I'm sure Eric will be asleep. Then I tiptoe upstairs and into the bathroom.

I avoid looking straight in the mirror but can't help noticing differences, which my brain catalogs as changes. My hair hits my shoulder blades now, and the corkscrew curls I get so many compliments on have become barely more than waves. The tattoos on my arms are missing, of course. I don't look at my ankle, but I know that tattoo is missing too.

In the bedroom I undress in the dark, my hands going confidently to the dresser drawer where I keep my pajamas, and ease into bed. Eric lies turned toward the wall, breathing deeply. I keep far enough away that I can't feel his warmth on the sheets.

My eyes don't want to stay shut. I stare at the ceiling until colored lights explode in my vision. I'm thinking about art school.

The ankle tattoo was a lark. It was spring of my first year and a few of us were hanging out in the dorms, drinking from a fifth of Smirnoff someone had brought. I had my feet in the lap of another first-year student, named Aaron, who was from Wisconsin and with whom I'd had sex once. At some point he got hold of a pen and doodled a design on the inner part of my ankle, over the bone.

"Hey," said Linnea, leaning forward, "that's kinda cool."

I was comfortably buzzed, higher on the feel of Aaron's hands on my skin than on the vodka. I couldn't keep still. We were in that uncertain place where I wasn't sure if he would come back to my room that night, where I wasn't sure if he'd text me the next day if he did. It was at once thrilling and tedious. I bent my leg toward my face so I could examine what he'd drawn. "Yeah, it is," I said. "I guess it's on there forever, since you drew it in Sharpie, asshole." I nudged Aaron's chest with my foot, not quite a kick, and smiled.

He grinned and I knew he'd be in my bed later. I felt like I'd won something. "You should get that tattooed on you," he said. "It'll be worth some money one day."

Across the room, Linnea snorted. "What, she's gonna cut off her foot and sell it to a collector?"

Aaron shrugged as if to say *Maybe*. I don't remember what his work was like; he was a sculptor, not an illustrator. I do remember his confidence, as well as the alarm in his eyes the next week when he saw I'd actually gotten the tattoo done. We'd run into each other on the street, each heading to a different class.

I couldn't see what the big deal was. I'd been thinking about getting a tattoo anyway, and here was a cool design already drawn on. But he assumed it was about him. "Don't you think it's a little weird?" he asked. *Obsessive*, he meant. His eyes flicked down to my ankle, still oozing and itching, the thick black lines almost three-dimensional. We'd been texting back and forth sporadically since that night, but I hadn't mentioned the tattoo. I'd figured I would surprise him.

I was proud of how well it had turned out, glad for the unseasonably warm day that let me display it, but he was acting like I should be ashamed. My chest tightened with anger. "I don't know. I mean, it's done now, right?"

Aaron shifted his weight, rubbed the back of his neck. "Yeah, well . . . maybe we should take a step back. I'm not really looking for anything serious right now."

"Neither am I!" It came out louder than I'd intended, and I saw the answer in his eyes: *Whoa, crazy girl.* "Man, fuck you. It's just a tattoo," I said, and stomped away. He avoided eye contact whenever I saw him after that.

In the bed I share with my husband of five years, whom I followed to Michigan State even though I had a full scholarship to the Art Institute of Chicago, I squeeze my eyes shut and roll farther away from him. I call up every detail of my memory of that night: the flush on Aaron's cheeks, the mandala tapestry on the dorm room wall, the lone sock peeking out from under the bed. (Whose room were we in? I can't remember the person's name now, and it bothers me.) The gnawing of the needles on my skin the next afternoon, more irritating than painful until the tattoo artist hit bone. The broken-glass edges and smooth curves of the design itself. My anger and disappointment when Aaron assumed the worst about me, a sinking feeling of betrayal, deeper for not being entirely unexpected.

All of that happened. It happened to me. The evidence is missing, but I know it to be true.

7

Day Two

I WAKE UP CURLED AT THE EDGE OF THE BED, AS THOUGH EVEN in sleep I was trying to keep out of the way of any errant arms or legs. I'm alone.

Morning light strains into the room through a screen of leaves. I half sit up, listening. The house is quiet and feels empty. Bear, stretched like a furry black-and-tan rug on the floor by Eric's side of the bed, thumps his tail on the carpet.

Eric must be at the gym: he always goes on Saturdays. The knowledge is there in my brain, too well-worn to be remarkable.

I lie back and wonder what I should do next.

A run. I go running most mornings. I've done it since . . . holy shit, since college. I began around the time Eric started going to the student fitness center four times a week. It's been a constant for my whole adult life, at least *this* whole adult life. No wonder I feel such a deep sense of comfort when I think about it.

A memory floats up that my running practice was part of the argument Eric marshaled in favor of getting a big dog instead of a small one: Bear would guard me from the legions of crackheads and rapists swarming the suburban streets. Men always want to make an emotional decision seem rational.

In practice, Bear is more a hindrance than a help. He pulls on the leash, then stops short to let out a trickle of urine or investigate a scent. "Bear! Come!" I yell for the tenth time, two miles into my run, and pull up when I see he's squatting to one side of the path. I've forgotten to bring plastic bags. When he's finished I look around guiltily—my route, a trail through the woods behind our house, is secluded but looks well traveled—and use a stick to roll his creation into the underbrush.

My surroundings seem familiar, but I'm not completely sure of my course, and I end up running in circles. It takes me a while to find Oriskany Way and my house again. Eric's still not home when I let myself in, however, and I feel a twinge at how much this simple fact relaxes me.

Before I get into the shower, I steel myself and look directly in the mirror. It's the same body—the birthmark on my inner arm is still there, the constellation of moles on my stomach—yet different. No tattoos, but I knew that. In Chicago I don't walk as much as I used to since I bought a car, so in the last few years my stomach has developed a comfortable pooch and my thighs have begun to rub together when I walk. In moments of insecurity about this, Linnea (who has the metabolism of a sixteen-year-old boy) says it shows I'm enjoying life. I mostly agree. Life's too short to worry about how your ass looks in a pair of jeans.

The body in my bathroom mirror is narrow in comparison, softish about the hips and belly but with lean, well-developed calves and thighs. My breasts, robbed of excess fat, are smaller. Even my face is thinner. I can't stop staring; it's like facing a twin I was separated from at birth. But when I raise my hand, the woman in the mirror raises hers too.

I stay in the shower a long time. It's strange washing long hair, having it tangle in my fingers. Shaving my armpits, I cut myself on a hollow under my arm that wasn't there before, but the hot water feels good. My lungs open up in the steam. I hum a tune, enjoying the reverberation of my voice against the tile. By the time I turn off the water, I feel a little better.

I wind a towel around myself, still humming my melody from the shower, but stop short in the bedroom doorway.

Eric's in there, buck naked.

I gasp, averting my eyes. He's got nothing I haven't seen before, but the sudden, enforced intimacy is shocking. Eric, holding the dresser for balance as he tugs off his gym socks, whips his head around. "Jeez, you scared me," he says, and makes no effort to cover himself. Why would he? We walk around naked in front of each other all the time. Usually, I don't even wear a towel from the bathroom to the bedroom.

I don't wear one here. In Chicago, with two roommates and one bathroom, I do.

I focus on his face. "Good workout?"

"Sure." He bends to scoop up his discarded gym clothes and I look away again, feeling vaguely repulsed, holding the towel tight around my chest. I don't want to get dressed in front of him. "Did you and Bear go running?"

A flare of irritation lights in my stomach. It feels familiar, yet more a part of this new Kelly, my separated-at-birth twin, than a part of me. So does the thought that surfaces: *He can't resist making sure I took the dog with me like a good girl.* "We did. I had to stop every twenty feet to pull him away from the shit he kept trying to roll in, and nobody even *tried* to rape me."

Eric compresses his mouth into a line as if I'm a toddler working up to a tantrum. "I see your mood hasn't gotten any better since last night." He turns to drop his clothes in the hamper, and I sneak a glance. He has a nice ass. All those squats. But his tone of voice, the way he's acting like I'm the one who's being unreasonable, makes me want to slam something.

"My mood is fine. I'd just like to go for a run without a fucking babysitter."

"What's with the swearing?"

I'm too surprised to be angry. This is the way I talk. *Mouth like a sailor,* Linnea always says, and I laugh and correct her: *Mouth like a* motherfucking *sailor.*

But then I realize (*remember*) that it's *not* the way I talk. It had to do with Amalia. Somewhere along the line, between meeting Eric's poised, accomplished mother and marrying her son, I gave it up. I can't get used to these small proofs that I'm not the person I was.

I cover my unease with bluster. "Is there anything else I'm doing wrong today? Anything you want to get off your chest?"

Eric blinks, a line appearing between his eyebrows as he stares me down. Then his forehead smooths. He walks toward me, his flaccid penis bouncing a little with each step. "I'm sorry. You know I just want you to be safe." I'm barely listening. We've had this argument before. When he gives ground it always means the same thing: he's going to touch me—take my arm or give me a hug—and then he's going to kiss me, and then we're going to have sex. Except we're not, because I'll scream if he lays a hand on me right now. I won't be able to stop myself.

I edge past him to the closet, and pull out a striped maxiskirt at random. "I'm not helpless. I can take care of myself." I hike the skirt over my hips, still clasping the towel around my chest. "Can we please talk about this later?"

Eric sighs. "Yeah. Sure." He goes into the bathroom, and my heart rate slows back down to normal.

Dressed and downstairs, I give myself a stern talking-to. I have no reason to be afraid. My husband is not the enemy. All of this about another life in Chicago is . . . I don't know, an early midlife crisis. I've reached the age of twenty-nine without achieving any of my adolescent dreams; maybe I've gone all *Yellow Wallpaper*. Or maybe my life in Chicago is the real one and this house, this marriage, is the delusion. My secret yearning for domestic bliss (so secret even I didn't know about it) has triggered me to construct an alternate reality in my mind where I've married some random dude from high school, while my body is strapped to a gurney, pumped full of antipsychotics.

Stop it. "Okay," I say out loud, but my hands are shaking so badly I almost drop the eggs taking them out of the fridge. I set the carton on the counter and slide down until I'm sitting on the floor. Bear comes up, nosing at my face anxiously until I stroke his head. "It's okay," I whisper, to myself as much as to him. "It's okay, you're fine. You're fine. You're gonna be just fucking fine." I put a fierce emphasis on the word *fucking*: Eric will just have to deal with the new, potty-mouthed me.

By the time he comes down, damp-haired and smelling of soap and (thank goodness) fully dressed, I've pulled myself together enough to scramble eggs. "Do you want some?" I ask him, nodding toward the pan.

He shakes his head, goes to the pantry, and takes out a container of protein powder. I turn back to the stove. The rattle of his shaker cup, the hiss of cooking eggs, fill the silence between us.

"Have I done something?" His voice startles me. He's turned

away, head down, the smooth curve of his freshly shaven cheek making him look like a little boy. I feel an incongruous rush of affection for him. "I don't know, you just seem . . . We had this big party for you because you said you felt isolated. And then you act like we're putting you out." His voice has a whiny edge to it, making my temper flare again. This is a variation on a theme. From what I can remember, most of our recent arguments can be boiled down to: *I do so much for you and it's never good enough.* He works long hours so I don't need to have a nine-to-five. He let me have the second-biggest bedroom for my office, never mind that it's on the shaded side of the house. He doesn't hound me about having kids, just drops increasingly obvious hints. He makes allowances for me, tolerates my failings, lets me do my thing. Up to a point.

But in this place, he's all I have.

"I'm sorry," I say. "I didn't mean to act like that . . . I had a great time, really. I don't know what's wrong with me." The relief on his face when he turns is so strong it startles me. He crosses the kitchen, puts his hands on my shoulders, and kisses my forehead, and waves of emotion wash over me in a way that's becoming familiar: the urge to nestle into his arms, the urge to squirm away.

"Oh shit, my eggs!" Smoke pours from the pan on the stove, and I jump to turn off the burner and dump the mess into the sink. The eggs are ruined, but it doesn't matter. My appetite's gone.

8

I SPEND THE AFTERNOON DOING RESEARCH.

I tell Eric I'm reorganizing the closet in the spare bedroom, which has the desired effect of getting rid of him. As soon as he's gone to his "office," the alcove downstairs where he keeps his computer, I start tearing through photo albums. I'm not looking for memories. I already have those. I recognize the faces in the pictures, remember where and when most of them were taken. Prom, Senior Skip Day, the first years of college, before we stopped printing out snapshots. A few from our courthouse wedding. But those memories feel as though they belong to someone else. What I'm searching for is some emotional connection to the life I find myself living. But even with my entire history laid out in front of me, I'm unable to feel that it's mine.

I have the bed covered with memorabilia, photos and old birthday cards and handouts from college we kept for some reason, when Eric opens the door. I jump, my hands twitching with the compulsion to push everything into a single pile to hide what I've been doing.

"I see you've made a lot of progress," he says dryly.

I laugh, the sound high-pitched and unnatural. "I got sidetracked."

"Little trip down memory lane, eh?" He advances into the room. "Find anything interesting?"

I could ask him if I've fallen and hit my head in the last few days. I could ask him if he too remembers another life in which we never got together.

My stomach flares with adrenaline as he bends to inspect the loose photos I've separated into stacks. In one pile I've placed pictures of the version of me that married Eric; the other contains photos that could be from the life where I wound up in Chicago. The latter are mostly from the first three years of high school: me clowning around with my three best friends; me in my homecoming dress with the princess sash over my shoulder, curls trailing from my updo. On top of the pile lies a snapshot of me and Dave Kowalczyk, my boyfriend the first half of junior year. In it, Dave looks at me, a swoop of dark blond hair falling into his eyes, while I grin into the camera. Picking up the photo, Eric lets out a *heh* as if he's recalled something mildly amusing.

"What?"

"Dave Kowalczyk," Eric says, contempt in every syllable. "Did I ever tell you what he said after you guys broke up?"

"You talked to him?"

"No." The word comes out on a snort, a meaning in it I can't decipher. Scorn mixed with . . . longing? Jealousy? Dave was a lot more popular than Eric in high school. He had a band. They were awful, of course, but his being a musician—another creative person in a place where creative people were in short supply— gave him a cachet that sixteen-year-old me found irresistible. "I was walking behind him and his drummer in the hall and he was talking about you. How you'd dumped him, though he didn't admit that. And he said, 'It doesn't matter. Plenty of other girls in this school would be happy to suck my dick.'"

I laugh a little. Dave had cried when I broke up with him. Kept texting me for weeks, until I told him I'd speak to my brother if he didn't stop, not that Nick would actually have done anything, and Jeff had moved out by then.

But of course Dave wouldn't let anyone else see that pain and vulnerability. He'd lash out, in whatever small way he dared. Or maybe he'd never really felt that much for me, and what Eric had heard was nothing more than hurt pride. "That's just how guys talk, or at least they did back then."

Eric shakes his head. "I'd never have talked about you like that. He wasn't good enough for you." He glances at the photo of me and Dave once more, his nostrils flared with distaste, and tosses it into the trash can next to the bed.

"Hey!" I retrieve it and lay it back on the pile.

"You really want to keep that?" There's a note in Eric's voice I don't like.

"He was part of my life. Just because it didn't work out doesn't mean I want to forget about him."

Eric looks at me like I'm speaking a language he doesn't understand. "But why dwell on things? Why not start over, move on?"

"I'm not *dwelling*. I'm—" I can't find the words to explain. "Every experience teaches you something." Eric tilts his head, still skeptical. "It's not like I'm planning to go find him. I definitely got an upgrade with you." I reach out and rest my fingertips on his wrist, just for a second. I keep being unsettled by how normal it feels to touch him.

But it works. His face lights up. He sits next to me on the bed and flips through the photos, placing Dave's on the bottom.

"Wow, I haven't looked at these in years. Remember this?" He holds up a picture of the two of us, standing in front of his dorm at MSU with our arms around each other's shoulders, looking impossibly young.

"My mom took that." The memory pierces me: move-in day, freshman year. The August heat, heavy as a wet blanket. I swallow, feeling cold. I could ask him whether he feels guilty that I gave up my scholarship. I broke up with Dave because he wouldn't stop complaining when I chose to paint instead of hanging out with him, but my relationship with Eric was what really killed the artist in me. I just didn't see it at the time.

"Our first apartment," Eric says, flipping through more photos. Most of these have no people in them, just bare rooms. They must be the move-in pictures my parents took to verify the initial condition of the apartment. I have no idea why we printed them out, or why I've kept them for so long. He stops on the last one, the only one with me in it. I look sweaty and irritated, my hair in a messy topknot, and I'm holding out my hand in a warding gesture. My mouth is open. *What are you doing?* I might be saying, or *Don't take my picture!* As I stare at my younger self, something surfaces in me, more impression than actual memory: Eric and me in a face-off across that same apartment living room, now crowded with our furniture and books and the art I'd hung on the walls, the accoutrements of our life together. A life that was collapsing because he'd done something unforgivable.

I can't remember what it was. All I can remember is him taking a step toward me, his hand extended, *Please, Kelly, please,* and the fury that rose inside me, the crash of the vase I picked up and threw at the wall behind him. It was a squat blown-glass thing I'd bought at a student art fair. Now it sits, unbroken, on the nightstand of this very guest room.

Suddenly the room feels too small; or it feels too small to be in with him.

I burst from the bed and hurtle out the door, down the stairs. He calls my name, but I don't stop.

I'm not quite panicked enough, or brave enough, to take the escape the front door offers. Eric catches up to me in the kitchen, where I'm hanging over the sink drinking a glass of water. His face is unreadable. I can't tell whether he noticed anything upstairs.

"I was going to go to the store," he says. "I figured I'd grill for supper."

I set my glass on the counter. "Sounds good."

"Do you need anything?"

I almost laugh and say, *You're not gonna find what I need at Meijer's.* "Nope, nothing. Thanks."

"Okay. I'll be back." His hand drifts toward my head, as though he's going to pet me like Bear, then dips to give my shoulder a little squeeze. I wait until I hear the garage door close behind him before heading back upstairs to what we call my studio, a polite fiction. The room shows no sign that an artist works in it. My easel and canvases sit in the closet, brushes and tubes of acrylic paint stacked neatly in clear plastic containers on the shelves, out of sight. They've been stored there since we moved in. The room is an office and nothing more.

I sit at the desk in front of the ultrawide monitor, another gift from Eric. The amount of money my graphic design work brings in doesn't justify state-of-the-art equipment. I don't bother looking at the photos Eric and I have posted online: if ink on paper won't give me what I need, pixels on a screen aren't going to.

I search for possible causes of false memories, memories that don't match up with reality. The lists that come up, on medical sites of varying legitimacy, are not comforting: epilepsy, brain tumors, schizophrenia, PTSD. The memories I'm concerned about have nothing to do with childhood, and most of them aren't particularly traumatic. But I learn that memory itself is fungible, even in people who don't have mental illnesses. I already knew how different people remember events differently based on their perspectives, and there've been more than a few nights when my friends had to tell me the next morning what I did and said. But the research I uncover now describes "normal" test subjects' perfect recall of occasions that never actually happened; childhood sexual abuse is the most well-known example, but researchers have also planted more innocuous scenarios in the heads of some of their subjects, who never know the difference until they're told afterward. It's unsettling to learn that memories can be vivid and convincing and completely false.

That can't be what's happening.

On impulse, I google Linnea Flood Chicago. A results page comes up with links to old articles about the Chicago River flooding. I put quotes around my friend's name and rerun the search.

The top result is a review of the exhibition that opened last night, at the gallery where Linnea is showing.

I sit back in my chair, hand clapped over my mouth. I wasn't expecting her to exist, was afraid to hope.

The review doesn't mention any mysteriously disappearing attendees at the opening. I skim it, then move on to her social media accounts and anything else I can find about her. Selfies of her and Bobby in restaurants, at openings, at the beach, in front of the Bean at a summer concert. A puff piece on her parents (generous donors) in the SAIC alumni magazine. Blurbs in the class notes, each announcing a more prestigious achievement. Her life has gone on the same as I remember, the only difference being that I'm not in it.

I study her photos for signs that she has a different best friend, that someone else has taken my place. I don't see any. I was the one who approached her our first year: we had Art History 1001 together and I plunked myself down beside her and started talking. Linnea is well loved, but mostly from afar. Even as a teenager she projected an aura of accomplishment, an untouchable quality. But I was confident enough, and midwestern enough, not to be intimidated.

After combing through everything, all the way back to her online portfolio from our senior year, I minimize the browser window and listen to my shaky breath.

Minutes pass. I bring the window back up and start typing in website addresses: my social media profiles, my portfolio. It's all either missing or confirms my identity as Kelly Hyde, a freelance graphic designer based in mid-Michigan. I google Kelly Holter artist Chicago. Nothing. Not that there was much online about me before, but the discovery chills me. I remember being there, being that person. Not even twenty-four hours ago, I was she. But every shred of information that proves it has been erased.

Or never existed.

The gallery is the demarcation line. If I can walk through the events of last night, everything will become clear. I'll discover a way to reverse this, find the rabbit hole and climb up it, back into my old life.

I have to go to Chicago.

9

ERIC COMES BACK FROM THE STORE WITH A PAIR OF PORTER-
houses the size of Frisbees. "I know you won't eat this whole
steak at once," he says, "but you could have leftovers. Make a
burrito out of it or something."

I was too distracted before to process what Eric meant when
he said he'd grill, but of course it would be meat. He plops the
steaks into a glass dish and begins patting salt and pepper onto
them, causing blood-tinged liquid to ooze out and pool in the
bottom of the dish. The sight of the raw meat jiggling under his
fingers, so obviously part of a dead creature, sends a frisson of
disgust through me.

I could tell him I'm a vegetarian. I could say, *Actually, I've
decided to stop eating meat.* Easy.

But Eric's one of those people who don't think they've eaten
unless the meal includes some kind of animal flesh. It'll turn into
a Discussion, for which I am Not in the Mood, so instead I
say, "Thanks. It'll be nice not to have to worry about lunch tomorrow," and turn away, feeling like a spy who's evaded interrogation.

"I'll make a salad," I say, going to the fridge.

"Sure." He doesn't sound excited about the idea. "I noticed
you're not eating a whole lot lately. You're not on a diet, are you?"

A *diet*? "You know me better than that."

"Good." Suddenly he's right up against my back, making me jump. He wraps his arms around my waist and squeezes. "I like you with a little meat on you."

His breath on my neck triggers the unsettling blend of attraction and repulsion I've been feeling for him since last night, a warmth spreading in my midsection that belies my urge to pull away. I let out a nervous bark of a laugh. "Are you fondling me with meat juice on your hands?"

He chuckles. "Sorry. Can't help it." He kisses me on the cheek and turns to the sink. "But you are feeling okay, right?" he says after he washes his hands.

Leave me alone, growls some deep, sour part of me, and then the rush of guilt comes, because he sounds genuinely concerned. "Yeah, fine!" I say brightly, opening the fridge, which tells me I need to buy "Meijer . . . two . . . percent . . . reduced . . . fat . . . milk!" and that my "Gulden's . . . spicy . . . brown . . . mustard!" is about to expire. I yank the produce drawer open and rummage for the half-full bag of mixed greens I somehow know is in there. "Can we turn off these reminders? They drive me nuts."

"Sure. Didn't I show you how to do that?"

"I forgot how." I find the greens, a cucumber, a plastic bag of wilting julienned carrots. "You didn't happen to pick up a tomato, did you?"

"I did not." The *you didn't ask me to* is unspoken, but I hear it nevertheless. "I'm gonna go fire up the grill." He goes out through the sliding glass door, leaving the meat at the edge of the counter, where Bear could easily jump up and have himself a nice dinner. I consider letting him; then I relent and move the dish back.

I watch Eric out the window. He looks untroubled, absorbed

in his task, like he doesn't sense me watching him at all. This is someone who says things like *fire up the grill* unironically, someone for whom a steak dinner at home with his wife is a good Saturday night. A simple man, as they say. Still, I can't help but feel like he's performing.

He's hiding something.

There's nothing in his behavior I can put my finger on, and God knows I've been extra-paranoid this weekend. But the thought rises from the dark bottom of my brain, cold and quiet and utterly certain. He knows something about what happened last night. And he's trying as hard as he can to

(*pretend it's not there*)

act like he doesn't.

What am I going to do about it? Accuse him of acting weird and demand to know what's going on?

Yes.

You know what'll happen if you do that, I say to myself. Eric will give me a concerned look and tell me I need to get out of the house more. And if I insist on a truth for which I have no evidence, if I tell him everything I've been living . . .

He will freak out. I'm sure of that now, more sure than I was last night. He will try to solve the problem inside my head, and that doesn't end anywhere good.

Monday, I promise myself between calming breaths. As soon as Eric leaves for work, I'm heading to Chicago. And there, one way or another, I'll find out what I need to know.

After Eric comes back to fetch the steaks, I follow him outside, and sit at the patio table with a beer. The air feels crisp and it's that perfect time of day when the sun has mellowed but the mosquitoes aren't out yet.

In my other life, I haven't had red meat since my parents took me to Outback to celebrate my art school scholarship. Even smelling it used to make me a little nauseous, but now my mouth waters. By the time Eric finishes the steaks, my stomach is growling like it's trying to digest itself. He slides them onto plates and they actually look appetizing, not at all like the damp, quivering lumps of muscle and fat they were an hour ago.

I try a bite and flavor bursts on my tongue: salt, freshly ground pepper, umami. My eyelids actually flutter. "Oh my God."

"Good?" Eric has the hint of a smile that means he's pleased. "Not too done?"

"It's perfect." I take another bite, then a sip of red wine from the glass I poured after finishing my beer. The contrast is immensely satisfying and sensual. "Mm. This is really good."

"I can tell." Now he looks amused, and I feel a flicker of annoyance.

"Well, dig in, this isn't a porno," I say lightly, and Eric chuckles and cuts into his meat.

"This is nice," he says through a mouthful, gesturing with his fork. "We should eat outside more often."

"Yeah." I've lit citronella torches to keep insects at bay, but farther out in the backyard the fireflies have begun their evening dance. The woods beyond them look otherworldly in the twilight, shadows pooling beneath the trees, until someone jogs down the trail in a high-vis jacket and spoils the effect.

The trees trip a memory in my brain. My back pushed against the rough bark of an oak. Hands in my hair, loosening my ponytail. Sunlight through the canopy making shadow patterns that dance along with my heartbeat.

I feel a thrilling drop in my stomach and seem to hear a male voice, low and amused, saying, *I like this route.*

It's not Eric's voice.

I close my eyes, trying to remember. Trying to see the speaker's face. This memory isn't like the other new ones. It's like an image seen through lake water, except with all the senses. Just the one impression was clear: the roughness of the bark, the softness of lips on my throat. The timbre of the voice, vibrating things deep inside me.

"You okay?" Eric asks. He's got a worried look on his face, which is justified considering how weird I've been acting.

I give him a sheepish smile. "Yeah, fine. I was away with the fairies," I say in a fake Irish accent. Eric smiles uncertainly, like he doesn't get the reference. I cut another bite of steak, though after the first few mouthfuls it doesn't taste as good.

"I was thinking we could take a trip," he says. "Maybe a long weekend sometime this summer."

I swallow my steak and ask, "Where do you want to go?" What I'm thinking is, *I could be back in my life by then.*

"Up north? We could get a place on one of those little lakes. You remember my dad's toast last night? How he was saying marriage is like a garden, you have to water it and take care of it . . ."

He's giving me a mild yet penetrating stare, like he can see every thought in my head.

Ask him. Ask him what's happening.

"What about Chicago?" I say.

His brow wrinkles. "Chicago?"

"Yeah! It'd be fun to visit a big city. Stay in a nice hotel, check out some art galleries . . ." *See if my roommates still live in my apartment . . .* "It's only a few hours away."

"That sounds expensive." He smiles, but his leg has begun jittering under the table. My heart speeds up.

"And a cabin on a lake isn't?"

Eric blinks and looks at me more closely. His eyes narrow and his mouth purses up into a W shape, but before he can ask a question his phone, sitting next to his plate, vibrates with an incoming call. *Peter Nedelman.*

"Huh." He answers cautiously, like it might be a telemarketer instead of his best friend from high school. His face changes as he listens to whatever Peter's saying on the other end.

"Just a second," he says to Peter, glancing at me, and he stands and goes into the house.

Left alone in the flickering light from the torches, I think about the way Eric blanched as soon as Peter started talking. I sneak to the sliding glass door and nudge it open a couple of inches. Eric's voice floats faintly from the living room. "Why do you think I have a connection?"

They could be talking about anything, anything at all. Fantasy baseball. Online fandom. Illegal drugs. Yet my heart speeds up and goose bumps erupt on my arms. "Nothing," he says, and I can hear the tension in him.

Bear, who's been nosing around for scraps under the table, bounds up and puts his face to the crack in the door as though he's listening too. He whines to be let in, drowning out whatever Eric says next.

"Hush," I tell Bear, stroking his head. He quiets.

". . . I promise you, I had nothing to do with it," Eric's saying. "I still don't know why you would—"

Peter interrupts him, loudly enough that I can hear his voice through the phone, a room away. I can't understand what he's saying, but he sounds pissed. He goes on for a while, and after he stops Eric takes a moment to reply.

Finally, sounding chastened, he says, "Peter, I'm sorry, but I can't help you."

Peter says something else, and then he must have hung up, because Eric appears in the arch between kitchen and living room before I can back away from the slider. Our eyes meet through the glass. Quickly, I pull the door open so Bear can wriggle through it. The dog bounds up to Eric and sniffs his feet as though they might be covered in meat drippings. "He wanted in," I say weakly.

Eric comes outside, giving me a vague, shell-shocked smile as he passes. He could have just received news of a family member's death, or that he won the lottery. He takes his plate, still half-full, into the kitchen.

"You're done eating?" I ask. Usually he cleans his plate.

"Yeah. I'm not that hungry."

I grab my dishes and follow him in. He moves like a sleep-walker, dumping half a porterhouse into the garbage.

"Bear would probably love to eat that," I say.

"Oh. Right." He leans down to peer into the trash can.

"It's okay. He can have mine."

"Are you sure?" He looks up at me, blinking as if to clear some obstruction in his vision.

"Yeah." I place my steak in Bear's food bowl. Bear picks it up delicately in his mouth and carries it into the cream-carpeted living room, where he can make the maximum amount of mess while he devours it. I'm too distracted to stop him.

"So, what was Peter calling about?" I ask, keeping my delivery casual.

"He just wanted to catch up." Eric holds out his hand for my plate, and I give it to him. His hands shake a little as he soaps it with a sponge. Does he think I don't see?

"Is he still with that guy Gary?"

Eric's mouth opens, then closes. "Um . . . yeah, as far as I know. I didn't ask."

"So what'd you guys talk about, if not your lives?"

My sarcasm goes right over his head. He shrugs. "Work. Video games."

I reexamine the few sentences I heard, what they could mean. What would Peter need help with that would involve Eric? I might be making something out of nothing. They were probably talking about a quest in some role-playing game. But Eric's still scrubbing my plate, though the traces of food are long gone, and he won't look at me.

He and Peter used to code together in high school. Peter even went to the trouble of establishing an official coding club, though he and Eric were the only members. They would set up their laptops in the cafeteria at lunch, and I remember being moderately amazed that no one bothered them. Peter was the rare person who actually didn't give a shit what people thought of him, rather than just pretending. It was like he emanated this force field of indifference that kept the school's designated assholes from messing with him.

After graduation he went to Stanford—I'm sure the coding club looked great on his college applications—then worked in Silicon Valley. Why did he come back here? His father got sick, I remember that, and he'd been recruited by one of the companies in the innovation district . . .

"Where does he work again?" I ask.

Eric glances at me. I pick up the dishcloth and start wiping the counter. He finally puts down the sponge and turns on the faucet to rinse my plate. "A startup. It's called Genie." He turns off the water and places the plate in the drainer with exaggerated care, then stares at the rest of the dishes in the sink as though he's not sure what to do with them.

"Genie." I move to the counter by the stove, still keeping an eye on Eric. "Like the spirit that grants wishes, genie?"

"Yeah . . . because the app's a digital assistant. It'll do whatever you want. You know, 'Your wish is my command.'" He does air quotes. "It's supposed to be smarter than anything that's come before it. It has some special features . . . I don't know much about it." He's trying to sound casual, but I see his jaw clench through his cheek, his fingers gripping the edge of the sink like he's trying to keep himself from making a break for it.

"It sounds right up your alley. Has Peter let you try it out yet?"

"That's kind of what he was calling about." There's irony in his tone, or there would be, if Eric had an ironic bone in his body. Immediately after he speaks, his shoulders stiffen, as if he's said more than he meant to.

I keep wiping the clean counter. "Oh?"

Eric doesn't say anything.

I go to the sink to rinse out my dishcloth, and he lets go of the edge and leans back so I can reach the faucet. My shoulder brushes against his. From the corner of my eye I see him swallow, his eyes lowered.

"So you're going to be his . . . what do they call it, his beta tester?" I wring out the cloth, fold it, and lay it on the counter next to the sink.

"We'll see," Eric says. He's started breathing again. "Can you check if there's anything left outside?"

I return to the backyard to gather silverware and glasses. My mind skips ahead to when I can be alone. I'm not sure if Genie has anything to do with my situation, but there has to be a reason Eric's so keyed up about it. And there was no mistaking the expression on his face after that call, before we both rearranged our expressions.

He's terrified.

10

AFTER WE FINISH CLEANING UP, IT'S EASY ENOUGH TO DISAP-
pear into my office. Eric barely seems to register it when I tell
him I've got some work to catch up on and he shouldn't wait up.
"Don't stay up too late," he says, and heads to the TV room with
Bear and a bag of peanut M&M'S.

Genie is actually spelled *gnii,* no initial capital letter, the de-
scender on the *g* morphing into a wisp of smoke that curls around
and above the wordmark. Meant to evoke smoke issuing from a
genie's lamp, I suppose. The company's tagline ("Your wish.
Our command.") makes me roll my eyes so hard my head tips
back.

Other than the branding, I don't find much. The company is
only a couple of years old. They haven't released a beta version
of their software yet, so there are no reviews. The few articles I
can find exude a sense of mild surprise that a startup so far off
the beaten path has managed to secure sufficient venture capital to develop yet another digital assistant in a crowded market.
They put this down to the company's founder and CEO, a charismatic yet mysterious figure, oddly shy of publicity for the leader
of a tech startup. I can't find any interviews with or photos of
him. One "profile," which the writer seems to have pieced together

using a mix of public records and pure speculation, asserts that the CEO is a former Green Beret and his military discharge was other than honorable.

The company itself is similarly secretive, its offices guarded by private security that turns away reporters, the staff bound by draconian nondisclosure agreements. The consensus in the tech press is that this behavior is slightly more paranoid than most but not completely out of the ordinary, and that gnii is up to something special and bears watching.

I search Peter Nedelman gnii and the only relevant result is his name on the staff page of the company's bare-bones website. I substitute Eric's name for Peter's and get nothing. There's no association between Eric and gnii at all, at least not one that's findable on the Internet.

Just like there's no association between me and anything in my old life.

It's tenuous. I might be drawing connections where none exist. But it's the only lead I have.

I need to get in touch with Peter, but I don't have his number in my contacts, and his email address isn't on gnii's website. Nor does he maintain any social media accounts that I can find. I search some of the other names on the staff page, thinking I might reach out to one of them, but they don't have any online presence either, not even old Facebook accounts. What *is* it with this company?

Eric has Peter's number. I could simply ask him for it, though that would be like wearing a T-shirt that says I OVERHEARD YOUR PHONE CALL EARLIER AND I'M SUSPICIOUS OF YOU. And he always keeps his phone locked. I picture myself palming it just as he's set it down after checking the weather forecast, or pressing his fingertip to the sensor while he's asleep. It wouldn't be hard. But it would be easy to get caught, and getting caught would mean questions I don't know how to answer.

With a sigh, I close the browser window. None of this will matter a couple of days from now anyway. By then, I'll be back in Chicago.

Back in my life.

IN THE MIDDLE of the night I wake up with Eric curled around me, his breath damp and sour on my neck. I ease out of his grasp and go to the bathroom. For a moment I consider packing a bag, getting in my car, and heading west on I-69. I'd arrive in Chicago with the sunrise. All that keeps me from it is the knowledge that tearing off at three in the morning would be an excellent way to notify Eric that I've gone round the bend. Better to stick with my original plan and wait until he goes to work on Monday.

There's no way I'm getting back to sleep, so I pad down the hall to my office. My studio. It's as good a time to paint as any.

The ritual of setting up easel and canvas, preparing paints and brushes, is the most comfort I've experienced since the night of my birthday. My brushes aren't bad, though I can't do much about the paints, which are amateur quality for sure. The smells bring me forcefully home, though a new smell tickles my nose: dust. The tops of the stretched canvases in the closet are furred with it.

I choose soft, floating music, since I can't play anything loud without waking Eric, and get started. I learned figurative work in art school, of course, but I've always gravitated toward abstract painting. Deceptively simple, emotion vibrating through some indefinable communion in the light between the color on the canvas and the eye of the viewer. Or at least I like to think so. Maybe my paintings communicate less than I think they do, or nothing at all to anyone but me. That would seem to be the case, judging by the resounding indifference to my work.

But there is no work, not here. This isn't the studio in Chicago I share with Linnea, where I have a rack full of finished paintings. And something's wrong. My fingers are stiff; my feet can't find the right stance. I never realized how much of painting is muscle memory.

That's not all it is, though. Everything I learned at art school about how to translate my vision into something tangible—knowledge that had become second nature—is in my brain. I can feel it, just beyond my reach. Normally it surrounds me like the air I breathe, but now when I try to grasp at it, it becomes smoke.

I stand back and examine what I've done so far. It's shit. It looks like a fifth grader's art project. It looks like it was painted at one of those BYOB moms'-night-out studios. It looks exactly like something a bored housewife would paint.

Rage wells up in my chest. My foot flies out and kicks the leg of the easel out from under it. The easel teeters drunkenly, then throws off my canvas and topples sideways, collapsing with a smack like a bundle of kindling being dropped. The canvas lands facedown on the carpet with a wet plop. I feel a mean satisfaction, like I've given that asshole painting exactly what it deserves.

A muffled exclamation comes from down the hall, then footsteps. The door opens and Eric squints against the light, his face soft and mole-like with sleep. "Everything okay?"

The draft from the door cools my hot face. "Yeah. My easel fell over." My voice comes out rusty.

Eric blinks. "Your easel fell over? Is there paint on that?" He nods at the face-planted canvas.

"I'll clean it up."

"Yeah, good." He focuses on my face. "Why were you painting in the middle of the night?"

"Got inspired, I guess." My throat catches, and I try unsuccessfully to clear it.

"Oh. Well, maybe the painting will end up being cool. Like a sponge painting or something." He extends his hand. "Leave it 'til morning. Come back to bed."

"No, I should get the paint off the carpet before it dries."

His hand hangs in the air a moment before he withdraws it. "Do you need help?"

I definitely need help, but not the kind he can offer. "I can handle it. Thanks." He wavers, seems to be deciding whether to step into the room. "Go back to bed." He obeys, turning away and shutting the door. I hear him shuffle back down the hall.

He's unconscious again by the time I return to our room. Before I can sleep I have to form the blankets into a ridge in the middle of the bed, a barrier between us.

11

Day Three

I GUESS ERIC AND I ARE ONE OF THOSE COUPLES WHERE THE man always drives, because when we leave for supper at my parents', he goes straight for the driver's side of his car.

Where M-21 turns into Main Street on the approach to Andromeda Creek, a sign notifies travelers that they are entering the sister city to Aulendorf, Germany. LIKE NOWHERE ELSE! claims the sign, but Andromeda Creek is indistinguishable from hundreds of other small towns in the Midwest. Downtown boasts a scattering of squat brick buildings with plate-glass windows, along with a few Beaux-Arts relics from the time of the town's founding in the nineteenth century. A soccer field, a couple of bars, and the annual homecoming parade furnish entertainment. There used to be a gourmet ice cream shop—it's where I had my first job—but the last recession killed that off. The rest is farmland and subdivisions.

Andromeda Creek is like a hundred other places. But something about your hometown calls to you, sends a vibration through the air that matches your heartbeat. It's part of you, even if you hated every minute you spent there, which I didn't. This was a great place to grow up. It was a great place to leave.

Most people born here never do. They graduate from high school and carry on working their family farms or businesses, sinking deeper into debt every year. Or they get retail or service industry jobs, since the auto plants aren't hiring anymore. The ones who go away to college come back, marry their high school sweethearts, and settle in the suburbs, opening medical or law or accounting practices in Davis City: safe, steady work. I know of only a few classmates who've taken the newly available tech jobs at companies that seem to rise and fall with the regularity of the harvest. People here might appreciate the increased business, but they look a little askance at anything new.

I did leave, I tell myself as Eric drives through town. I'd been planning to since I discovered in sixth grade that you could go to college for art, that it was possible to paint pictures for a living. No one had told me that before. I'd had a vague idea that people in olden times had managed it, though I had no inkling of the patronage system supporting the Renaissance painters or the fact that most of the Impressionists had lived in a continual state of hustle, destitution at their backs. I knew only that their work appeared in the exhibition catalogs Ms. Gore, the art teacher, kept on the art-room bookshelves.

Ms. Gore encouraged me from the start. The idea of teaching adolescents has always seemed soul crushing to me, but she displayed genuine enthusiasm for showing my classmates and me how to mix paints and work with oil pastels. Still, it must have been dismal: the assembly line of poorly proportioned still lifes to grade, the constant rustle of laughter from the kids in the back who thought art was their time to goof off. I can only imagine what it was like for her to look over the shoulder of the one-in-a-thousand student with talent.

I was that student. It's not arrogant for me to think that: I had to have talent to get as far as I did. But I've wondered, the past couple of years, if that was enough. How much of my progress was because of simple determination? In the art world, no one cares how hard a worker you are. It got old, always being passed over, often not even being considered. Watching my friends from art school—the ones who could afford to go on to MFA programs—garner prizes and write-ups and incite decorous collector feeding frenzies, while my paintings gathered dust in the shared studio space for which Linnea paid much more than half the rent. The roommates who left dishes in the sink and food clogging the drain. The increasingly exhausting side hustles; dealing with gig apps designed to penalize me for the smallest infraction and squeeze out ever more money for their makers. More and more, after I got home from cleaning gutters in Winnetka or moving someone into a twentieth-floor apartment in River North, I'd flop onto the couch and stream some comedy or drama, something distracting and completely disconnected from my life, instead of going into the studio and making work.

I think I might have been getting tired.

But that beats what I am now: confused, frightened, possibly delusional. My entire adult life, more than a decade of discovery and uncertainty, might be something I made up in my head. I *wish* my most pressing problem were worrying about selling the next painting or how I'm going to pay my electric bill this month. *There's been a toxic spill,* I think as Eric and I pass Petersson's Drugs, Creek 'Tiques, a boarded-up Cosmic Hobby Shop. *I've got lead poisoning.* There must be some explanation for my opening a door in Chicago and walking through it into Davis City, Michigan, and logic says it's almost certainly not that it actually happened.

We pass the cross street leading to the middle and high schools, nestled alongside each other next to the park, and Eric takes my hand as though he's sensed my unease. I glance at him, startled, and he's smiling. "I always think about history when we go by here," he says. I'm a little preoccupied with history myself. But he means the class we shared junior year, when we paired off for a research project.

"Oh, right." (*Thanks for saving my ass with that history presentation. Keep in touch!!*)

"That was when I really got to know you. Though I'd had a crush on you for years—you knew that."

"I didn't, actually." My lips feel stiff. "I didn't know until you asked me out."

I'm telling the truth. I don't recall his exact words that day, just the confusion they elicited, shading to not-altogether-unpleasant surprise, which ceded the conclusion: *Ahh, what the hell.* I've never told Eric this. It seemed unkind to say I'd never thought of him that way, and I fell in love with him pretty quickly after that. Didn't I?

Then there's the alternate history, where he never asked me out at all.

He gives me a sidelong look and squeezes my hand, then puts his back on the wheel. "I can't believe you didn't know on some level."

At the second and last stoplight in town, Eric turns left; then he turns right, then left again, onto a dirt street of clapboard houses built for factory workers who'd wanted a taste of small-town life and had been willing to make the commute to the city. In fifth grade my friend Katie Spence made a comment about my house being small and I learned the difference between my family's version of middle class, where we ate Hamburger Helper twice a week and my two older brothers shared a room in our semifinished basement, and other people's. I didn't speak to Katie for days. But I never felt looked down on: babysitting and a part-time job earned me enough money to buy some of the right clothes, and I took full advantage of the school's well-funded extracurricular activities and art classes. I got a scholarship to art school. I made good.

But I didn't.

The recessions hit my parents' neighborhood hard. Several houses sit empty, boarded up, and the remaining homes are pointedly well maintained, with fresh paint and aggressive window-box pansies. I wonder how much money Andromeda Creek's schools have for art classes now.

Eric pulls up behind my dad's truck with HOLTER ELECTRIC painted on the sides. As soon as he cuts the engine, the side door of the house opens, spilling out light and the smell of pot roast and Dad, beer in hand. "Hey! Here you are!" He always acts like he wasn't sure if we'd make it.

He hugs us both. My parents love the shit out of Eric. He's completely unlike their own sons: reticent where Jeff and Nick are brash, conscientious where they're carefree. It would be different if he'd been theirs to raise. Dad would have found fault with Eric's lack of interest in sports, while Mom would have worried that he didn't have enough friends, but a son-in-law's fitness is defined differently. They've decided he'll take good care of me.

Walking into my parents' house is like going back in time to high school. It's the first really familiar place I've been since Friday, and I relax a little. Dad hustles us through the galley kitchen, where Mom, stirring green beans on the stove, gives us each a one-armed hug. "Beer's in the fridge," Dad says to Eric.

"That sounds great," I say, and Eric glances over quickly enough that I can tell he's surprised. I bend into the refrigerator. "Don't you guys have anything besides alcoholic water?"

"There's red wine," Mom says.

Ugh. I've had enough red wine for a while. I grab a can of Coors. "Eric? You want one?"

"No, thanks." He points to the smart speaker sitting on the kitchen windowsill, playing a pop-country song. "When did you get that?" he asks my mother.

"Jeff brought it over last week. He won it in some Internet contest, and they've already got one . . . I don't really know what to do with it, though, other than listen to music. Oh, and I asked it what I should set the oven to. Three twenty-five, it said! No way is that high enough. I went ahead and did three fifty."

"I'll have to adjust your privacy settings," Eric says. "You know those things are always listening, right? They record everything you say to them."

Mom laughs. "Anyone listening to us would be bored out of their minds. Ooh, that's nice." Her hand swoops in to pluck at my new necklace, which I haven't taken off since Eric put it on me. I'd almost forgotten it was there. "Birthday present?"

"Yeah."

Her eyes glitter. "Are these real diamonds?"

"Mom!"

"They are," Eric says, looking more pleased than offended.

"You done good, Eric." She pats him on the shoulder. "All right, get out of here. Let me cook."

I slug half my beer as soon as we've sat on the overstuffed couch in the living room, where the TV is playing *SportsCenter*. Dad parks himself in the La-Z-Boy next to the wall where my and my brothers' senior portraits hang, immortalizing our unfortunate fashion choices. Our baby pictures used to decorate the dining room, but my mother has packed those away in favor of her "grands," painstakingly ensuring an equal number of photos of each child. Ashleigh and Kaleigh in the bathtub; Malik in the bathtub. Malik in tae kwon do gear; Ashleigh (or Kaleigh) in a glittery leotard; Kaleigh (or Ashleigh) in her T-ball uniform brandishing a tiny bat. In the kitchen, the refrigerator is covered in their drawings. My mother has never displayed any of my work, beyond taping my own childhood drawings to the fridge. Once I got serious about art, she stopped wanting anything to do with it. She thought I was being frivolous, was sure I'd end up working service jobs for the rest of my life.

My dad gabs to Eric about baseball, about going to games at the old Tiger Stadium at Michigan and Trumbull when he was a kid. Totally different experience from Comerica Park. Eric never got to go to Tiger Stadium, did he?

"I never went inside either of them," Eric says.

"Really? Living in Dearborn, that close, and you never went to a game?"

Eric shrugs. "My family wasn't into baseball."

Dad sits back in his chair, his expression and sympathetic headshake saying plainly, *You don't know what you were missing.* "Kelly never liked going to games, either."

Eric looks at me with interest. "Really?"

"I didn't *dislike* it. Baseball's so boring to watch, though. I'd rather watch soccer." Plus my brothers would fight over literally everything for the whole trip (who rode in the front seat in the car, who snagged the better view at the ballpark, who was hogging all the popcorn) and I always felt bad, because my dad was spending so much money to make us all pissed off and tired, but he had this romanticized view of baseball games from his childhood and wouldn't stop taking us to them.

"I don't know how you can say baseball's boring," my dad says, and launches into an explanation about some esoteric stats thing.

"It's almost ready!" Mom calls from the kitchen.

Eric pops up like he's on a spring. "Need any help?"

"Sure, hon, you could set the table. Kelly, will you get everyone ice waters?"

Setting the table was always Nick's job, along with drying the dishes afterward. Jeff cleared and scraped; I washed. I still hate washing dishes. I trail Eric into the kitchen to get the glasses while he fetches the plates, the three of us crowding the narrow space. "No Jeff tonight?" I ask Mom. I don't bother asking about Nick; I figure he had enough family time on Friday.

"No, the girls had something for dance. Or maybe it was gymnastics. Nick said he might bring Malik over." Mom glances at the clock on the oven. "It's not looking good, though." She opens the oven door and gives a little grunt as she lifts the roasting pan, struggling with it. I project my vision seconds into the future, when the pan tips out of her hands and crashes to the floor, spattering the linoleum with meat and potatoes and ropes of grease. Then Eric is steadying the pan, taking it from her, setting it on a trivet on the counter.

"Thanks, hon," Mom says. She's breathing harder than I'd

like. I've been trying not to think of the news Dad dropped on me, back in my other life. Not during my birthday call, but on a separate one a few days earlier.

(I didn't want to ruin your birthday, Bug.)

Mom looks fine now. Maybe a little pale.

I watch as she spears the roast with two big forks and lifts it onto a serving dish. "Dr. Walter says I'm going through hormonal changes," she says, noticing my attention. "Hoo-boy, Kelly, are you in for a ride in another twenty-five years."

"Is he sure it's just hormonal? Has he run tests?" I turn away to fill the water glasses. My parents still have those yellow pebbled-glass ones from my childhood that made milk look spoiled.

"Help me with those drippings, will you?" she asks Eric as she pulls a skillet out of the cabinet and flour from the pantry. Eric pours the meat juice from a corner of the roasting pan into the skillet, where she whisks it into gravy. Vicky Holter doesn't do vegetarian options, as she made abundantly clear on my occasional visits home from Chicago.

Just as we're sitting down, we hear the sound of a car settling into park on the street outside. "Nick's here," my mother says, popping up to grab another couple of place settings. She never gives my brother any grief about his small rudenesses, like showing up late for supper. Nobody does, except for Jeff. When we were younger, I resented that Nick got away with so much, but eventually I just accepted it. And learned as many tricks as I could from him.

"Hey-hey!" His voice floats through the house, his feet stamping on the stairs inside the back door.

"Nicholas! You made it!" My father half rises from his seat, beckoning. "Get in here."

"Let me just set these in the fridge real quick. Kelly? Eric? Do either of you want a real beer?"

I crane my neck to see into the kitchen, where Nick holds up a six-pack of IPA. Speaking of tricks: bringing alcohol is one of his more reliable ones. "Yes, please," I call. Eric declines. He doesn't drink much. Nick hands me a beer and opens one for himself; he must be anticipating the freedom of handing Malik off to his mom after supper.

Malik, shadowing Nick, submits to my mother's hugs and kisses and cheek pinches with stoicism. He's a quiet kid, more self-possessed than shy. As he comes into the dining room, I notice he's clutching a knitted stuffed giraffe with long eyelashes that's wearing a pink ribbon around its neck. He sits and sets the giraffe beside him.

Nick loads up his own plate, while my mother fixes Malik one before she serves herself. Oblivious, Nick and my dad begin a loud conversation about baseball, which Nick played in high school. The volume level is nothing compared to Eric's family dinners, from what I remember, but I take a glance to see how he's reacting. He stares at a point on the table just beyond his plate, eating Mom's pot roast like he's tunneling under a wall.

I remember being surprised when, after the first time I had him over for supper, he let slip that he found Mom's cooking bland. He bought his lunch at school every day, and when we went out he ate fast food like everyone else, but I didn't know yet that his dad was a decent amateur chef. *I'll have to have him cook for you,* Eric said, his ears flushing pink the way they did when he was excited or embarrassed. This was the week after prom and two days after our first real make-out session, when articles of clothing had come off. We'd been dating three weeks. Was I in love with him by then? Maybe. On my way to it.

Malik's pretending to feed his giraffe with morsels of meat from his plate. "How come you didn't bring her to my birthday party?" I ask, putting a joking lilt into my voice.

Malik's utterly serious hazel eyes meet mine. "Gerald's a boy."

"Oh! Sorry, Gerald."

"And he doesn't like spaghetti."

Kids are so weird.

I return to my own dinner. I've taken a small slice of roast and filled the rest of my plate with carrots and potatoes and green beans, though it hardly matters because the root vegetables are permeated with gravy, the beans cooked in bacon grease. Except for the steak last night, I haven't eaten meat since I was eighteen, but my stomach accepts it without complaint. Apparently Michigan Kelly is used to it. Still, I can't bring myself to do much more with the beef than shred it with my fork, hiding it under some crushed potato.

"You're not eating," my mother observes. "You're not on a diet, are you?"

Haven't these people ever heard of body positivity? "No," I say, "I'm not on a diet."

"Good. We've got carrot cake for dessert."

"When did you have time to make that, Vick?" my dad says. "I thought you were supposed to be—"

"Packing?" Mom interrupts. "I'm done with that already."

"Packing for what?" I ask.

"Your dad's taking me up north. Nice, huh?"

"Up north? As in a vacation?" The last vacation my family took was a camping trip to the Grand Canyon when my brothers and I were still in elementary school. We had an old army tent that reeked of mildew and was so cramped that Jeff, Nick, and I ended up fighting over who got to sleep outside in the hammock.

Mom smiles at my dad, who looks sheepish. He doesn't like to take time off work.

"When did this happen? When are you leaving?" I ask.

"We just decided a couple days ago. We're leaving tomorrow, coming back Friday. You can actually get a condo for pretty cheap, if it's during the week."

If travel isn't my parents' thing, a spur-of-the-moment trip is even more out of character. "Won't it still be kind of chilly?"

"We're just going to Traverse City. Plenty to do there, even if it's too cold for the beach."

"I wanted to take her to Florida," Dad says through a mouthful of potatoes.

"People don't need to see me in a bathing suit."

Dad waves his fork at Eric and me. "You guys should go on vacation. You know, get it in while you're still young." *While you're still childless,* he means, because apparently all pleasure and fulfillment in life end as soon as you reproduce.

"We were just talking about taking a trip," Eric says. "Chicago, right?" He turns to me. His face is placid, brows raised in polite inquiry, but his voice sounds half an octave higher than usual. "Nice hotel? Art galleries?"

I give a false laugh. "So you do listen to me."

"Chicago, that's where you had the scholarship, wasn't it?" Dad says. "The Art Institute."

"I was so relieved when you gave up that whole art school idea," says Mom. "It was so pie-in-the-sky. Though of course nobody could tell you that at the time."

I didn't give it up. Doesn't anyone remember except me? But my dad is masticating his way through his pot roast, the subject all but closed in his mind, as Mom nods in a self-satisfied way that makes me want to go scream in the street. Eric's the only one who's still looking at me, waiting to see what I'll say. I feel caught in his gaze. I swallow, and even that small movement feels like a giveaway. Am I swallowing the way *his* Kelly would swallow? Am I acting different, strange?

Is he onto me?

The thought makes my heart beat faster. Not because Eric would think I was having some kind of mental breakdown—though that would be bad enough—but because he might not.

"I'm going to Vegas next month," Nick says. "It's gonna be pretty sick." He goes on, talking about the casinos and buffets he plans to hit, how he and a group of his friends have been planning this trip for months. As usual, nobody minds his bringing the talk around to himself. I'm actually grateful for it.

I glance up and Eric's still looking at me, but his eyes flick away as soon as he sees me notice. Unable to stand any more, I pop up and start clearing plates. My mother starts to rise as well. "No, sit down, Mom, I've got it."

She subsides into her chair but can't keep herself from saying, "Why don't you leave those until after we have dessert?" As if I could eat cake right now. Maybe Michigan Kelly would listen to her. I don't.

In the kitchen, I start to fill the sink with soapy water and scrape the food remnants from the plates. Nick slips past, heading outside for a smoke without fetching me any of the dirty glasses or silverware from the table, but it's Eric I'm annoyed with for not helping. He knows I hate doing dishes.

He knows.

Maybe not everything. But Eric's not stupid, and if Peter's call last night had anything to do with my situation, he'll be on high alert. The only reason he hasn't confronted me is that he's not sure. But he's watching me, looking for signs. And he's been probing, in his oblique way. *Have I done something?*

He'd better not try to keep me from leaving tomorrow.

A fork jabs the pad of my thumb under the water: hard enough to startle, not hard enough to really hurt, but I gasp and cry out. "Everything okay in there?" Eric calls, turning sideways in his chair. Mom has her hand on his arm. She's probably boring him silly.

A possibility occurs that sends relief and disquiet washing through me in successive waves. An explanation for my parents' suddenly deciding to go on a trip together. A justification for Eric's monitoring of my emotions, my reactions, that doesn't involve his knowing about the other life in my head.

And a connection between that life and this one. Out of everything that's different, one thing that's the same.

"Hey, Dad, could you bring me those serving dishes?"

"Sure, Bug." Dad drains his Coors and carries in the dishes. As soon as he's in the kitchen, I pounce.

"What's with Mom?" I keep my voice low enough to be lost in the rush of rinse water running in the sink. "She almost dropped the roast taking it out of the oven."

"We'll talk about it later, okay?"

"She's sick, isn't she?"

The animation goes out of my dad's face like someone's snatched it. His shoulders sag, and I know. *I know.*

He sets the dishes on the counter and—after glancing into the dining room to make sure Mom's still chattering to Eric—lays his arm across my shoulders in a half hug. "She has breast cancer. Stage two."

The words are like a sly, distorted echo in my head. "Stage *two*?"

He nods, solemn. "It's not as bad as it sounds." He doesn't know how bad it could be. "It's treatable. She's having a lumpectomy as soon as we get back from Traverse City . . . we'll find out after that if she needs chemo and radiation. It's outpatient, but I've gotta work that day. We could probably use your help."

"Was she ever going to ask me? Because, you know, that would involve telling me what's going on." I manage to sound normal, even put out.

"She didn't want to ruin your birthday. You know how she is when she gets an idea in her head . . ."

"Yes. Yes, I do."

In the dining room my mother stands and says, "Who's ready for cake?"

"Don't make a big deal of it, okay?" my dad says, before she comes in.

12

"YOU'RE QUIET," ERIC SAYS ON THE DRIVE HOME. I HAVEN'T SAID a word since we got in the car.

My hands twist together in my lap.

"Everything okay?"

I run my pinky fingernail under my thumbnail, jabbing the unprotected flesh, and stifle a gasp. "You knew about my mom, didn't you?"

"What?"

"That she has cancer?"

He turns his head and looks at me, horrified, and a different kind of horror drifts through me. He didn't know.

The car vibrates as we rumble over the reflectors at the verge of the road. "Eric!"

"Sorry!" He whips his head forward, rights the car.

"I didn't mean to tell you like that. I really thought you knew."

His face is drawn tight. "Why would you think that?"

Because you've been hiding something from me. "I don't know. I'm sorry."

"It's okay." He takes a breath and lets it out in a short, hard sigh. "Is she going to be all right?"

"I don't know. She has to have surgery." And suddenly I'm

crying, noisy, ugly sobs that feel torn from my chest. It's because of her diagnosis, though there's a dash of relief in there as well. *Stage two.* Mostly, though, I'm crying because I've been holding all this in for two days, my reaction to this huge, scary, inexplicable change in my life, and now it's coming out in the only way it can. I want to go home. I just want to go home.

"Hey," Eric says, putting his hand on my leg. "Hey." I can feel him vacillating over whether to pull over and comfort me. I want him to, but at the same time I don't want the heat of his attention. I cover my face with my hands and hold my breath until the sobs stop.

"I'm fine," I say, wiping tears. I'm not fine, but I will be.

Tomorrow. Going to Chicago feels like an escape chute out of this life.

We arrive at the house, let the dog out, get ready for bed. Eric watches me from the sides of his eyes, worried in a way that makes my skin crawl. After we get into bed he pulls me into his arms and holds me for a long time.

"She'll be okay," he says.

"How do you know?"

He doesn't answer, because there is no true answer other than *I don't.* Instead, he kisses me. I let him kiss me a second time, and a third, and then I turn over, away from him, breaking the circle of his arms. His hand follows me, stroking down my side and coming to rest on my hip.

"I'm exhausted," I say. The hand withdraws. Hurt radiates off him, but I don't have it in me to do anything about it.

"I love you," he says.

I murmur an answer and pull my knees into my chest. After a while his breath lengthens and deepens and he sleeps. I can't.

My mother's sickness is the first thread I've found between this life and the one that might exist only in my head. It's a twisted thread. The week before my birthday, my dad had called me in Chicago in the middle of the day. He'd gotten right to it. Breast cancer, he said in a hushed, even voice unlike any I'd heard from him before. Stage four. Aggressive course of treatment. A long way from giving up, a darn long way. He'd wanted to wait until after my birthday to tell me, but they weren't sure how long . . .

He'd stopped there. I took refuge in questioning him. When would treatment start? Should I come home? But I paused too long before asking that one. I knew returning to Michigan to help my dad and my brothers was the right thing to do, but I really, really didn't want to.

"No, no. No need for you to come home yet," he said, and a belated stab of hurt went through me. Did she not want to see me, her only daughter? Had our relationship deteriorated that much? "Come visit when you can. But she wouldn't want you to uproot your whole life." He went silent, leaving an opening of more than adequate size for me to insist. I didn't. Instead, after I got off the phone, I went out and got so shit-faced I couldn't stomach alcohol again until the night of Linnea's opening.

Chicago Kelly's mother had stage-four breast cancer, a virtual death sentence. Michigan Kelly's mother has a manageable disease. There's no logic to it: it's not as if it was caught earlier here. Same time period, same medical care. Different outcome. It doesn't make sense. Nothing here does.

13

Day Four

I PACK AS SOON AS ERIC LEAVES FOR WORK. TOOTHBRUSH, moisturizer, running shoes, a few days' worth of clothes. More than that seems like too much of a commitment. I'm on the freeway by midmorning, sailing along until I hit an inexplicable series of traffic jams at the Indiana-Illinois border, as if the universe is throwing up obstacles. Well, fuck the universe.

My plan, such as it is, is to retrace my route through last Friday night as closely as possible, which means starting from my apartment. I'm not sure what I expect to find. I'm half hoping something similar to what occurred on my birthday will happen now, only in reverse. That would make everything a hell of a lot simpler.

Traffic crawls and then flies. Scrubland and strip malls give way to a Lego landscape of narrow houses with neat little garages tucked behind them, which merge into taller buildings with jutting porches. On a Monday afternoon, parking in my neighborhood is easy. I look for my car—the car I have in Chicago, a ten-year-old Civic named Hortense—but it's not in its usual spot. This doesn't bother me as much as I would have thought, because I'm so happy to be home. It's one of those early spring days that makes you glad to be alive, all fresh breeze and bright blue sky. The city luxuriates in it, as though it has a sense memory of hunkering down against bitter winter winds. Even though the temperature is barely over fifty degrees, everyone I see on the street wears short sleeves and smiles at me as we pass. It's only friendliness, however: I don't run into anyone I recognize. It feels like I've been gone much longer than a weekend. I pass crumbling brown brick houses, side by side with the squared-off granite and glass of the newly rehabbed. From somewhere down the block echoes the rhythmic punch of a nail gun, the whine of a saw.

The sidewalk in front of my apartment is empty. My building's not directly on the street, but behind it: an old coach house converted into two flats, reached by a narrow, gated passageway between buildings. As usual, the lock on the gate is broken. I stop at the entrance and thumb open a couple of mailboxes: empty. The mailboxes have never had names attached, but years ago someone put some local band's sticker on one of them. It steadies me to see it's still there.

My steps slow as I approach my building, as though a magnetic field repels me. No reason not to see, I tell myself sternly, and continue into the little concrete courtyard. I can see changes right away. Instead of the picnic table my neighbors and I dragged in from an alley, a wooden kitchen table sits warped and faded from the weather. Drifts of discarded plastic bottles and cigarillo ends have built up in the corners. I want to look up at my balcony, but I keep my eyes lowered until I've mounted the stairs.

On my porch I keep potted plants, most of them in some stage of progress toward death; a couple of deck chairs, also gleaned from an alley; and a thrift-store coffee table I decoupaged. Now the space is half-filled with a jumble of toys and shoes of various sizes. I knock on the storm door. I can hear music inside, loud and bright. I knock again, hard enough to make the door rattle, and the volume of the music goes down.

The inner door opens about a foot, wide enough for me to view the face and shoulders of a woman in her thirties whom I've never seen before. Her expression is guarded. "Yes?"

"Hi!" I put on a smile. "I'm sorry to bother you . . . I used to live here." I don't even know what I want: to go in and see other people's stuff where mine sat three days ago? It's not as if this woman has my roommates or my cat stashed inside.

She eyes me silently, and I wonder if she understands English. Then she says, "Are you sure you have the right place? My mother-in-law's been here since the eighties," and I feel like an asshole. For a second I consider the possibility that she's right and I've wandered into the wrong courtyard. But the sticker on the mailbox, the familiar slam of the broken gate . . . And the shapes of the buildings themselves: I could draw the way they cut into the sky above from memory.

"¿Mami?" A little girl sidles around her. "¿Quién es?"

The woman answers in Spanish. The girl looks up at me shyly and I give her a small smile. *See, I'm harmless.* This spooks her; she turns and darts back into the apartment, pushing the door wider as she goes so I can see inside. My living room walls hold an assemblage of gallery posters, band flyers, the work of friends. In this room, framed photos march a ruler-straight line near the ceiling: a black-and-white of a bride and groom, a color shot of a different bride and groom. School pictures of a dark-haired boy in a series, growing older from left to right, and a studio portrait of him a few years younger, holding his little sister as an infant.

"This apartment's not for rent," the woman tells me, with a coil of steel in her voice that suggests the question has come up before. "They're rehabbing the building down the street; I think those apartments are about to be listed. Try there." She steps back, starts to close the inner door.

"You said your mother-in-law's lived in this apartment for a long time?"

Her impatience is palpable. "Yes, since she moved to Chicago. My husband grew up here."

"Does she remember—is she here? Can I talk to her?"

The woman shakes her head. "She's not well."

From a bedroom—my roommate Leni's, the largest—comes a voice: "¿Daniela?"

"Momento, Mami," Daniela calls. To me she says, "I have to go."

"One second!" Without thinking, I reach for the storm door's handle. Daniela's eyes widen, and I pull my hand back. "Who lives downstairs from you? Is it a couple? James and Kevin? Tall, skinny dude, short guy with a beard—"

The voice comes again, querulous: "¡Daniela!"

"I have to go," Daniela repeats. She slams the inner door and locks the dead bolt.

I stand for a moment outside my apartment, which is not my apartment, then descend the stairs slowly. On the way down I think about knocking on James and Kevin's door, but they won't be home; they both work during the day. I'm not sure I could handle it if someone else answered.

Or if one of them answered and didn't recognize me.

I feel better once I'm back on the street, bathing myself in the atmosphere of the city that's been my home for more than a decade. *The gallery.* I'll follow my plan. Like I did on Friday night, I'll take the Ashland bus south, lock onto whatever magic brought me here, and ride it back to my old life. Will I even remember this odd, fractured period? I feel a flicker of regret for the closeness with my family and the warmth of Eric's, for Eric himself. Something's there, some turbid well of emotion for him under my fear and uncertainty, but I'm too focused on my goal to examine it.

I walk down the street with purpose but get turned around on my way to Ashland Avenue and find I have to concentrate on tracing a route that I usually take automatically. I *lived* here, not seventy-two hours ago. Earlier, being in Chicago felt like coming back home, but now I feel conspicuous in my too-new Converse and mall clothes. I'm afraid that if I stop walking someone will ask me if I need directions. I make a turn, then another, and before I know it I have no idea where I am.

No one's around. Warehouses and parked cars surround me. It's eerily silent, or as close as you get to it in the middle of the city; tiny sounds magnify themselves against crumbling concrete walls covered in graffiti. The sun goes behind a cloud, desaturating the colors in the landscape. I walk onward, feeling faintly ridiculous, scanning for the next turn so I can work my way back to something recognizable.

Movement, from the corner of my eye, a block behind me. It could be a pigeon or a stray cat. It could be someone getting into their car. But there's something furtive about it that makes my skin prickle and my heart rate surge.

Someone's following me.

The thought sounds oddly calm inside my head, but my breath sticks like hot taffy in my lungs. I clutch the strap of my bag, more to ground myself than out of any expectation of holding on to it. This feels more dire than an impending mugging; this feels existential, like the darkest part of a dark fairy tale. A metallic taste fills my mouth; a stain like smoke spreads in front of my eyes.

I keep walking, numb, until the street ends in a waist-high wall and a chain-link fence, beyond which I-90 cuts a swath through the neighborhood. I'm boxed in.

A kind of panicked torpor comes over me: an urge to stand at the wall, staring at the freeway, until whoever—whatever—is behind me catches up. Instead I make an about-face and plunge down the street the way I came, walking in the middle, unable to turn my head left or right. I feel like I'm wading through hip-deep water. The soles of my shoes flap against the pavement. If I break into a run the hunt will be on; the horror in my sub-imagination will pounce. The sun emerges, bathing the street in a bilious yellow glow, glancing shards of light off car bumpers. The crabgrass forcing its way between cracks in the sidewalk shines a cancerous green. A finger of sweat strokes the curve of my lower back. Any second someone will step into my path, a hand will descend on my shoulder, a voice will ask me for a cigarette. Any second now.

Nothing happens.

I reach the point where I saw the movement, then the next block and the next, and no one accosts me. A car turns onto the street, so I veer onto the sidewalk, feeling dizzy and unreal. In the middle distance I can see people walking, normal people with legitimate business, not shadows for me to jump at.

Eventually I find my way to Chicago Avenue, and the grid snaps back into place in my head. My route to Ashland and the bus stop is easy enough to remember. I can even pinpoint the area where I got lost: I've walked past that street hundreds of times. I should have known exactly where I was.

14

THE GALLERY'S CLOSED.

MONDAY BY APPOINTMENT, the lettering on the door says. I lean in to peer through the plate glass, cupping my hands around my eyes. It's darkened, empty. I almost let myself get discouraged, but the real me is so close. I'm right here in her city, and she soon comes surging back. I whip out my phone and punch in the number printed on the door below the hours of operation. I can hear a telephone ringing through the glass, echoing, at the same time as I hear it ringing through my phone. Both sets of ringing end in a recording that invites me to leave a message.

When I speak I attempt to summon the appropriate sense of entitlement, to project the assumption that whoever checks the voicemail will return my call immediately and will be happy to open the gallery for me that very afternoon. I try to sound like the sort of art connoisseur who would show up wearing a hoodie and tennis shoes and not think anything of it.

But that's not quite good enough. I walk around to the alley, find the back door, and ring the bell. Amazingly, footsteps approach and the door chuffs open wide enough for a guy to stick his head out. He's about my height and almost as slight, dressed in a slim-fitting charcoal suit with a fuchsia pocket square, and he's waxed his mustache into curlicues at the ends. I remember him from Linnea's opening—he was the one hovering at her elbow half the night—and I knew him slightly before that. He came out of art school a few years behind me and Linnea and he's been kicking around the scene since then, but I can't recall his name.

He quite plainly doesn't recognize me. "Yes?" he says, looking me up and down with dismissal in his eyes. "There's a café down the street with a public bathroom."

I straighten my back so I stand half an inch taller than him. "I don't have an appointment, but I wondered if I might have a quick look at the Linnea Floods." His eyes are already glazing over. I change tack, turning on the charm. "I've heard they're amazing."

He responds to my smile with a closed-lipped one of his own: he's not convinced I'm anyone he needs to be nice to. Why would he be? I look like a soccer mom from Kenosha, with my frizzy hair and leggings and my purse from T.J.Maxx slung across my chest. I should have thought ahead and dressed the part, assuming my closet in Davis City contains anything approaching the part.

"Sorry," he says, not remotely regretful. "I'm booked up this afternoon. We're open to the public tomorrow at ten."

"But I'm only in town for the day. I just flew in from the West Coast—" The door is already thumping shut.

Never mind. I'll come back.

I head north toward my car, walking the whole route this time. What next, now that the plan's been derailed? It's past noon and I haven't eaten since the bowl of cereal I had this morning. In a café where I used to bring out-of-town guests for brunch I sit at the bar, ordering a vodka soda to go with my tempeh tacos, and plan my next move. In the bar mirror I can see flyers tacked to the wall behind me for clubs, rock shows, art openings. There's still one up for this year's Artbash, the student exhibition at SAIC. I should go there while the buildings are open, to verify that I still recognize the places where I used to spend time when I was new to the city. Or better yet, get a copy of my transcript. Hard evidence.

I finish my lunch, pay, and leave. The drive downtown is stop-and-go, knotted with traffic. Leaving my car in the garage at Millennium Park, I walk down Columbus Drive past the museum. As I approach the angled concrete-and-glass blocks of the Columbus building, where the student studios are, I feel a disconcerting sense of familiarity mixed with foreignness. I used to practically live in this building; now I'm a visitor.

But that would have been the case anyway. It's how any alums would feel after years of separation.

Inside, the smell is the same as I remember—linseed oil, the chalky tang of clay—which makes me feel more like myself. I'm intending to go upstairs and check out the painting studios, but instead I find myself wandering past the seminar rooms. Most of the doors are closed, but through one that's slightly ajar I see tables arranged in a discussion-aiding square, holding attentive students who sit in the same ways and the same spots as Linnea and our friends and I used to, though the fashions have changed some.

A voice drifts out, and though I'm still too far away to hear what it's saying, its timbre plucks a string of memory in me.

The answering voice is louder, authoritative, its owner young and male. "I don't know if I'd call her *feminist*. She's actually participating in her own objectification."

I drift to a stop, listening. A third voice, also young but female, chimes in. "But if she's objectifying herself, it's on her own terms. Like with Sex Pictures? Those works, they're supposed to—"

"Yeah, I *know* what they're supposed to do," the boy cuts in.

"Let Raina finish, Jasper," the first voice says, patient but with an edge. I definitely know the woman who's speaking. I creep until I can peer through the small window in the door. The instructor is turned sideways, facing the room, but I recognize her. She's a painter I worked with when I was here, Julia Wheat, who also taught art history.

"They aren't supposed to be *titillating*. They're supposed to make you uncomfortable?" says a dark-haired girl, the same one who was talking before. "And, like, she's playing different roles? So it's not really *her* that's being objectified. She's performing femininity, subverting the male—"

"The male gaze, right." Jasper can't resist finishing her sentence. He reminds me a bit of Aaron, Aaron of the disappearing ankle tattoo: same good looks, same air of disdain for everything. He's even wearing a beanie.

"You're right, Raina," Julia says a little pointedly. "And keep in mind, Sherman is taking on a multiplicity of roles behind the camera as well. Photographer, obviously, but also set dresser, makeup artist . . ."

"So she's in control. She's empowered," says Raina.

"Right. And though Cindy Sherman has denied being a *feminist* artist, it's worth thinking about the reasons an artist might feel pushed to resist that labeling. Especially in the era we're talking about."

Another girl speaks up. She's outside the slice of room I can see through the window, but her voice has an air of ponderous profundity that makes it sound like she did a few bong hits before class. "So in each photo she's a different person . . . but there are always those moments between, when she's not one thing or the other. What is she then?"

"Naked," says Jasper. People laugh, but Raina throws him a scornful glance.

"Well . . . that was retro," Julia says dryly, drawing a friendlier laugh than Jasper got. "It's about that time, folks. I'll see you Wednesday."

I wait outside the door while the students gather their things and leave. Most of them pass me without a glance. When I step into the room Julia looks up with interest but no recognition.

"Hi," she says. I fight against a swell of disappointment. There's no real reason she should remember me. She goes through dozens of new students every year. Except, I recall in a rush, she did remember me the last time we ran into each other. It was a couple of summers ago at a friend's group show, and she came up and asked how Linnea and I were doing. I can still feel her cool hands on my elbows as we kissed cheeks, the flush of warmth and pride. I'd liked her, wanted her to think well of me, and was happy at the indication that she did.

"You're still here," I say.

She smiles uncertainly. "Are you an alumna?"

"Yeah. Yes, I am." It feels good to say it. "Kelly Holter."

Still not a flicker. If anything her smile grows more dubious. But she looks me in the eye and says, "Oh, right. How've you been? You were photography, right?" The old fake-it-'til-you-make-it: I've done it plenty of times myself.

I smile. "You don't remember me, do you?"

Her mouth opens as if she's going to deny it; then her lips press together sheepishly. Her head turns sideways in a half shake of affirmation.

"It's okay. Sometimes I hardly know myself if art school ever happened."

She nods, her eyes widening—in concern? Or just sympathy? "But that's why you came back. To remind yourself."

"I guess so. Some of the things I remember, though, nobody else seems to." I don't know why I feel like I can unburden myself to her. Maybe it's because she's part of my old life, if only glancingly; and once I start it's hard to stop. "I'm not sure whether they're real or I'm making them up."

"Memory is subjective," she says. "We all prioritize different experiences. Doesn't make it less true if nobody else bothered to remember it."

I only wish that applied to my situation.

"That's where the best work comes from, you know," Julia goes on. "The things you notice that no one else does. Are you making work?"

"That's part of the problem."

She nods again. "I had a feeling." Her gaze sharpens, and anticipation stirs in me; she might recognize me after all. But she just glances at her smartwatch. "Look . . . Kelly, right? I've got a free hour. Did you want to get a coffee?"

I'm tempted. But she should remember me and she doesn't. Revealing who I really am now would only make it awkward, and I can't tell her the whole truth. "I can't, but thanks. It was nice to see you."

Her smile is sincere, if uncertain. "You too."

At the door, I turn back. "So what are you? When you're not

one thing or the other?" I'm thinking of the last bit of the class discussion, but also of my own predicament. "If you're not artist or subject, are you just . . . nothing?"

The regular-person response to that would be that nobody is unimportant. Everybody means something to someone; everyone matters. But in the world where Julia Wheat lives, where I used to live, that's not necessarily true.

"I don't think so," she says. "Maybe you're figuring out which one you want to be." She smiles, like she's making a joke, but she's helped me more than she knows.

"Thanks," I tell her, and leave.

I'm tempted to walk through the museum, but I want to check with the school's registration and records office before it closes, so I take Monroe, with its view of skyscrapers gilded by the afternoon sun. Dodging swarms of tourists making their way from Michigan Avenue to the lakefront, I'm overwhelmed by the time I reach the teeming, building-shaded streets west of the park, as if I'm truly a denizen of the suburbs knocked back by the hustle and bustle of the big city. Being part of a crowd used to soothe me, but now I feel my breath coming faster. The same sense from before of being watched—being followed—creeps over me. I'm not alone here—I'm surrounded by people; I'm safe. But what if someone really is stalking me? What could any of these strangers do?

I go so far as to step out of the flow of foot traffic and scan my surroundings. I get a few passersby doing the glance-and-look-away in response, but no one seems inordinately interested. I don't recognize any of the faces. Still, as soon as I start west again, I feel that crawling sensation between my shoulder blades. I practically throw myself through the Sullivan building's glass doors. My heart pounds as I board the elevator, which would make an excellent trap. Fortunately several other people, all seemingly focused on their own errands, get in with me.

Upstairs, in the registration and records office, a secretary sits half-hidden behind a translucent glass wall. I reel off my student ID number from memory and she types it in.

"Hmm," she says, "I'm not finding you. When did you say your dates of attendance were?" I tell her. "I'm not seeing a Kelly Maureen Holter," she says, her face clouding, a thread of suspicion in her voice. I am pranking her; I am wasting her time. Then, abruptly: "Oh, wait! Here you are." Every nerve in my body extends. Even though I hoped for proof, it's still a shock to get it. "You're in the admitted-never-enrolleds."

Never enrolled. I let out a shaky breath, the blare of adrenaline fading, leaving me wrung out. *Never enrolled.*

"You graduated with a BFA?" The secretary looks up at me uncertainly, with the care of someone who has realized the person across the desk is not all there, round the bend, a few sandwiches short of a picnic. "Are you sure it was at this campus?" Her tone conveys that she deals with artists all the time and can maintain professionalism in the face of myriad eccentricities, but actual mental illness falls outside her job description.

I take a deep breath and remember my commencement ceremony. Afterward my dad hugged me, speechless for once, his eyes moist. We went out for dinner with Linnea and Bobby and their families, a whole crowd of us.

I say, "Yes, I'm sure. Could you look one more time, please?"

My certainty revives the secretary's faith in me. Her fingers fly across the keyboard, and she mutters as she descends into more esoteric depths of the system. "Maybe in the department records . . . Could you have been filed under your middle name? But no, your ID would turn that up . . ."

Meanwhile, my resolve drains away. Even if she did find my transcript in some database backup from long ago—which she won't—I can't paint. My memories of art school are just that—memories, pictures, electrical impulses in my brain. I haven't retained anything useful. I have nothing to go back *to*: no apartment in Chicago, no contacts in the art world. Somehow I've made the switch into being a different person, and the person I am now, Kelly Maureen Holter Hyde, never attended the School of the Art Institute of Chicago. Never graduated. Never even left Michigan. I feel faint, but it's not the dizziness of my two lives spinning together in my head; it's my nerve, collapsing.

"I'm sorry this is taking so long," the secretary says. "What I can do is file a records request, and we'll go through everything, including the backups. It might take a few weeks."

"You don't need to do that." My voice sounds far away.

"Are you sure? We can—"

"I'm sure. Thank you so much for your time." I turn and walk away. I don't remember taking the elevator, but then I'm out on Wabash, heading north, my feet moving on their own. I drift up the street, looking at my surroundings without really taking them in. It's all so familiar: the buildings, the train overpasses, the way locals and students jaywalk while tourists hover stubbornly at the curbs until the lights change. But even the other me hadn't come downtown in months. It's familiar because it's entrenched in my memory, not because I've lived it recently. Or ever, if that secretary is to be believed.

Every feeling I have fights against what I learned in that records office. I walk faster, passing Madison, then Washington, glancing down ravines of white stone buildings. Beyond them I imagine the rest of the city, the neighborhoods spreading out. People I know, my friends, going about their business.

Homesickness for our studio—Linnea's and mine—burrows into me. The studio is cavernous, impossible to heat, with eighteen-foot ceilings and huge single-paned windows. Even on a warm day it's like a brick refrigerator, and in winter you have to wear layers and fingerless gloves. In the morning the light is bluish; right about now it'll start shading to gold. If Linnea's there, bass will be vibrating through the space from speakers that cost more than my entire wardrobe (she has the trust fund kid's conviction that life's too short for inferior-quality anything), and she'll have a cold mug of coffee on the table, well away from her rinse cup. My best friend. I feel an ache at the thought of her, elegant even in a paint-stained T-shirt and jeans out at the knees. I need to hear her voice, hug her, laugh with her. I need to make sure she exists in the form I remember her.

At the same time I'm dreading it. Will she have a different studio mate? What if I go up and someone else is installed in the northeast corner of the room, some other girl who befriended Linnea their first year of art school? One who took the scholarship I left on the table? The thought elicits a gnawing, possessive jealousy, but more than that, it stings to think another person could step so easily into my place. Not a substitute, but a replacement.

What if Linnea doesn't recognize me?

I don't entertain the thought longer than a few seconds. Of course she'll recognize me. I'm her best goddamn friend.

15

I TAKE THE STAIRS, AS I USUALLY DO WHEN I'M NOT CARRYING anything big in or out of the studio. There's a freight elevator but it takes forever, groaning and clanking as though it'll give up and plunge to the bottom any second.

I'm calm until I hear muffled bass filtering through the door. Then my heart speeds to a gallop. I press the buzzer and the volume of the music halves; I buzz again, a short burst, to make sure Linnea has heard. Footsteps approach and I close my eyes like it's the scary part of the movie.

The door opens. I wait for what feels like a long time. Then Linnea says, "Hi."

She's too calm. Our reunion should have been a flurry of embraces and questions: *Where the hell have you been; what happened; you scared the shit out of me, disappearing like that.* But when I open my eyes her face is composed, polite, expectant. A slight bit of wariness in her eyes but she's open to me. She's so kind: Chicagoans, she and I agree, are much friendlier than New Yorkers. I want to hug her so bad.

"Can I help you?" she says. Disappointment crashes through me in a sick wave. I truly thought she would know me.

I never came up with a cover story. "Hi! I know this is . . ."

Weird? Stalkerish? I smile too widely, then dial it back so I'm not showing *all* my teeth. "I saw your exhibition, and it really resonated with me." I'm playing the art fangirl, but what else can I do? It's the least creepy of all my creepy options. "I was talking to—" Not the little snot who opened the door. Who's Linnea's dealer? Marcie? Markie. "Markie, and I mentioned I'd love to meet you. She told me your studio was here."

Linnea's gaze sharpens. "Markie gave you this address?"

"I hope I'm not interrupting." I keep smiling, affecting an entitlement I've never felt. Maybe she'll think I'm a collector, a Silicon Valley one-percenter. I peer past her into the studio. What I can see looks the same as I remember: crumbling layers of paint over plaster walls, the windows open to let in the street noise. Her easel stands angled toward the light. Sketches flutter on the wall, dozens of them, overlapping like paper shingles. I glimpse what had been my side of the room, the leg of a table taking up what was open space before.

"I always like to talk to people who appreciate my work," Linnea says dubiously, making no move to invite me in.

That doubling feeling hits me again: the difference between now and the last time I was here, who I was then and who I am now. It's a wave, drowning me. I stumble and sag against the wall.

"Whoa, hey, you okay?" Linnea steps out into the hall, taking me by the arm, and leads me inside, where my legs buckle and I crumple onto the couch. My head is pounding, my mouth filling with rich liquid like I'm going to throw up. I take deep gulps of air, but I still feel like I'm suffocating. "Hold on," she says, and after a minute she comes back with a glass of water. The glass isn't one of the thrift-store ones I bought for the studio. This is heavier, the glass infused with bubbles. She probably ordered it in a set from Williams-Sonoma. I drink the whole thing and she takes it from me, refills it from a bottle of water she's brought over, and gives it back.

"Man, you turned white as a ghost," she says.

"Sorry."

She shakes her head, flaps a hand. Sits down next to me. "What's your name?"

"Kelly." My left thumb crosses my palm to stroke the rings on the fourth finger. It feels like an old habit. "Kelly Holter." I watch for a reaction to my maiden name, but she gives none.

"I'm Linnea Flood. But I guess you knew that already." We smile wryly at each other, and I sense the spark: oh yes, we would have been friends. "So, where you from, Kelly?"

I almost blurt out the truth. It's been a long day and my defenses are at their lowest, but I catch myself in time. If I can't have her friendship, I at least want her respect. "Michigan," I say. "Between Flint and Detroit." It's all flyover country as far as she's concerned.

She looks confused. "So, are you with a gallery, or . . . ?"

"I'm not really in the art world," I admit. "I just saw your stuff and liked it and wanted to talk to you. I'm sorry I busted in on you like this." I set my glass on the floor, for lack of anywhere else to put it, and stand. "I should probably go." The words open a wedge into another time, remind me of late-night phone conversations with Eric our senior year in high school, him murmuring so his parents wouldn't hear. *I should probably go,* I'd say, and then we'd talk for another hour. Another wave of dizziness breaks over me, and I have to close my eyes and take deep breaths.

"Nuh-uh," Linnea says firmly, gripping my elbow. "You sit right back down." Her fingers are cool and strong, a little rough.

I don't have any resistance left. We sit and I stare at her bare feet. Her toenails are painted a smooth aqua: color won't stay on her fingernails, even gel polish, but her pedicure is always on point. I feel like I should be asking more questions. My memories of art theory and history pulse in my brain, but I can't grab hold of them to build a conversation.

"I used to paint," I say. It's not a lie.

"Oh. For real?" She smiles politely, unsurprised. She thinks I'm a hobbyist, a dabbler.

"I had a scholarship to art school," I go on, and her eyebrows rise: now she's impressed. "At the Art Institute, actually. But, um . . ." It seems petty to blame this on Eric. "Everyone thought I should go to school for something more practical."

Linnea nods sympathetically. This is a topic she and I have gone back and forth on before. Financially secure from birth, she believes people should follow their dreams and do what they love. I spent years beating into her head that not everyone has the option.

But I did have the option, and I gave it up. "I really regret not going," I tell her, the closest I can come to *You were right.*

"That's too bad. You could still paint, take some art classes." Linnea's no Pollyanna. She's not going to tell me I could have a career, starting out at my age.

"I suppose. I'm a graphic designer, so that's something. Not really the same, though."

"No," she says, so emphatically it makes me smile. She can't fathom a life of making work to order, for commercial purposes. I used to be envious of her money, her built-in connections, her ability to paint full-time without the need for a side hustle. But at least then we were on the same planet; now we live in different universes.

My gaze drifts to my half of the studio. Instead of my easel, the area is sectioned off with a large table, half taken up by a tabletop printing press. Another table, holding printmaking supplies, occupies the space along the wall where I used to store finished paintings. Prints hang in a row on a wire. Bobby's stuff.

The door clanks open, making me jump, and Linnea's boyfriend shoulders his way in, dressed in his usual raggedy T-shirt and joggers and maroon Chucks. His head almost brushes the top of the doorway. Bobby's built like a damn refrigerator—he gave up a football scholarship at IU to go to art school—but he's one of the gentlest people I know. *Knew.*

"Hey, baby, I got us some—" He hefts a plastic bag, which drops to his side when he catches sight of me. Then something happens that shocks me, considering the day so far. "Oh! Hey!" His face breaks into a wide smile and he bounds over, joyful as a puppy, like I'm a good friend he hasn't seen in years.

I rise and almost hug him out of pure habit. But then he stops, his face screwing up in confusion. "Oh, sorry, I thought you were . . ." He shakes his head, light flashing off his glasses, and gives a little laugh. "You know, I'm not sure who I thought you were."

"This is Kelly," Linnea says. "She came by to look at the work . . . She was at the gallery and Markie sent her over."

"Huh, so Markie's just giving out your address to any . . ." He winces. "No offense," he says to me, nothing but politeness in his face. I feel like I've lost something irretrievable. "Baby, you need to have a talk with her, though."

We all look at one another uncomfortably until Bobby breaks the silence. "You look so familiar!"

"Maybe I have a doppelgänger."

Bobby's laughter rolls out richly. "I've got one too. He's in the NFL! I had a guy come up to me on the street who was so sure I was him. Refused to believe I wasn't. I had to let him take a selfie with me to get him to go away."

I remember when that happened, how we laughed about it. Three days ago these people were my best friends, and now they're strangers. But I still feel the same pull toward them. I've spent most of the day coming to terms with the idea that my life in Chicago wasn't real, but now it's not so cut-and-dried.

"I got a bunch of food, we've got beer in the fridge," Bobby says. "You're welcome to join us." I'm tempted. It would be so easy to stay, to pretend we're all friends again. I wonder if Bobby's being so nice because he thinks I'll buy one of Linnea's paintings, or if he feels the same affinity I do. Maybe friendship can cut across different lives.

Linnea says, "Do you want to see what I'm working on?"

"I'd love to." I've already seen it, of course, but I follow her to the other side of the room with trepidation. It doesn't make sense that her work would be different because of my absence. Still, other things have changed in seemingly random fashion. She might be painting Campbell's soup cans now.

It's a relief to see that the half-finished painting on her easel is the same one she was working on the last time we were in the studio together. Linnea watches me study it as though what I think matters.

"This is part of a new series," she explains. "It's different from the work being shown right now . . . I got the idea a few weeks ago." She smiles, looking almost embarrassed. "It came out of nowhere, which hardly ever happens. Usually I'm incubating things in my head for months. But one night I was supposed to meet Bobby for drinks and I ended up staying here sketching 'til three in the morning." She motions toward the wall where the overlapping sketches hang.

I remember that night, because I was here. I ended up leaving to meet Bobby and Rowan, a twenty-four-year-old bass player I was sort of seeing. I walk over to the sketches but don't touch them. Linnea doesn't like her stuff disturbed. "I don't suppose I could buy one of these?"

"Sure. I mean, you can just have one." Her voice ripples; I've amused her. "Any one in particular?"

I raise my hands toward the wall—"Do you mind?"—and, with Linnea's permission, riffle through the layered papers. My hands meander like a dowsing rod, but the goal is never in doubt. I recognize the sketch I want immediately. It's the first one, the one I saw over her shoulder that night. I wasn't doing anything—drinking a beer, stretching a canvas—but I went and looked as soon as I felt her drop out of our desultory conversation. It's exactly the same as I remember.

"This one?" I ask.

She nods once, approvingly. "It's yours."

I take it down carefully. Linnea goes over to the little office area, a desk shoved up against the wall, and gets a poster tube for me. "Let me give you something for it," I say. Linnea shakes her head. She's got great career sense but little concept of money. "Well, thanks. Thanks very much." I feel awkward now, like it's time for me to leave. My near-sleepless night and the day are catching up with me, and I doubt Bobby and Linnea's hospitality will extend to letting me crash on their couch. I need to find a hotel room and gather myself for the gallery tomorrow. It seems pointless to go through with the rest of the plan, but I came all this way. I should at least try. "I've taken up enough of your time."

Bobby, setting out Chinese food cartons on the drainboard by the big sink, looks up. "No, hang out! Have some food!" But I hear hospitality in his voice, not friendship.

"I can't. But it was great to meet you both. Here—" On impulse, I dig in my bag for one of my business cards, the ones that say HYDE DESIGNS, and hand it to Linnea. I want to leave some kind of thread connecting us.

Bobby comes over and hugs me, a real Bobby hug, safe and all enveloping. "It's so weird, I really feel like I know you," he says.

"Me too."

Linnea walks me to the door and, after a second's hesitation, gives me a hug too. Hers is more reserved. "You sure you're feeling okay?"

"A hundred percent better."

"All right. Take care."

She closes the door, and I'm alone in the echoing hallway. I should be relieved that Linnea and Bobby can go on without me, that they can be happy and productive and the same as they've always been, but I'm devastated. How can she not miss me? I miss her. I miss the person I was when we were friends. I miss my life.

It's gone is all I can think. *It's really gone.*

16

IT'S ALMOST DARK OUTSIDE. I KEEP AN EYE OUT AS I WALK TO MY car, but I don't get the spine creep of being followed. Most likely it was just my imagination, earlier. The stress of everything. I'm trying to stay optimistic, but increasingly I feel as though returning to the gallery will be an empty ritual, an attempt to drum up magic where none exists. What's more plausible: that I stumbled onto some kind of portal to another life, or that I did too many drugs in my formative years? What will I do if nothing happens at the gallery? Go back to Luigi's and try to take the trip in reverse? Get my mother to plan another surprise party?

My thoughts are jumbled, like the half dreams that seep in when you're sliding toward sleep. I'm so tired. Maybe it was a mistake to come to Chicago. All the evidence points to my memories of my life here being false. The other family in my apartment. My missing tattoos. The missing school transcripts. Linnea . . .

Bobby. He *knew* me. It's enough of a discrepancy to make me doubt.

I'm at my car. I get in and lock the doors but don't start it yet. I need to figure out my next move, but my mind stubbornly tries to pick out connections between my conflicting sets of memories. Thin places in the border between two lives: Bobby seeming to recognize me. The sticker on the mailbox outside my apartment. Linnea's work, the same as I remember.

I've had my phone turned off all afternoon to conserve the battery, and now I turn it back on to search out a hotel for the night. It bubbles with notifications of missed calls and text messages. Eric, asking where I am. My mother, asking the same. Eric must have texted her. Guilt stabs me: Mom is supposed to be enjoying her vacation up north with Dad, and instead she's worrying about me. I have her last message open, so I reply to her first: I'm fine. Talk to you soon. XXOO

I begin a message to Eric. I'd forgotten about him; not Eric himself, exactly, but it hadn't occurred to me that I'd need to account for my movements to him. Where I was going, I thought, he wouldn't be an issue.

I've barely started to frame what to say to him when my phone rings. "Where are you?" my mother asks.

"I'm fine," I tell her.

"You said that. Have you called Eric back yet? He sounded pretty worried."

"I was just about to text him when— Wait, he *called* you?" Eric hates making phone calls, especially to people he's not comfortable with. Like my mother.

"Yeah, with his voice and everything. He wanted to know if you'd been in touch with us. Why didn't you tell him where you were going?"

Because I didn't think I'd be back. "I just went for a drive. I felt like getting out of the house, so I drove to west Michigan. To the lake."

"Lake *Michigan*?"

"Yeah." It's not a complete lie.

An ambulance screams by on the next street over, drowning out the first part of her answer. ". . . like you're at the beach."

"What?"

"I said, it doesn't sound like you're at the beach."

"I'm on my way home. I pulled over to the side of the road, I didn't want to use my phone while I was driving."

"You should get one of those self-driving cars."

"Yeah, sure, as soon as my Christmas bonus comes in." Tired and demoralized, I don't feel like editing myself.

"You know, Kelly, if you got a real job, then you'd—"

"Mom, I don't want a self-driving car." Though one would be nice, right about now. I blink the exhaustion from my eyes.

"But you'll call Eric, though?"

"As soon as I get off the phone with you. Look, I'll let you go, you're supposed to be on vaca—"

"How can I relax when my daughter's missing?"

"I'm not *missing*. I just went for a drive. Mom, you're talking to me right now, and I'm obviously fine."

"Well, you need to be talking to your husband. He sounded like he was ready to start calling hospitals. Or the police. Is something going on with you two?"

"No! Why would you say that? Nothing is going on. We're fine."

"I'm just asking."

"Well, you don't need to worry. You and Dad enjoy your trip."

"Call your husband," she says, and hangs up.

I don't call Eric. I'll text him soon—I'm not a monster—but first I want to find somewhere to stay. I return to my hotel search, but thoughts of my mother nag at me. Maybe it was my fault her illness was worse before. Maybe, as her wayward child, I stressed her out so much it affected her health.

If I somehow became Chicago Kelly again, would I be killing her?

"That's ridiculous," I say aloud. I don't sound very convincing.

My phone chirps with a text from Eric. Your mom texted me. What's going on? Are you coming home? Please answer me. I thumb the screen dark but the words glow in my brain, his anxiety plucking at me until it becomes my own.

Another text comes in. He's not going to let me be. Why would he? I'm his wife.

With a groan of frustration, I drop my head back against the headrest. This is it, the last straw. I have to admit that Chicago is a dead end. Everything I've experienced on this trip points to the truth that's been seeping into me since the switch: my life with Eric is the only one that exists. The only one that ever existed. I hadn't realized how much I'd counted on finding proof that I wasn't always the kind of person who would settle for a lesser life, for a partner who would gently but effectively hold me back from pursuing my dreams. But there's nothing, and staying here isn't going to change that.

I let out a sigh and reply, OMW home. Phone dying. See you soon. Then I turn off my phone before he can answer.

THE DRIVE BACK to Michigan takes forever. I'm so tired that automatic actions—blinker, lane change—become events I have to plan out. I stop at a gas station and buy a twenty-ounce coffee, dumping in sugar and hazelnut creamer to cover the scorched taste, and that props me up enough to make it home. The garage door registers my car's approach and opens automatically, as though ushering me into the house.

Eric's the first thing I see when I step into the kitchen. He's slumped in a chair, elbows on his knees, but he jumps up as soon as the door opens.

"You're okay." He sounds like he can't quite believe it. His voice is hoarse, as though he hasn't spoken in several hours, and his eyes are red-rimmed, his hair standing on end like he's been pulling his hands through it all night. Remorse wakes tenderness in me. It's unexpected, this feeling. For the past three days I've been thinking of Eric mostly as an obstacle to avoid. "Why didn't you let me know where you were?"

"My phone died." It's a good thing I left my overnight bag in the car. Thinking is like wading through mud, and I need to tread carefully: I'm too exhausted to fight, and once Eric starts he won't stop until it's resolved. He definitely took to heart the advice about never going to bed mad.

He looks at me a second longer, then covers the distance between us in a single step and gathers me up in his arms. I breathe in his end-of-day smell, soap and deodorant with an edge of sweat, the pomade he puts in his hair: a comforting smell, one that animates deeply inscribed patterns in my brain. For the first time, I don't feel like pulling away from him.

He draws back first, kissing my forehead before he releases me. "You should text your mom and let her know you got home."

Mom. A feeling of wanting to cry climbs up my throat. I shuffle past him to a chair and drop into it.

He folds his arms across his chest, his face neutral. "Where did you go?"

If my mom texted him, I'm pretty sure she would have told him what I told her; he could be trying to catch me in a lie. "I got restless this afternoon and went over to Grand Haven. Walked along the beach for a while. I ran out of gas on the way back . . . I wasn't paying attention. I guess an astronaut died today." I give him a weak smile to go with my weak joke, hoping to lighten the mood.

It doesn't work. He frowns. "Did you take a ride with someone?"

"No. I'm not stupid." An edge creeps into my voice. "I walked to a gas station and got a can. It wasn't that far, it just took a while."

I force myself to meet his eyes. His are soft but steady.

I have the overwhelming feeling he knows I'm not telling the truth.

Why doesn't he call me on it? Why isn't he angry? "You should have texted me," he says, his voice as soft as his gaze.

"I told you, my phone died."

"You could've called from the gas station."

"I was tired, Eric, I didn't think about it. I just wanted to get home." Finally I look away, though I can feel his eyes trying to draw mine back. Maybe he can sense the shape of what's happening inside my head. Maybe he's afraid, as I am, that I'm losing my mind.

I massage my aching forehead. I have memories of being happy and at ease with him. But what's real, those memories or the others?

He goes to stand by the sliding glass door, staring out at the dark backyard as if he can see something other than his own reflection. "When I got home and you weren't here, I thought . . ." His head jerks, like he's trying to shake away the worst possibilities.

Jesus Christ, it's not like I'm dead in a ditch somewhere. It's not like I left him.

But you tried to.

"I'm sorry," I say, keeping my voice even. "I was thoughtless. I should have told you where I was."

He nods in a helpless way, as though he doesn't trust himself to speak, and turns more fully away from me. It occurs to me that I've never seen Eric cry. I hear his breathing hitch and feel guilty again, this time for being annoyed. He's got every right to be upset: I disappeared for hours, without warning or explanation. I'm not used to the rules of being in a relationship. The basic courtesy of letting your partner know that nothing terrible has happened to you if you're not where you're supposed to be.

But my body seems to know how I should react. It pulls me toward him, toward physical connection. I'm not stupid enough to think a hug will fix everything. But everything I knew is gone, and I feel as though I've been driving myself, holding myself up, for much longer than a few days. I need someone to hold me up for a change. Something in me senses that Eric's up to the task.

And I want to give him comfort, too. It's an elemental misery, to see him in pain and do nothing about it. I stand and go over to him, putting my arms around him from behind, and it feels like something I've done many times before. He stiffens as if in surprise; then his body relaxes and he turns and hugs me hard.

"I'm just glad you came back." His shoulder angles awkwardly into my face as he kisses my hair. "Kelly . . . Kelly . . ." He says my name over and over, like an incantation, like if he repeats it enough times he can prevent me from disappearing again. The vulnerability of it touches me to the quick. Responding to the same instincts as before—the impulse to touch him, the need to comfort and be comforted—I lift my chin and kiss him.

He drags in a breath that's almost a gasp and his arms tighten around me and he kisses me back, hungrily, like he was waiting for me to start. I wasn't going for seduction, but suddenly I'm fully awake, skin tingling, desire bringing a crystalline surge of awareness. I slide my hands under his shirt and up his back. His skin feels smooth yet oddly coarse under my fingers, familiar and yet new.

He's breathing harder. He presses his mouth to a spot under my ear. "You have no idea how much I love you," he says, which seems like an odd way of putting it.

17

I KISS HIM AGAIN. FAMILIAR, NEW.

I have memories of sex with Eric, but that's not the same as direct experience. The smell of him, the taste of his mouth. A remembered frisson isn't the same as the goose bumps that sweep over my arms and the abrupt drop in my stomach. He feels it too. He takes my face in his hands and kisses me like he wants to devour me. I'm surprised to feel none of the aversion he provoked in me before, only a need to get closer. *What are you doing?* says a voice in my head, but it's remote, irrelevant.

I tug at his shirt, one of the plain white tees he wears to work under polos and button-downs. He lifts his arms so I can drag the shirt over his head; he shivers at the touch of my hands on his bare chest. I glance over my shoulder at the table, wondering if it will support our combined weight, but then the darkness outside captures his attention. There's nothing out there but woods, but he says, "Let's go upstairs." His voice is still rough, but for a different reason now.

I lead him from the kitchen. At the bottom of the stairs, he takes my wrist and pulls me back to him. A minute later my shirt and bra are gone, his hands on me, his mouth so hungry on mine I can't snatch a breath. He pushes us both up the stairs, sliding along the wall, kissing all the way up. His need makes my blood sing. We stumble to our room and sink onto the bed, fumbling at the rest of our clothes. His mouth on my neck, my breasts, between my legs, I come in seconds. He kisses me again and I taste myself. I reach down to guide him in.

"Oh fuh . . . Kelly," he gasps, and a kind of wry triumph spreads through me. I've made him swear, made him start the word even if he didn't finish it. He doesn't, usually, out of some combination of prudery and ex-Catholic guilt. I close my eyes in the blackness of our room, moving with him, reveling in his heat, feeling waves of sensation diminish and build up again. His heart pounds against mine, my heart speeding in response.

Then, abruptly, he stops.

He springs away from me. "Oh God," he whispers. He's breathing hard, and not from exertion or arousal. "Oh God, what did I do?"

"What?" I half sit up, startled. "What is it? What's wrong?"

"It's okay," he says quietly, as if to himself. Then he asks me, "Did you start taking your pill again?"

I reach out and find flesh: his leg, folded underneath him. I can see him dimly in the light from the window, which admits a slight glow from the streetlamp. He swipes his hands over his face.

"My pill?"

"Your birth control." A thread of impatience in his voice at my failure to keep up. The lucidity splinters what's left of my desire, though it doesn't touch my confusion. Had I been taking birth control? Certainly not since Friday. It never occurred to me. I've been so wrapped up in my situation, and when I lived in Chicago, I was never in a relationship long enough to get past condoms. But now other memories blink on in my head, memories from

(*my real life*)

this life. I remember myself, this new me, telling him a couple of weeks into a new cycle that I'd never started the month's pack of pills. He'd been bringing it up so often that I'd put a touch of resentment into my manner of announcing it. *We'll leave it up to fate,* I said, knowing that would drive him nuts. I'd been sure he would want to plan our child's conception like he planned everything else, download an ovulation-tracking app and optimize my diet, any way he could take control of an inherently uncontrollable process. But the smile of quiet happiness that spread over his face had disarmed me.

Now my mind rebels at the implications. Now would be a very, very bad time to get pregnant.

But Eric doesn't know that.

"Why would I have started taking birth control again?"

He lets out a long, shaky breath. "I think it's okay. I didn't . . . I think it's okay. I should've thought ahead, though, I should've gone . . ."

"Gone where?"

"Nowhere. Nowhere. It's fine. I just meant to talk to you, that's all. I've, uh . . . I've been thinking, and I'm not sure we should try right now after all."

"Okay." We're in agreement there. But his panicked about-face is troubling. He was the one who wanted this house, with its three bedrooms and fenced backyard. "But why are you freaking out?"

"I'm not freaking out."

"Eric . . ." I move my hand up his thigh and, finding his

hand, fold mine over it. "You're freaking out." *You scared the shit out of me,* I want to say, but then he'd make a comment about my language and not take the sentiment seriously. I don't know how I know this, but I do.

"I just don't think we should wing it. You need to get checked out . . . you know, medically. I do too. Just in case."

"Just in case what?"

"There's lots of things that can go wrong. Genetic abnormalities. Problems with your . . . equipment."

I laugh. "My *equipment*?"

"I just want to make sure everything goes well."

"But that's not something you can make sure of. There aren't any guarantees." I think about stories I've read and heard. Miscarriages and stillbirths. Birth defects. A friend of Linnea's and mine who'd gotten married and moved out to the suburbs almost died after giving birth last year, even with the best medical care available. No guarantees.

The room brightens as the moon emerges from behind a cloud, its light filtering through the small windows. In the shadows it makes, Eric's face looks like a sculpture, like something inanimate.

"Well, then, maybe it's too big of a risk," he says. "I think you should go back on the pill."

"*You* think *I* should go back on the pill?" I pull my hand away. "Or we could just not have sex. How about that?" I'm not serious, not completely, but I don't like his tone. I scoot to the other side of the bed, negotiating the twisted sheets with care, and stand. Fuck this. I'm going to take a shower, and then I'm going to sleep. In the spare room.

"Kelly. Wait." A rustle as he crosses the bed, then a thump, and he's beside me. "Please," he says, though I haven't moved. Chicago Kelly would have been out of the room already. But I'm a different person now: gentler, more hesitant. "I'm sorry."

"For what?" I'm fiercely glad to hear my voice come out cold and strong.

"For . . . telling you what to do." He sounds like he's guessing, but I let him take me in his arms anyway. My tiredness hits me again, all at once, and I lean against him. Which it seems he takes for forgiveness, because he lets out a sigh and starts rubbing my back. "We have to stick together," he murmurs. "We can't let these things tear us apart."

What things? We had a minor fight. It's over. Though maybe it shouldn't be. Words bubble in my throat, wanting to come out, but I'm beginning to understand the dynamic here. Eric loses his mind at any indication that all is not perfect; then we smooth the conflict over as quickly as possible.

"It's been a long day." I back out of his embrace. "I need a shower. We both need some sleep."

"You'll feel better in the morning," he says, as if I'm the one who had a meltdown. He kisses me on the forehead, dismissing me, and turns toward the bed.

I don't bother with a long shower, but he's asleep by the time I return. Sprawled on his back, face turned slightly away in profile. How can he sleep, when he was so upset fifteen minutes ago? Unless he's only pretending to sleep. He doesn't react when I slip into bed next to him. I slide a hand over his shoulder, watching his face. His eyebrows twitch and he lets out a half-conscious *hmm*, but that's it.

As I watch his chest rise and fall under my hand, examining the angles of his sleeping face, it strikes me that Eric is a beautiful man. I feel an upwelling of pride, familiar and yet not, that he's *my* beautiful man. And I made him.

Of course, he did most of the work, but he wouldn't be the person he is without me. Who drew him out, back when we were just classmates sitting next to each other? Who made him feel like he might have something to say that people wanted to hear? In college I was the one who collected our friend group: it was "Kelly and Eric," not "Eric and Kelly." He embraced weight lifting around the same time I took up running to get rid of my freshman fifteen. He joked that he needed to level up to keep my eye from wandering, but he repeated it often enough that I knew he was at least partly serious. After graduation I dragged him to networking events, for my professional community and his, and although he would always be introverted, by then he'd developed enough confidence and social skills to make his own connections.

He'd been a painfully awkward adolescent, gangly and mute in social situations. I remember being surprised when he asked me out, and then again at how much I enjoyed myself with him. Outside of school he was different, more confident. He kept his car clean. He didn't behave like the other boys I knew, with their horseplay and dick jokes and their self-imposed need to show a detached front so nobody would say they were whipped. By then I'd learned the aloofness was a sham, but that didn't make it any less irritating.

Steeped in the affectionate sarcasm of my group of friends, I hadn't known earnestness could be so refreshing. I'd never thought I could date someone who wasn't into the same things as me, but I'd also never felt so appreciated for who I was. Eric wanted me in a way no one else had. Sometimes, even years into our relationship, I'd catch him looking at me with an expression of muted awe, like he couldn't believe his luck.

He treats me like a fucking queen, I remember telling Katie Spence during senior year when she asked why I was with *Eric Hyde, for Christ's sake, when you could have any guy you want.* Most guys that age just wanted you to suck their dicks and watch them play guitar or football or video games; Eric wanted to watch me. I remember feeling like that was a special and precious thing, something worth holding on to.

Maybe that's why I gave up on art school. I remember, almost like it really happened, the immediate crash after the high when I got my scholarship notification. For the first time I saw my relationship with Eric as something holding me back, which horrified me. He wasn't an *obstacle.* He was a *person* who loved me, who was willing to endure the pain of separation so I could fulfill the dream I'd nurtured since I was eleven years old. Even so, I suspected that the choice between going to art school and staying closer to home was a choice between losing Eric and keeping him.

So I chose to keep him.

Did you?

The sly voice in my head won't shut up. It whispers to me of another narrative, parallel to the ones I know: the life where I've been with Eric since high school and the life where I never was.

You left him, the voice says. *Don't you remember?*

It's too murky. I can't plumb that memory; it's like a dream I barely remember, no more than a breath of a feeling. Regret mixed with an exhilarating sense of freedom, of *What now?* Then it's gone.

I remember my first real job after college, as a graphic designer at an advertising agency that closed down after I'd worked there a couple of years. I remember a hurried wedding: unemployed, I'd lose my health insurance at the end of the month, and we were going to get married eventually anyway, so why wait? I remember moving to Davis City when Eric got a job offer from the community college there, as an instructional designer. He hadn't told me he was applying; he said he'd been sure nothing would come of it, and I had no reason to disbelieve him. It was a big step up in his career. A step toward what? I'd had a blurry vision in my head in which Eric and I moved to Chicago together and I designed by day and painted by night, while we lived the life of a cool young couple in the city, doing cool things. It turned out Eric's vision was entirely different.

I remember being mildly alarmed, when we started looking at houses, by the attention Eric paid to school districts and whether there were "other families" around. He seemed to operate on the assumption that our own family would show up any minute. It wasn't that I didn't *want* kids. Unlike in Chicago, where I never even thought of motherhood, in this life I sometimes daydreamed about having a child. It was a pleasant vision: Eric and me elbow to elbow, gazing into our sleeping newborn's face. What did that face look like? The baby I conceptualized was nameless, sexless, with sturdy little limbs and curling hair of indeterminate color. I couldn't—or didn't want to—get a handle on the reality of what our lives as parents would be like. Neither of my brothers' versions of fatherhood seemed ideal. Nick had Malik only every other weekend. Jeff and his wife, on the other hand, were completely wrapped up in family life, Andrea especially, in a state somewhere between infatuation and servitude. Conversation revolved around the most minute facets of behavior and well-being: hours slept, ounces of breast milk consumed, volume and consistency of excrement. It defied logic that I could be entrusted with the life of a human being when I couldn't even keep a houseplant alive, but the loss of identity was what really freaked me out. Andrea had changed all her social media profile photos to a picture of their older daughter holding their younger one, as though erasing herself from the record. The volition of it unsettled me: she'd undergone a transformation so complete that she could do this of her own free will and see nothing strange in it. Who could say the same thing wouldn't happen to me?

I remember after we moved into the house on Oriskany Way and Eric started dropping weekly hints about "trying," I suggested we get a puppy.

I suppose I should have told him my doubts and fears and listened to his. That's the advice I'd give a friend, if I had any friends. Maybe it's good advice for my current problem. Just dump it on him: *Hon, I've got a second life in my head and it's driving me mad.*

I want to shake him awake and tell him right now. Ask him, *Why? Why is this happening to me?*

18

Day Five

I WAKE SLOWLY, FEELING MUTED SUNLIGHT AGAINST MY EYELIDS and the warmth of Eric's leg pressed against mine. He sleeps like a little kid, breathing deeply, his eyes screwed shut.

With a sharp inhale, he blinks them open. "What time is it?"

"I'm not sure."

He cranes his neck to check the bedside clock and groans. Then he looks at me and his face freezes up, just for a second, and I can see him remember what happened last night and calculate how he should act. He decides to smile and stretch, his hand diving beneath the sheet to curl around my waist. "Mm. Maybe I'll call in sick." A lick of his morning breath reaches my nose. With it comes a sense of unreality that for years—for *years*—this stranger has been the person I sleep next to every night.

I turn my face away, but that just makes him start kissing my neck. "I could go get some condoms . . . or we could—"

"I have to get some work done today." I try to say it kindly, but his lips freeze on my neck. Though I can't see his face, I can imagine its wounded expression.

He pushes himself up and off the bed without looking at me. "I guess you need to catch up, after yesterday."

Ouch. The dig turns my guilt to annoyance. It was wrong to worry him, but I won't keep apologizing for it. I lie silent as he stalks to the bathroom and somehow manages to make the shower turning on sound passive-aggressive.

I roll over and put my feet on the floor, equivocating to myself. Even if I wanted to spend the morning in bed, I don't have the time. Now that I've slept I need to process everything that happened in Chicago. Figure out what it means, if it means anything. And I need to pursue my lead: Peter.

But first, now, I'll have to put energy into smoothing things over with Eric. It's natural for him to feel rejected, but he doesn't have to be such a baby about it. His behavior makes me aware of a hard stone of resentment inside me, layers of sediment that have built up over the years. Does Michigan Kelly feel like this all the time?

I pull on shorts and a singlet, figuring I'll go for my run after I talk to Peter; plus Eric doesn't need to know about the change in my routine. When he comes downstairs, I'm standing at the kitchen sink, drinking a glass of water. He doesn't pause on his way through the kitchen, his steps actually speeding up as he nears the door to the garage, and I realize he's going to leave without saying goodbye.

An incongruous rush of guilt sweeps through me, so strong it's almost dread. *You can't let him go without making things better.* The thought comes from some foreign part of me: the woman who's been living in this house, with this man. She's the one who crosses the room and places her—my—hand on Eric's shoulder. His shoulders stiffen and I think he's going to pull away, but then he lets me draw him close. I kiss him. His lips stay rigid at first, but then they soften, opening. His arms slide around my waist. He kisses me like we're in some epic film, practically picking me up off the floor. His words from last night come back to me: *You have no idea how much I love you.* Mixed with that strength of feeling, the kiss is intoxicating.

"Don't you want breakfast?" My voice is husky, not quite suggestive.

He blinks and sucks in a breath like he's waking from a nightmare. There's blood in his cheeks, his eyes dark, and he says, "I'm not hungry," and pulls away. He won't look at me. I haven't done enough penance yet, for disappearing yesterday or for rejecting him this morning. My temper flares. I'm about to say something sharp when he looks at me, a small smile on his face like he can tell what I'm thinking, and says, "I'll see you tonight." His voice is also husky, also not quite suggestive.

Then his eyes go distant. "Love you," he says, and leaves me at the door.

I feel unbalanced but intrigued. His small manipulation shows he's capable of more than just pique, that he has an interest in keeping me on my toes. After all, in a long-term relationship, the element of surprise is the first thing to go.

19

I DON'T KNOW EXACTLY WHERE PETER LIVES, BUT I KNOW WHERE he works. Davis City doesn't have any picturesquely defunct auto factories, so 1832 Innovation Park is built around a former dairy farm on the outskirts of town. Driving up the curving entrance road toward the old barn, now painted a fresh red, I see sunlight glinting off its tin roof and newly installed windows. I wonder if it still smells like cow shit inside.

The new buildings are designed to look farm-like as well, creating a pastoral scene from a distance. However, the silos and outbuildings are actually offices and retail spaces, the latter still mostly unoccupied, with parking lots tucked discreetly behind them. Gnii occupies the whole of what looks like a modern farmhouse, set apart from the rest of the district. When I park next to it, I see that the building's features—clapboard exterior walls, window frames, brick chimneys—are all 3D printed on huge sheets of glass. The illusion isn't quite realistic—the "windows" are opaque, the "front porch" oddly flattened—so it's a little like a stage set, and in a real-life setting it falls straight into the uncanny valley.

This building and location both track with what little I know about gnii, their reputation for hiding in plain sight.

As I approach the entrance, two large panes of the porch sweep aside. Inside is an atrium, where the walls and ceiling glow with filtered light. Here's where the farmhouse illusion ends. Beyond a reception desk, the atrium cuts off at a solid wall with a sturdy metal door in it.

The man at the desk makes eye contact and recognizes immediately that I don't belong. "Mornin'," he says. "Can I help you?"

I tell him I'm here to see Peter Nedelman, wondering at the same time if it's the best idea for me to create a record of my having been here. It ends up not mattering, however, because the receptionist—or the guard, actually, since he has a gun holstered on his hip—checks something on his console and tells me Peter hasn't come in yet. He asks if I'd like to wait. There's a seating area, a fake midcentury modern furniture grouping clustered to one side, but the guard's manner is vaguely discouraging and my urge to fly under the radar hasn't gone away. *Yet,* the guard said, which means Peter's expected to come in at some point today, and I might get more information out of him if I catch him off guard.

"No, thanks," I say, smiling. The guard smiles back. "I was just around and thought I'd say hi." I leave before he can get any ideas about questioning me.

This whole place is probably rigged with cameras. I walk toward a coffee cart, trying to look like I'm not inspecting the gnii building. The way the district is set up, Peter could park in any number of places, so staking out the building's entrance is my best chance to intercept him. That won't work if the staff uses a separate door, but I didn't see one when I arrived. I buy a black tea and settle on a bench with my phone and a view of gnii's front door.

I've drunk my tea down to the dregs by the time Peter finally shows up. He's walking fast, clutching the strap of his laptop bag and looking preoccupied. I have to call his name twice before he turns, and as he does, he's got a *This better be good* look on his face.

The expression melts away when he sees me.

In high school, Peter and Eric looked enough alike that they could have been cousins. Same height and build, both with dark hair and eyes. Peter wore glasses and dressed like his grandmother picked out his clothes, while Eric lived in an endless succession of baggy jeans and T-shirts under rumpled button-downs, but they gave the impression of being a matched set. Now Eric dresses better and outweighs Peter by a good forty pounds, but there's still something about Peter that reminds me of Eric. A watchful reserve, a faint air of contempt, like he knows he'll always be a little on the outside of things but he doesn't care because he's better than all of it.

That reserve comes down over his face like a mask, but before it does, I see an emotion I can't identify. Shock, maybe, or anger. That's it: Peter's pissed off that I'm here. But why?

"Hey, Kelly," he says neutrally. "How're you doing?" *What are you doing here?* his look says, and I want to shake the truth out of him.

I start with the facts. "Eric was kind of upset after you guys hung up the other night."

Peter's control slips, scorn surfacing on his face. "He talked to you, huh? Well, he should be upset. You can tell him I don't feel bad for him. And you can tell him he's a coward for sending his wife instead of facing me himself."

So that's why he's mad. He thinks I'm here to intercede for

my husband. "Eric didn't send me here. I came on my own, because—" If I tell Peter how little I know, he won't give me anything, so I need to be careful. I step closer, thinking back to what I overheard. "What made you call him that particular night? What is he helping you with?"

"Eric's not helping me with shit. He's leaving me to clean up his mess all on my own." Shaking his head, Peter makes as if to walk away.

"What mess?" Desperate for answers, I drop the pretense of knowing anything. "What did he do? What happened on Friday?" Peter recoils from me. I make a grab for his arm and get the strap of his laptop bag, pulling it off his shoulder. He catches it just before it slaps against the concrete. "Peter, weird shit has been happening to me."

My words, plus whatever he sees in my face, make him stop and focus on me. "What kind of weird shit?" Looking around, he makes a quelling motion with his hand. "No, wait. This isn't a good place to talk."

"How about inside?"

He chuckles humorlessly. "Definitely not there." The door of the glass farmhouse slides open, drawing our gazes toward it, and two young guys wearing hoodies and jeans come out. "I gotta go in," he says, lowering his voice, "but let's meet up later."

"Six o'clock at the Brazier," I say, the time and place rolling off my tongue. It's an old dive out on the highway, where my friends and I could sometimes get served when we were in high school. Outside of deer-hunting season, no one goes there except underage drinkers and middle-aged alcoholics, which makes it the perfect place for a clandestine meeting.

"Can you make it any later than that?"

"I want to get home before Eric does."

Peter's eyebrows jump. "Eric doesn't know you're talking to me?"

"He doesn't know anything."

The hoodie guys are close enough to greet Peter. "Oh good, you're back," one of them says. "I wanted to ask you . . ." He glances at me and shuts up.

"How about you ask me when we get inside?" Peter says, in a friendly work voice with something behind it, some kind of tension or maybe simple authority. As his coworkers pass us on the way to the coffee cart, I notice neither of them looks like he's slept much lately. Peter gives me a smile with too many teeth. "It was great running into you," he says, and goes to step away.

"Peter," I say, with enough urgency to make him stop. I pitch my voice so his coworkers won't hear. "Do I need to worry about Eric?"

He looks me in the eye. "I'm not going to lie to you. He could be in some deep shit."

"No. I mean, do *I* need to . . . *worry*?" For some reason I'm hesitant to put what I actually mean into words, so I try to do it with emphasis. Peter gets it. His eyes widen in an unguarded expression of surprise.

"No," he says, horrified. "He would never—you're the most important thing in the world to him."

"So I can trust him?"

He narrows his eyes and opens his mouth, then pauses, thinking about how to answer. Before he can, one of his coworkers calls over asking if he wants a coffee.

"Sure," he calls back. "I can get it, though." To me he says, "See you tonight," and hurries off.

It's not until I'm back at my car that it occurs to me to wonder why I picked the Brazier as a meeting place, when I haven't been there in more than a decade. Or how I knew without thinking about it that Eric will be at the gym after work tonight and won't miss me unless I get home too late. I can almost discern a memory behind the suggestion, a reason I spoke with the thoughtlessness of habit. But when I try to reach deeper, the memory flickers out.

20

WHEN I GET HOME, I BRING IN MY OVERNIGHT BAG FROM THE car. It doesn't take long to unpack, and soon I've got everything put away except Linnea's sketch. I take it into my office and remove it from its tube, smoothing it out on the desk. It looks as familiar as it did in Linnea's studio. A message from another life, calling me back.

Above my desk hangs a large bulletin board, where I map out projects with sticky notes and sketches and attach magazine ads torn out for inspiration. It's the closest thing to a work of art I've made in this house. The papers rustle gently every time the air moves, making the board seem like a living thing. I tack Linnea's sketch to it, near the top so it won't get covered up, angling the pins so they won't pierce the paper. I have the idea that it will serve as a reminder—but of what, exactly? That I used to have dreams?

There must be some reason I'm here. To save my mother's life, or maybe there's another purpose for me in this house, this marriage. Maybe Eric and I are meant for each other, and what happened to me on my birthday is the universe correcting some cosmic mistake. The almost physical yearning I feel for my life in Chicago will do me no good, but I still need to know *why*.

The sketch helps, a little. It reminds me that this life isn't the only one that's possible.

You could leave, says the voice inside my head, the one that sounds like my old self. *You can't get your old life back? So fucking build a new one.* It sounds like my true self. But is it? I think about packing up my stuff for real—the look on Eric's face when I tell him I'm leaving—and my insides sink.

You're not really going to stay, are you? With him?

It isn't just my dread of confrontation, or even that I don't want to hurt him. Inside myself I sense a cautiousness that wasn't there before, a reluctance to take a step into the dark. Maybe it's Eric's influence. He's been with this version of me for so long. And I do feel something for him, from him: a warmth, a glow, a comfort. The intuitive sense that he's on my side, even if I can't tell him everything. Something like what Linnea and I had, with the obvious added dimension.

Chicago Kelly hadn't spoken to him since high school. Had barely thought about him. Yet now I feel as though he was there all the time, a part of my life whether I knew it or not. I remember our coming to this house for the first time after we closed on it, driving straight from the attorney's office. It seemed so strange that the place was ours, that we could tromp through its empty rooms unsupervised. We brought our bedspread and pillows and slept on the floor in our new bedroom. I felt self-conscious while we had sex, as though the previous owners might still be hanging around.

I also remember another moving day, when I was still in art school. Linnea and I had found an apartment together: a narrow column of rooms with views of brick walls and thin slices of sky. It had a claw-foot tub in the bathroom, and the drain stopped up if you took a shower longer than five minutes. Linnea could have afforded a better place, but my pride wasn't so beaten down as to accept a situation where she would be paying twice as much rent as I would. I can hear our laughter as we moved into that apartment, manhandling box springs and bookshelves up the stairs and through the doorways. We had friends helping us move (including Bobby, who'd just broken up with his high school girlfriend and with whom Linnea was beginning, shyly, to flirt), and the atmosphere was that of a party. Music was playing; we'd filled the fridge with cheap beer. It was a hot day, and I remember the smell I carried on myself by evening, sweat and the sour breath of alcohol-induced dehydration. I remember the coolness of the sheet I spread over my mattress without tucking it in, how good it felt to collapse and let the tired springs take my weight.

That moving day feels as real as the one with Eric. More real. But how can that be?

Another memory surfaces. Didn't I see him once during art school, at one of my student exhibitions? I close my eyes, trying to envision it, and the patterns of leaf shadow from my office window form imprints on my eyelids. I picture the gallery on State Street full of light and people. I stood in a cluster with my friends, wondering if this was what showing would be like when it was for real. It was winter, the sun setting early. A slanting beam filled my eyes with fire. And then, turning my head, I saw him.

He was behind a column, slouching. (Trying to avoid being seen?) I thought, *Wait. Isn't that . . . ?* Someone started talking to me before I could finish the thought, and he'd disappeared by the time it occurred again. And honestly, though I'd liked him well enough in high school, I hadn't been so attached that I'd go looking for him in a crowd. I hadn't even thought of the incident again until now.

Maybe that's because it never happened, and this is one of those deceptively detailed yet false recollections, like in those memory studies, constructed around nothing more than suggestion.

But what if he *was* there? What if he was there to see me?

The thought sends a shiver through me, as though someone might be watching me right now. I imagine myself from the back, the way someone at the door would see me. My hair pulled into a bun, exposing the back of my neck. I whirl around, confronting the open door. No one's there.

Of course no one is. I shake the feeling away.

21

DURING THE AFTERNOON I DO MORE DIGGING, WITH DISAP-
pointing results. No "kmholter" exists in the School of the Art
Institute's online portal, not that I was expecting to find myself
there after yesterday. The documents in the filing cabinet downstairs all support my current life: marriage license, home and car
maintenance receipts, diploma from Michigan State. I pull on
the cabinet's bottom drawer and find it locked. I don't know
where the key is.

Eric's desk sits downstairs as well, his computer used mostly
for playing video games and downloading shows and movies. In
the top drawer, I find a small silver key wedged into the front
corner next to a roll of Scotch tape and more pens than we'll ever
use. It opens the locked filing cabinet drawer, which holds tax
records and the deed to the house. I lock the drawer, replace the
key, and hesitate before pulling Eric's desk drawer the rest of the
way out, running my fingers over the edges and bottom. Nothing but the smooth fake wood of the drawer itself. What am I
looking for? Surveillance photos of me from my other life? Furtively, I search the rest of his desk, turning up an assortment of
orphaned cables, a defunct trackball, a half-empty bag of Sour
Skittles. I wake up his computer and try guessing the password,

but none of my attempts get me in. Not wanting to lock it down, I stop after a few tries. I go through the desk one more time, checking the back side of his monitor and the bottoms of the drawers and keyboard, but I don't find a helpful sticky note of passwords or any other information.

I'm restless, and I've still got hours before my meet-up with Peter. A run will settle me down.

I leave Bear at home. It's not as if Eric will ever know, and anyway I never *promised* him I wouldn't run alone. Taking the dog is something he imposed on me. It's not that he's domineering; he just cares about things I consider too trivial to pursue a conflict over.

Unburdened, I stay out longer. I run a big loop around our neighborhood and up the trail through the woods behind our house, then wind through BellaVista, the newer subdivision next to ours, then retrace my path down the woods trail in the other direction, toward home. Doris, our next-door neighbor, told me the forest used to extend a mile or more to the west, crisscrossed with trails and teeming with birds and squirrels and sometimes deer. Her kids used to find arrowheads. Most of the trees were razed to make way for BellaVista, reducing the area to a narrow strip of toy forest and a single path running parallel to Oriskany Way. As I run down it I see rooflines through the budding trees, but if I focus my eyes closer I can pretend I'm in the wilderness.

It's a gorgeous day, sunny and crisp, and I marvel at my body's efficiency, the effortless collaboration of heart and lungs and limbs, small machines working to power a larger one. Chicago Kelly got out of breath climbing the stairs to the El. I should be exhausted after the long day and late night and my eventful morning, but I feel full of energy, buoyed by the promise of answers. When I see Peter tonight, I'll make him explain every-thing. He'll know how I could have gone straight to my apart-ment, even though there was another family living there. He'll know why I got lost in my own neighborhood, why my best friend treated me like a stranger even though her boyfriend seemed to recognize me. He'll be able to tell me for sure if my life in Chicago was real.

And if it was, maybe he can tell me how to get back to it.

The possibility doesn't comfort me as much as it should.

You're the most important thing in the world to him, Peter said. In Chicago, I was never anybody's number one. I had support-ers, friends who would drop everything if I needed them, but in the most fundamental ways, I was on my own. Most people would say I've got it better now. I have a nice house, a job where I make my own hours, and an objectively hot partner who smooths my path through life in every possible way. If he's somehow responsible for what happened, then what was he tak-ing me away from?

Struggle and doubt. Minimum payments on the credit card balance. Inconsiderate roommates. The constant sense of being passed over, of time running out.

And a constant sense of possibility. Moments of brilliance that told me why I'd chosen that life. This life, I didn't choose. It was chosen for me. But would it be so bad if I had to stay here?

I remember the look in Peter's eyes when I asked him if I could trust Eric. He stopped himself from saying an automatic yes, because he didn't know the answer any more than I do. Maybe he doesn't have the other answers I'm looking for either, but I have to believe he knows *something*.

I need to find out what happened to me. To know for sure if

this is real or all in my head. And if it's real, then I want to know who did it to me.

WHEN I GET back to my street, a moving truck idles at the curb in front of the vacant house kitty-corner from ours, filling the air with exhaust and engine noise. Doris is camped out in her front yard, pretending to fuss with her rosebushes. She waves me over and I approach with a sense of impending amusement, wondering what she'd say if I told her she forgot her binoculars.

"Have you seen them yet?" She points her gardening shears at the new neighbors' house. I shake my head. "The property manager told me the wife teaches elementary school—no kids, though—and the husband's a real estate agent. Makes you wonder why they're renting." She tilts her head. "I'm glad someone's finally living there, though. An empty house brings down the whole— Ooh!" Her flat blue eyes flick over my shoulder, widening. "I bet this is them."

We watch the approach of a gunmetal BMW: a rare import in a state where the Big Three automakers hold sway. It makes a wide arc around the moving truck, pulls into the driveway, and comes to a stop.

The woman who emerges from the passenger side is a perfect match for the car. Tall, with dark hair in a pixie that accentuates her elegant neck and cheekbones, she moves with grace balanced between control and effortlessness. She props her sunglasses on top of her head, regarding Doris and me, then turns away before I can wave. Her gaze runs along the roofline of her new home as she says something to the man getting out of the driver's seat.

He's more prosaic-looking. Attractive, certainly, in the inoffensive manner of a Ken doll or a B-list actor (broad shoulders, strong jaw, sheaf of dark blond hair), but there's nothing about him that makes me want to look twice. "Well," Doris murmurs, "they're a handsome couple."

The man turns his head and sees me and Doris rubbernecking. Unlike his wife, he acknowledges our presence, with a smile that animates his entire face. My hand and Doris's rise in tandem, a perfunctory, neighborly wave. We'll probably never do more than that. I might never even know these people's names unless Doris takes the trouble to ferret them out.

But then I think: *Why shouldn't I know them?* In Chicago I was friends with all my neighbors, despite the urban tendency to keep to one's own little sphere of acquaintances, and it was because I made the effort. "I'm gonna go say hi," I tell Doris, stepping off the curb. She trails me across the street, delight coming off her like perfume. I'm doing her work for her. "Hey there," I call to the man, who's seen me coming and is waiting for us, still smiling. The woman pivots and an expression of irritation flits across her face.

Just as quickly it's gone, replaced with a guarded smile. "Hello," she says.

"Welcome to the neighborhood," I sing out. I should be carrying a plate of cookies. "I live across the street. Kelly Holter. Hyde! Kelly Hyde."

The woman shakes my hand in the limp-fingered way some women have. I try not to judge her for it. She's no less beautiful up close, towering over me in three-inch heels. This is an elementary school teacher? "Diane Rowley," she says.

"Adam Rowley," says her husband. "Great to meet you."

He's one of those big guys who's more graceful than he looks, and he's rounded the car almost before I'm aware of it. Up close I see his eyes are a brilliant blue, though a smidge too close together for movie-star flawlessness. His hand, when I shake it, is warm and dry, large enough to envelop mine, the handshake firm but not crushing. I get a strong sense that I've seen him before, that I know him. But it's not as if my déjà vu has been especially trustworthy lately.

"Where did you guys live before?" I ask.

Diane looks at Adam, waiting for him to answer. "Ann Arbor," he says, after just enough of a delay to make it slightly awkward.

"Oh, Ann Arbor is heaven on a stick. Dick and I go down every summer for the art fair," Doris gushes. "I'm Doris Vredevoogd. I live across the street." She flaps a hand at her house. "What brings you to Davis City?"

There's another brief silence, which Diane and Adam both break at once, talking over each other. They break off, and then Adam nods for Diane to speak, giving her a tight smile.

"Ann Arbor is a . . . competitive environment in many ways," Diane says, holding eye contact with her husband.

"Right," he confirms.

"If you'll excuse me, I should make sure our furniture made it in one piece. It was nice to meet you both," Diane says. Without waiting for an answer or looking at me or Doris again, she turns and clicks up the walk into the house.

Well. Apparently someone's not happy about moving to Davis City.

If Doris noticed the tension between them, she gives no indication of it. "So, I hear you're a real estate agent," she says. "It must be hard to set yourself up in a new town, huh?"

Adam does something weird: he completely ignores her, as if she hasn't spoken, and turns to me. "So, you're a runner?"

I blink, surprised at the shift in topic. "How did you know?"

He makes a gesture up and down me, his eyes following. His gaze isn't remotely lecherous, but it heightens my awareness of my altered shape under the slight polyester shorts and singlet. "Oh, duh," I say, my cheeks warming.

"I run too . . . well, I used to. I've gotten fat and lazy." He pats his flat stomach. Then his face lights up. "Hey! Why don't we meet up tomorrow morning? I'll dig out my running shoes. I need to get back on the wagon."

The thought pops up that Eric won't be able to complain about my leaving the dog at home if I've got a running buddy. "Great idea," I say.

"You don't mind? I get bored as hell running by myself." He grins at me, the kind of smile that pulls you along with it. I can't help but smile back, and the feeling that I know him touches me again.

"Not at all." We set a time and I leave him to Doris, who looks ready to pry his life story out of him with her shears. I go inside feeling optimistic, lifted by the prospect of a new friend.

22

I ARRIVE AT THE BRAZIER EARLY, WANTING TO BE IN POSITION before Peter shows up. This bar is steeped in memory for me. My friends and I didn't come here often, maybe half a dozen times during high school, and nothing earth-shattering ever happened, but those visits feel foundational to our friendship. The four of us would pile into a booth, me and Alicia on one side, Nicole and Katie on the other. We'd order a bucket of bottles, whatever was cheap, and sip with deliberately casual expressions, as if nonchalance would keep an overzealous bouncer from noticing how young we were. (There were never any overzealous bouncers at the Brazier, which was part of the attraction.) By going to this place, we might have been looking for the kind of adventure people seek out when they go to punk clubs or buy drugs off the street, but if so, we never found it. The usual clientele couldn't have been less interested in high school girls slumming.

As the door closes behind me, something else pushes at the edges of my thoughts: the more recent feeling of familiarity from earlier. Less defined than my memories of our high school antics, but it's there.

The bar is perpetually dim, neon lit, and fairly quiet on a

weekday evening. A woman gossips with the bartender, and a pair of semi-drunk middle-aged men debate the merits of the Tigers' starting lineup in raised voices, but I can barely hear them over the jukebox. The more introverted regulars slump on barstools at decorous intervals from one another. I don't want conversation, so I order a Bell's and take it to one of the booths along the wall where I can keep an eye on the door.

I figure it's about fifty-fifty whether Peter will show up. He didn't seem eager to talk to me at all until I mentioned last Friday. I no longer have any doubt that our problems are closely related. It's a hunch, but I feel that gnii is somehow bound up in what happened to me. How Eric fits into that, I don't know. But Peter seems convinced that he does.

While I wait for him, I drink my pint and scroll through search results on my phone, looking for information about digital assistants like gnii's app. The market is dominated by the same tech giants who've been around forever, which makes it difficult for a smaller, newer company to break in without a distinct advantage. The holy grail they're all seeking is artificial general intelligence, the ability for a computer to process information like the human brain does. To make inferences and connections without having to be trained for every possible situation, to translate humans' idiosyncratic utterances into actionable commands. A few apps have come out purported to have cracked it, but those have been quickly exposed as having human backup, an army of poorly paid techs to catch and fulfill commands in real time when the AI fails to interpret them correctly.

What if gnii is the one app that's actually reached its goal? Nobody outside the company seems to know everything it can do. What if its developers have figured out how to affect reality in material ways, to literally change people's lives? There has to be some added dimension, some feature being kept under wraps. *Your wish. Our command.*

Or maybe all the secrecy is just covering up a whole lot of nothing.

Peter is fifteen minutes late, twenty. A couple of the bar sitters finish their after-work drinks and leave; others come in to replace them, with an air of settling in for the night. The noise level stays fairly constant. Someone's cued up an old Morphine album on the jukebox, and the sound of it plucks at the recognition I felt when I first came in. I've been here recently. Not with my friends but by myself, sitting in a booth waiting for someone just like I am now.

The turbulent darkness of the music, all smoky sax and chaotic bass, creates impressions in my mind, flashes lit in neon chiaroscuro. Emotions burst inside me like small fireworks. Excitement and a sense of danger, but not the elemental danger I've been feeling. Something more pedestrian, yet with the power to shake my life to its foundations. Growing inside me is a sense of confusion, of dislocation, not in space but in time. Not *Where am I?* but *When is it?* It's not that I don't know what day it is, or what I'm here for; it's more that my certainty about those facts seems based on faith instead of evidence, and my faith is slipping. I'm still watching the door, but I'm no longer sure what I expect to see when it opens.

Who am I waiting for?

The sounds around me seem to have been turned up. The crack of pool balls hitting one another, the cackle of the woman at the bar, the song playing on the jukebox. *We should've kept it every Thursday Thursday Thursday in the afternoon . . .* a song about infidelity and the threat of violence, about keeping within the limits of things, letting them go when they've run their course. The space next to me in the booth feels empty, like it's bereft of someone who should be sitting there. A larger body than mine, bulkier, taller, someone who won't hesitate to enter my space, to reach for me underneath the table where no one can see.

No one can see. I hear a silky murmur, feel warm breath on my ear and my neck. *And so what if they do?* A thrill goes through my entire body, making my breath catch, making me bite my lip. The music gets louder, howling to a dark crescendo, increasing the pressure in my head until I have to slide out of the booth and bolt for the nearest escape.

That turns out to be the bathroom. The door locks with a ridiculously large bolting mechanism, as if the bar has had problems with people breaking flimsier locks. I throw it shut and the dingy walls close me in with my dull reflection, backlit by the ceiling fixture. I pat water on my face, then lean on the sink. When I close my eyes, I see an image like the smoke from two vast fires, miles apart but burning to meet each other, and the smoke is the memories from different lives. Or maybe it's more than two fires. Maybe the whole world is on fire. The smoke— the memories and under-memories—curls and billows until I can't tell where any of it comes from.

Go home, my inner voice says. *Go home to your husband.*

When I think the word *husband* I see Eric's face, shiny with tears. Eric who doesn't cry. I hear his voice in memory, not the words he flung at me but the sound of it, ragged, accusing, despairing.

That never happened.

It's true. When I think back over my memories of this life, my Michigan life, I can't remember Eric and me ever having a blowout like that. Our fights are more controlled, resentful things. And I've never cheated on him. I would definitely remember that.

And yet. The impressions keep crowding in until I realize it's something about this place, that it won't let up until I leave.

I haul the bathroom door open and hurry out the back exit, past the scratch-off-ticket vending machine and the tiny hole of a kitchen. The cool evening air clears away some of my confusion, but I don't stop until I'm in my car. Fortunately I've got my bag and phone with me, because I'm not sure I have the courage to go back inside. If Peter's there, if he showed up while I was in the bathroom, I'll just have to follow up with him tomorrow.

I crank the engine and roll down the car windows, pulling out of the lot with a spray of gravel under my tires. The farther I get from the bar, the more blessedly empty my head feels. But as I turn into my subdivision and drive down my street, I become aware that this too is familiar; this is something I've done before. I've felt the same twist of dread in my gut at seeing the garage door up, seeing Eric's car already inside, knowing I haven't beaten him home and explanations will be needed.

I'm steeled for anything, especially after yesterday, but all I find is Eric peacefully setting out Chinese food containers on the dining table. "Oh, hey," he says, when I walk in. He seems less worried about where I've been than about sidestepping Bear, who's underfoot hoping for a beef-and-broccoli windfall.

"Thanks for getting food," I say, dropping my purse into a chair.

He glances up, smiling. "I stopped by the store too." His eyes touch mine and linger, imbuing his words with more than sur-face significance, though I have no idea what he could be trying to tell me. Then he says, "I got some condoms," which makes the whole puppy-eyes routine make more sense.

Unfortunately, I'm too nervous to play along. "Didn't you go to the gym?" I ask, noticing he's still wearing work clothes.

He frowns. "I was tired. I'll go tomorrow."

"Won't that throw off your whole routine?" I'm not really serious, but Eric launches into an explanation of how he works different muscle groups each gym session, so it's fine for him to go two days in a row. I go to the fridge and fill two glasses of water, snapping, "No," when the fridge asks yet again whether I want to re-up on water filters. "Didn't we turn these off?" I ask Eric. "These reminder things?"

"Oh, right." He steps up behind me, pushing a sequence of buttons on the panel. "Should be good now. We can drink as much dirty water as we want." I wait for him to move away but he kisses my cheek, his hand lighting on my shoulder. "So where'd you go?"

There it is. "Just to meet a friend for a drink." It's easier to lie when I'm not looking at him.

"Oh? Which friend?"

I don't hear anything beyond simple curiosity in his tone, but my hackles are still up. "Katie, from high school." The lie slips out easily, even as I think of Peter saying *He could be in some deep shit.* I should find a way to tell Eric about Peter's warning. But I need more information first; at this point I don't even know what the threat might be.

"I didn't know you still talked to her." Finally Eric backs away from me, going to sit at the table.

I follow him, bringing our water glasses. "I haven't seen her in forever, but she texted me this afternoon. She wanted to check out that new cocktail bar downtown." Then I realize I'll have to make up more lies about how she's doing and what we talked about. "She actually . . . she didn't show up. Her husband ended up having to work late, so she couldn't get away, with her kids and everything."

I dig into the Chinese food. Naturally, everything Eric ordered has meat in it.

"So you went to the cocktail bar by yourself?"

"Yeah, I had one drink while I was waiting for her. Then she texted me saying she couldn't make it. You know how she is." I roll my eyes.

"Do they let you smoke in bars now?"

"No, why?"

"Because you kind of smell like smoke."

I lift a hank of my hair to my nose and, yeah, there's that Brazier smell, decades of sunken-in cigarette residue from before a smoking ban was ever thought of.

"Huh." My mind races. "I did walk right past some people smoking outside." I pick through a container looking for vegetables, trying to hide my agitation. I can't do this, this *lying* thing. Again I hear Eric's raised voice in my head. I can't do it, but I have.

I glance at him. He's watching me with an expression like he's trying to figure out a puzzle, and not a fun one. *I haven't done anything wrong,* I want to say, but with this unexplainable guilt inside me there's no way it'll sound convincing.

I try on a smile. "Did you see we have new neighbors? I met them. They seem nice. I'm going running with the guy tomorrow.

It's a couple, they're from Ann Arbor. Diane and Adam . . ." What is going on here? Eric's the one with secrets, but I'm the one eluding his questions.

I watch for his face to relax, but it gets tighter and tighter. "I wasn't going to ask you where you went," he says, cutting me off midsentence. "I didn't mean to."

Silence unspools. He stares at his chopsticks, chomping them closed, open, closed, then lays them across his bowl. He sighs. "I need you to tell me where you really were."

"What do you mean? I told you, I went downtown—"

"No. You didn't."

How do you know that? But saying that would give me away. Anger flares in my stomach at the position he's put me in, the trap he's made for me. I stare at him, hardening my expression so he knows he's fucking with the wrong person, though he still won't look at me. "I know last night was upsetting for you, but that doesn't mean you get to accuse me of lying."

"I'm not accusing you of—"

"You are. You just called me a liar."

Blood flushes in his cheeks. "Kelly, I—"

"Eric, I went downtown to meet Katie. I had one drink. She texted me to say she couldn't make it. And then I came home. To you." The words come quietly, orderly, one after another like little stones dropping out of my mouth. "I don't know what else to tell you." And that part, at least, is true.

He looks up at me, his eyes wide, and I can see how much he wants to believe me.

"Show me her texts," he says. "If what you're saying is true."

That's easy. "I'm not going to show you her texts." I push back from the table and carry my bowl and glass to the sink, waiting for Eric to say something. He just sits there, stiff and straight, his back to me. I can feel the tension in my own body, the way I have to consciously unclench my jaw, and I want to be done with this fight; I want to be out of this room.

"If we can't trust each other," I say, "then I don't know what we're doing here."

Eric doesn't move or do anything to indicate he's heard me. I take the leash from its hook by the front door. Bear comes to me and I clip the leash to his collar. I open the door and we head out into the night.

23

Day Six

ERIC'S GONE WHEN I WAKE UP.

We didn't speak last night after Bear and I got back. As soon as I walked into the house I could feel Eric's presence filling it up, feel him waiting downstairs for me to come and continue our pointless argument, but I wasn't in the mood. I'm never in the mood. So I ignored his blaring silent message and went upstairs and went to bed mad.

I didn't think I'd be able to sleep, but I was so exhausted that I don't even remember my dreams.

Eric's side of the bed is rumpled, which means he did eventually sleep there, or at least lie there. I drop my head back onto my pillow. It's earlier than I usually wake up, but Bear is in the room and the house is silent.

Eric probably just went to the gym or headed into work early. But I can't rid myself of the sense of wrongness. We had a fight, he knew I lied to him, and now he should be here and he isn't. I've got enough to contend with—I still haven't talked to Peter, and I still don't know what the hell happened to me at the

Brazier—and the last thing I need is Eric acting like a fucking wild card.

It isn't only that. Last night I wanted nothing to do with him, but now I wish he were here, his warm body stretched out next to mine, so I could drape my arm over him and nuzzle my face into the soft space underneath his jaw, so that even if he was still upset when he went to bed, even if I was still upset, we could work it out through touch instead of endless and bloodless circles of discussion. I'm not sure why that feels like something that would be safe, after last night, except in my head I keep multiple versions of Eric as well as myself. There's the Eric from last night who questions me about where I've been, who watches my every move. And then there's the other Eric, who loves me, takes care of me, only wants me to be happy. The Eric I can soften with a touch, whether he'll admit it or not.

No messages from him on my phone. After vacillating a few minutes, I text him. Hey. Let me know you got into work, ok? Neutral, yet with a subtle communication of my displeasure at his taking off without speaking to me. He doesn't answer right away, so I assume he's sulking.

I lie back in bed, watching morning light leak into the room. I'll have to go back to gnii and see if I can intercept Peter again. Teach him to dodge me. But before that, I remember with a small flush of pleasure, I'm going running with Adam, my new neighbor.

I get out of bed, get dressed, drink a cup of tea and some water. A few minutes after nine, I head outside to find Adam already stretching in his driveway. "You're making me look bad. I thought you said you were lazy," I call as I cross the street, and he grins. Interacting with him feels comfortingly normal, a welcome chance to step outside the strangeness of my own problems.

"Aw, your dog wants to come," he says, looking over my shoulder.

I turn around. Bear has his paws up on the sill of the living room window and is barking his head off. "You do not want Bear to come with us, unless you're collecting dead squirrels."

Adam sets a faster pace than what I'm used to, but not so fast that I'm dying. I think about asking him to slow down, but since I can still carry on a conversation I decide it's good for me to push myself. He's not even breathing hard, despite telling me he hasn't gone running in over a month.

"So why did you and Diane move here?" I ask, curious about what might have led a couple like Adam and Diane to leave a relatively cosmopolitan college town for suburbia.

"The parents at Diane's school were out of control," Adam says. "Nothing was ever good enough for their little snowflakes. And before Ann Arbor she was teaching in Ypsilanti, which is a mess in a whole different way. I should know, I grew up there."

"Really?" Ypsilanti, a few miles east of Ann Arbor, is the town's down-on-its-luck sibling. Finding out it's Adam's home-town makes me see him differently, as more than the ex–frat boy I assumed he was. "Did you go to U of M?"

"Eastern. Go Green!" He thrusts his fist in the air with a mocking laugh. "I moved to Ann Arbor after college, though, to start my rock-star-slash-bartender career."

I'd never have pegged him as a musician. "What did you play?"

"I was the frontman in this nu-metal throwback band. I used to think the dude from Godsmack was totally badass."

"Everyone has bad taste when they're young," I say with a

laugh, and Adam narrows his eyes as if he didn't expect me to agree with so much enthusiasm. I move on quickly. "Is that how you met Diane, at one of your shows?" I can imagine Adam posturing on stage with a microphone, but try as I might, I can't see sleek, self-contained Diane rocking out in the front row.

"She wasn't there by choice." A flash of white teeth in his tanned face. "She came with another guy and ended up leaving with me."

"Must've been a pretty bad date."

At that Adam throws his head back and laughs so loudly it startles me. "Must have. So, what about you? How did you and . . ."

"Eric." I haven't mentioned him before now, but I'm wearing a wedding ring and single people aren't exactly common in this neighborhood.

"How did you and Eric meet?"

"We went to high school together. One day in junior year he up and asked me out after soccer practice." Recounting this memory feels strange, like I have to reach back and rummage around in my head for it, yet I can almost feel the chafing of my shin guards. "He took me to see a Broadway show in Detroit. Had everything all planned out."

"Wow," Adam says. "Guys like that ruin it for the rest of us."

I laugh. "He's always gone out of his way for me." It strikes me that, after the fight Eric and I had last night, the way I'm talking about him now would be a front even if I weren't going through an existential crisis. But that's what you do in a marriage: you smooth out the messy parts for other people.

"So, what does he do?"

It rankles a little to have Adam ask about Eric's work when he hasn't asked about mine. Maybe, since I'm home on a weekday morning, he assumes I don't have any.

"He works at the college. He's an instructional designer." Not that anyone knows what that is.

But apparently Adam at least has an idea, because he says, "So he works with computers. Does he do any programming on the side? App development or anything? Seems like that's where the money is . . . not that I know anything about it."

"If you knew Eric, you'd know he's not the most ambitious person in the world." It comes out sounding more spiteful than I intend. "I mean, he doesn't care that much about money."

"Nothing wrong with that, right? We need worker bees too. Not everyone can change the world."

His tone is positive, but the words rub me the wrong way. Though I've had thoughts along those same lines, wondering why Eric doesn't want more out of life, I don't like hearing Adam dismiss him so easily. He doesn't even know Eric.

"You know, I didn't mean anything by that," Adam says when I don't respond.

"Oh, of course!" I smile, rushing to smooth things over. "I know you didn't. And you've got him pegged, really. He's got his own little corner of the universe and that's just fine with him."

"Nothing wrong with that," Adam repeats. We turn onto the forest path, which is just wide enough to run abreast. A screen of leaves turns the light greenish: once they're fully grown out it'll be another world in here, cut off from the neighborhoods on either side. Here and there trash lies on the ground, cigarette butts and bottle caps, the deflated balloon of a used condom. It's probably teenagers. This is the place Eric's thinking of when he asks me to take Bear along on my runs.

The rest of the run slips by. Adam and I talk about music and our younger days, me careful to tell only stories from Andromeda Creek. I don't mention that I used to paint. I arrive home energized. I haven't enjoyed myself this much since before last Friday.

"This was great," Adam says as we arrive back on our street. "We should definitely make it a standing thing."

"I agree. Tomorrow? Same time, same place?"

"I'll be here." He holds up his fist for me to bump. "That dog sure does miss you," he says with a laugh.

I look over at my house, where Bear is back at the window, barking desperately. "He just doesn't like it when I do fun things without him. Eric's the one he really loves."

As I let myself in Bear crowds the door, whining and sniffing at my legs. "Jesus, Bear. Be cool." I can feel the stress returning, the carefree conversation slipping away. An unexpected wish cuts through me: that my life really were this simple and I really were just Kelly Hyde, freelance graphic designer. I could go about my day, satisfied in the knowledge that I'd made a new friend, looking forward to nothing more momentous than my husband's return home and maybe a weekend trip up north. If I were that person through and through, there'd be no reason to lie to Eric, no reason to distrust him.

It's tempting to try to sink into it. To subsume these other memories, these other parts of myself trying to come to the surface. I could throw myself into this life, build community here, make friends. I'd be someone who talked to her family all the time, who had a close relationship with her in-laws. Eric and I could even have kids. People do it every day.

It would never work. The other memories are too insistent.

When they take over it's a full-body experience; it's terrifying. But what if my other life really is nothing more than a delusion? How would I stamp out something like that? Therapy. Drugs, possibly. I'd have to commit to the reality that's in front of me. I'd have to tell Eric what's going on. He would help me.

I'm still thinking about it as I go upstairs and shower, then stand before the mirror to detangle my long hair. If Eric knew what was going on in my head, he wouldn't be angry at me anymore. He's a good husband, kind and attentive. I'm attracted to him, maybe even love him. Who's to say we wouldn't be blissfully happy if I threw in with him for good? If the last few days have taught me anything, it's that I can't go back. There's nothing to go back to.

Just then the room seems to shift, not physically but inside my head, in some indefinable way. Do the lights flicker? It's more like my *vision* flickers. Ink springs up on my arms: watercolor tattoos, the same ones I had in Chicago. My hair shortens, corkscrewing. It's so clear, so real, that I cry out and drop the comb.

Then it's gone.

Feeling dizzy, I bend and pick up the comb. My ankle is as devoid of ink as it has been since the switch. But if I'd looked a moment ago, I'm almost sure the tattoo would have been there.

I stare at myself in the mirror, willing the ink to reappear, the flicker to reoccur. Nothing happens.

It was real.

Maybe I can't make it happen again right now, but it *did* happen. I've never been more certain of anything. I can't give up yet.

I take a fistful of my hair, tugging on it. Then I open the cabinet and take out the scissors I keep for trimming split ends.

I trap a lock between my first two fingers, sliding them down until I have the length I want, and snip just below them. A damp chunk of hair falls into the sink and divides itself into strands, while the part that remains on my head springs upward like it's been freed. I take another lock and snip again, then another lock, another snip. I drag the comb through my hair, arranging it into sections so I can see what still needs to be cut. The sink fills with a soft brown nest, creating a visible indication of progress, as I watch my neck and shoulders emerge. I'm shedding a part of myself I don't need. With every snip, I feel lighter.

AFTER ANOTHER SHOWER, I head back to gnii. The same guard as yesterday is at the desk, but when I say, "Hello again," he gives me a blank look. Some people can't see past a haircut, though it seems counterproductive for a security guard to be so unobservant.

"Is Peter in yet?" I ask.

He doesn't glance at his console. "There's no Peter who works here."

Come again? "Peter Nedelman," I say, smiling. "He's a developer?"

"Not here. You must have the wrong building."

I feel my smile fade. The guard's giving me a steady glare and a distinct *Get lost* vibe. I don't believe him for a second.

The door behind me sweeps open and one of the coffee guys from yesterday—at least I think it's one of them—walks in. He nods to the guard and walks briskly toward the metal door to the restricted part of the building.

I say, "Hey, remember me?"

He looks genuinely freaked out, but he pauses. I press my advantage, stepping toward him. "Tell Peter to message me. Kelly. He's going to want to hear what I have to tell him." I take out my phone to transfer my number to the guy's contacts.

The guard stiffens when he sees me reach into my bag. "I'm gonna need you to leave now, ma'am," he says, coming around the desk.

"Okay, okay, I'm going." I move away from him, toward the exit, and make the transfer. The guy jumps a little as his phone chimes in his pocket.

As soon as I'm outside I start shaking. I head blindly into the main part of the district, my only aim to get out of sight of gnii's glass farmhouse. The walkway curves past an engineered-plank barn, its wide windows showing pretty people busy at standing desks. A ramen stall. A retail space, empty, still dirt floored behind the plate glass and FOR LEASE sign.

What the hell just happened? The guard and Peter's coworker, they recognized me. Someone told that guard to get rid of me if I came back. He wouldn't have reacted the way he did otherwise. Why would Peter be dodging me, when I could give him another data point to help with his problem?

Did Peter get fired? Is that why he didn't show up last night?

Or it's all fake, and I never actually came here yesterday. It's another false memory, like my life in Chicago and my feeling that I've been meeting someone at the Brazier. Or my visit here did happen, but then something changed. The world went through another shift.

I'm trying as hard as I can not to feel like I'm losing my shit.

My phone chirps with a text message. It's from an unfamiliar number. Local area code.

Probably best you don't show up here again, the message says. I'll get in touch with you

Peter. I message him back. How come you didn't show up last night?

My phone chirps again. Message could not be delivered, it says.

Now I turn and look back the way I came, where I can just barely see the gnii building glittering in the sun. Peter's in there. The answers to my questions—at least some of them—are so close. But I can't get to them.

24

NOT KNOWING WHAT ELSE TO DO, I GO HOME AND SIT DOWN TO work. At first it seems strange that I can shift so easily into a flow, working on a design for a wedding invitation, but then it's a relief. Bear lies on the floor behind me, thumping his tail on the carpet every time I speak out loud, which I tend to do while working. Time slips by, I'm not sure how much.

My phone vibrates on the desk, making me jump. Thinking it'll be Peter, I grab for it, but it's Eric. Want to have lunch?

Disappointment pierces me, then annoyance at his follow-up: I thought we should talk.

He's not going to let it go.

The last thing I need is to have him re-interrogate me about where I was last night. But maybe I'm wrong about his intentions. If he means to apologize, I should give him the chance.

Or I could interrogate *him*.

OK, I reply.

Great, pick you up in 20

Which means he's already on his way. No discussion about what time might be good for me, or where we're eating. Eric likes surprising me. It's part of how he shows love, by arranging things for me, making many of the small decisions that comprise our life together, and it does make life easier. But in my current mood, I'm irked that he assumes I won't want a say.

I text him back. Let's get sushi

It's a small thing, a tiny thing, but it's a choice.

If you want sushi in Davis City, there's only one place to get it outside of a grocery store. Sushi World sits in a strip mall between Subway and FedEx Office, its polarized windows smeared with neon paint advertising five-dollar California rolls and two-for-one Tiger beer during happy hour. Inside, it looks like a sports bar, with wood paneling and flat-screens mounted to be visible from every seat. When Eric and I walk in the place is empty, despite it being the tail end of lunch hour on a workday.

A bored server tells us we can "sit wherever" and takes our drink order. Eric gets iced tea; I get a Kirin, because why not? Every table is outfitted with a console where you can order drink refills and pay your bill when you're finished. I could get drunk without having to talk to the server again. These consoles were common in Chicago, but I didn't see them at Luigi's.

Eric's been distracted since he picked me up—he doesn't seem to have noticed my haircut—and as soon as we order, he gets to the point. He straightens in his seat, squaring his shoulders, and says, "I'm sorry about last night. I basically called you a liar, and that was inexcusable." He speaks precisely, formally, like he's practiced it, looking down at his clasped hands. His gold wedding band a muted gleam. He has a flexible silicone one, I know, that he wears when he goes to the gym.

My first thought is that it's laughable how seriously he's treating this, when he knows damn well I was lying.

Then, paradoxically, a bubble of irritation expands in my chest. As if his apology has given me permission to get angry.

"I've been . . . going through some stuff," he goes on. He seems to realize how much tension he's putting into his hands and releases them from each other. "I know I need to work on it. But that shouldn't be on you."

"No. It shouldn't." The forcefulness in my voice makes him look at me; then he drops his gaze back to the table. "I meant what I said, about us trusting each other." *And I don't know if I can trust you.*

But, and I'm surprised at how strong this feeling is, I want to.

Eric nods. "I know, and you're right. Absolutely."

"What kind of stuff have you been going through?"

He pushes the lemon slice around the rim of his iced tea glass. "Just . . . you know when you realize certain things might not turn out the way you wanted them to, or be as easy as you thought?"

I let out a dry chuckle. "You mean adulthood?" Eric's face falls a little, and I soften my tone. "What things?"

He hesitates, mulling over how to respond. "Sometimes at work," he says finally, "we'll get a project, and issues keep coming up, and keep coming up, until I start to wonder if the whole thing was cursed from the start. Like maybe there's some reason we shouldn't be doing it, and all these problems, that's the universe trying to tell us."

"So you're having problems at work?"

"No, work's fine."

I think of Ruby saying Eric should have been a software developer. "If you want to do something else—"

"I don't," he says, abrupt. Done with the subject.

I take a sip of my beer before I speak. "Does this have anything to do with why Peter called the other night?" I let my eyes flick up to his face, which is carefully blank. "I feel like there's something you're not telling me." Understatement of the year.

"Kelly—"

"You don't have to shield me, or whatever it is you're doing. I'm a grown-up. What's going on with you?"

"Lately, I feel like . . . I keep trying and trying to make everything right, and it still goes wrong."

"What do you mean? What's going wrong?"

He pulls in a breath, lets it out in a sigh. "I just want us to be happy." He sounds so forlorn. He reaches across the table and takes my hand, and I let him. "You are happy, right?"

My anger has dissipated, and it seems like saying no would be an attack. Was Michigan Kelly happy, before last Friday? Was I happy in Chicago? Probably, maybe, but most of the time I was too busy to notice. *Happy* implies an end. A state of being, not doing. But the times in my life when I've felt true happiness— uncomplicated contentment, unassisted by drugs—it's dawned on me fleetingly, during pauses from everything else. A sudden breaking through the clouds while I'm on the dance floor, or in the midst of roughing out a new painting, or just before falling asleep. Happiness is not an emotion that remains at constant levels. It's a moving target.

What would it take for me to be happy, here?

"You shouldn't worry so much about me," I say. "You're not responsible for my happiness."

He shakes his head. "That's not the way I see it. I do feel responsible. Because I—" He squeezes my hand. "I don't want to think about what my life would be like without you in it. I know that's selfish. We both know you'd be fine, if we'd never gotten together."

There's bitterness in his voice. He wants me to deny it. "So would you," I say, but he's already shaking his head again.

"I'd be . . . a different person," he says. "And not a very good one." He watches his thumb stroke mine. "You said I need to trust you. But would you tell me if something were wrong? With us?"

He's got me there, whether he knows it or not, but there's no way I can explain my situation to him without sounding delusional. And I sense a resistance in him: he's asking me to open up, but he doesn't really want to know what's inside of me. Not if it doesn't match his idea of what he wants out of life.

The server drops off our sushi, slamming the platter on the table an inch from our clasped hands. "Could we have—" I begin, but she's gone before I can finish. "Jesus," I mutter.

"What did you want?"

"Just some small plates." And another beer. Another three beers.

"I'll find some." He slides out of the booth. I survey our lunch, which glistens with different-colored sauces. The chef has formed sliced cucumber and pickled ginger into the shape of a duck, or maybe it's supposed to be a swan.

Eric comes back from the bar with two plates, two monkey dishes for soy sauce, and a Kirin. "I figured you'd want another beer."

"Thanks." That's Eric for you. He's always been good at anticipating my wishes. A curio I admire at an art fair will show up under the Christmas tree, or I'll mention my car has a blown taillight and the next day it'll be fixed. I appreciate it, but his diligence makes me feel a sneaking guilt. A better wife would stalk her husband, looking for opportunities to please in return.

The interruption seems to have disrupted Eric's pensive mood. He tucks into our sushi like he's starving, but I don't have much appetite. The alcohol is starting to make me drowsy as well.

"Do you remember when we started going out?" I ask, lightly, as if I'm indulging in some idle nostalgia.

He swallows what's in his mouth. "Of course." He laughs a little, which I understand, because it would be surprising if he didn't remember. Our first date was an elaborate undertaking for a teenager: dinner and a show in Detroit. *Les Mis.* I remember wondering what he would have done with the tickets if I'd said no. But I was pleasantly surprised by how easy our rapport was, and how much more attracted I was to him at the end of the night than at the beginning. He had a way about him, a surety that seemed to belong to a much older man. That night, I realized both how much he liked me and how much I could like him in return.

"You'd been planning that for a while, hadn't you?"

Eric's dimples come out with his smile, the same boyish, slightly bashful smile that charmed me on that first night. "I didn't want to kill any astronauts." It's our joke, but I find it jarring to hear him say the word *kill* in this context.

"You were trying to impress me."

Eric pauses with a slice of volcano roll en route to his mouth. "All guys want to impress the girl they like. It's a caveman thing." I scoff and he sets his bite down on his plate. "I wanted to stand out from the crowd. I mean, I knew you didn't hate me, but it didn't seem like you saw me as someone to date. I wanted to change that."

"How long had you been thinking about this?"

He starts picking apart the ginger-and-cucumber swan/duck with his chopsticks. "A while."

"Months? Years?"

"Yeah."

"Which one? Months or years?"

He grimaces. "What is this, an interrogation?"

"No, I'm just curious." I give him a flirtatious smile, the one he says makes me look like I'm getting ready to eat him. "You must've been thinking about it for a long time, though. You had your speech all ready when you came up to me. You—"

Then a memory intrudes, so vivid it makes me stop talking.

IT WAS MY seventeenth birthday. We were headed to the school parking lot after soccer practice—me, Katie, Alicia, and Nicole—planning to go over to Katie's, since her parents didn't get home until after five. I was feeling a little flat, had felt that way all day, because my birthday hadn't felt as special as when I was younger, but as with most of my negative emotions I covered it up and pushed through it.

We were walking to Katie's Jeep, bullshitting as usual, when suddenly Eric Hyde was in our path. I remember noticing how stiffly he held his body. I'd veered to one side to let him pass before it registered that he intended to speak to us, that that had been his purpose all along. Idly, I wondered what he wanted. I didn't know him well, and he wasn't the type to walk up to a bunch of girls and start shooting the shit. Nice enough guy, but painfully shy.

"Hey," he said.

Katie, who'd already started to go around him, turned back and eyed him suspiciously. Alicia and Nicole looked at him in surprise. He was looking at me; he was talking to me. So I smiled, summoning Sweet Kelly, Homecoming Princess, and greeted him in return.

"Are you . . ." He swallowed. "Are you having a good birthday?"

"It's been all right." I was surprised he knew it was my birthday. Earlier, in history class, he'd hardly even acknowledged me, let alone wished me happy returns.

"Um, good."

Katie let out a snort. Eric's head jerked at the sound, and a dart of irritation shot through me, aimed at him more than her, perversely. Why was he keeping us here? Why couldn't he either spit out what he wanted to say or let us all get on with our lives?

"So, when's you guys' next game?"

It was Katie who answered. "Tuesday." Her voice a hammer strike, hard and scornful.

"Oh, cool." Eric's mouth stretched into a grimace. In my peripheral vision I saw Alicia and Nicole exchange glances.

"Did you, um . . . so what are you guys doing for prom?"

"I think we're just going as a group," I said. A horrible suspicion had taken root in my mind, planted by Eric's refusal to look in Katie's direction and her general status as one of the more lusted-after girls in school. *Why couldn't he have a crush on Alicia?* I fretted. *At least she'd be nice to him.*

"Or we might not go at all," Katie put in.

Eric chuckled. It came out as a choked rasp. "Yeah, prom's kind of cheesy."

"How would you know?" Katie fired back.

"Uh, I don't— I mean, I was just—"

"Jesus, Katie, be more of a bitch, why don't you," I snapped. I'd grown less patient with her in the past year: her superior attitude, her need to exclude and put down anyone who didn't come up to her esoteric standards. It was so *juvenile*. And I was ready to be done with this martyrdom of a conversation. Eric was obviously in misery, and I wanted to put him out of it. "You know what we need to do?" I said to the others. "We need to look for dresses. I want to try them on, I don't just want to look at them online."

"Yes!" Bless Nicole.

"Okay, let's go to Katie's and take showers, and then we'll go to the mall." I moved toward Katie's Grand Cherokee and my friends followed, leaving Eric openmouthed and desolate but, I assured him silently, better off. "Bye, Eric!" I called over my shoulder. I'd have to warn him off Katie—discreetly—when I saw him in class.

But the next day he showed up late, something he never did. Same thing the day after that, and for the next two weeks. Come to think of it, we never really talked after that, other than quick hellos when we ran into each other, which didn't happen often. And then I went to art school.

This happened on my seventeenth birthday. But also on my seventeenth birthday, my three best friends and I walked to the parking lot after soccer practice. Eric called to me, took me aside, and asked me if I wanted to go out with him sometime. I was surprised, but not unpleasantly, and I said yes. *Sure*, actually. *I'd love to.* Sweet Kelly, being sweet.

After I left him (he looked more stunned than happy) I joined my friends in Katie's car. Katie looked at me in the rearview mirror, one side of her mouth twisting up. "So, what did Eric Hyde want with you?"

"He asked me out."

She snorted. "What'd you say?"

"I said yes." With a shrug, I looked out the window, ignoring the quiet rustle of surprise from the others.

"Seriously? You're gonna go out with him?"

I turned my eyes back to Katie's in the rearview, staring her down. When Eric had asked me out I hadn't felt any special impulse toward or away from him, no attraction or repulsion. We moved in different circles. I knew he wasn't popular, but he seemed like a decent guy. And it would make him happy. I figured we'd go out once and never again. But Katie's scorn pushed me toward him, made me want to rebel by being into him.

"Yeah," I said. "Seriously. Are you gonna drive, or . . . ?"

She made a face, cranked the engine, and pulled out of the parking lot.

"EARTH TO KELLY," Eric says. He's smiling, his equilibrium recovered, but I'm thrown. Before my seventeenth birthday, I have one set of memories. Through childhood, middle school, and freshman and sophomore and most of junior year, the milestones sit neat and linear in my head, as much as memories can. Until Eric and I got together. After that, there are two versions of every rite of passage: prom, graduation, leaving home. Doubles laid side by side.

All this flies through my mind in the space of a few seconds, and the realization follows even more quickly: everything hinges on Eric and that conversation we had after soccer practice on my birthday. *Two* conversations. One painfully awkward, the other resulting in our going out together. Did they really take place at the same time on the same day, or am I confusing things? I don't think I'm confusing things. I don't know why I haven't tried to find the point of divergence in my memories before. The fact that it's related to Eric's and my relationship makes me more sure than ever that he's the key to all this.

"Do you remember?" I ask, before I can talk myself out of it.

His brow knits in confusion. "Do I remember what?"

"There was . . . another time." I'm having trouble putting it into words. "You tried to ask me out . . . before. I didn't realize that's what you were doing, but . . . you don't remember?"

He gives me a questioning look, picks up a piece of sushi roll, and stuffs it in his mouth.

"You came up to us after soccer practice," I say. "You asked us what we were doing for prom. Remember?"

He shakes his head.

"On my birthday."

He swallows. "I did ask you out on your birthday."

"No." My voice comes out forceful. "My birthday was when you came up to us, and Katie was mean to you, and then we left to go shopping for dresses." I'm sure of it now. Except he's also right. We're both right. How can we both be right?

"Katie never did like me very much, did she?" Eric takes a sip of his tea, thinking. "Wait! I remember now. I did come up to you guys. And yes, I meant to ask you out, and chickened out. This was a couple weeks before your birthday, though."

"No, it was *on* my birthday."

"Are you sure? I specifically remember thinking about how it would be your birthday in a couple weeks. And when I came up to you *again,* on your birthday, I remember thinking the first thing I had to do was get you away from your friends."

I open my mouth to tell him, *Yes, I'm sure, I'm goddamn fucking sure,* because of course I remember this right; he's the one remembering it wrong.

He nods. "Yeah, now that I think about it, that's the way it happened." His eyes touch mine, and I get the impression he's checking to see how his last statement landed.

I want to keep pushing. I want to insist that both occurrences are real, the one when Eric asked me out and the one when he didn't, and see what he has to say for himself. But I can feel the other Kelly, the one who has always inhabited this life, stirring deep inside. What led her here? I don't know; I have memories, impressions, but it's like they were placed in my head. I don't have access to her entire thought process. What did she want? What would she do, if she were here?

She loved Eric. Did she fear him as well?

I watch him as he awkwardly chews a too-large mouthful, holding his hand in front of his mouth, then washes it down with iced tea. He smiles sheepishly. "You have to eat it in one bite to get all the flavors."

I can't imagine him being violent. I don't have any memory of him hurting me. *That's not how he operates,* says a part of me that knows things I don't, or just haven't thought of yet. I think of the way he acted last night, his disappearing act this morning. The way he was the one to decide when the time was right for us to talk again. The way he controls me without seeming to. From deep inside comes the knowledge that if I push, he will push back. He'll insist on his own version of the truth until I believe it too, or at least convince him I do.

He's afraid, the voice says. Afraid of what? No answer to that.

"You should eat more of this," he says, gesturing toward the platter with his chopsticks.

"I guess I'm not that hungry." I take a sip of my second beer, noticing a spreading warmth in my neck and shoulders. I'm getting a buzz. I'll probably sleep half the afternoon after Eric drops me off.

"You know, if you got pregnant, you wouldn't be able to drink that," Eric says, nodding toward my bottle. "We wouldn't be able to go out for sushi either. It's one of the things pregnant women aren't supposed to eat. Sushi, deli meat, soft cheese . . ."

I have no idea why Eric would know these things. Or why he's bringing them up in the first place.

"I'm not planning on getting pregnant," I tell him.

He looks at me. "Okay."

"You made your position on it pretty clear the other night." I take another drink. "Just because I don't want to go back on the pill doesn't mean I'm going to secretly get knocked up."

"I never thought you would do something like that."

Why not? You obviously don't trust me for some reason.

"I do want kids," he says. "I just want to make sure everything's okay with us first. Physically."

"You said that." I don't mention that we also might want to make sure our marriage isn't going to fall apart.

"Yeah." He shrugs, looking away. "I mean, I don't have any reason for thinking there'd be a problem. I just want to be sure."

Something about what he's just said sets off my bullshit detector. But why would he think something was wrong? And if he did, why wouldn't he tell me?

"You know," I say, "it's not a requirement for us to have kids."

He smiles. "Tell that to my parents."

"No, really. It's not something you do for other people. I've been thinking we should . . . wait and see." Which is a mild form of what I've really been thinking, which is that I've never been that interested in procreating. Not the real me, anyway. Even Michigan Kelly seemed like she was considering it mostly to make Eric happy, and because what else would she do? But especially now, it seems impossible.

"Wait and see what?" His expression clouds. He lays his chopsticks on the edge of his plate. "I thought . . . this is just a pause. I mean, eventually, we do want kids. We agreed. Once we know both of us are okay, there's no reason we shouldn't try."

"Unless one of us decides we don't want to." I feel a falling away inside myself, but that's just this new version of me asserting herself. *We'll be fine, whatever happens,* I tell her. *We don't need him.*

He looks genuinely confused. I wonder if this is one of the things he was talking about earlier that wasn't as simple or easy as he wanted it to be.

"We were supposed to keep trying," he says, his voice hardly more than a whisper. Like he's talking to himself, not me.

"What do you mean?" I ask him.

His expression clears, and he blinks as if he's just noticed I'm still here. "I don't want to make you do anything you don't want to do."

"I'm not saying I definitely wouldn't want a baby. Just . . . it's not a given."

"I always thought you felt the same about it as I did."

That's what you assumed, I think. *Maybe you saw what you wanted to see.* That could be true of a lot of beliefs Eric holds about me.

"But if you don't want to have a baby, then we won't. End of story," he says.

"I'm glad to hear you say that."

"Not that I wouldn't keep trying to convince you." He smiles then, his most charming smile, the one with dimples. I'm surprised by the anger that flares up inside me. In that second, I hate him a little.

He's still looking at me, like he expects me to come back with some bit of banter. Then his eyes narrow, his smile fading down to about halfway. "When did you cut your hair?"

25

Day Seven

THE NEXT MORNING, WHEN I OPEN THE DOOR, A FOLDED NOTE falls from where it was propped on top of the doorknob. *Can't make run today. Buyer called for 2nd showing. See you tomorrow AM?* I decipher the scrawl at the bottom as *A. Rowley.* He's left a postscript with his cell number. Despite this I feel a ridiculous sense of rejection, and the glow of our interaction yesterday is all but gone.

After I get back from my solitary run, I call Katie Spence. She's Katie Boyer now, and she's been on my mind since I used her as an excuse for Eric. We rarely see each other, even though we both went to MSU and then moved back to the area, but it's possible she'll be able to shed some light on my situation. Plus I could really use a friend.

She picks up on the seventh ring. *"Kelly!* I've been meaning to text you. Sorry I couldn't make it to your birthday dinner thing. Happy belated." Her voice competes with a cartoon babble and the whine of what sounds like a hair dryer. "Maddie! Honey," Katie says, muffled, "turn off your vacuum cleaner;

Mommy's on the phone. Madilynn. Turn off your vacuum cleaner. Please turn off your vacuum cleaner. Okay, one. *Two.* If I get to three, the vacuum cleaner's going in time-out. Two and a *half.*" The hair dryer noise cuts off. "*Thank you,* honey. Kelly! What have you been *up* to?"

"I was wondering if you wanted to grab lunch. Maybe somewhere near you?" Katie lives in what its developer calls a mixed-use community: a sprawl of newly built smart homes next to a sparsely tenanted commercial plaza, which itself bleeds into Innovation Park. It's within walking distance of gnii's offices, not that that factors into my desire to go there.

Her voice takes on a saccharine quality I remember from high school, although she never directed it at me back then. "Oh, that would be great! I was just thinking we needed to get together." I hear a wail in the background, and she snaps, "Mason! We do not hit!"

A small child whines, "Maddox won't give me back my—"

"When someone takes our toy, we ask for the toy back. We don't use violence with each other, even when we're angry."

Another whine, something about the Hulk.

"Maddox, please give Mason back his Hulk— Mason! *No!* Do you want a spanking?"

"If some other time would be better . . ."

"No, no, you're fine. Did you want to get coffee? There's a Starbucks right by our playground. I was going to take the kids over after lunch, they're kinda going crazy in here." Another screech drives her point home. "Mason! That is *it,* young man. I gotta go," Katie says to me. "See you in a bit?"

I agree with more enthusiasm than I feel. This is what I'm reduced to: sweeping up scraps of time with people I no longer have anything in common with. I think about Katie in high school, her razor-sharp wit and almost psychic knowledge of what everyone we knew was up to. Those skills might translate well to parenting, but she's the last person I'd think of as maternal.

An hour and a half later I arrive at the playground, which teems with shrieking kids under the bored eye of the rent-a-cop posted at the entrance. Katie, clutching a tall green-logoed cup, stands in a knot of women. Despite their varied shapes and sizes and hairstyles they have a uniform appearance, with well-moisturized faces and athletic wear that looks as though it's never seen sweat.

Katie sees me and peels off from the flock. "It's been for-ever!" She hugs me with one arm, patting my back with a stiff hand. "You look amazing! Did you get your hair cut? I love it!"

I reach up and touch my curls. When I asked Eric yesterday what he thought, he said he'd forgotten how curly it was when it was short. "It looks good on you, though." He sounded as if that wasn't the same thing as him liking it.

I'm fairly sure Katie's being sincere with her praise. Katie always treated me with more care than she did the rest of our classmates. I was one of the few—along with Alicia Kang and Nicole Petersson, the other two members of our tight quartet— who escaped her constant derision of people's too-tight jeans, their crookedly applied eyeliner, their awkward ways of walking. Maybe that's why we were such good friends: I felt privileged that she wasn't mean to me. I'd like to think I tempered her more hateful impulses, or at least called her out when she was overtly cruel.

"You look great too!" I say, though she looks tired and doughy and her expression has settled into a permanent pout of smug dissatisfaction. Or maybe that was always there, and now it's just more apparent. Her features and body haven't changed much, but she used to have something, a distinguishing spark. Now I'm not sure I'd recognize her if I hadn't been looking.

She brushes highlighted strands of hair out of her face. "Oh good, you got coffee," she says, nodding toward the cup in my hand but not noticing the tea-bag string dangling over the rim. Chicago Kelly drank coffee black and as strong as she could get it, but the first time I tried a cup after arriving here, I almost spit it out from the bitterness.

I don't bother to correct Katie. "I bet it's convenient, having it right here."

"You bet. I'd mainline caffeine if I could."

"There should be a bar right next to the Starbucks," I say, grinning, but Katie just lets out a halfhearted *heh*.

"So," she says, "what have you been up to?"

"Oh . . . same old." This conversation feels like shoveling snow, burying any thought I might have had of coming out with my story, and the atmosphere is discouraging as well: the children running in mad circles, their mothers shooting us curious glances, and Katie's own prosaic life. Even when we were younger, she never voiced any desire to break out of our surroundings. She liked being in a world where she knew the rules. High school offered enough drama for her, and she seems to have the same attitude toward suburban life.

I'm selling her short. She's still one of my oldest friends. We have a whole catalog of shared experiences, inside jokes I could invoke. Even in my memories of living in Chicago, when I hadn't spoken to her in years, I thought of her fondly. Our history connected us in a way continued interaction never could have, especially once we'd started to grow apart. The memories were idyllic, and staying in contact would only have eroded them.

This Katie, twenty-nine-year-old Katie in the flesh, is not someone I can immediately trust. I ask her how she's been, and I can tell she's been waiting for the chance to talk about herself. "I'm *so* busy. It'll be nice when the twins start school in the fall. I don't know what I'm going to do with myself. I mean, I'll be room parent of course, and there's the PTA, and we might get them into travel baseball, but . . ." She waves a hand, as though the idea of so many vacant hours in the day defies description. "I hope they'll be okay in kindergarten. They're so *active*."

I scan the playground. With a gun to my head, I wouldn't be able to pick out Maddox and Mason from the swarm of sleek-headed, shouting little white boys. I feel a prick of guilt: I'm a bad friend, and I don't even have the excuse of parenthood.

"So! What about you and Eric?" I'm confused until she reaches out and pats my stomach. "You two would have the cutest babies. Oh my *God*," she gushes, as if she's never imitated Eric's stiff posture or made fun of his haircut or harped on how skinny he was, how awkward, didn't he eat, didn't he know how to talk? (He ate as much as any seventeen-year-old, and he was tongue-tied around Katie because he knew she didn't like him.) I remember having to defend him multiple times during our senior year. Alicia and Nicole weren't as bad. They couldn't understand why I liked Eric— loved him—but they accepted him as long as he didn't take me away from them too much. Katie, though: she had a real problem with Eric's lack of social capital. It reflected badly on her.

Her attitude got a little better after graduation, and better still after Eric developed some social skills and put on forty pounds of muscle in our first years of college. But now her erasure of the past sets me on edge. I wonder how she'd react if I said, *Actually, until last week I was single and living in the city and painting and I'd pretty much decided I never wanted to have kids, but suddenly I have this whole different life and I'm afraid my husband wants me to turn into you.*

"It'll happen when it happens," I say, sounding sharper than I mean to.

Her eyes go wide and soft, pitying. "You know, we had trouble at first. Then they put me on Clomid and bam—twins! Have you talked to your ob-gyn? Or maybe you need to get Eric checked out." Like he's a faulty car. "But there's so many things they can do."

Her words sound like a distorted echo of what Eric said at lunch yesterday. "I'm not trying to get pregnant right now," I say sharply.

Katie furrows her brow and says, "Oh, sorry, I thought you were for some reason." Of course Katie, who always manages to put the worst face on things, would take it as a judgment of her own choices.

I change the subject, taking the opportunity to probe a little. "It's funny how life goes in directions you never expected, though," I say. "Remember I had that scholarship to art school?"

"Oh, right, you used to be all into art," Katie says. This gives me a shock. A week ago I had a BFA; now I'm someone who *used to be all into art.* "God, wouldn't it be weird if you'd moved to Chicago after we graduated? We'd never have been roommates!"

I study her face for signs of confusion or alternate threads. A recollection of her other freshman roommate, maybe, about whom she used to text me constantly. (She called her the Goth Princess, GP for short. *OMG GP is blasting her moany-ass music again. I'm gonna murder GP if she doesn't stop microwaving fake meat in our room.*)

There's nothing.

"I think a lot about what would be different if I'd gone," I say, giving Katie a significant look.

Which she misses completely. "Well, you and Eric probably wouldn't still be together. People always break up when they go to different colleges. Oh God, do you remember that knock-down-drag-out Brian Hamp and Danielle McKim had over winter break senior year, when she found out he was cheating on her with some slut from Saginaw Valley? Whose party was that at?" Katie gets a nostalgic look in her eye, then purses her lips into a smirk. "But yeah, there was no way you were gonna leave your schmoopy behind. You guys were attached at the hip the entire last year of high school. So nauseating. I remember Alicia was pretty gung ho for you to go to art school, though, since she was all into theatre. Oh!" She leans toward me, eyebrows raised dramatically. "You saw her post. Right?"

I didn't: online, I've been focused on stalking myself and Linnea and researching gnii. When I shake my head, Katie assumes the gleeful look she used to get when she was about to deliver an especially juicy piece of gossip. "She got married. I mean, 'married.'" She does scare quotes with the hand not holding her coffee cup. "To a *woman*."

For a second I'm confused. Alicia came out to me years ago, when we went out for drinks while she was in Chicago doing a play. She doesn't splash her orientation all over social media—when she first started acting, she worried it would keep her from getting what she called "the fuckable-girl roles"—but she's been dating her now wife, Michelle, for half a decade.

Then it hits me: in this life, I'm one of the people she's kept it from. Alicia and Michelle invited Chicago Kelly to their wedding, but there's no invitation pinned to the bulletin board in my house in Davis City, because I've chosen to live in a place where some people still get bent out of shape over same-sex marriage. I've let Alicia drift away. I can't be trusted to be an ally.

The two realities split apart, double, and slam together inside my head. Disoriented, I collapse onto a bench. Katie sits next to me, her expression melting from triumph to concern. "I didn't realize you'd be so shocked."

"I'm not shocked. I just got a little shaky for a second. I think I've had too much caffeine."

"Oh! You should eat something." Katie digs in her huge handbag, hands me a slightly smushed granola bar, and tears open a second one for herself. "I guess now we know why she never had a boyfriend."

"It's not like us straight girls had a lot of options either."

"You've got that right," she says, more in solidarity than as truth. Katie was rarely without a boyfriend in high school, though she never got in so deep that she fell out of our group, the way some people neglect their friends when they get into relationships. "Except for you, with Eric. Somehow you picked the best one."

Her voice carries a wistful note, which keeps me from pointing out that unlike her, I wasn't dating for status. "How are things with you and Matt?" I feel guilty for not having asked before. Bad friend.

She sighs. "Oh, fine. I mean, sometimes I feel more like his maid than his wife. And he works all the time—I mean *all* the time. His office is within walking distance of our house, so you'd think he'd make it home for lunch every once in a while, but no. I take care of the kids all day every day, then put them to bed by myself and fall asleep alone on the couch."

I sit up. "He's in the Innovation Park? He doesn't work at gnii, does he?" Maybe Matt could get me in touch with Peter.

Katie scoffs. "He wishes. You know, their AI is supposed to be able to do all this *Star Trek* shit? He told me one time that they're supposedly working on, like, teleportation or time travel or something. But *his* company does email marketing. I doze off whenever he starts trying to explain it to me."

"Teleportation? Time travel?" Those things have a lot in common, thematically, with magical portals to alternate lives.

"I don't think it's true. I think someone was having a little fun with him at happy hour. Oh yes, he goes to those. Calls it 'networking.'" Out come the scare quotes again. "Honestly, I'm at the point where I'm afraid to drop in on him at work because I don't want to catch him sexually harassing some twenty-two-year-old marketing girl."

She throws the sentence out like a joke, but the forlornness behind the admission snaps me back to reality. "Seriously?" I ask.

She looks at me, and I remember how our real conversations used to come about, dropped without warning in between the discussions of bands and shows and our moms and who was hooking up with whom, all the things we talked about to fill the endless hours we had to wait before the onset of adulthood. But those things were also real: they mattered; they took up space in our thoughts and our lives, even though nobody ever thought anything a teenage girl cared about could be important. Guilt brushes against me again, for the near contempt I've been feeling toward Katie, the way I've dismissed and reduced her. A bit of the old trust sparks in her eyes, and I can almost hear the words building inside her head.

Then she tosses her hair and laughs, retreating behind an eye roll. "No, I'm just being stupid. Honestly, I can't complain. All I can say is, enjoy the romance while you've got it. Eat that, will you?" She motions toward my still-unopened granola bar.

Obediently, I tear open the wrapper and chew on the gluey mixture of oats and raisins, washing it down with tea. A tiny blond girl in rhinestoned pink leggings—Madilynn, Katie's three-year-old daughter—scurries over with a child's unerring instinct for the availability of junk food. "Mommy, I'm hungry," she says in a grating singsong.

"We just had lunch, honey."

Like a switch has been flipped, Maddie pushes out her lower lip and starts to sniffle. "But I'm hungry!" If her eyes weren't full of actual tears, I'd swear she was faking.

"Well, you wouldn't be hungry if you'd eaten your lunch. You can have some almond butter crackers when it's snack time."

This shatters what's left of Maddie's chill. Her voice cycles up into hysteria. "I don't want ammon' butter cackers. I wan' a ganola bar!" She wails, square mouthed, as her legs buckle underneath her and she collapses into the playground mulch like a tiny bereaved wife.

"Maddie." The edge in Katie's voice is familiar to me from high school: it means she's about to get mean. "Madilynn Avery. Stop this right now, or we go home and have a time-out." Maddie continues crying and flailing at the wood chips. Katie stands, her mouth a tight line. "Okay, let's go. *Maddox! Mason!* Come on, boys! Your sister's making us go home!"

She scoops up Maddie and tucks her under one arm like a purse full of snakes. "It was great seeing you!" she says to me, sweetly, over the sound of Maddie's screams. "Don't worry about getting pregnant. It'll happen for you, everything always does."

They go one way and I go the other. I can hear Maddie crying all the way down the street. I suppose my situation could have been worse: I could have landed in Katie's life.

I take a detour through the main part of Innovation Park toward gnii. I don't quite dare to try going inside again, which would be useless anyway if what Peter told me is true, but I walk between the fake barns and silos and stand within sight of the glass farmhouse. I take out my phone and text the number Peter messaged me from. I'm outside if you want to talk. I really need to talk to you.

Message could not be delivered

No sense in waiting, then. But I stay a moment anyway. I'm not sure whether I'm hoping Peter will see me and come out, or I just want to make a point. To show whoever might be watching that I'm not scared.

As I walk back toward my car and the residential end of the park, I pass by the Starbucks again. I take an automatic glance in the window, and a charge of recognition goes through me as my eyes touch Adam Rowley's through the glass. I lift a hand but he turns away with a hastiness I think, a second later, that I must have imagined. Maybe he didn't recognize me. Was it even him? I peer through the window, but the man has melted into the depths of the coffee shop and I'm not going to go inside to check. Probably it wasn't. There are plenty of tall blond guys in the world.

26

Day Eight

WHEN I MENTION TO ADAM THE NEXT MORNING THAT I SAW HIM in Starbucks, his forehead creases in thought. "I'm pretty sure I was showing a condo on the other side of town yesterday afternoon. Yeah, I remember now." He gives me an easy grin. "I must have a doppelgänger."

In the NFL, I think, remembering Bobby's laugh when he told the story about someone mistaking him for a football player. Dizziness wafts through me.

We run together the next couple of days, into the weekend. I already feel as though I've known him much longer than I have. Maybe it's my lack of other friends, but it's nice to be comfortable with someone so quickly. I end up telling him I used to paint, and about the art school scholarship. As a former musician, he understands the bittersweetness of giving up a dream in exchange for stability. Yet our runs are the one part of the day when I barely think of the other life in my head, or what Eric might have to do with it, or Eric himself, really. It's good to spend time with someone I can just talk to, without worrying about what everything means.

Every afternoon I take Bear for a walk, to make up for leaving him home when I run and because without exercise he'd be even more out of control. The walks are frustrating for both of us, with Bear continually tripping me up or pulling on the leash. Dogs are always *demanding* things. I miss having a cat, the companionship without obligation. Meeks never jumped up on me or peed on the floor in excitement. Food, water, a clean litter box, and a warm lap were all she needed.

That life recedes further from me every day. As I finger the edges of the pictures in my head they seem to fade, replaced by my new memories, until I can't tell which are the originals. Instead of making me more settled in my life here, this makes me feel unmoored, like I don't truly belong anywhere.

One day I've just gotten the leash down from its hook, sending Bear into an agony of tail-sweeping anticipation, when the doorbell rings. He loses his shit, howling and scratching at the door until I drag him back so I can open it. It's Diane Rowley, in a white sleeveless blouse and houndstooth gardening gloves with boots to match, looking cool and crisp despite the heat outside. And startled, once Bear greets her.

"Bear! Down! I'm so sorry."

"It's fine. Hi, dog." She gives me a tight smile and pushes Bear's nose out of her crotch.

"He's so *rude.*" Finally I get control, clipping the leash to Bear's collar and hauling him back. This is not the impression I wanted to make on my new neighbor.

"I wondered if you had any plant food."

"Oh, do you garden?" Obviously. I can feel my face stretching in a foolish smile. She must think I'm an idiot.

"I'm doing a little planting." Her gaze darts around the foyer and into the rooms beyond it, as though she's looking for someone else who might be in the house. "I'm trying to make this place feel more like home."

"So you're all unpacked already?"

"Getting there."

"I don't have plant food, but you could try Doris. She grows roses. And I'd be happy to loan Bear out to you anytime. He's great at digging." I grin to show I'm joking, but Diane doesn't crack a smile. "We were about to go for a walk . . . do you want to take a break and come with us?"

Her face twitches. "I don't think so . . . but thank you for asking." She tacks on the last part grudgingly, and I feel a wave of dislike for her. Maybe she's one of those attractive people who never had to learn social skills, with everyone falling all over them no matter how they behaved. Bear makes a break for the open door, pulling me off-balance when he reaches the end of the leash. Diane smiles, but it's a look of private amusement, almost derision.

"Well, I better get going before Bear pulls my arm off," I say.

Diane takes my hint and follows me outside, shutting the door behind her. "I'll ask Doris about the plant food."

Bear and I are already halfway down the walk. "Okay! See you later!" I glance back to see Diane standing sideways on my porch stairs, looking intently at the house. As if she's got any room to judge my paint colors, when she and Adam still have a sheet tacked up in their picture window instead of curtains.

There's no sign of her in the yard when Bear and I return from our walk, nor do I see any new plantings in the flower beds around the Rowleys' house. The heat must have driven her inside.

27

Day Nine

ERIC'S PARENTS LIVE ON THE OTHER SIDE OF ANDROMEDA
Creek from my folks, in a subdivision where the houses look like
oversize beige blocks scattered on a slightly warped pool table.
Their house is the same one they lived in when Eric was in
school, the one they bought when they first moved to town. My
mother will occasionally comment that it must be nice to be able
to afford all that space, even with their kids gone. Amalia is an
executive at the hospital in Davis City and Tony co-owns a business with his brother Wayne, so I imagine they could afford
more if they wanted. Though I don't say that to my mother.

Ruby wasn't joking when she warned me to be ready for a
party tonight. Everyone in Eric's family who was at my birthday
dinner is at the house, plus his older sister, Christine, in from
California for the weekend, though I don't see her in the kitchen
with the rest of the women. Amalia and Dora, Ruby's mom, are
putting together a formidable spread. Daisy, who's married to
Ruby's brother Edgar, helps them while Ruby perches at the
breakfast bar with a beer. She hops down when I walk into the

room, and comes up to hug me. "Love the hair," she enthuses. "Get a drink and come sit by me. I'm just trying to stay out of everyone's way."

Everyone else compliments my cut too, except for Dora, who laments that it was "so pretty long." "Where did you have it done?" Amalia asks me.

"I did it myself."

She lifts her sculpted eyebrows. Obviously she's never considered cutting her own hair. From what I've gleaned of Eric's parents' history, she was the daughter of an attorney and had disappointed her parents twice: once by attending the University of Michigan instead of an Ivy League school, and again when she married the guy who always (somehow) managed to wait on her at the café where she always (for some reason) went to study. Tony's parents weren't much happier about his hooking up with some hoity-toity rich girl, so Eric didn't have much contact with either set of grandparents growing up.

"Well," she says finally, "you did a good job."

Even that crumb of approval gives me a warm feeling inside. Amalia has always seemed bewildered by me, an artist who doesn't make art, a woman with little professional ambition who nevertheless hasn't settled into having a family of her own. *What do you want to do?* she asked me once. I'd just given up my scholarship to art school and was still feeling sensitive about it, plus she gave off a fairly strong vibe that she thought I should have gone to Chicago, which didn't inspire me to be especially candid with her. I babbled something about wanting to support Eric, though I was wrong if I thought that would win me points with her. She's never been unkind, but I always feel as though she's keeping me at a distance. Possibly, she's waiting for me to fuck up.

I ask if I can do anything, but Amalia and Dora banish me to the barstool next to Ruby's as swiftly as they dismiss Eric to the back deck. "Your dad needs help grilling," Amalia tells him.

"Help drinking beer, you mean?" Ruby says with a laugh, then to me, in an undertone: "He's getting plenty of help from the rest of the men."

"So you take after him," Dora says, eyeing Ruby's half-empty bottle. She rolls her eyes over to me. "I've taught this girl every recipe, but she's useless in the kitchen. I don't know why Glenn puts up with it."

Ruby sips her beer. "Because he's a way better cook than me?"

"I'm not a great cook either," I say, to support Ruby.

"See, everyone has different strengths," Ruby tells her mother.

"Cooking is like anything else," Dora argues. "You get better at it the more you do it."

"Maybe, but whatever you might think, we're not put on this earth solely to feed men."

Dora clicks her tongue and gets back to slicing tomatoes for salad. The five of us keep chatting. Daisy's eighteen-month-old son, Daniel, lurches in looking for attention. She sits him up on the counter and tickles him while she talks to him in Tagalog, eliciting a string of adorable toddler giggles. Kids are cute, but I can't imagine being responsible for one constantly. Daniel's presence doesn't put much of a crimp in the conversation, though: talk soon bends toward the men, and it isn't necessarily complimentary. But even the complaints seem comfortable, a way for us to connect rather than express any serious grievance.

Christine bustles in, wearing a black silk turtleneck shell, full makeup, and athletic shorts. "Oh, hey," she says when she sees me. "I didn't hear you guys come in. I had an 'emergency' call."

She does air quotes, rolling her eyes a little, then gives me a pro forma hug. She and I haven't gotten much chance to be close: she's a few years older and moved away right after high school. Against type, since she was part of the cheerleading / student council / homecoming court crowd, like me, but her coming out a couple of years later pretty much explained that decision. Now she's followed in her mother's go-getter footsteps and works as a recruiter in Silicon Valley. She reminds me a lot of Amalia, only with sharper edges.

She takes the last empty barstool, and she and Ruby start shoptalking across me in a language where eighty percent of the words sound identical to English but have slightly different meanings, and twenty percent have been replaced with deliberately opaque acronyms and abbreviations. I tune out, finishing my beer, enjoying the relaxation my lowered tolerance affords me, until I hear the word *wormhole* come out of Christine's mouth.

"What?" I say, breaking into her sentence.

"Are we boring you? Sorry," Ruby says.

"No, what were you talking about?"

"Just some of the work that's going on right here in li'l ol' Davis City," Christine says, affecting a Southern accent.

"Technically, Greater Davis City." Ruby picks at the label on her beer bottle with a smooth navy blue fingernail.

"I had a candidate who told me—*strictly* on the down low, of course"—Christine widens her tastefully black-winged eyes at me—"that at his last job he'd been working with an AI that taught itself how to construct an Einstein-Rosen bridge—a wormhole, for us nontechnicals—and then send itself information through it."

"You know what a wormhole does, right?" Ruby asks me, trying to peel her label off in one piece.

"I've watched *Star Trek*," I say, and to her skeptical look: "Okay, I haven't. But it's, like, space travel, right?"

"Theoretically, which was the only area in which wormholes were *thought* to exist, it connects two distant points in the space-time continuum," says Christine. "Or it could also be two points in different universes."

"I don't know what that means."

"It means," Ruby says, scrunching up her face as the top layer of her label separates from the bottom, "that there's a company in the Innovation Park that's sitting on a way to facilitate instant travel through space and time."

"Only of information," Christine clarifies. "The theory is that the future version of the AI sent instructions for how to open the wormhole to the past version."

My heart has started to pound. This is too similar to the rumor Katie told me for it to be a coincidence. "Which company?"

"Not mine," Ruby says glumly.

"Can't say," Christine says. "My candidate would get sued into oblivion. He really shouldn't have told me, but I think he wanted to make sure I was suitably impressed with his résumé."

"Why would he leave?" Ruby wonders plaintively.

"Because the founder's a psycho? Perfectly charming until you get to know him, apparently. We get a lot of those in my industry," she tells me as an aside. "So you guys can't say anything either, or *I'll* get sued into oblivion."

Ruby sighs. "I guess I'll just have to apply at every company run by a charismatic man-child. And there are so many."

"Tell me you won't," Christine says. "This dude's supposed to have had competitors surveilled, blackmailed—"

"Just another day in tech," Ruby says, waving a hand.

"I heard he had someone run off the Zilwaukee Bridge. I'm taking that one with a grain of salt, but it still doesn't sound like anything you want to be involved with."

"But *time travel*," Ruby groans.

"What about time travel?" Eric asks, coming into the kitchen.

"I was telling Ruby she'd like this show Courtney and I've been watching, but she can't get past a little bit of tropiness," Christine says, not missing a beat. Amalia gives her a raised eyebrow across the counter but says nothing.

"I thought you didn't have time to watch TV," Eric says. "Anyway, Dad sent me in here to clear counter space. He's about to bring in the meat. What am I allowed to move?"

Amalia and Dora start shifting things around. "I need more room!" Tony announces from the entrance, holding a platter of slow-roasted pork shoulder. "The master needs to work his magic."

"And 'the master' would be you?" Amalia puts her head to one side and fixes him with a fond look while he sets the pork on the counter. "Back off, maestro. It still needs to rest."

"I know that," he says testily, but with no real heat, and Amalia pats his arm. They're comfortable with each other in a way that makes my heart squeeze. "So, Kelly, how was your first week being almost thirty?"

"You're not supposed to ask that," Dora interjects. Tony waves a dismissive hand.

"Pshh, she knows I'm not calling her old. Nowadays, they're just coming into their prime, right? Now, when I was your age . . ." He turns away from the counter, hunches over, and shuffles a few steps, pretending to be a decrepit old man. When he was my age, he was raising two young children and working fifty-hour weeks while Amalia went to night school for her master's degree. Not even ten years later, he had a thriving business of his own. You'd think that much stress and hard work would weigh someone down, but I can't think of my father-in-law without hearing his laugh.

He lets it roll out now, full and rich. I've never heard Eric laugh like that, with such a complete lack of self-consciousness. He looks like his dad, but he got all of Amalia's seriousness with none of her composure. With Eric there's always something going on under the surface, some unexpressed judgment or unsatisfied longing. I remember it intrigued me when we first started going out, the puzzle of figuring out what he was thinking, what he wanted, all the more because I quickly discovered I was one of the only people who could really soothe him. I didn't even have to do much, just be present. It was a rush to have that power.

"Don't let my son bring you down, though," Tony says, as though he can see what I'm thinking. "He was born old, but you've still got some fun in you, eh?"

"Oh, totally," I say. "I keep him on his toes."

"She does," Eric confirms, slipping an arm around my waist. I hadn't noticed him come up behind me.

Tony tips two fingers at me in a salute. "Good."

With the pork sufficiently rested, Tony shreds it, which makes me reflect on the number of times since my birthday that I've been served hunks of meat. But Eric's family would definitely notice if I didn't eat it, so I place a small portion on my bun with some sauce.

Dora zeroes in on my plate. "That's barely even a sandwich! You're not on a diet, are you?"

"Nobody diets anymore," Christine says. "It's all about intermittent fasting now."

"Intermittent what?"

Christine explains the concept while I load up the rest of my plate with side dishes. Eric's family doesn't stand on ceremony for these dinners. We eat off paper plates around the kitchen island and table, everyone grabbing seconds and thirds as they wish. The conversation is loud and spirited and I'm the quietest person in the room except for Eric, and not just because I'm somewhat auxiliary. I'm thinking hard about what Katie said the other day, what her husband told her about gnii. Teleportation, she said. Time travel. And now Christine, with her tales of . . . what did she call it? An Einstein-Rosen bridge. What if something like that is responsible for my life switching? What if I got caught up in some kind of time warp caused by malfunctioning software? It seems impossible. But it's almost comforting, because if that's what happened, then at least I know that what I'm experiencing is real.

If that's what happened, then Eric might not have had anything to do with it after all. He doesn't have a connection to gnii except for Peter. But I can't get that phone call out of my mind, or shake the feeling that he's involved somehow.

I look down at my plate and find it empty. The pork, like the steak last week, was delicious.

28

AFTER SUPPER, I HELP CHRISTINE, RUBY, AND DAISY CLEAN THE kitchen while Glenn, Edgar, and Eric hang out with the kids in the great room. Flora, Daniel's four-year-old sister, is teaching him how to do karaoke with the app on the TV. Edgar dances with them, the baby in a carrier on his chest. It's adorable.

With the dishwasher running, the pots and pans drying on the rack, and the counters wiped down, we four go out into the great room with drinks. "Karaoke time!" Ruby announces. "Everyone's taking a turn."

"No way," Eric says.

Ruby smiles wickedly. "You just volunteered to go first, cuz."

"You go first. I'll go after you."

"Fine, fine."

Ruby sings a Prince song, which brings the older adults in from the back deck. "Ooh, I love this song," Dora says, raising her arms and shimmying her hips.

"I'm not sure it's appropriate for children," Amalia says doubtfully as Ruby swings into the chorus. Ruby's dancing with Flora, who sings along with her: *Cream, get on top . . .*

"It's fine, it goes right over their heads." Daisy waves a hand.

Eric is saved from having to go next by his uncle Wayne, who insists on going after Ruby and sings an old country ballad that makes Dora fan herself and blink rapidly. "I haven't heard this song in years!" Wayne's performance inspires Dora to take the mic from her husband. "I can sing any song? How do I pick?"

Ruby shows her how to do a voice search, which is growing increasingly difficult in the noisy room. Eric, sitting by me on the couch, leans over and murmurs in my ear, "We should take off soon."

"You just don't want to have to sing," I say. I don't want to be rude and leave early, but I'm hoping the karaoke party breaks up before my turn comes. I'm not shy conversing with people, but I hate performing. Something about having all that focused expectation on me, even with something low stakes like this, makes my heart race and my palms sweat and my head feel swimmy. The memory comes to me that when Eric and I did our history project together in high school, he volunteered to do the presentation despite his own distaste for public speaking. This was before we'd started going out, but I didn't have to tell him how much presenting scared me. He just stepped in. That's how tuned in he was to me, and how considerate.

He looks at me now. "You don't have to sing if you don't want to. Don't let them pressure you."

I shrug. "It's supposed to be fun, right?"

He raises an eyebrow, which makes him look more like his mother.

When Dora's song is over she tries to hand the microphone off to Amalia, who demurs. "I've got to finish cleaning the kitchen."

"We did everything, Aunt Amalia," Ruby sings out.

"One of the young people needs to go. Kelly!" She turns

202

toward me, fixing me with a classic mom look, the eagle eye that won't be refused.

"I haven't thought of a good song yet," I say weakly, fiddling with my necklace, which has become a kind of worry stone; the contrast between textures on the front and back of the pendant, the rough and the smooth, is satisfying.

Beside me, Eric shifts. "I've got one."

"Really?"

He reaches over and squeezes my hand, his gaze carrying a warmth that kindles an answering glow in me. It reminds me that he's willing to take hits for me, and it makes me feel taken care of, safe in a way I remember feeling but haven't felt since I arrived in this life. He lets my hand go and, standing, takes the microphone from his aunt.

I don't know that I've ever heard him sing. Surely I would remember. It's an old song he chooses. He stands motionless, staring at a point on the wall, as the intro trills through the speakers, brushes and strings and agogo. When he sings, however, his voice comes out strong and sweet and his body moves naturally. *Sign your name across my heart, I want you to be my lady.* He's no Terence Trent D'Arby. Even still, I can't look away from him. I have to concentrate on keeping my breathing even.

Everyone claps when the song ends. Edgar whistles and yells, "Dang, Eric!" which makes the drowsing baby on his chest startle. His wife and mother both shoot him dirty looks.

"Why don't you ever serenade me like that?" Daisy asks.

"That sounds like a challenge," crows Ruby, plucking the mic from Eric's hand and pressing it on Ed, who refuses to take it.

"I've got the baby," he protests.

"I'll take him." Daisy goes for the buckles on the carrier.

"No. Absolutely not. I can't sing. I had too much to eat."

Everyone heckles him, but halfheartedly. It seems like they're over karaoke. Eventually they let it go and the adults drift out onto the deck. I go with them. The sun has set and the sky's darkening, the air soft. Summer's coming. A mosquito bites me, a sharp sting on the back of my neck, and I brush it away.

"I don't think I've heard Eric sing since the last time he went to mass," Amalia says. "That would be, what, when he was eighteen?"

"Seventeen," Tony says. "After high school we didn't make him go anymore."

I remember going with them at Christmas, senior year. Eric was never religious that I know of, and his parents weren't particularly observant, but they still dragged him to church on the holy days. He hadn't sung, though.

I also remember another senior-year Christmas, which I spent scrolling through my phone while my mom played carols on the radio and roasted every drop of juice out of a twenty-pound turkey. My friends and I texted about how bored we were, but I secretly enjoyed the enforced laziness.

Eric puts his arm around me and I lean against him, the position feeling habitual. I'm tired, but the older generation is just getting started. We listen, kids eavesdropping on grown-ups' talk, as Tony and Wayne reminisce about their youth in Hamtramck and about their parents, who've moved to Florida. People I've never met, but their stories bring them to life.

I finish my beer, then wander inside. The downstairs bathroom is occupied; I can hear Flora singing inside. She'll probably be a while. I go upstairs and use the bathroom there.

Farther down the hall, the door to Eric's old room is ajar. His parents haven't kept it like it was in his teenage years, though he wasn't big on decorating even then. Now, as I poke my head in, the walls are bare, any personal effects packed away in the closet. The bed is still the same twin-size one Eric slept in when he lived here.

I flash on a memory of us in that bed. We were in it together only a handful of times: his parents, like mine, had a strict door-open-at-all-times policy. But I remember this instance in particular because it was right after I'd told him about the scholarship. Suddenly our relationship seemed endangered, worth taking risks for, so I'd made him skip school with me so we could talk out the issue.

Fuck it out, more like, I think, and smile to myself.

This little bed. Only a supplement to fumblings in the front seat of his car, stolen moments in people's parents' bedrooms at parties. We never had the luxury of space and time and privacy until we went away to college.

I was lying awkwardly in his arms, wanting to shift into a more comfortable position but not wanting to move too much, not wanting to distract him. *People who go to different colleges always break up,* he said, and I knew it was true even as I countered, *But we won't.*

Still, I was already wavering. It would have been different if we'd never gotten together. I'd have been happy to get out of Andromeda Creek. I would have left and never looked back. But I wanted it both ways: the life I'd always imagined for myself, plus him.

He thought a moment, then said, *You could do art at Michigan State. East Lansing might not be as distracting as a big city.* I was a little irritated that he'd shifted right into problem-solving mode, but he'd also started scratching my back, which he knew I loved. And we did, after all, have a problem that needed solving. MSU would be a poor substitute for the Art Institute. On the other hand, Eric would be there.

Why does it have to be so hard? I complained, flopping my head down on his chest. He kept scratching my back, started kissing me, pulled me on top of him. For the next few weeks, I remember, he went on a charm offensive. He'd always treated me like gold, but he stepped it up during that time. Sweet text messages every morning before school. Dinner dates at Luigi's. Once, a single rose waiting on my pillow when I came home from soccer practice. His actions were all the kinds of things that would impress a high school girl, and I knew exactly what he was doing, but it worked anyway. Because really, I'd already decided.

Now, though, looking at the bed in the half-light falling in from the hall, I remember something else, like a shard pushing into the first memory, splitting it open. In that shard Eric and I don't talk at all; he lies woodenly next to me and says nothing even though I know his thoughts must be racing as fast as mine. I resent that he's being so immature, that he can't understand how important this is to me. Does he expect me to give it all up for him? And how strange that you can lie in someone's arms, as physically close as it's possible to be, and yet they're gone, travel-ing in a place where you can never follow.

I decided, lying in bed that day, that I would go to art school even if it meant I'd lose Eric.

I decided I couldn't stand the thought of losing Eric, that I would go to Michigan State.

I went to art school. I didn't go to art school.

I did. I didn't. What did I decide?

And then another shard calves from the first, another memory of us in here. Earlier. Was it earlier? Around the same time. We're still in Eric's bed but on top of the covers, fully clothed, because his parents are home. And because I'm sobbing like all my dreams have been snatched away from me.

Eric strokes my hair. *Maybe it happened for a reason.*

For a reason? I repeat back to him in acid tones. *What, like, God didn't want me to go to art school, so he sent a computer glitch that withdrew my application?*

Of course not. Eric keeps stroking my hair, but I'm mad at him for being so unruffled, and at his parents for being downstairs and seeing me with puffy red eyes, and at *my* parents for refusing to let me take a year off and reapply next year. *But maybe it wouldn't have been the right place for you anyway.*

What is the right place for me?

With me, he says, and surprisingly his saying that is the first thing that comforts me at all.

The memory swirls inside my head. I search for the rest of it, for what followed after that, but I can't remember. Because it's not real; that's not the way it happened. There was no computer glitch. I got in, I won the scholarship, and I rejected it. I made the choice to stay in Michigan. Didn't I?

My hand whips out and turns the light on, making everything fall into the unequivocal present. Eric's bed has a different comforter and more pillows now. It's been moved under the window, when before it was against the wall. His old desk, which was always covered in a mountain of junk, is clear. The room doesn't look at all like it did when he slept here.

My pulse thrums just above my collarbone as I walk in and open the closet. I survey a largish cardboard box on the floor, labeled *Eric*. His childhood and adolescence distilled to three cubic feet. He doesn't have any memorabilia at our house that I know of; he's not big on nostalgia. For him, high school wasn't fun. It was something to get through.

The box is closed with alternating flaps but not taped shut. Raising the flaps, I find the sorts of objects that are of no use but hard to throw away. A small photo album, nearly empty. A Fossil watch, stopped. A red mortarboard, unadorned except for the tassel with our high school graduation year dangling from the button on top. Eric's diploma is in there too, inside a black leatherette cover stamped with his name. I recognize our yearbook from senior year and lift it out with the idea of seeing what inscription I wrote Eric in this life. Though I can remember some things with photographic clarity, I can't remember that. I'm pretty sure it wasn't an offhand note about history class.

Something silvery glints from the bottom of the box: a loose flash drive, the kind that was ubiquitous when we were in high school. There are no other electronics in the box, no dead phones or old laptops, no tangle-corded headphones. Small and easily overlooked, the drive could be something Eric's mother missed when she was separating junk from stuff he might want later, but it seems odd for it to be in with sentimental things.

As I'm fingering its edges, I hear footsteps coming down the hall and, on impulse, slip the drive into my jeans pocket.

"There you are," Eric says from the doorway.

I turn and smile, trying not to look shifty. "I came up to go to the bathroom and got sidetracked . . . I wanted to see if you still had our yearbook." I hold it up.

"Wow." He comes into the room and takes the book from me. "I can't believe this is still here. This is great." He riffles through the pages, stopping on one of the end flyleaves, which is covered with my handwriting. He reads it to himself, smiling.

"Can I see?" I ask when he's done, and he hands it to me. The inscription is long and must have been written after I made the decision to go to MSU, because I'm talking about the future, how I'm looking forward to our having more quality time at college (the phrase *quality time* surrounded by little squiggles of innuendo), how glad I am that we'll be together forever. It's full of the drama and bombast of high school feelings, without a hint of uncertainty. I have no memory of writing it.

"We can take it if you want," Eric says.

"It's probably safer here." I slip the book back into its box. Eric doesn't even glance into the closet, doesn't seem concerned about what else might be in there or what information it might reveal. The flash drive in my pocket probably holds nothing more interesting than homework. He turns back toward the room and smiles, shaking his head. "I can't believe we both fit in that bed."

"We fit in a twin bed in your dorm room, too. Beggars can't be choosers."

"True." He goes over and sits down, patting the comforter beside him. "So . . . wanna fool around?"

A laugh peals out of me, loud enough to be heard downstairs, if anyone's listening. I cover my mouth with my hand. "Do we have to keep the door open?"

"Let's not."

I close the door. It doesn't have a lock. I bet Eric wished it had, back when he was a teenager doing what teenagers inevitably do. He's such a private person. For some reason the thought of him furtively masturbating, maybe thinking about me, turns me on. I go over and he puts his arms around me, holding me between his knees, and I bend down and kiss him, my hair brushing his face. We do that for a while, kissing, his hands drifting under the hem of my shirt. It feels good, partly because I know it won't go past a certain point. We're not going to have sex in his childhood bedroom, behind a door with no lock, with his family downstairs. At what age does it become passé to kiss and touch with your clothes on, for hours? When does making out become a means to an end?

When his hands migrate around to my front, I pull back. "They're going to send up a search party."

He sighs, laughs. "You know . . . I'm kind of tired. It might be time for us to go home."

He pulls me in for one more kiss and then we go downstairs and say our goodbyes, which are sped along by the fact that Edgar and Daisy's baby has woken and the party is breaking up, but still take twenty minutes. We drive home. We go to bed at the same time for the first time in nearly a week.

AFTER THE LAST time, I thought Eric might be hesitant, but he's not. At all. Except for his pausing to put on a condom, it's like he doesn't even remember.

He's propped on his elbows, over me in our bed. It's dark; I can't see his face. He dips his head to kiss me under the ear, then nips my earlobe. When I moan he laughs lightly and does it again.

"You want it, don't you?" he whispers in my ear, with almost no breath, like he's pulling something out of me rather than pushing air in. It makes me shiver. "You want me?"

"Yes."

"Say it."

"I want you."

He sighs, a long shaky breath of lust that in a different context would sound like relief. We shift our hips together. A little breathy sound comes from his throat as he moves into me. His larger body covers mine, anchoring me, weighing me down. Weight can feel smothering, or sheltering, or—like now—the tension between the two can excite me. I can't *make* him let me up. But he would if I wanted him to. He'd do anything I wanted. That's the power I have.

He rears up and I can feel him studying me, though I can see only the glint of his eyes. It's as if he's trying to look into my brain. What is he looking at? What is he looking *for*?

I laugh uncomfortably. "What?"

"I just . . . love you."

I feel too seen, or maybe not seen at all. The people we love, it's hard to see them as more than constructs of our own longings. To see past our own desires to the people they actually are and love them anyway. That's a big part of why Chicago Kelly always ended up single again eventually.

I ask, "Why?"

He gives a small chuckle of confusion.

"Why do you love me? Why me and not someone else?" In my other life there were several people who, had things gone differently—had one or the other of us been willing to *be* a little different—I could have stayed with forever, or at least for longer than I did. Partly I'm asking myself: *Why Eric?* What made me end up with him in *this* life?

"It's always been you. There was never anybody else."

"But why? What was it about me?"

"I don't know, you had this . . . quality, there was something . . . I felt drawn to you."

What he's describing isn't my experience with him. I can remember specific features that attracted me to the people I dated in Chicago: a wicked sense of humor, onstage swagger combined with offstage shyness, a pair of bright blue eyes. I can't identify any with Eric. He asked me out, and then I fell into a relationship with him. It's almost like I was in love with him before I realized what was happening. There's an inevitability to my memories, as if our relationship couldn't have gone any other way, even though I remember a reality in which it did.

Did I love him only because he wanted me to so much? The possibility terrifies me. But I can't rid myself of the emotions that tie me to him, the feeling of being bound by both love and habit, the obligation to continue what the other me began.

He takes my silence for the end of the conversation. Starts to kiss me, then collapses down, buries his face in my neck, and breathes in. His body heavy on mine, stirring. I push myself against him and he moans and starts to move. Closing my eyes, I let my head fall back, using my hands on his hips to spur him faster. A groan escapes him, some combination of pleasure and frustration, and he slows his movements, resisting me. Now we're in a struggle. Me against him, him against biology. I open my eyes and meet his with a challenging half smile, as though I'm just being playful, as if this isn't setting the tone for the remainder of our relationship. However long it lasts.

I don't try speeding him up again. Instead I move my hips in an exaggerated circle, thrusting hard at the top, taking him in as deeply as I can. He lets out a noise like he's been stabbed, but in a fun way. I do it again, and again, until he gives in to my rhythm. I can feel the wave coming toward me, washing through me, and a moment later it catches him too.

He rests on me, boneless, though I can tell he's holding part of his weight back. "I love you so much," he mutters.

It feels like this sense of well-being will last forever. The oxytocin glow, my roommate Leni used to call it. *I never put too much stock in the oxytocin glow,* she'd say after one of her weekly conquests. *It's a trap.*

Yet I hear myself say, "I love you too."

He falls asleep in minutes. I lie beside him, drifting, until I remember the flash drive. It's still in my jeans pocket, my jeans on the floor. I open my eyes, then close them. I'll get it in the morning.

But what if he—

I slip out of bed. I don't want to accidentally throw the drive in the wash. That's all.

No. I don't want Eric seeing it, recognizing it. I don't know why. But if he asks about it, I don't want to have to explain why I took it, because I don't know that either.

My office desk doesn't have drawers, and the various catchall baskets and bowls I have sitting on its surface seem too exposed. I stash the drive in one of the bins in the closet where I store art supplies. Then I can sleep.

29

Day Ten

WE START OFF THE NEXT MORNING WITH A FIGHT.

I come out of the bathroom to find Eric holding my phone. "The neighbor guy texted you," he says. "He can't run today."

And why are you reading my texts? I pluck the phone out of his hand. Adam's message explains that he has to go out of town for a few days. Some "emergency" with the in-laws, he says, with an eye-roll emoji.

Trying not to feel too disappointed, I put on my running clothes. Eric lets me get down the hall before he calls, "You're taking Bear, right?"

I freeze at the top of the stairs. I can hear Bear's tail thumping on the carpet at the mention of his name. "You know, this is a safe neighborhood." I enunciate more than I need to. "That is why we bought a house here. Nothing bad will happen if I go for a run by myself."

Eric comes to the bedroom door, Bear at his heels. "It's not that I think anything's going to happen. It just makes me feel better knowing it won't."

"What makes you so sure? It's not as if Bear's some attack

dog. All someone would have to do is throw him a steak and he'd be like, 'Go ahead, rape her.'"

"That's not the way it works. These guys go for the easy targets."

"*These guys?* Who, the rape gangs roaming around?" When Eric and I argue, my voice rises, while Eric's gets quieter and more infuriatingly reasonable. "Bear won't run on a leash. He's too busy sniffing around. When I take him with me, I don't get to run. You know how cranky that makes me." I force a smile, which doesn't make me any less irritated.

"So train him to run on a leash."

"You train him! He's *your* dog." Which isn't true, strictly speaking, since everything is *ours*. "*You're* the one who wants me to take him along." Eric just looks at me until I give a windy sigh and clap my hands. "Come on, Bear! We're going for a fucking run." Bear scrambles to his feet and bumps past me as I go down the stairs.

"There's no reason to get mad," Eric calls.

"There's no reason for you to be so controlling!"

"You know they picked up a transient in those woods behind the house last week?"

"He was probably taking a walk!" Bear wriggles ecstatically around my legs, tail fanning. At this point I'm ready to give up on the idea of a run altogether, but I don't want to be in the house. "The world is not full of danger! I don't need a man or a dog protecting me at all times!"

"Kelly, I'm looking out for you because I love—"

"You don't *need* to look out for me! I can look out for myself." I clip the leash to Bear's collar, then stumble over him as his gyrations block my path to the door. "Goddamn it, Bear!"

"You don't have to swear at him."

"I'll swear if I goddamn want to!" I feel like a teenager as I slam the door, but Eric's overprotective-dad routine brings it out in me. I don't know why he's like that. In Chicago (*if that was even real,* my brain supplies without my approval) I lived in what he would call peril every day of my life, and yet here in Michigan is where I feel a nameless danger. Call it inertia. The lure of well-stocked suburban grocery stores, the false security of knowing everyone by sight, even if you've never spoken. On the next street over lives a woman about my age whom I see most days on my walks with Bear. She goes up and down her front walk, moving at a stately pace, back and forth from the door to the street. She wears yoga pants and fuzzy pink slippers. Down and back, down and back; I've never seen her leave the property. Maybe she's agoraphobic. Maybe she's overmedicated. Maybe she has a baby who wails and arches its little back in rebellion when she tries to strap it into the stroller. I've tried to make eye contact but her gaze slides past mine, focused on the horizon, as though she's pretending to be somewhere else.

Bear pulls up short, fascinated with some scent in the grass, but I drag him mercilessly down the street. I feel desperate. I feel like scratching my skin off, as though I can scratch off this smothering new life along with it and emerge as my former self. I feel like if I don't find out what happened soon, I'll be stuck: my life settled into gelatin around me, cool and soft, putting up a resistance to any movement.

When I return home, Eric's mowing the front yard. A blurred bird shape of sweat spreads across the back of his white T-shirt. I remember being surprised, when I first recognized him in the restaurant on my birthday, by how broad his shoulders had become. Pivoting into a new row, he catches sight of me and waves, giving me a smile of uncomplicated happiness, like he's forgotten all about our argument. Like he's been pleasantly reminded that this is his life.

I wave back. Then I hurry inside and upstairs to my computer.

THE FLASH DRIVE'S encrypted. I try every combination of personal information I can think of, various permutations of Eric's birth date, my birth date, bearhyde, even our zodiac signs. Nothing gets me in. What could be on it that he wanted to hide, or keep safe?

It's perfectly reasonable for someone to password protect their electronics. And Eric's cautious; it drives him nuts that I don't use a passcode for my phone or computer, that I won't accept a little bit of inconvenience in exchange for security. I remember Eric and Peter coding together in high school, laptops open in the cafeteria, the library, sitting on the floor outside the auditorium. The coding club of two. It could be one of their old projects on the drive. But why wouldn't it have been thrown away?

I bet Peter could hack into that flash drive in ten seconds.

I stare at the log-in screen, the cursor blinking in the password field. With two fingers I type in g-n-i-i, and I hold my breath as I hit Enter.

Wrong password.

gn!i gets me the same message, as do yourwishourcommand and gniiyourwishourcommand. I wish I could code one of those scripts that cycle through thousands of possibilities in a second.

I try gniibearhyde. I try gnii with Eric's birthday, July 10.

Outside, the roar of the lawn mower dies away. I hear the rattle of Eric rolling it into the garage.

I switched lives on my birthday, April 29. I try gniiapril29, gniiapr29. Wrong password, wrong password. I try gnii0429.

A window of files opens on my screen.

"Yes!" I yell, my voice too loud, echoing off the walls. When I go to open the first file, however, a dialog box pops up telling me it's encrypted and asking for my key file or password. The password I used for the drive doesn't work.

Footsteps on the stairs send a rush of adrenaline through me. I yank the drive out of the port, palming it as Eric opens my office door and pokes his head in.

"Hey, did you eat yet?"

"Not yet." My heart's powering a dance party in my chest.

"Do you want to go out? I could go for some barbecue."

Yet another plate of meat. "I'll probably just grab something later, but don't let me stop you."

A frown creases Eric's forehead, then smooths as he comes into the room, stands behind me with his hands on my shoulders, and kisses the top of my head. He smells like grass and sunshine and sweat. "You shouldn't work so hard," he says. "What are you working on?"

We both look at my monitor, which, fortunately, shows the front page of a news website. I can see Linnea's sketch without having to raise my head; I wonder if Eric has noticed its appearance on my bulletin board.

If he has, he hasn't mentioned it.

"I'm kind of feeling my way into a new project." The plastic oblong of the flash drive slicks my palm with sweat. I fight the urge to make sure it's not showing between my fingers.

He chuckles. "Must be nice to be able to take your time like that."

"It's called discovery," I say, a little tartly. "It's an important part of the process."

"Take a break. We'll go to that salad place you like."

Something splits apart in my head. Which version of me is he talking about? Does he know there are two? "I'm not hungry."

"You can't not eat. You need to take care of yourself."

"Why do I need to take care of myself, when I have you to take care of me?"

His hands tighten on my shoulders, making me turn my head and look up at him. His expression is intense—eyes narrow, jaw tight—but not easily readable. He could be annoyed, or wounded, or in the grip of some stronger emotion that he wants to hide. As soon as his eyes touch mine, he relaxes his jaw and turns the corners of his mouth up slightly. He bends down and slides his arms around me. Kisses my hair, the side of my neck. His warmth flows into me, the smell of sunshine. "Always," he says in my ear. "I'll always take care of you."

I don't know how to respond. He means it, every word.

He kisses my cheek once more, then straightens. "I'm going to take a shower, and then we're going to lunch," he says. "Can you be ready in fifteen minutes?"

I sigh, giving in. "How about half an hour? I need a shower too."

As soon as he leaves, I turn my hand over in my lap. The drive pulses there, tempting me, though I know I can't read the files on it. It feels like a risk to try to look at it even with Eric busy elsewhere in the house.

No connection between Eric and gnii, yet *gnii* is in his password. My birthday is in his password.

I remember the day he proposed. It was the morning after

the last, bitter happy hour with my newly unemployed coworkers from the advertising agency. Eric and I had gone to breakfast so I could drown my hangover in grease. There was no public display, no kneeling in the aisle of the IHOP, not even a ring. He just took my hands across the table and told me, *I want to take care of you.* The memory doesn't feel like mine—not quite—but I can easily visualize the earnest look on his face when he said those words. I remember I barely thought about it before saying yes. By then, it seemed like a foregone conclusion. I didn't feel like he was expressing a wish to contain me; I didn't feel as though I was giving up control of my life. All I felt was relief at letting part of my burden fall on someone else.

But now, on the other side of the consequences of that choice, I'm more aware that letting someone else do the work, letting them make the decisions, means they grow accustomed to doing so. Opting out of responsibility means giving up control.

I don't know how Eric would react if I tried to take that control back.

30

Day Eleven

MOM'S LUMPECTOMY IS SCHEDULED FIRST THING IN THE MORN-
ing. I'm exhausted after lying awake half the night, my thoughts
running on a track between worry for her and curiosity about
what could be on the flash drive. Eric had a restless night too,
tossing and muttering in his sleep, and both of us have dark
patches under our eyes, but when I ask him how he slept he
smiles and says, "Fine. You?"

"Fine."

He gives me a steady look, which tells me he didn't miss my
sleep disturbances any more than I missed his. I wonder if he'll
ask me what I'm really worried about. Just the surgery, or something more? But he says only that he'll try to leave work early so
he can come check on me and Mom, after I take her home.

"You don't have to do that. I know how busy you are."

"Not that busy." He leans in and kisses my forehead. Despite
everything, I enjoy the sensation of his lips, their warm stamp
on my skin.

Dad brings my mother to the hospital but doesn't come in,

since he can't stay and Mom doesn't want him to pay for parking. My brother Jeff—bless him—shows up bearing a plastic box of bear claws from Meijer's bakery and two large coffees, mine loaded with cream and sugar so I can drink it. I need the caffeine after skipping my morning run. Nick is MIA, naturally, most likely sleeping off his kid-free weekend.

We're sitting in the waiting room, waiting for the nurse to call Mom back for surgery prep, when I hear the approaching click of heels on the floor. My mother, who's sitting across from me, looks up and a complicated ripple goes over her face, resolving into a welcoming, if slightly stiff, smile.

"I wanted to make sure you were settling in okay," comes Amalia's musical voice from behind me. Eric must have asked her to look out for us. She's VP of finance here, so she doesn't have much to do with the medical side, but I suppose the surgeon is unlikely to leave a scrap of gauze inside anyone under her protection. We chat a few moments, during which she actually says to the receptionist, "Take good care of my friend Vicky. Okay, Taneisha?" Taneisha answers with good grace that makes it clear she considers Amalia a benign presence, but I'm still slightly appalled at the blatant, if generous, way Eric's mother throws her weight around at work.

Not coincidentally, Mom gets called back less than a minute after Amalia disappears into the admin suite. "You should go," my mother says to Jeff as she stands. "I know you've got work." She'd never say anything like that to me, of course.

"I took the morning off," Jeff says. He's a contractor, an electrician like my dad. Dad used to have the idea that the two of them would go into business together, but Jeff ended up working for the city since they give him paid time off.

Mom smiles. "Your dad never would have done that. Here I am in the hospital, and he's out on a job." Which isn't completely fair, seeing as how he just took a week's vacation, but she's not wrong. My dad sees himself as a provider first, last, and always. So does Jeff, but he likes to be around every once in a while.

We've been waiting to dig into the pastries, since my mother can't eat until after surgery. Once she's out of sight, Jeff gets a bear claw for himself, then hands me the container and a napkin. "Mom's right, though," I say to him. "There's no reason for you to hang around."

He shrugs. "Least I can do after all the bullshit she's put up with from us."

It's a throwaway remark, but when I was younger, I wouldn't have expected even that level of self-awareness from Jeff. He's never been introspective. Maybe that's why he's adapted to adulthood so well: he does what needs to be done without thinking too much about it. He was the same way in high school, only the priorities were different. Then, he played the part of the amiable jock; now he fills a different role. Life does that, shapes you into things, either sharpening or smoothing you.

"Besides," he goes on, "we've got to make up for Nick being such a flaky bastard."

"He could be a lot worse." I don't have much room to judge. In my other life, I was the flaky bastard, the sibling who lived hours away and skipped as many visits as she could reasonably avoid. There's no way Chicago Kelly would be sitting in this waiting room.

It strikes me that I'm grateful to be here.

"Besides," I say, "you didn't even get him a coffee."

"Because I knew he wasn't going to show up!"

"But I could have drunk it."

Jeff laughs and fakes putting me in a headlock.

"Hey, watch the coffee!"

It's nice to catch up with no one else around. Jeff mostly tells me about the funny things his daughters do, and I'm charmed to see him so obviously smitten. I can't help thinking that's exactly how Eric would be if we had a girl of our own.

The time passes quickly. After a couple of hours the surgeon, a tiny blond woman, comes out and tells us the surgery went as well as it could have. The mass in my mother's breast was localized and relatively small, and we should know in a few days whether the cancer has spread.

"We used to have to wait weeks," the surgeon comments. "But we've made a lot of advances."

Jeff scratches the back of his neck. "So, what do you think? Are you optimistic, or . . . ?"

"I can't make a definitive prediction yet. They'll call you back to recovery when she's less groggy."

When we see Mom, I ask, "How was your nap?"

"They told me to count back from ninety-nine. I got to about ninety-seven and I was . . . whoosh." Her eyes aren't quite focused. In the hospital bed, wearing a faded green gown, she looks diminished. Sick. Her feet, wearing fuzzy hospital-issue socks, stick out from the bottom of the blanket. I tuck the blanket around them.

"That surgeon looked like she was about twelve," Jeff says. He's ill at ease, glancing up every time he hears a voice from the other side of the curtain surrounding our area.

"She's very brisk, isn't she?"

"Well, we don't need her for her social skills," I say. We sit awhile longer on the uncomfortable chairs, Jeff and I scrolling through our phones. Soon, Mom perks up enough to ask for hers. Nurses and aides walk in and out, checking vital signs and drainage and other mysterious medical things. After a while, one brings an evil-smelling tray, which Mom picks at and pushes away.

"We'll get some real food after they discharge you," I say.

"Whenever that is."

Finally, the nurse comes in with discharge instructions. I listen carefully, since I'm the one driving Mom home and getting her settled in before Dad gets off work. After that there's another half hour of waiting and paperwork before Mom can get dressed and wheeled down to the exit. I pull my car up and Jeff helps her into the passenger seat. "Bye, Mom," he says, then leans down to look through the door at me. "See you, Bugface."

"Bye, Assface."

"Kelly!" Mom yells, and Jeff gives me a smirk.

I roll my eyes, feeling fourteen again. "Say hi to Andrea and the girls for me."

On the way to Mom and Dad's house, I pick up her prescriptions and some sandwiches. She doesn't like what she calls "ethnic" food: her taste runs to the bland and filling. She says it's because of her Irish ancestry. At the house I get her set up on the couch and bring her two Vicodin and a glass of water.

She waves them away. "I don't need those."

"Mom, the nurse said to stay ahead of the pain."

"But I see on the news all the time about people getting hooked on opioids, and that's how it starts. They have an injury, or—"

"You're not going to get addicted taking them for a few days." I shake the pills at her like I'm shaking a stick at Bear to tempt him to chase it. She makes a face but relents, swallowing them with a tiny sip of water, as if there's some value in conserving it.

We watch TV, trading remarks about the afternoon shows.

After a while Mom drops out of the conversation, sagging into the couch cushions. I tuck a blanket around her and adjust the blinds so the sun won't shine in too strongly.

"Thanks for looking after me, Bug." Her eyelids flutter. I kiss her on the forehead like she's a toddler going down for a nap, and she smiles sleepily. "Love you, sweetie."

"Love you too." I turn off the TV and listen to the birds and squirrels and traffic outside the open windows.

"Hey, Mom?"

"Mm."

"What if I'd moved away? Gone to art school?"

She makes a confused noise, like she's trying to figure out where this came from. I wouldn't mind knowing that myself.

"Would you have been mad at me?" My voice is quiet, so when she doesn't answer, I assume she's fallen asleep.

Then she inhales, noisily. "Huh? No, course not, sweetie."

"But you were," I say almost inaudibly. "You thought I was wasting my life. Don't you remember?"

No answer, except her steady breathing.

From my purse on the dining room table, my phone makes its incoming-message chirp. My mother doesn't stir, so I get up to check it.

Can you meet me right now?

The number is unfamiliar, but it has to be Peter.

I glance into the living room, where my mother's still deeply asleep. I shouldn't leave her on her own, but Peter's been so evasive I'm afraid he won't give me another chance if I pass this one up.

As I'm weighing my options, the dining room wall catches my eye. Specifically, the photos mounted on it.

Weren't there pictures of Malik up here before?

There were. I remember looking them over when we were here for dinner, noting that each kid was equally represented. Now I scan the little gallery and see a photo of Ashleigh (or Kaleigh) in a T-ball outfit, her sister in a gymnastics competition leotard wearing an unsettling amount of makeup, a toddler giving a baby a shampoo Mohawk in the bathtub. The two girls cover the wall. I don't see any nail holes or spackle to indicate the moving of frames. Something flickers through my mind, the feeling of things shifting, and from the bottom of my eye I seem to see color springing up on my arms, then disappearing. The photos blur.

Dizzy, I drop into a chair and press the heel of my hand to my forehead, trying to massage away the headache blooming there. When I look up, the gallery is the same as it was last Sunday. I stare at the photos, daring them to change again. Were they really different when I came in here, or was it all in my head?

I focus on Malik's tae kwon do portrait, his small face solemn as he performs a side kick. I remember Nick at my birthday party, smiling as he watched Malik chatter with his cousins and more or less patiently helping him sound out words on the kids' menu.

But conflicting memories underlie those. Nick was out smoking when I came in—I remember that. We'd run into each other by the back door of the restaurant and talked for a few minutes before Eric found us. I don't remember what we talked about. For the rest of the night he'd skulked around the edges of the party, leaving well before the bill came. Alone.

Peter's message waits on my phone. What if these strange

deviations, these palimpsests of reality, are connected to something he did? Something he's doing even now?

What if they're caused by something *I'm* doing? The idea is ridiculous, impossible, but so is instantaneously switching lives. A week ago, all I wanted was to find my way home, but now I feel like a giant who turned around and accidentally flattened a house. Any choice I make—any choice at all—might hurt someone.

Outside the window a cardinal calls, a distinctive *chia-chia-chia* like a car alarm. Maybe I don't have a choice. Maybe everything will change regardless of what I do, and I'm about to be spun away, back to Chicago or somewhere else entirely, some new, scary place. I curl my fingers around the edge of the table as if that could hold me here. *Chia-chia-chia.* They mate for life, cardinals.

The bushes rustle and the bird's call changes to a metallic *chk-chk-chk-chk-chk,* a warning. Maybe something's trying to get at its nest, one of the feral cats that stalk the neighborhood. A breeze wafts through the window and caresses my cheek. The dining room remains solid around me, unchanged.

If I respond to Peter's text, will it tip some kind of balance? Which way?

Mom will be groggy and weak when she wakes up. Rattled if she finds me gone. But she's completely out. And Dad will be home in an hour.

Chicago Kelly would go.

Maybe whatever I decide is what I'm meant to do.

I answer Peter. Where?

31

HIS REPLY COMES BACK IMMEDIATELY, NAMING A CHAIN BAKERY
I never go to, with counter-service soup and sandwiches. The
kind of place my mother would like.

I respond, Give me 20 min. I'll have to push it, but I can make
it if there's not too much traffic.

This morning I slipped Eric's flash drive into an inner pocket
of my bag. I just wanted it with me. I still haven't had the chance
to try opening the files without Eric around. Maybe Peter can
give me some insight into its contents. I haven't decided whether
I want him to see it, whether I trust him, but I'm glad I have the
option.

I scrawl a note for my mom and leave it on the coffee table,
where it'll be the first thing she sees if she wakes up, next to a full
glass of water and a banana. I leave another note for my dad on
the dining room table. I don't text him, because I don't want to
have to explain.

Driving too fast on back roads, I try to piece together what
I've learned so far. I'm almost sure gnii is the startup Christine
was talking about on Saturday. Along with Katie's husband, that
makes two people who are relatively in the know and have heard
rumors of the app's futuristic capabilities. Only rumors, but

what if gnii can change the past? What if someone used it to change mine? And why would they do that to me?

Maybe it wasn't intentional; maybe I'm collateral damage.

I arrive at the bakery a few minutes late and walk in through cinnamon and yeast smells, nodding at the greeting from the boy behind the counter. They still have counter people here; they haven't replaced them with touchscreens.

Peter might have left. But then I see him, sitting in a banquette that faces the door, watching my approach. He gives me a little wave, a coffee cup in front of him but nothing else. I'm disappointed; I was hoping he'd bring his laptop and we could check out the flash drive together.

I slide into the chair across from him, asking, "What happened to you the other night?"

"I'm sorry about that. I couldn't get away, and I didn't have any way to let you know."

"Why couldn't you just text me?"

Peter's blinking a lot as he talks. "I hadn't gotten another number yet, and I didn't want there to be a record of a text from my real phone to yours. Just in case."

"Just in case what? Am I in some kind of trouble?"

Peter opens his mouth. Closes it. Opens it again. Says, "I really hope not. But you were saying something about weird shit happening?"

"Yeah. Do you know anything about it?"

"I might. Why don't you tell me what's going on?"

With everything that's happened, I'm past worrying about his thinking I'm cracked. "I was an artist," I tell him, "in Chicago." I tell him about going to Linnea's opening. How I started to feel weird. Sick. He starts nodding then. I tell him about going to the bathroom to get some space, opening the door, stumbling through into another life. How I remembered, eventually, everything that had happened to me in both lives. How they're both still there, uneasily coexisting in my head.

"That's not supposed to happen," Peter says.

"What's not supposed to happen?"

"If you didn't initiate, you're not supposed to be an observer."

"An observer of what? What am I observing?"

Peter looks down at his coffee cup. A tiny streamer of steam rises from the spout on its compostable plastic top. "You've never used gnii, have you?"

"No. I'd never heard of it before a week or so ago."

"And this . . . switch . . . happened the Friday before last?"

I nod.

"What time?"

I shrug. "Seven fifteen? Seven thirty? It wasn't late."

"Chicago time?"

I nod again.

"Eight thirty here. Yeah." He sounds like he's confirming something to himself. "But what I don't understand is, why do you remember so much? Years."

"It goes back to my seventeenth birthday."

Peter blinks. "Your—*what*?"

"That's where my memories split off from each other." I tell him the date, which makes his mouth fall open.

"Do you think that's significant? That both things happened on my birthday?"

His head wags back and forth, not quite a shake. "I don't know." Brow furrowed, he gazes over my shoulder into space.

"Did gnii do this? I know it does time travel." I don't, not for sure, but this is a time to be assertive.

He shakes his head. "Gnii doesn't—"

"Don't bullshit me."

My voice comes out louder than I intend, making Peter blink again. A man a few tables away glances at us, then looks away quickly.

Peter speaks quietly, leaning toward me. "I was going to say that gnii doesn't let you go back that far. Not even close."

"How far does it let you go back?"

"Minutes. Enough to change small things. Well, usually."

I sit back in my chair. Minutes. And I've got twelve *years* of the wrong life in my head.

"From what we can determine, it's a fail-safe. To preserve the stability of the timeline." He huffs a laugh. "Well, I guess now I know why we're getting all those error messages."

"Error messages?"

"Yeah. reWind's broken, since Friday before last. We couldn't figure out why."

"What's reWind?"

"That's what we've been calling the time-travel function. No idea if Marketing's gonna go for it or not, once we're ready to beta test. If we're ever ready to beta test, now."

"Marketing?" I'm incredulous. "You're going to *sell* time travel to people? Anyone's just going to be able to go back in time and change whatever they want?"

"We're making it safe," he says. "It's not like it really lets you change that much. There are other fail-safes built in too."

"It changed my whole fucking life, Peter!" I whisper-scream, not wanting to attract more attention.

"Yeah. Well. It's not supposed to do that." He scratches his eyebrow. "And if we're developing it, then I can guarantee that someone else is too. Or at least trying. We need to be first." He glances at a notification on his smartwatch. "Shit. I gotta go." He starts to slide out of the banquette.

"No, wait!" I need to tell him about my tattoos reappearing and about the photos of Malik. "It hasn't stopped happening since last Friday. There've been a couple of times when—"

"Look, we're gonna fix this," he says, standing up. "Maybe in a few days, you won't remember any of this anymore."

Terror, pure terror, shoots through me. "I won't remember any of what?"

"The residual memories," he says, waving a hand like my other life is nothing.

"How is that fixing anything?"

"Well, you'll be able to move on with your life. In this reality." He looks at me like he doesn't get why that would be a problem. As he takes in my horrified expression, understanding seems to dawn, a little. He says weakly, "I mean, Eric's a good guy, right?"

"That's not the point." But his mentioning Eric reminds me. "Why did you call him last weekend?"

"I can't get into that right now. My boss will lose his shit if he gets back and I'm not there. Half the time he's out of the office doing God knows what, the other half he's on a rampage . . . This week's been a nightmare."

"You think Eric did this." I stand, blocking Peter's path. "I told you something you didn't know, didn't I? I helped you. The least you can do is tell me that."

Peter's mouth tightens. "Yes. Yes, we have reason to believe Eric's responsible. Which is why I have to go, so I can work on fixing this, so a world of shit doesn't fall on him, and you along with him."

He's in a rush, but my decision is instant. "I have something else that might help." I dig in my purse for the flash drive. "I found this in Eric's stuff. I'm not sure what it is, I haven't read it, the files are encrypted. But it has something to do with gnii. Maybe you can get in. Look at it and let me know." I give him the drive and tell him the password, which makes him raise his eyebrows.

"Thank you," he says. "I'll be in touch."

I feel a pang of regret, letting the flash drive go. It's possible Peter's lying, that he'll never get back to me and I'll never find out what's in those files. I almost ask for it back. Instead I step aside so Peter can get by.

He steps past me, then pauses. "If you care about Eric, you might want to warn him." He's halfway to the exit before I can ask him what that means.

32

ERIC CALLS WHILE I'M DRIVING HOME. "HEY," HE SAYS. "SORRY I didn't come by. I got pulled into a meeting."

It's strange to hear his voice sound so normal, given what Peter just told me. It's even stranger to hear mine. "You didn't miss much. My mom took a nap."

"Good. How's she feeling?"

I give him the status report, and he says he'll pick up some dinner. "What do you think about Luigi's?"

"Fancy."

"You're worth it." I can hear that he's smiling and something in me responds to it, warming, unfurling. I'm reminded of the love-bombing campaign he carried out when he was trying to persuade me to go to Michigan State with him instead of art school. "What do you want, chicken Marsala?"

I hesitate, then say, "Sure. Thanks."

"Okay. See you in a bit. Hey," he says, as if something has just occurred to him, something important he needs to ask me, and my heart jumps in my chest. I think about how he knew I wasn't downtown the other night. I'm suddenly sure that he knows I wasn't where I was supposed to be just now, either.

"I love you," he says, and I feel silly.

I love you too. I can tell he's waiting for me to say it back. I push it out in a mumble, and we hang up.

They're just words. I've probably said them to him hundreds of times. Can you love someone without truly knowing him down to his core? Maybe not every thought that passes through his mind—no one can know that. Eric has no idea what's been going on in my head for the past week and more, and I don't doubt he loves me. But at least, if you love someone, you should know how he's likely to respond to certain situations, certain stimuli. Like how I knew Eric would think something was wrong if I didn't answer him the way he expected.

If you care about Eric, you might want to warn him.

That *if.* Peter seemed awfully comfortable with the idea that I would look upon my husband as a stranger, even after I'd told him I remembered our entire history. Or maybe he didn't want to make assumptions. He must have seen—anyone could have seen—that I was upset about what happened to me. *We have reason to believe Eric's responsible.* I still don't know what that means, what Eric is supposed to have done. I don't know what to warn him about. Peter's boss, the psycho CEO Christine had heard those rumors about? The man who supposedly had someone run off a bridge? It sounds like something out of a Mafia movie.

When I arrive home, Eric's not there yet. I let the dog out, tell our speaker to put on some music, and empty the dishwasher. The normalcy of the work soothes me. I look at the device sitting on the countertop. Something like this is supposed to let a human travel through time? How does that even work?

Only information could be sent, Christine said. Gnii sent code and specifications to an earlier version of itself, and that information became part of it, the later version integrated with the earlier one. If it could send code, what about thoughts, memories, knowledge, personality? Sent where? From a later version of a person to an earlier one.

Bear bounds up to the sliding glass door and starts barking to be let in. A few seconds later, Eric's car pulls into the garage. I let him get inside and set dinner on the table before I open the slider. Bear runs up to Eric and crashes into his hip, whining joyfully at being reunited with his favorite. Dogs are supposed to be good judges of character; if a dog dislikes you, then there must be something shifty about you, something wrong. But I think Bear would be friends with anyone who fed him.

Eric removes containers of food from a brown paper bag. He's wearing a button-down shirt with the top button open and the sleeves rolled to his elbows. I can appreciate the sight of his exposed forearms, the neat dark shadow of five-o'clock beard on his jaw, even as I wonder what's going through his head. What he's not saying.

"How was your day?" he asks me, which is the most innocuous question possible, but it feels charged.

"Long."

He glances up quickly, as though he's heard something in my voice. Then his face softens into sympathy. "It's hard dealing with health stuff."

I saw Peter today. The words stay locked behind my teeth. Eric is acting so normal, so husbandly. He moves into the kitchen, grabbing plates and silverware, even though the restaurant packed compostable plastic utensils with the food in the bag. He sets them out on the table, then goes back and fills two glasses with water. The whole time I'm watching him, my back to the corner. The food smells good, and my stomach rumbles.

"Sit down and eat with me," Eric says. "Tell me how your mom's surgery went."

I sit and lift a portion of chicken and pasta onto my plate. I have the sudden strong feeling that we've sat here before, talking about my mother's breast cancer surgery as we ate takeout from Luigi's. Déjà vu. That's all it is.

"I'd rather talk about your day, to be honest."

He shrugs, twirling his fork in linguine. "Same old, same old."

"Do you still like your job?"

Another shrug as he swallows what's in his mouth. "It's fine."

"Fine. And that's okay with you?"

"Why wouldn't it be?"

"Is that really all you want out of life? A job you don't hate that pays the bills?" I sound petulant, angry almost. Distracted, I reach for a glass of wine that's not there. I thought I'd poured myself one just before sitting down.

"My job's not the point. My job enables everything else I want to do."

"And what is that?" The wine was something different. Something from one of those half memories, the not-memories, that have bled through to my conscious mind so frequently in the past week. Eric and I sat here, this same night, having a different conversation. I took a sip from my wineglass and it tasted funny, like the wine had gone off, even though I'd just opened the bottle.

"Take care of you. Maybe have a family eventually, but . . ." His face clouds, then clears. "We'll see. Why all the questions?"

I can't stand it. I get up, go into the kitchen, and open a bottle of cabernet from the rack on the counter. I pour some into a glass. It tastes fine.

"Forgot something?" Eric's looking at me with amusement.

"You want some?" I know he won't. He shakes his head.

I know now that what happened to me is real. So why can't I say it?

I go back to the table, though I no longer feel like eating. "Don't you ever think about how your life could be different, if you'd made different choices? Or if . . . if you could go back and live your life over again. Knowing what you know now." That's the closest I can get to coming out with it. I watch him while I say the words. I see the moment he looks up at me; I see the flicker of awareness in his eyes. He knows that I know. But what is it, exactly, that I know?

He sets down his fork. His hand's trembling a little. He's still watching me, drawn back, like he's both anticipating and afraid of what I'm going to say next.

I saw Peter today. Those words would be the start, the ax that would break the ice and let all the rest flow out, but I can't make myself say them. Why can't Eric make this easy on me? He's the one at fault. Why doesn't he say something, confess? Unless Peter and I are both wrong, and there's nothing for him to confess.

Or there is, but the illusion that we're a normal couple in a happy marriage is too precious for him to smash. What might he do to maintain it, to enforce it?

When it becomes clear that I'm not going to speak, he smiles. "Well, sure. I could work on Wall Street and drive a Ferrari. But I don't want that. I have everything I want." His eyes arrow into mine, making it obvious what one of those things is.

Would I be a better person if I'd chosen this life from the beginning? Chosen home, chosen Eric. Been focused on family rather than work. Or would I be like Katie, self-interested and provincial? I can't ever know.

33

Day Twelve

THE NEXT MORNING, I PUT ON MY RUNNING CLOTHES WHILE
Eric gets ready for work. It's funny how the routine is so established in my body that I don't feel right unless I've had my
daily run.

"I'm not taking Bear," I tell Eric.

We're in the bathroom; he's shaving. Only his eyes move
toward me in the mirror. He takes a breath, like he's getting
ready to argue, then lowers his razor and nods. "I'm sorry I was
so uptight about it. It's your choice."

Damn right, I think, but this is obviously a concession for
him, so I give him a kiss on the side of his mouth that doesn't
have shaving foam around it and wish him a good day.

Heading outside, I'm surprised to see Adam stretching in his
driveway. He perks up when he catches sight of me. "Ready to
get your ass kicked?"

I grin, happy to see him. "I was just going to ask you the
same thing."

Doris, next door, waves and hallos at us from her front yard.

Adam gives me a covert eye roll, then turns his sparkliest grin on her and says, "You should run with us sometime, Doris. This girl'll have you in the best shape of your life within a week. Either that or kill you."

"Oh, I'll stick to gardening," she says, blushing under her visor. "You guys have fun, though."

"More like torture. You should be happy I'm here at all," he says to me. "I had a client call, wanting to look at a house. The perfect excuse, but I put 'em off until this afternoon."

"I'm honored," I say with a smirk.

"Hey, that reminds me," Doris breaks in. "I wanted to ask you . . . I've got a friend who wants to sell her house and move into something smaller—her husband passed away last year—"

"Have her call me." Dropping all pretense of friendliness, Adam nods curtly and sets off down the street. Startled, I follow him, tossing a farewell over my shoulder to Doris. "That woman," he says when I catch up, "annoys the shit out of me."

"Oh, she's harmless." Not wanting to get into a neighbor-trashing session, I change the subject. "So, your in-laws are good?"

"What?"

"Your in-laws. Their emergency got resolved?"

"Oh. Right. Yeah, they're fine. They were just being dramatic." He doesn't elaborate. He seems distracted, his mood less sunny than usual, so of course I feel duty bound to cheer him up. I tell him about karaoke at the Hydes', exaggerating for comic effect. In my version, Amalia nearly faints with shock at the sight of her three-year-old grandniece singing along to Prince. Then I fall silent. The weather's a preview of midsummer, the humidity making it hard to breathe, let alone talk.

I'm debating whether to bring up my mother's surgery, since

Adam hasn't asked about it. Honestly, I'm a little miffed that he seems to have forgotten. Then, as though he's read my mind, he asks, "How'd your mom's surgery go?" He seems as though he's switched into a different mode, warm and caring, giving me his full attention as I answer his question. I feel a rush of warmth, especially when he tells me to let him know if there's anything he can do. He sounds like he means it.

Eric's gone by the time I get back, and I go through the rest of my morning routine. Shower and dress, tea and toast and a banana. I text my mother, asking how she's feeling. She replies that she's great, good as new. No, I don't need to come over today, unless I want to—which I probably don't, considering what a rush I was in to get out of there yesterday. I ignore the dig and tell her I'll stop by tomorrow.

I sit in front of my computer and try to do work, but I'm distracted. I fall down a rabbit hole (wormhole?) of research about the possibility of time travel, though *research* might be a generous term. I can't understand half of what I read, at least the stuff that seems to have been written by non-crackpots. It's all physics, formulas, light cones and tachyon particles and farfetched theoretical scenarios that begin, *If one twin boards a spaceship that travels at the speed of light and the other twin stays on Earth . . .* None of it applies to me or my situation. Most physicists seem to believe human time travel, especially into the past, is difficult to impossible. Maybe they're right, and Peter is messing with me for fun. Maybe I'm delusional after all. I rub my forehead, trying to get rid of the headache that's settled in since this morning.

Right then, my phone rings.

34

IT'S A CHICAGO NUMBER, WHICH IS THE ONLY REASON I PICK UP.
"Hello?" I'm ready for a spam caller, but there's silence on the
other end. "Hello?" I think about my mom's stories from when
she was a teenager, when her family had a landline without caller
ID and boys in her class thought it was fun to make heavy-
breathing prank calls.

Then someone says, "Kelly?"

I recognize the voice instantly.

Hope flies and flops in my chest in a fraction of a second,
flops so hard it leaves me dizzy.

"It's Linnea Flood. From Chicago, the painter? You came to
my studio?"

I know, I want to say, *I know it's you.* But the words are stuck.

I must have left something behind. My business card doesn't
give my home address; she's calling to get it so she can ship the
forgotten item. *How thoughtful,* some inane part of my brain
simpers. My friend is so lovely, my lovely friend who will never
be my friend again.

"I'm sorry to call . . . This is so weird." The last part comes
out lower, muffled, as if she's talking to herself. "I was trying to
put it in a text . . . or an email . . . but it sounded too bizarre."

Her voice seems to fade in and out, along with my vision. I listen harder; I think of enchantments in stories, magical melodies that transport people into parallel worlds, and grip the edge of the desk. My eyes move up to her sketch, still pinned to my bulletin board. Its edges lift in the breeze from the window, showing it to me from different angles. That's my talisman. That's my totem.

Linnea says, "I remember you."

YOU REMEMBER ME?

Like, *remember* me remember me?

Hey, remember when we had that dinner party?

You took it so seriously. Like you were channeling your mother doing one of her fund-raising galas. I was all, let's just get some cheese and crackers and wine and call it good, but you said no, it has to have a *theme*. It has to have a *rhythm*. So we trawled thrift stores until we found a trove of black velvet Elvis paintings and old vinyl 45s. We designed invitations, glued them to the records, and hand delivered them. We made a playlist of blues and gospel and fifties rock, Elvis and Chuck Berry and Muddy Waters and Rosetta Tharpe, and called the party Theft.

(I mean, we *were* art students.)

Of course, it all fell apart after the first hour because our friend Ray had the bright idea to bring an eight ball. Nobody ended up eating much. Fun party, though.

That was a good apartment. A good year. We lived together only that one year before you and Bobby moved into the place in Pilsen. It feels like a lot longer, though, right? Time is tricky:

it stretches out when you're young and compresses as you age. My four years of art school felt the same, subjectively, as the seven years after graduation.

I thought we'd grow apart. After you moved out, and then again after we graduated and your career started taking off and mine didn't. But you stuck by me. I must have had some value for you apart from history and loyalty, which will carry a relationship only so far. When it comes down to it, people don't stay friends unless they each have something the other needs. That sounds so transactional, but we were never like that. There was never any sense of obligation between us. But maybe you're one of the reasons I was so hesitant to give up on being an artist: I was too afraid of losing you.

"I REMEMBER YOU," she says.

There's a rhythm in my ear. I'm distracted trying to puzzle out where it's coming from before I realize it's in the phone; Linnea must be playing music in the background.

I have to say something. "You do?"

"I woke up this morning and everything was *there* in my head. You and me being friends, the apartment . . . K, what the fuck's going on?"

"I don't know." I feel like this news is still far off but approaching fast, ready to slam into me.

"You remember me too, right? That's why you came to see me?"

"Yeah." And there it is. Relief so strong I almost burst into tears. This is real; it's all real. I've spent so much time trying and failing to prove my other life existed, and Linnea's confirming it. "I was afraid I was going crazy." I can hear my voice shaking.

"How long has this been going on for you?"

"Almost two weeks." It seems like so much longer. Time getting up to its tricks. "We need to talk. Like, in person."

She laughs. "Yeah, I was about to tell you . . . I'm already driving, actually. I'm coming up on Indiana right now. You'll have to tell me where you live."

There's no way I can sit here for three and a half hours waiting for her to arrive. We agree to meet up in Battle Creek, which is midway between Davis City and Chicago and has a twenty-four-hour doughnut shop where I've stopped on multiple occasions to fortify myself for a visit home. I don't want to hang up; I feel like she's going to disappear as soon as I can't hear her voice anymore. "How's your showing going?"

"My . . . ? Oh! Good, I think. That one painting sold, the one Bobby called the redheaded stepchild? Some dude from Austin bought it."

"That's great."

"Sure." I can almost hear her shrug through the phone. "Do you . . . ? Are you . . . ?" Am I painting, she's about to ask. Am I making work. But then she swears loudly at someone on the road with her, and I am saved. "Shit, traffic's getting *hairy*. I better let you go."

"You're not going to forget about me as soon as you hang up, are you?" I'm ostensibly joking, but she must hear something in my voice.

"It's gonna be all right, K. We're going to figure this out."

It's not her certainty that calms me down so much as hearing her use her old nickname for me. She really does remember. She isn't going to forget.

"Of course we are," I say. "I'll see you in a couple hours."

I rush to let Bear out, bring him in, and get on the road before anything can stop me. As if anything could stop me.

35

THE ONLY CAR IN THE DOUGHNUT SHOP PARKING LOT WITH AN
Illinois plate is a Tesla, and Linnea drives a Lexus. Nevertheless,
I see her as soon as I walk in. She sees me too and stands, open-
ing her arms. We hug for a long time.

"I missed you," I say. Tears push at the backs of my eyelids.

"I missed you too." We sit at the booth she's staked out with
two coffees and a half dozen mini–heart attacks. "I mean, just
since this morning, but it was intense. Like a panic thing. I woke
up thinking I'd had this nightmare that we'd never met, never
been friends. Then I realized it was real, and I had to run to the
studio during rush hour to find your business card."

"But you didn't know me when I came to your studio?"

"No. I'd never seen you before. I was actually kind of annoyed that Markie would send some rando up there."

"But you never get annoyed! You're an angel of patience." I
smile across the table at her.

"I am." She smiles back and takes a large bite of a chocolate-
iced doughnut sprinkled with M&M'S. Chewing, she pushes
the box toward me.

"What, these aren't all for you?"

She laughs. "I didn't eat breakfast! And you know I'm getting a dozen to go."

She polishes off the M&M'S doughnut in four bites and starts on a second that looks even more monstrous and delicious, with chocolate cake covered in green frosting, ribbons of caramel, and chocolate chips. I take a nutty doughnut and a sip of coffee, which shocks my still-unaccustomed taste buds with its bitterness, and nod out the window at the shiny black Tesla. "Is that your ride?"

"Yep."

"Did you just buy it?"

Her mouth is full of doughnut, but she gives me a quizzical look, which I'm guessing means no. I don't know why everything in Linnea's life would be the same except her car. And, of course, me. But maybe there are other differences too. I know her, but I don't know her life. Not this version of it.

"So you don't remember having a different car."

Still chewing, she shakes her head.

"I wonder why you would remember me all of a sudden." I think about what little I was able to learn from Peter last night, how he and his team are working on fixing what went wrong with gnii, and "fixing" my residual memories. This must be the result of one of their attempts. "What about Bobby? Does he remember me?"

"Nope. I mean, he remembers you coming to the studio, and thinking you looked familiar, but he didn't wake up with the whole history in his head like I did."

"If something had happened to put things back the way they were, I'd be in Chicago right now," I muse. "Or at least Bobby would remember me. So you talked to him about this?" I'm surprised.

"Well, I had to, so he would know why I was having an emotional breakdown at eight in the morning. And I would have told him in any case. I trust him. He's not going to say I'm crazy or making shit up. He offered to call in sick and come with me, but I told him not to." Bobby, like the old me, has to work for a living. Apparently that hasn't changed.

I don't know what else might have, though. I would hate to think I've had a hand in disrupting Linnea's life. For some reason I feel like it's my fault, like I caused it, and have to blink back tears.

"Hey." She reaches across the table and touches my wrist. "What is it?"

"You're still okay, right? Your life hasn't been turned upside down in the last twenty-four hours, has it?"

She shakes her head. "Not that I'm aware of, other than having a best friend I didn't know about until this morning."

"Well, you've still got Bobby. That's one thing. How's your career?"

She smiles, ducking her head self-deprecatingly. "My career is fine."

Relief washes through me. "Which means it's still on fire."

She rolls her eyes at me. Linnea has a very expressive eye roll.

"Don't. I need to know you're okay."

Her face softens. "I'm okay."

"Good."

"How did this happen for you?" She wipes her fingers on a napkin, dives into her voluminous canvas tote, and brings out a Moleskine notebook and a sky-blue fountain pen. No cheap implements for her, and no electronic note-taking either. I'm not sure how I feel about having any of this written down. But that's one advantage of analog: the record can truly be destroyed if we decide it needs to be.

The shop is empty except for us. Even the woman who was behind the cash register when I came in has disappeared, into the back. I give Linnea an abbreviated version of events on my birthday and since then, including my inconclusive search for answers and my conversations with Peter. As the words *time travel* leave my mouth it strikes me how preposterous all this must sound.

"Back up," Linnea says. "So you're saying there's an app that's a *time machine*."

"Um . . . yes?"

She snorts, eyeing me like she thinks I might be messing with her. Then, seeing my face, she nods. "Okay. Okay, I'm gonna go with that. So how did that cause . . . this?" She makes a swirling gesture around her head, flicking a hand to encompass me, both of us, our entire lives.

"I think what we're in now is an alternate future. The one that would have happened if I'd started dating Eric junior year and never gone to art school. And I kind of got transported into it all at once, instead of living it from where it split off from the other track."

"And me all of a sudden remembering our friendship is because Peter's messing around trying to fix this gnii app."

"That's what I assume. And that's not the only thing that's changed since I got here." I tell her about my tattoos reappearing, then disappearing again, and the bleeding through of memories that aren't really memories. "Whatever's happening, it started on my birthday and it's still going on. Peter thinks Eric caused it. He has evidence that Eric's involved, but he hasn't told me what it is."

"What do you think?"

"I think Peter's more worried about keeping his job than helping me."

"But about Eric."

"He has at least some part in it." I tell her about finding the flash drive. "I don't know what's on it—the files are all encrypted—but it was in his stuff and *gnii* was in the main password. Along with my birth date. So I'd say that's pretty incriminating. Plus I just have a feeling he knows something. Sometimes he's fine, but other times he seems nervous. Like he's waiting for the other shoe to drop."

"And you said you guys met in high school?"

"We were acquaintances. We hardly saw each other outside of school until he asked me out, and that's where my memories split." Track one: I go to art school. I meet Linnea. I live in Chicago. Track two: I date, then marry, Eric. I stay in Michigan.

"That's got to be weird, suddenly being married to some random dude."

"Yeah." The word comes out on a laugh, but the sound of it makes Linnea look up from her notebook.

"Are you okay? He's not, like, raping you every night, is he?"

"No, no. The sex, it's . . ." I feel my face get warm. "It's actually the least complicated out of everything. Though he's really careful about using condoms, and that's new. He doesn't want me to get pregnant, for some reason."

"Well, you don't want to get pregnant, do you?" For the first time, she looks at me like she doubts my sanity.

"Fuck no."

A smile flits across her face, disappearing quickly. "And you haven't talked to him about this whole thing."

I shake my head.

"Why not?"

I brush the peanut bits off my half-eaten doughnut, herding them into a pile on a napkin. "Like I said, he might have caused it."

"Wouldn't that be a reason to ask him about it?"

"It's not that easy."

"K." Her tone makes me look up from my denuded pastry. "Are you afraid of him?"

"No! I don't know." Wiping my hands, I accidentally tear a napkin in half. "He's never done anything to make me think he'd hurt me. He obviously loves me, and I . . ." Love him? Do I? "I guess I've been worried that if I tell him what happened, he'll think I'm having some kind of delusion."

"Or he'll act like he thinks it, even if he knows you're for real."

I don't want to admit that possibility, but I can see it playing out. "Maybe."

"Tell me this. What would he do if you told him you'd remembered this whole life you had back in Chicago and you were leaving him to pick it up again?"

"He'd be upset. Obviously."

"But what would he *do*? Do you think he'd try to have you committed?"

"He wouldn't be able to do that unless I was 'a danger to myself or others.'" I do air quotes. "Right?"

"He could say you'd tried to kill yourself. Or threatened him. He could say anything he wanted, and most anyone would believe him over you. Police, doctors. They believe men, not crazy women."

"I don't think he'd do that."

"What if the alternative was losing you?"

Eric worships me; I know that. And whatever apprehensions I have about him, he's never been abusive. But what if I step too far out of line? What if I threaten to blow up the life he (*we*) built? I don't think he'd try to cage me, but prisons and cemeteries are well populated with women who thought they knew the men in their lives until it was too late.

I say, "I don't even know if I want to leave him."

"What do you want?"

That hits me like a challenge, but all I see on Linnea's face are worry and sympathy. The question only feels confrontational because I've been so remiss in asking it of myself.

I take a drink of my coffee, now lukewarm, and wince at the taste. "I don't know. I've been so wrapped up in trying to figure out what happened that I haven't even thought about how I'm going to move forward."

Linnea nods. The door beeps as it opens to admit a pair of mustached men wearing work boots and faded jeans. They look like contractors. One is huge, overflowing the stool he takes at the counter, while the other is more compact, like my dad. The counter woman comes out from the back and greets them like they're old friends.

"Do you have anyone close by who could help you if you needed it?" Linnea asks.

"Sure. My parents. My brother Jeff's in the next town over. If the shit really hits the fan, my running buddy lives right across the street." It feels like overreacting to discuss worst-case scenarios when it comes to Eric. But there's also risk in shaming myself into not reacting at all.

Linnea sputters. "Your *running* buddy? You're a runner now?"

"Apparently."

She wipes up crumbs with her napkin and balls it up. "You could come back with me."

"To Chicago? Right now?"

"We've got the spare room. You can stay as long as you want."

It would be simple, in a way. I could take up my previous life, or a simulacrum of it. Hang out with Linnea and Bobby, take art classes and get back into the rhythm of painting. Try to be Chicago Kelly again.

Except I wouldn't be. No matter how much I might feel like it on the inside, I'm not that person anymore. I haven't been to art school. Nobody knows me except Linnea; not even Bobby remembers me. I'd be an outsider, Linnea's bumpkin friend, there on her indulgence. Faced with the option of trying to slot myself back into my old life, all I can see are the reasons it won't work.

And then there are my entanglements in Davis City. Not just Eric, though my feelings about him are complicated enough for several Russian novels. I've committed to helping look after my mother, at least for the next few weeks. This goes deeper than my being stuck in someone else's life and needing to get back to my own.

"I really appreciate the offer," I say.

"But you're not going to take me up on it."

"That would be hiding. This isn't just about me anymore." Something crystallizes in my head, something I hadn't consciously thought of until now. "More things are changing, and I need to find out what's causing it. How to stop it from happening again."

"Okay. But you know that involves talking to your husband, right?" She shakes her head, smiling. "That's still so weird. You, married."

"I know, right?" I nod slowly. "You're right, though. It's not that I'm afraid to tell him, I just . . . don't know how to start." That's not completely true. My heart doesn't race when I think about bringing this up with Eric. I don't break out in a cold sweat. But I can't imagine saying the words that would need to come out of my mouth.

"What if I come home with you? In case you need some backup."

I start to make doubtful noises, but Linnea says, "You know what I think, why I remember you when Bobby doesn't?"

I shake my head.

"I think it's because we're connected. No matter what happens, how reality might change, we're linked. We're there for each other. That's why your instinct was to come find me. Not to get all woo-woo, but the universe knows what it's doing. You don't have to take all this on by yourself."

I let out a sigh, and it feels like putting down a burden. "Okay." Linnea goes to the counter—she wasn't kidding about that dozen to go—while I gather up our trash.

A text comes in from Eric. Hey what are you up to?

I pull in a breath. Logically, I know there's no way Eric could know I'm *up to* anything, but I'm extra paranoid in the context of my and Linnea's conversation.

Want to get lunch?

When Linnea comes back I'm staring at my phone, weighing how to answer him.

"What's up?" she asks.

"Eric texted me."

"Is that . . . not normal?"

"No, he texts me all the time." But that little tickle in the back of my head is tickling away, trying to tell me something is, indeed, up.

My phone chirps in my hand. Or I could bring something home . . .

Where he'd find me gone. Which would mean a confrontation, which needs to happen sometime but preferably not the second I walk in the door. I dash off a quick reply: I just ate. Tomorrow we can have lunch I promise!

Linnea's looking at me with concern. "You okay? You about hit the ceiling when that last text came in."

"I'm fine. Let's go." I give her my address, but it turns out I hardly needed to. She sticks right behind me the whole way home.

36

WE ARRIVE IN DAVIS CITY IN MIDAFTERNOON. BY THE TIME I'M driving down my daytime-deserted street, my high from Linnea's return is all but gone. I pull into the garage and rest my head on the steering wheel, just for the moment it takes Linnea to pull up behind me. I don't feel well. Emptied out, like I've spent a night without sleep or failed to drink enough water, but I've still got a lot to do before I can rest. I lift my head and a familiar wave of dizziness passes through me, but nothing seems to change. Linnea's still here, which is all I care about right now.

I wonder what Eric will think when he gets home from work in a couple of hours and sees her car. As Linnea and I approach the door that leads from the garage into the kitchen, the sound of Bear's frantic barking filters through. Which is strange: he usually greets me or Eric with ecstatic sniffing and tail wagging, but no noise. Maybe Linnea's unfamiliar voice riled him up.

He lunges at me as soon as I open the door. "Holy fuck!" Linnea yells. I get it closed again without shutting him in it, but he keeps barking—a high-pitched *Get out of here, evil UPS man* howl—and underneath it I can hear the scrabble of his toenails on tile as he attempts to batter his way through the wood.

He's *my dog*. I try easing the door open again and he snaps at me through the two-inch gap. "Bear, no!" He cowers at the authority in my voice, and I open the door another few inches. Did we skip his last rabies shot? I put a foot in the house and he gives me a warning growl. Another step and he raises the growl a notch, using it to string together several more barks. He's scared, crouched on the kitchen floor with ears laid back and tail between his legs, and a scared dog is a dangerous dog.

"Does he want a doughnut?" Linnea asks.

"Let's try that." Otherwise the house will be off-limits until Eric gets home. I don't want to think about what we'll have to do if Bear's still freaking out then. Linnea goes to her car. "Hey, buddy. Hey, sweet boy. It's okay, it's just me." My tone is gentle, making his ears prick up and putting a pause to his growling, though his tail stays down. I reach out my hand and the growl returns, lower this time.

Linnea hands me a ball of dough dusted with powdered sugar. I break off a piece and slide it across to the dog. "Here you go, sweet boy." He gives me a suspicious look but tongues it up off the floor; the tip of his tail rises. I keep feeding him bits of doughnut until he lets me come into the room. When I sit at the kitchen table he comes to me, nosing at my hand, where I have the last piece. "I guess we're friends again, huh?"

Linnea steps inside and Bear turns toward her, growling, until she holds out a chunk from another doughnut. Then he likes her too.

"No chocolate, right?" I say, and she nods. She sits next to me and gives him the rest of her doughnut. Once that's gone he flops down on the floor, sighing as if in relief. He's doing his best impression of a rug, but I haven't missed that he's blocking the path to the rest of the house.

"Guard dog, huh?" Linnea says. "This neighborhood must be tougher than it looks."

"I don't know why he's being like this. He's usually totally gentle."

"Lot of weird shit happening today."

"Yeah." I wonder whether Bear's behavior is part of the pattern. If there even is a pattern.

We sit and talk, acting as casual as possible. After a while Bear relaxes enough to drink from his water bowl. He drinks it dry and stays calm when I stand up to refill it. On my way back to the table, I fetch Linnea and myself beers from the fridge. We've earned them.

Bear comes over and lays his head in my lap, fanning his tail back and forth. I don't know if he recognizes me, but he seems to have decided I'm a friend.

"How do you want to handle it when Eric comes home?" Linnea asks.

"I guess I'll just tell him there's something we need to talk about."

She nods. "Direct. That's probably best. Then we can all sit right here and figure this out. It's always possible he's innocent, and he's been noticing things too and didn't want to say anything 'cause you'd think he was losing his mind."

"I wish I could believe that." I take a sip of my beer. It's still three-quarters full, but the alcohol is already unscrewing the tension at the base of my skull. "Thanks for coming back with me. You didn't have to do that."

"Yes, I did."

I let that go. "While we're here, I should see if I can find anything on Eric's computer, if his password matches the one on the thumb drive." I scratch Bear behind the ears, making the movement of his tail speed up a little. "If Bear will let me go downstairs."

"I can babysit Bear. You got anything healthier than a dough-nut for me to give him?"

I find a bag of salmon-flavored dog treats. Bear pulls up into a hopeful sit as soon as he hears the rustle of plastic, following the bag with his eyes as I hand it to Linnea. He plants himself in front of her, looking over only when I take a step toward the stairs. He eyes me as if to say, *Hey, friend, don't rob the house, 'kay?* but he stays put.

I take my phone downstairs with me so I'll know if Eric texts again. No joy on his computer; I should have known he'd be too careful to use the same password for everything. I try a few other configurations, but I'm about to give up and head back upstairs when I receive a notification that someone's trying to send me a file.

It's a zip archive. A text message comes in right after it: It's what we thought. There are more files but these give me enough to go on for now. Will send more when I open more.

I accept the download to my phone and extract three files. When I first opened the flash drive, all the files were named with long strings of random characters; they must have been part of the encryption, because now one is named session.docx and the other two are numbered.

It's what we thought, Peter said, which I take to mean that Eric is responsible for what happened to me. And I'm about to learn exactly how.

Now that I have the answers in my hands—some of them, at least—I'm scared to look.

I take a breath, let it out, and open the first file in the list.

0429.docx

I may as well write up a session sheet. I guess this counts as a testing session. An extremely long-term and definitely unauthorized one, but who knows, maybe my report will be useful to someone, years from now. It's clearer than ever that none of us really knows how reWind works, no matter how much we might think we do. Only gnii knows, if an AI can be said to "know" anything.

I'm still kind of numb. I can't believe I'm actually here, back on Kelly's birthday. Everything looks different from how I remember. Or it looks the same, but it feels different because *I'm* different. I'm 12 years older on the inside.

She said yes. (!!)

I read the file twice, then once more, bits of sense filtering in. My birthday. April 29. The file names are dates.
I'm 12 years older on the inside.
She said yes.
This was written on my seventeenth birthday. The day Eric asked me out, the day my life split into two. That's the day he traveled back to.
He did this on purpose.
Maybe my report will be useful to someone.
Eric's way more deeply involved in gnii than Peter and I thought.

I move on to session.docx.

session.docx

Tester Name: Eric Hyde

Report date: 04/29

Date and time of session start: 04/29–1747

Charter: Attempt to disable reWind's built-in time horizon
restriction by using previously injected code (invoked by the
trigger phrase [REDACTED]). Analyze gnii's ability to
interpret context clues to discern the user's intent and
desires. Test reWind functionality in use cases where
commands do not refer to precise time periods.

Intended behavior:

• When a command is given that does not comply with safety
  restrictions, gnii issues an informative error message.

• When a command is given with insufficient context or no
  explicitly defined destination, gnii requests user to clarify
  command or restate in a way that complies with its schema.

Risks:

• Command may trigger application crash, requiring a hard
  reset of device.

• Jump may be further than intended or to an undesirable destination.

• Jump may cause undesired changes in user's worldline or others.

• Desired changes in worldlines may not be possible.

• Despite unspecified destination, logs may still provide enough information for a pursuer to follow.

Issues:

• Nonspecific temporal destination means less lead time once user arrives at destination; user needs to be fully prepared for whatever action they wish to take.

• Intensity of adverse physical/psychological effects (dizziness, nausea, vomiting) increases with temporal distance traveled. In concert with the previous issue, this makes immediate physically demanding actions difficult. However, the effects may diminish with repeated trips, similar to what we've seen with short jumps.

Notes:

Using the instance of gnii contained in the smart speaker in testing pod 2, I invoked reWind functionality using one of the standard wake words. After using the trigger phrase (REDACTED) to circumvent time horizon restrictions, I issued a deliberately imprecise command ("I want a do-over with Kelly Holter"). Gnii fulfilled the command with no error, putting me at a temporal destination 12 years previous, which was the intended result.

Bugs:

• Discomfort (dizziness, disorientation, nausea, vomiting) is much more pronounced with a longer jump.

• The ability to get around the time restriction is in itself a bug.

• TODO: Note differences in historical events.

• TODO: Monitor for anomalies in current states of reality.

The clinical language knocks me back. It reads as though the disruption of my life was barely a consideration. Maybe it's because the Eric who wrote this, the Eric who worked at gnii, wasn't the same as the one I know. I remember him saying he'd be a different person if we'd never gotten together. The man who wrote this report was the one who'd grown into adulthood without me.

But he didn't want to be. He wanted this, his do-over, so much that he was willing to risk his job and whatever life he'd built for himself. Was it because he wanted to become a better person, or was he obsessed with what might have been? The journal entry, and the report, gives the impression that he'd been building toward this from the day of his failure with me, years before he even knew traveling back was a possibility.

I feel the weight of the forces against me, an implacable will against which my own amounts to no more than water filling the container it's poured into. The monstrous thing is that, as I read the remaining file, I can hear the words in Eric's voice, as if he's reading them to me. As if he's confessing.

0430.docx

Asking Kelly out worked because I'd planned every word. So going forward, I just need to resist the temptation to wing it. Everything will be set. The tickets, my route, where to park, how to get to the restaurant and the theater on foot. That's the easy part.

I've come up with conversation topics, everything from world events to movies (I had to look some of those up), but that's just to head off any awkward silences. I figure if I can get her talking about herself I'll be golden. It was funny seeing her in class today, knowing what I know. I couldn't go into the classroom early to talk to her like I used to. I was too afraid I'd say something to ruin things, or she'd take it back.

I only went to school at all because my parents would keep me home all weekend if I didn't. I forgot what it's like to have other people running your life, but I can't say I miss my "freedom." It hasn't even been 48 hours, and my other life already seems like something that happened to someone else. Good riddance.

It occurs to me that Eric's one of the only people in the world with the same experience as me, a second life in his head. It didn't blindside him, he welcomed it, but he must have had some idea of how disorienting it would be. How afraid it would make me. And he did it anyway.

The feeling of betrayal pushes through me like nausea, and I know I can't stay here.

When I stand a wave of dizziness knocks into my head, splotches of black and chartreuse bursting before my eyes. I lurch through it, upstairs to tell Linnea we're leaving as soon as I can pack the essentials. I want to be gone before Eric comes home.

Bear meets me at the entrance to the kitchen, his tail drawing a lazy arc back and forth. It's the same casually friendly greeting he always gives me when I've been home all day and I come into a room where he is.

Other than the dog, the kitchen is empty. "Linnea?" My voice sounds unnaturally high, on the verge of tears. I call up the stairs to the bedrooms. "Linnea!" No answer. Silence surrounds me like a layer of dust, the silence of an empty house. I run back through the kitchen and open the door that leads to the garage.

My car is still parked there. Linnea's Tesla is gone.

I slam the door, then drag it open again, as if by some magic her car will reappear.

I fumble my phone out of my purse to text her, but she's not in my contacts. The number she called me from isn't in my recent calls. I stare at the screen in confusion for several seconds before it dawns on me. Whatever shifted overnight that let Linnea remember she was my friend, it's shifted back. Or into a different configuration. Which means that whatever's going on hasn't stopped.

Linnea's number isn't in my phone because she never called

me at all. Everything that happened today—the call, the meeting in the doughnut shop, her coming back here with me—happened in another reality, one that, somehow, I no longer inhabit.

Peter said, *We're gonna fix this. Maybe in a few days, you won't remember any of this anymore.* But I do remember, and it fucking hurts.

"No," I moan, choking up. I feel it all over again, the same pain I felt when Linnea opened the door to our studio and I found myself looking into the face of a stranger. But no, this is worse: I'd gotten her back, her friendship and support, someone else who knew and didn't think I was deranged. I had hope, and now it's gone.

A sick dread rises in my throat. I whirl around, run upstairs to my office, and stop in the doorway, staring at the empty spot on the bulletin board where Linnea's sketch was definitely, definitely pinned this morning. The blood drains from my extremities, leaving my fingers cold. It hums in my head like angry bees.

I want to collapse on the floor and sob. I want to scream and kick holes in the walls. But I can't give in to my feelings right now. I need to get out of here before Eric comes home from work.

The sense of urgency propels me down the stairs and through the kitchen, where I stumble over Bear, who whuffs reproachfully and scrambles to his feet. "Stay," I tell him.

I snatch my purse from the table, open the door, and run for my car, just as Eric pulls up in the driveway.

37

MY FIRST INSTINCT IS TO SPRINT PAST ERIC'S CAR. OR BACK INTO the house, out the sliding glass door, through the backyard, and into the woods. But his eyes lock on mine through the windshield, freezing me in place. His expression is blank: he could be anything from terrified to exhausted to indifferent.

Why is he here? It's the middle of the afternoon. He's not supposed to be home yet.

Maybe it isn't Eric's fault that Linnea was snatched away after I'd gotten her back. But even if he didn't cause it directly, he's at the root of it. I look at him and all I can see is everything I've lost.

I think about how I've spent the last week and a half—or the last twelve years, if my second set of memories is the one that's real—soothing and pleasing and fucking and trying as hard as I can to love him. Rage fills me like smoke billowing inside glass.

"What the fuck have you done?" I yell, stomping toward his car. He jumps visibly, his eyes going wide. *"You tell me what you've done!"*

He unbuckles his seat belt, opens the door, and unfolds himself from the driver's seat, his hands reaching out. I step back and he stops short of touching me. "Kelly." His voice is faint.

"You need to calm down. I can't explain anything with you screaming at me."

"Don't fucking tell me to calm down. Where's Linnea?"

His face, already an unhealthy grayish color, goes even paler.

"You know! You know what's going on!" Some faraway part of me notes that I'm crying, sobbing. I should stop that; it makes me sound hysterical.

"Let's go inside and talk about this." He tries to take my arm and I jerk away from him.

"I'm not going anywhere with you."

"Please. Please, I'll tell you everything, let's please just go in the house." He catches my gaze, his eyes huge and dark and pleading. "Kelly, I never wanted to— Everything I did, it was because I loved you. Can you believe that?"

"No, I fucking cannot! You've been lying to me this whole—"

"I don't know what's going on either," he says. "Something's happening, and I don't—I don't know if it's me, if it's something I did, something I set in motion. But I don't know how to stop it." He breaks into a sob at the last part, and something in me breaks too, seeing his face, and some of the anger leaks out of me. He's not evil. He's as scared as I am.

I can hear Bear barking from inside the house, and I wonder if he'll attack us if we try to go in. That's when I realize I've made my decision, at least for now.

"Fine," I say. "I'll go inside with you, if Bear will let us." Eric gives me a questioning look, but I don't bother explaining. "You're going to tell me everything. Everything," and I poke my finger at his chest. Then I pivot and stalk into the garage, not waiting to see if he's behind me.

Bear lets us in. He jumps all over Eric, but in affection.

270

Maybe he's having his own version of a crisis, or he assumes that since Eric is home it's dinnertime, because he won't stop whining and butting up against Eric's legs. Finally Eric gives in and gets his food.

As Eric deals with the dog I notice that my beer bottle and Linnea's, which were sitting on the table earlier, are gone. I look in the fridge and I can't be sure, but I think they're in there, full. I take out one of the bottles, open it, drink.

"I'll have one of those," Eric says from behind me. I hand him a beer. He can open it for himself. I walk past him, to the dining area, and stand at the sliding glass door, staring into the backyard and the woods beyond. He stays on the kitchen side of the room. Doesn't want to spook me, maybe. Doesn't want me trying to run off.

He says heavily, "How long have you known?"

I think about how I want to answer that question, the answers I want to elicit from him. I don't want him thinking he can slip into omissions and half-truths.

"About the time travel?" I say. "Since last night."

He closes his eyes and puts his cold beer to his forehead, then brings it down and takes a long drink. "So that's why you were asking about what if you could live your life over again?"

"It started on my birthday, though."

"I knew it. I knew something was off with you."

I don't like the smug note in his voice. "What was *off* is that my entire fucking life had just been turned upside down. I think I handled it pretty fucking well, considering."

He frowns, and I swear to God, if he says anything about the double f-bombs I will walk straight out of this kitchen, drive away, and never come back. But he just asks, "What do you mean?"

I tell him, briefly.

"Oh," he says, his shoulders sagging as he leans against the counter. "Oh, Kelly. You must have been so . . ."

"Confused? Disoriented? Terrified? Yes, all of those."

"I didn't know it would . . . I had no idea that's how it would be for you. New worldlines are supposed to be transparent to nonobservers."

"What the fuck does that mean? Just tell me what you did."

"It's a long story."

"We've got all night." I motion toward a dining chair.

Eric sits. Bear lays his head in Eric's lap, wagging his tail.

"You remember me trying to ask you out, that one time. On your birthday."

"So that did happen."

"Yes. And then I was so embarrassed I never talked to you again. And you moved to Chicago, and I tried to forget about you, but I couldn't." As Eric talks he strokes the dog's head, plays with his ears. "I knew I was being pathetic. But you have to understand . . . I've never been good at people. Especially girls. Women. There was never anyone else who showed the slightest interest in me. And by my late twenties, I just . . . I'd gone to college, but I was working help desk jobs I hated. I was living in this awful apartment with this awful roommate. I felt stuck. I was lonely. My life was empty, you know?

"Then Peter got me a job back home, here, in Innovation Park. This company called gnii."

"Who made an AI time machine," I say. Eric's head jerks up. "Yeah, I talked to Peter." Which reminds me. "One other question. Have you been keeping track of where I've been going?"

He takes in a sharp breath, like he's going to say something, then presses his lips together. I can see the guilt in his eyes.

"You said you were going to tell me everything," I remind him. "And whenever I go somewhere unexpected, you call or text or show up."

Bear whines at the slackening of Eric's attention, and Eric starts petting him again. Not looking at me, he says, "I, um, installed a GPS tracker on your phone."

My heart sinks. "When?"

"You lied to me," he says, as if that justifies it. "And I was worried about you. That night you disappeared, I was imagining all kinds of . . . I needed to be able to find you, in case something happened."

He hasn't answered my question. He's trying to steer me into the assumption that he installed the tracker after I came back from Chicago, but he still won't look at me. I think it was there before. I think he knows I went to Chicago, which means that since last week, he's known—or should have known—that I remembered at least something of my old life. And he said nothing.

"I wish you would have just said something that first night," he says. "I could have helped you, explained things to you."

"I was afraid you'd think I was crazy. If you could tell something was off with me, why didn't you come clean?"

"I don't know. I guess I was afraid of being wrong. I shouldn't have installed the tracker without asking you. I'm sorry."

His apology, inelegant as it is, seems sincere. And there's still a lot more I need to know. I take the chair next to his, setting my beer on the table. "So, back to the time machine," I say, the words sounding laughable.

"I'm surprised Peter told you about it."

"I had to hound him for a few days. That's where I went most of the time, by the way, to meet Peter. He was skittish about talking to me."

Eric nods. "I could see him being nervous. He'd be violating his NDA. Some places aren't so serious about secrecy, but gnii definitely is. It's kind of like a cult."

"It was like that when you worked there?"

"Definitely. Complete with the narcissistic dictator." His face darkens.

How Eric felt about his boss isn't my concern. "So, you get a job at gnii. And what, on your first day they show you around the office like, 'Here's the coffee maker, here's the time machine'?"

He shakes his head. "I wasn't working on reWind at first. That was kind of a need-to-know thing. They had me doing quality assurance, user testing, on the digital-assistant functionality. It was a lot more interesting than the work I'd been doing before. I actually got to use my brain, and the people I worked with were nice. My parents were happy I was living close by again.

"And then Peter brought me onto his team. They were starting to do QA on reWind. He thought he was doing me a favor." Eric picks up his beer like he's going to take a drink but then sets it back down and starts drawing his fingernail down the bottle, leaving streaks in the condensation.

I've finished mine already, but I still feel perfectly clear-headed.

Eric's gone silent. "Go on," I prompt him.

He makes a move like he's reaching for my hand. I pull it away, into my lap.

"Have you ever wanted something really badly?" he says. "Like, okay, if I can just have this one thing, then I'll be happy forever, I'll never ask for anything else." His hand is still half-extended across the table, as though he's forgotten it belongs to him.

"Yeah, that's how I felt about going to art school."

He flinches, obviously wounded. I don't care. Except I do. His pain distresses me, no matter how much I try not to let it.

"Just tell me," I say.

"I'd spent the last twelve years thinking that if I just had another chance to ask you out, if I could just do that one thing over, then my whole life would be different. Better. This is going to sound really creepy, but I used to look at pictures you'd posted online, of you hanging out with your friends, and pretend I'd been there with you. Like I was just outside the frame, or I'd gone to get you a drink or something right before they took the picture. Like I'd been in your life the whole time.

"And then I start working with a time machine."

He stops. Letting that sink in, I guess. I pick up his beer, which is still mostly full, and make eye contact. He motions acquiescence, and I drink off a third of it in one go. Still feeling clear and sharp. Still no cushioning numbness.

"Part of the problem was that reWind wouldn't do what I needed it to. You could only make short runs, no more than a couple minutes. It was a fail-safe. But I started tinkering around, writing test scripts but really trying to see if there was a way I could build in a backdoor, make it so I could make a longer jump. Part of my job was penetration testing, making sure the app was secure, so it was easy to justify if anyone asked. But I never documented my backdoor code. I just included it without telling anyone. I didn't even know if it would work. That was the other thing: I was scared I'd end up somewhere else, somewhere I didn't want to be. I couldn't use a specific date and time as my destination, in case someone read the logs and decided to follow me, so it was a real possibility."

I get the impression that he's enjoying drawing out the story. He's never been able to talk about this with anyone, not even Peter, and it must be a relief to unburden himself. "Apparently it worked just fine, though," I say. "How did you get it to do that?" I consider telling him I've read his report and his journals, or whatever they are, but decide against it. Let me be the one to withhold information for once.

"I told it what I wanted to do, and it chose a destination that worked. Weak AI wouldn't be able to do that; it's too limited. But gnii, it can understand goals, it can problem solve. So I arrived on your birthday, a few minutes before I'd tried to ask you out the first time. I probably could have used a little more lead time, but then again I might have chickened out if I'd had time to think about it. So maybe gnii knew what it was doing.

"And this time you said yes, and here we are." He gestures around our kitchen.

"It's not that simple, though. My best friend from Chicago was here earlier. She remembered me. And then, all of a sudden, she was gone, and it was like she'd never been here at all. Her number's not in my phone anymore . . ." My voice rises, thinning out. If I don't stop talking I'm going to cry, so I shut up.

Eric looks at me like he's having a hard time not pulling me into his arms. And part of me wants his comfort, wants him to tell me everything's okay, even if it's a lie. A larger part can't stand the thought of him touching me.

"I think she's probably okay," he says. "If she was here, and then she wasn't, something must have happened that sent her back to her other timeline. We already know something's been screwed up. And that you remember things from different . . . from the other timeline. Linnea could be part of that."

"So she doesn't remember me anymore." I thought that might be the case, but it's dispiriting to say it aloud.

Eric doesn't answer, just sits there fidgeting.

I drink the rest of his beer. It's warm now, and it leaves a thick, sour taste in the back of my throat, but the numbness is starting to kick in. Or maybe it's just grief.

"Your backdoor," I say. "How did no one else figure that out? You worked in a company full of smart people. Not one of them thought of trying to travel back far enough to make some good stock picks?"

"I've wondered that myself. I don't know. We were still pretty early in development, as far as reWind went. Only a few people had access to it, and most of the ones who did were the kind of people who were in tech because they wanted to make the world a better place. The developers were trying to figure out why the AI had put in a fail-safe, but not so they could misuse the software. They were curious about it, but they were pretty sure there was a reason. Probably someone would have figured a way around it eventually.

"Sometimes I wonder if Peter put me on his team because of that. Like, not consciously . . . or maybe it was consciously. He knew I was still hung up on you. He knew I had regrets."

"Everyone has regrets. If you don't you're either an asshole or you're lying to yourself."

Eric half smiles. "But he knew I'd be motivated to push the boundaries, once I found out what gnii could do. Maybe he wanted them pushed. He just didn't want to be the one to do it."

"Boundaries." I force air through my teeth. "You act like you were all so principled, but you didn't even think about how any of this would affect the people outside your little bubble."

"No, we did. That's why we did so much testing—"

"I had a life, you know. It wasn't perfect, but I liked it. I had work, I had friends, people I cared about—" It hits me again, that Linnea's gone from my life, and the emptiness inside me is too big for me to cry. "You took all of that away," I choke out.

Eric looks stunned. "I, uh, I never . . ."

"You never thought of it that way? Yeah, you wouldn't, would you?"

"I just . . . I've been in love with you since seventh grade."

"You weren't in love with me, you barely knew me. You were in love with your idea of me." He opens his mouth to protest, but I roll right over him. "You thought being with me would make you into the person you wanted to be."

His eyes fall to his lap. "You don't understand."

"You've got that right."

"The way my life had gone, I couldn't see any way to fix it from where I was. And what you're saying about me not knowing you . . . that might have been true before, but not anymore. I know you now, I love you now. The real you."

"This isn't the real me! I never wanted this!" I sweep a hand to indicate him, being married, this life. It's somehow worse that he did what he did out of sincere regard for me, with no ill intent. That he manipulated events so he could have me.

"Then I'll make it up to you," he says. Before I can stop him he lurches forward in his chair and takes my hands in his. "Tell me how I can make it up to you, and I'll spend the rest of my life doing it."

I stare at him, too shocked to pull away. I can't even begin to explain to him how wrong he is. Does he think I'm going to give him the chance? Does he actually believe I'll stay with him?

"I should have been honest with you from the beginning. I know that now," he says.

"You mean you should have told me you were a time traveler when we were still in high school?" The idea makes me laugh.

One of his dimples makes an appearance in response. "I should have figured out some way to tell you. It's just . . . Kelly, you don't know how much of a relief it is to have you know." His thumbs stroke mine, his hands warm, the touch relaxing me despite myself. The sound of his saying my name, the intensity of his gaze, these things still have their power.

"Well, I'm glad you're relieved."

My sarcasm makes him dial his energy back a few notches. "I know it's going to take a lot for you to trust me again. But I promise you, whatever you need. What can I do?"

His eyes are as wide and earnest as they were the day he asked me out. A possibility wakes in me.

Help me go back to the beginning. Help me start over.

I can't get my life back, but I might be able to rebuild it. I could go back to before I turned down the scholarship and let all my dreams slip away.

Help me start over without you.

38

I IMAGINE SAYING IT, SNUFFING OUT THE LIGHT IN ERIC'S EYES.
How would he react? I remember what Ruby said at my birthday party: *He'd do anything you wanted.*

Not this.

But: nothing ventured, nothing gained. I say, "What if I
wanted to go back to when we were in high school?"

He drops my hands, and I feel the absence of his touch. He
leans back, frowning, but it's a thinking frown, not a hurt-
feelings frown. "It's possible. But we'd have to get access to a
device with the app and the reWind add-on installed on it, and
security's pretty tight at gnii."

I picture myself and Eric hiding behind the coffee cart at Innovation Park, waiting for some hapless nerd to walk by, then
knocking them on the head and stealing their entry badge.

"Plus reWind's not even working," he adds.

"Peter told me. How does he know that's your fault?"

"When he called, he said they were getting error messages
that implicate me. So even if we can get our hands on an instance of gnii, it'll be tricky to get a jump going. But Peter doesn't
know my trigger phrase . . ." Eric's in his own world, drumming
his fingers on the tabletop. "Yeah. Yeah, we could try using that.

Maybe Peter will give us access if I tell him I'll help him troubleshoot. Though that wouldn't explain why you'd need to be there."

It doesn't escape me that Eric seems unfazed by the prospect of lying to his best friend.

"Would your . . ." I grope for the term he used. "Would your backdoor code still be there?"

"Yeah, it persists across timelines."

"It does? How do you know?"

"I . . . well, I mean . . ." He gets flustered, but only for a second. "Gnii can send code to past versions of itself. I assume it's broken because of something in my code."

What he says sounds plausible enough, or at least as if he believes it, but it raises a mutter in the back of my mind. I don't know if I'm being paranoid, or if the sense that I need to keep my guard up and my eyes open is based on information my subconscious is taking in. It doesn't feel good or healthy.

I stand, shaking off the feeling. "So let's go."

"What, now?" He looks startled.

"Yes, now. When else?"

He shakes his head. "We're not going to be able to walk right into the lab. I thought we could wait until morning and go to Peter's house before he goes to work. He never goes in before ten."

"When I saw him he looked like he'd been sleeping at the office. We might not catch him at home. Besides, if security's that tight, is he going to be able to smuggle out a device with gnii installed on it?"

Eric's shoulders sag. "Probably not."

"So we have to go to the lab."

"But we can't just charge in there before we figure out what we're going to do."

"What's to figure out? We head for the nearest smart speaker and I tell it to send me back to my seventeenth birthday. Seems simple enough."

"But it's not that simple. Remember, reWind's broken. All of gnii is broken. Peter said it's been throwing errors on everything except the simplest commands."

"So we use your thingy, your trigger phrase."

Eric's getting more and more agitated. "But we don't know for sure if that'll work! I've never seen this happen before, where the entire app is having issues. The whole configuration could be different. There's too much we don't know, and when we make our move it'll need to be fast, so no one can realize what we're doing and stop us."

"You're stalling," I accuse.

"I'm not. I swear I'm not."

I grab my phone out of my bag. "Then you won't mind if I text Peter and tell him we're coming."

"Wait," Eric says. "If we go rushing off to gnii and we get stopped at the door, or we can't get reWind to work, then you'll be worse off than you are now. You'll be stuck."

I lower my phone. He has a point.

"Let me talk to him first," Eric says.

"Fine." I still don't trust him completely, but I appreciate that he's trying to spot pitfalls. Especially when he could let me blunder into them and be forced to remain here with him. "But I'm not waiting until morning."

My stomach chooses that moment to growl, loudly.

Eric smiles. "Can you wait until after dinner?"

I haven't had anything all day except two beers, half a dough-nut, and a bitter cup of coffee—and the doughnut and coffee might have been in a parallel universe. I'm starving. I nod.

In my hand, my phone makes its incoming-message chirp. In the instant before I look at my screen I'm full of the possibility that somehow it will be Linnea, that she'll have remembered me again. It's almost a disappointment to see the number Peter's been texting me from on the screen. No message this time, just another zip archive. More decrypted files.

"Who's that?" Eric asks, with just enough tension in his voice to make it more than an idle question.

I don't have a specific reason for not mentioning the flash drive to Eric, except that I feel the need to keep something in reserve. "Just my dad, telling me how my mom's day is going."

He's watching me with a tiny smile, a sardonic expression that looks out of place on him. "So . . . how's your mom's day going?"

I accept the download, then darken my screen. "She's feeling good. Up and around."

"That's great. That's really great." Eric's eyes find mine, and I wonder if he remembers how sick she was in the other . . . what did he call it? Worldline. He starts swiping through the delivery app on his phone. "What do you feel like eating?"

"We've got food, we might as well cook. We shouldn't let it go to waste." As soon as I say that I realize how silly it is. If things go the way we want, the produce in our refrigerator will never go bad. Those specific vegetables might never even come into exis-tence.

But Eric agrees. Maybe he wants to do something, anything, other than talk.

There's chicken and leftover rice in the freezer, so we start on a quick stir-fry. We fall into complementary roles, Eric chopping while I heat up the skillet. Other than the night we grilled last weekend, when he was mostly outside, I haven't cooked alongside him except in memory. I'm surprised by how comfortable it is, how routine. Each of us knows how to vacate the spaces where the other needs to be just at the right time. We touch each other without fanfare: Eric's hand grazes my shoulder to let me know he's behind me, I grasp him by both sides of his waist to cue him to move to the side. It feels seamless. It feels *married*.

I could tell myself I'm playing a part to get what I need from him, but I don't think that's completely true. This isn't nothing, this relationship. It's another thing I'll be losing, and part of me is sorry.

I've just turned off the burner when I sense Eric behind me. His hand brushes my back and it reminds me of my birthday party, how alarming it was when he slid his arm around my waist. But this time his touch is tentative, seeking permission. And the vulnerability he's shown me this afternoon has softened me toward him, rejuvenated the strange bond we have. I lean into him.

His arms settle around my waist, his chin resting on my shoulder. Next to my ear he says, "I don't know what's going to happen." Does he mean tonight, or after we succeed? When we're teenagers again?

"I don't either." I set down the spatula and rest my hands on top of his. *Married*.

"Are you sure about this?"

I stiffen. "You promised you'd help me."

"I will, it's just . . ." He pauses for so long that I squeeze his hands to prompt him. "You think everything'll be smooth sailing, because you know the future. But it's not always easy being the one who remembers."

A heavy silence falls between us. I feel an urge toward honesty: I should warn him it might not turn out how he wants. If this works, when I arrive, he'll have just traveled back from a different future, all hyped up to ask me out. He must know it's possible I won't say yes. That we'll be working at cross-purposes.

Or maybe he doesn't know, or won't allow himself to believe it, and if I speak it out loud he'll refuse to help me.

"I didn't think it would be so soon," he says, in barely more than a whisper. He could be talking to himself. His arms tighten around my waist, and he kisses the place where my neck meets my shoulder before letting me go. When he steps away, I miss his warmth.

We eat, not talking much. I'm mulling over what could be in the files Peter sent to my phone. It might confirm or expand on what Eric has told me, or it might contradict it. Either way, it's information I need, but I can't read the files in front of Eric.

He seems lost in thought as well. Our bowls are nearly empty before it occurs to me that I should have been trying to distract him, that he might be wondering what my plans are once I've arrived in the past. Whether they include him or not.

He takes my bowl to the sink and washes the dishes, even the ones that could go in the dishwasher. Maybe he feels the same reluctance I do to leave things half-done. Or he's trying to stretch out the time until he has to talk to Peter and make this real. I wipe the table, the countertops. I feel like I should be packing, but there's nothing to take with us. Nothing except the memories inside my head.

I watch Eric, the intentness and care with which he attends

to his task. A wave of nostalgia slaps into me, and I recognize again that some part of me will miss this once it's gone.

Maybe I will say yes when he asks me out. Something tells me I'll get only one chance; if I refuse him, he'll skulk away and never talk to me again, just like he did the first time. But if I say yes—

I could tell him the truth. We could walk into this with our eyes open.

The question is whether I can forgive him for something he'll have only just started doing. He'll have set it in motion, the theft of my life, but he won't have carried it out fully. Maybe I can stop him. Maybe we could make what we have into something worth keeping.

I can't help but wonder why he's so willing to help me. Does he feel genuine remorse for what he did? Is he really so unselfish as to risk losing even the memory of having me? One wrong word from me will pluck the linchpin from the plan he spent years making. He constructed his whole life around me. Or his idea of me.

Another possibility: he can't conceive of my telling him no because, on some level, he can't conceive of me as a human being with my own will, a will that might oppose his. He's counting on my acceptance of him. That's the only reason I can think of that he'd be on board.

He feels me watching him and glances over. The ends of his mouth curve upward, but his eyes are so solemn it doesn't register as a smile. He turns off the water and carefully places the clean skillet upside down in the drainer, carefully wipes behind the sink.

Outside the window the sun sinks behind the woods, the shadows of trees reaching across the backyard.

I give Eric the kitchen so he can talk to Peter, though really I want privacy to read my new files. I go upstairs to my office, leaving the door cracked so I can hear when Eric finishes his phone call. The fact that he's calling Peter rather than messaging him is a good sign, an indication that he's taking this seriously. He wants to nail things down right away, rather than waiting for Peter's answer.

The archive, when I extract it, contains four files. Two are dated—0315.docx, 0315-2.docx—but there's also a session2.docx and a session3.docx.

Why are there more session reports?

My body knows the truth before I do. My heart speeds up and a wave of adrenaline rises in me, like I'm a rabbit that's just realized it's being hunted. My hands shake, so I have to tap the screen several times before session2.docx will open.

This report is written in the same clinical style as the first. Eric lays out goals, risks, issues, effects; he expresses mild surprise that long-term jumps are still possible and proposes that gnii sent his backdoor code to a past version of itself. He notes that, as before, an imprecise command results in very little lead time to put a plan into action, and he theorizes that this is gnii's way of minimizing "collateral disruption," whatever that means.

It takes multiple scrolls through the file for me to take in any information at all. Mostly I'm just running my eyes over it, individual words and phrases jumping out but failing to come together into a coherent whole. Then, on the third or fifth or fourteenth pass, a single line buried in the middle of the file under the "Risks" section stabs straight into my brain:

—Kelly will find out what I did.

And I can't read any more.

I set my phone on the desk, gently, as if it will be startled and bite me if I move it too suddenly. I haven't darkened the screen, so Eric's words glare up at me. I can't look away from them.

He went back more than once. He was worried I'd find out. He knew what he was doing was wrong, but he did it anyway.

And there's a third session report.

After a minute, my screen winks out, the words *Kelly will find out what I did* winking out with it.

The sound of Eric's voice, drifting upstairs, filters into my consciousness. It's odd—shocking—to hear him sound so normal. Nothing has changed for him since I came upstairs. The one tiny platform remaining under him hasn't crumbled away. But his voice is louder than it was before—not like he's arguing, but like he and Peter are winding up their conversation. They've almost finished making their plan: the same plan, I realize, that Eric has probably had in mind since I started yelling at him in the driveway, if not before. The plan he's carried out at least three times now.

And when he's done talking, he'll come upstairs to collect me.

I feel flattened, like I don't have the capacity for shock anymore. My brain has become an information-gathering machine rather than a living organ that feels emotions. And right now, I need as much information as I can get. I don't think I can stomach that third session report, so I open the later of the two dated files.

0315-2.docx

Since Kelly left me, I've spent a lot of time thinking about the word she used. "Manipulative." OK, so maybe accessing her

288

account and withdrawing her art school application wasn't the most ethical thing I could have done, but manipulative? No. That makes it sound like I was just playing with her. Which couldn't be further from the truth.

I won't lie, it hurt that she found me so unnecessary she could choose art school over me. I was still working out my resentment, maybe, and exercising that power felt good. (If I had a therapist, they'd be proud of me for this breakthrough. Ha.) But it gave me an idea. Instead of doing what the old Eric would do, the clumsy, socially inept, "manipulative" Eric, this time I'll try a different approach. I'll be necessary. I'll be such a perfect boyfriend that she can't imagine life without me. I can't believe it took me this long to come up with it. Oh well, third time's the charm. Right?

THE ARROGANCE OF him. The entitlement. Apparently I hadn't discovered the big secret, but the smaller one was enough to make me leave him. So he thought he'd scrape off the canvas and start over. I feel an echo of the same righteous rage that must have risen up in that other Kelly before she stormed out. But then Eric clears his throat, too close, right outside the door, and I slam it down.

Getting mad at him won't do me any good. It never has before.

I slip my phone into my pocket as he steps into the room and says, "Peter's on board. He's waiting, he's going to let us in." His voice has a buoyant note, with no hint of the defeat I heard earlier. He's excited. Hyping himself up.

"Does he know what you're planning?" A slip: I should have said *we.* How many times has Peter helped him do this? He wouldn't remember, any more than me. Except I do: those flashes of déjà vu, so strong they were like hallucinations.

"He's worried," Eric says. "Now that they know for sure that long-term jumps are possible, his boss is all fired up to make them himself. *Optimize his life* were the words he used. Apparently."

So gnii's CEO is planning to make the prescient stock picks. "You could basically become immortal," I say, marveling at how calm I sound. "Keep going back over and over. Stay young forever."

Eric's brow furrows like that never occurred to him. Of course not: his vision's never been so grandiose. "That sounds like something he'd come up with." Dislike, so strong it borders on disgust, ripples over Eric's face. "He's not a good person. He doesn't care about anyone but himself. He definitely won't worry about keeping the timeline stable."

My eyes are pulled to the bare spot on the bulletin board where Linnea's sketch should be.

Eric goes on. "So Peter wants me to go back far enough that it won't matter. Go around the problem, basically."

I don't point out Eric's slip, that he said *me* instead of *us* or *you.*

"Why hasn't Peter done it?" I ask. "If he's so worried."

"He doesn't have access to my backdoor, and he hasn't been able to program a working one yet. Plus, like I said, it's hard being the one who remembers."

A text message comes in on my phone. It's from Peter. You're way more understanding than I would be, is all I'm saying.

"What's that?" Eric asks, his voice mild, as if he doesn't really care about the answer.

290

Peter thinks I've read all the files and I'm okay with what Eric's done, what he's planning to do again. Or he's telling himself I'm okay with it. What would he choose to do if he knew I wasn't? Which one of us would he help?

My thumb hovers over my screen, ready to reply, then moves to tap the power button and put the phone to sleep. I don't trust Peter that much.

There's another way. If I go into the lab with Eric, I can look and listen while he fixes whatever's wrong with gnii. Find out what his trigger phrase is and use it before he can. In order to pull that off, I have to keep Eric from seeing I'm onto him.

"Peter," I say. "He says thanks for convincing you to help."

Eric laughs, and I take a second to mourn our brief alliance. He glances around, his gaze catching on my darkened monitor. "What were you doing up here, anyway?"

"Just taking a last look around."

He looks at me, and I wonder what he's seeing. After a moment he says, "It'll all be here for you."

I feel like I can't breathe, but I manage a smile. "I know."

39

ON OUR WAY DOWNSTAIRS, ERIC PEELS OFF INTO THE BATH-room, saying, "I let Bear out, can you let him back in?" I nod wordlessly, not trusting my voice.

The sun has nearly set, sending streaks of pink and orange across the sky. As I walk through the kitchen the light switches on, making my reflection in the sliding glass door jump out at me. "Lights off," I bark, then peer outside, looking for Bear. Something seems to ripple in the air, a wind that doesn't move the trees. I hear Eric's steps on the stairs and start to say, *Did you feel that?*

Then I shut my mouth. Better to stay quiet, still, watchful. I don't turn as Eric comes into the kitchen. The refrigerator's voice makes me jump. "Your water filter is expired," it says pleasantly. "Would you like me to order a replacement?" Eric's filling two water bottles, as if we're heading out on a hike. "Would you like me to order a replacement? Would you like me to—"

"No, thank you," Eric says.

"I thought we turned that off."

"I thought so too. A glitch, I guess. Everything's made to break after a couple of years now."

I open the slider and call Bear. He doesn't come. I squint out into the yard; it's growing darker, but I can still see to the fence line. I don't see the dog anywhere. Trying to ignore the quiver deep in my stomach, I step outside. "I think Bear got out."

"What?"

"I'm going to go look for Bear."

I walk farther into the yard, calling, through a drifting constellation of fireflies. Something that sounds larger than a squirrel rustles in the trees beyond the fence, but no big dumb dog comes bounding up.

"Bear! Come!" At the fence, I peer into the woods. They're not a park, officially; the trail is maintained by volunteers. The trees are packed tight, saplings and underbrush crowding mature oaks and maples and elms. Probably a fair amount of poison ivy too.

I turn on my phone's flashlight, but that just throws everything outside its beam into greater darkness. Muttering a curse, I pocket the phone, grab the rail of the fence, and thrust my sneakered toe into one of the chain links. There's a gate but it's locked, with a padlock we don't have the key to.

How the hell did Bear get out? He's not a jumper. Or he never has been before.

It's been a long time since I climbed a fence. Kids climb fences, and criminals, and I'm neither. Thumping down on the other side, I realize belatedly that it doesn't matter where Bear is. Or it won't, where Eric and I are going.

But I don't feel right leaving him out here. I pick my way toward the trail, using my hands to balance against trunks, the ground soft and uneven under my feet. Thin branches whip my face and clutch at my hair and clothes. Finally I break through onto the trail, which is murky with shadows. It's too dark to walk without a light, so I take out my phone again. Its beam conjures different, sharper shadows just outside of my path. The fireflies are in here too, floating sparks in the tunnel of trees. They catch at bits of my attention, fading as soon as I focus on them.

I walk down the trail toward the main road, since that direction holds more interest—and danger—for a wandering dog. I forgot to bring the leash. After a couple of minutes I stop calling, stop walking, and listen. The woods at twilight are *loud*. Crickets, the rustlings of small animals finding food or sleeping places, diurnal birds twittering as they settle in for the night. An owl squawks its hollow cry and I tense, like any creature caught out where it shouldn't be.

When I start to walk again I'm conscious of how much noise I'm making, the crackle and thud of my footsteps, the sawing of my breath. I feel like an intruder. I need to find my dog and get out of these woods. "Bear! Where are you?"

"Everything okay?"

The voice comes from behind me, too close. I jump around in a circle, my feet leaving the ground and landing in something approximating a defensive stance. Light blinds me, coming from a source held at my eye level.

I angle my phone upward. And see, bleached white in overexposed brilliance, Adam Rowley's face.

All the tension runs out of my body at once, leaving me shaky. "Holy fuck, you scared me." I lower the hand holding my phone and shadows bounce off the trail, through the trees.

"Didn't mean to." He steps closer, looking around. "Did your dog get out?"

"Yeah. I don't know how. He's not normally, like, a Houdini dog." I laugh nervously, my heart still pounding.

Adam beams his light into the woods, and I notice he's not using a phone, but the LED on his smartwatch. "I'll help you look for him."

I'm about to say something polite and inane like *Oh, you don't have to do that,* then realize I actually could use his help. Plus it's a lot less creepy running around the woods in the dark when you've got a partner. "I can't figure it out. There's no way out of the backyard, but I haven't seen him at all since Eric let him out."

"You think he came back here?"

"I thought he did." But now I can't remember what my reasoning was, or if I even used any. If Bear found a way out, he'd be just as likely to nose into one of the neighbors' yards, or the street. Something drew me here. "Maybe I heard you walking and thought it was him."

"Yeah, maybe." Adam shifts his light around, inadvertently blinding me again. "Sorry," he says, when I shade my eyes. He's wearing a dark shirt and pants, and in the gloom his face looks ghostly, disembodied, his hair a gleam of antique brass.

"I don't know where he could have gone." I hear my voice waver. Until now I thought I was just looking for my escaped dog, but now I realize I didn't think that at all, not underneath. I knew all along that he didn't escape. He was never there.

That ripple, that wind.

I don't know what's happening.

"What's going on?" I turn and look at Adam. He's shining his light in my eyes again. When I raise my hand to block it, he reaches out and grabs my wrist. He pulls me toward him, dragging me back down the trail. His hand is strong and, I notice, gloved. It encircles my wrist completely. I can't get away. "What are you doing?"

He pushes my back against a tree, covering my mouth with his other hand, and I feel that hallucinatory sense of déjà vu, stronger than ever. "Be quiet," he says, his voice pitched low in a way that plucks at my memory. We've been here before, me and him, in this exact position. But it was different last time.

I struggle and he shoves my head backward, my skull cracking against the tree trunk. His hand covers my nose along with my mouth. "Stop it," he hisses, as chartreuse worms begin to squirm around the edges of my vision. I stop. The hand falls from my face but I still have to fight for breath as he pulls me stumbling along the path again. I look back, almost hoping for a glimpse of Bear coming to my rescue like Eric always thought he would in a situation like this. I dropped my phone back there and I can see its LED, shining up into the trees like a searchlight. It's the only light in the woods; Adam turned his off.

Eric, I think disjointedly, would not like this at all. He would definitely not allow this to continue.

Eric took my life away. Kept taking it. But just the same, the impulse to scream his name rises in me. If I could only get enough air. *You're panicking,* says the voice in the back of my brain, sounding detached and slightly contemptuous. *You'll never think of a way out of this if you don't calm the fuck down.*

I concentrate on my feet, on not tripping and falling, because Adam seems like he'd keep dragging my inert body by the arm. It helps to focus my attention on that one point. Don't fall. After a few moments I'm still panting, my breath ragged, but I'm getting enough oxygen that I don't feel like I'm about to pass out. We must be almost back behind my house by now. I can't tell for sure, it's gotten so dark, but Adam slows down. I open my mouth and drag in a breath to scream.

Light stabs through the trees. "Kelly?"

Adam changes position so fast I don't perceive the actual movement, only that he's now behind me. One steel-banded arm, the hand clamped over my mouth, holds me tight against him. His other hand pushes something hard and cold to my temple.

I blink, bathed in the glare from Eric's phone. Against my back I can feel Adam's chest rise and fall with his breathing, fast but controlled. The grotesque intimacy of it sends a shiver of disgust through me, and another wave of déjà vu. He lowers his chin a notch and says, "Turn that light off."

The light douses. Belatedly, I realize what has inspired such instant obedience. I stop trying to move at all.

"We're going in your house," Adam says.

"Yeah, okay." Eric's voice is flat with fear. His breath shakes. "Don't—"

"I don't want to shoot her out here. I won't, unless you make me."

"No." Eric's feet crackle in the underbrush as he turns and picks his way back toward our fence. Adam nudges me forward. Even though I understand the gun is still aimed at me, it's a relief not to have it pressed to my head.

Branches whip me in the face, worse this time since I can't see to avoid them. The ground sinks under me unexpectedly, making me stagger. I could fall, or pretend to, and try to crawl away and hide. But there's no guarantee I could move fast enough. Adam would shoot me like a dog. And even if he missed, Eric's right in front of us. Something tells me that even in the dark, he wouldn't miss a second time.

Or the first, for that matter.

"The gate doesn't open," I say when we reach the yard.

"Eric, you climb the fence first, then Kelly. I used to be Special Forces, and I've got pretty good night vision, so think about that."

Eric stops, half turning. "It *is* you."

Adam just snorts.

"Who are you?" I ask him.

"We'll talk inside. Climb the fence."

I manage to scramble over. Adam follows in what sounds like a single vaulting bound, too quick for us to think about fleeing. Besides, there's nowhere to go except into the house. Adam lets us walk in front of him, but I can feel the eye of that gun on my back the whole time.

As we enter the house, I half expect Bear to be bounding around our legs. The fact that he's not feels like a grievous loss. "Do you know where my dog went?" I ask when the slider is closed and locked behind us.

"Close the blinds and sit down," Adam orders. As Eric and I comply he moves around the kitchen, peering through the doorways into the living room and foyer. He locks the door going out to the garage. Then he says, "Hello, gnii. Call Diane, secure."

"What's up?" says a voice from Adam's watch a few seconds later.

"Good evening, my love. The Hydes have invited us over for dinner. Can you make it?"

"Be right over," she says, then adds, "Boss."

Adam smiles fondly. "She loves it," he says. Seeing that easy smile on his face, the same one he's given me numerous times while we've been running, plants a strange feeling in me. It's almost worse to see him acting like a human.

And then it catches up to me, the wake words he used for his watch. "You work at gnii."

He smiles as if what I've said amuses him. "I do, yeah."

"He's the CEO," Eric says.

"What? He's our neighbor. He just moved in across the street." I'm going over my interactions with Adam in my head, and none of them track with what I've heard about gnii's founder. Adam Rowley is open and friendly, with a self-deprecating sense of humor and a weakness for bad music. He can't be the borderline sociopathic leader of a tech company. And that's when it crystallizes for me: our friendship, which despite its newness has given me the most uncomplicated comfort I've had in this place, isn't real. The person Adam's shown me isn't real. I don't know what his reasons might be for renting a house in our neighborhood and posing as my friend, but Eric, scowling at him across the table, obviously has some idea.

His smile widens, sparkling in his eyes. "Yeah, we've been here about a week now. Isn't that right, Kel?"

Eric flinches, nostrils flaring like he's about to start breathing fire. His hands clench into fists. "Don't call her that."

Adam raises one eyebrow, the same side of his mouth quirking like the brow is pulling it up. "Easy, tiger, you act like I'm fucking her or something."

Gun or no, Eric looks ready to come up out of his chair, but right then the doorbell rings. I brace for Bear's announcing bark before I remember it's not coming.

"Are you going to get the door?" Adam asks me. I get up, moving slowly to disguise the fact that my legs are trembling. He follows me into the foyer with the gun. It's his wife, or rather his backup. Diane is dressed similarly to him in black jeans and a long-sleeve black T-shirt. No gloves, however. She doesn't bother with a greeting. "What we got?" she asks Adam, looking past me.

"Hyde's in the kitchen. He hasn't given me any trouble so far." Adam lays a hand on my shoulder and I stifle a gasp. "Dog is in the unknown zone."

Diane bustles past me into the kitchen, removing a handgun from a holster at the small of her back, underneath her shirt. She doesn't glance at Adam, or smile at him, or do anything that suggests they have an intimate relationship, and it clicks: her aloofness with me was never awkwardness. It was indifference. She was doing a job.

We follow her. "So, what are you," I ask, "his henchperson?"

She glances at me over her shoulder. "I handle security. In various capacities. You and your husband violating that security is why I'm here." She doesn't look overjoyed to have been taken away from whatever she was doing.

In the kitchen, Adam has me sit back down at the table by Eric. "What's the unknown zone?" I ask.

"Just a little joke between colleagues." He smiles at Diane, who has taken up a position between the door to the garage and the archway into the living room, where she can keep an eye on both me and Eric. Diane doesn't smile back. Her lip curls, subtly, as soon as he looks away.

I feel the same, but I can't say I'm sympathetic. "Where's my dog, Adam?"

"That's not his name," Eric says.

"Let's stick with it, though." Adam turns to me. "Your dog . . . I'm not sure. I was doing some testing earlier." He holds up his left hand, rotating it to display the smartwatch on his wrist. "I fully admit I might have broken some things." The boyish smile lights up his face again.

"You killed my fucking dog?"

The smile disappears. "I did not."

"You just wiped him out of existence," Eric says. "Be honest."

"That's not true. He could still exist, but somewhere else." Adam sits across from me and Eric, doing the douchebag thing where he turns the chair around and spreads his legs over it. Or maybe it's tactical: he doesn't want to be boxed in at the table. "Besides, you don't have much room to talk about being honest, Eric H. That is you, right? Username 'Eric underscore H'?"

Eric draws in a breath, then seems to think better of speaking.

"Don't try to deny it. You've been all over gnii's error logs since the Friday before last." Which means Adam's known about Eric's involvement since my birthday, since I arrived in this life. He moved into my neighborhood and befriended me purely to get to Eric. I think of the sheet hung in his and Diane's front window instead of curtains; they never meant to be there for long. If there hadn't happened to be a vacant house across the street, he would have found another way. The sense of disillusionment shouldn't sting so much, but it does.

"Plus I've read your session reports," Adam adds.

Eric flushes. His eyes shift to me, then away. My stomach churns, threatening to evict the stir-fry, and not only in fear of what violence Adam and Diane might do. It's because of me, because I gave Peter that flash drive, that Eric's being called to account.

"And the journals," Adam goes on. "Those were actually pretty informative. I might have my devs start taking more free-form notes when they do session-based testing, so thanks for that example. But they didn't tell me what I really wanted to know, which was how—"

"There's no way you could have read those," Eric breaks in.

"Where did you get them?" His voice is hushed with nerves, but calm, curious even, which sweeps away any compunction I might feel about being part of his downfall. In fact, the idea that he might never know angers me. Adam has the power to take Eric's life, but he won't make him feel his crime like I would.

"He got them from me."

Eric, Adam, and Diane all look at me.

"I found the thumb drive in your room at your parents'." I look Eric in the eye so he'll know I'm not ashamed, that I don't feel like I've done anything wrong. He looks away. "The files were all encrypted, so I gave the drive to Peter to see if he could open them. He decrypted them and sent them back to me. I guess he showed them to you too," I say to Adam. Whose eyes narrow, as though he finds me an interesting specimen.

"So you know," he says, "how many times your life has been overwritten."

40

ADAM'S WORDS OPEN DIMENSIONS IN MY MIND, POSSIBILITIES that seem infinite, like one of those expandable balls that looks like a mini-universe when you're on drugs, but really it's just plastic.

"All I really know," I say, "is that one minute I was a painter living in Chicago, and the next I was a glorified housewife in Michigan." I'm finding it difficult to separate this version of Adam from my friend, my running buddy who's so easy to talk to. "I was just trying to figure out what the hell had happened to my life."

A brief silence falls. Then Diane speaks up. "Wait. Are you saying you remember another timeline?"

"Yeah."

Adam's eyes widen. "So you're an observer."

"What's an observer? You guys keep saying that. I don't know what it means."

"Someone who's able to perceive the changes in worldlines caused by reWinds. Usually it's just one person, the one who initiates the jump, but . . . wow. This changes everything."

I don't like the way he's looking at me, like I'm a problem to solve.

Eric evidently doesn't either. "She has nothing to do with this," he says. "The only reason she remembers is because there's a bug somewhere."

"Which is your fault, according to the error messages we're getting," Adam says, his attention shifting back to Eric. "'Loop closure required.' 'Waiting for fatal discrepancy resolution.' Those mean anything to you?"

"Loop closure . . ." Eric's gaze drifts to the ceiling as he retreats inward. "The only thing I can think of is that last time I used gnii, it used a previous jump-off point as a destination. Kelly's birthday, her twenty-ninth . . . On my very first jump, I left from there, and on my most recent one, I arrived there from a year in the future. Gnii picked the exact destination point. I've always let it do that in order to save resources, so I didn't think it would be a problem."

"How many times have you done this?" Adam asks.

Eric's face abstracts again. After a moment he says, "Um, five." He clears his throat. Studiously avoids looking at me.

"That's more than you reported in the files on the drive."

"Yeah. Those are just the ones where I landed back in high school. I didn't write up reports on the other two. It seemed risky, and by then I'd . . . Things had changed."

"What changed?"

Eric glares at him. "I didn't feel like working for you anymore."

Adam does his simultaneous eyebrow-and-mouth quirk. "Why not?"

"I'd rather not say."

"You'd rather not say?" Adam purses up his lips like Eric did, mocking him. He'd been resting his gun on the table, but now he raises the muzzle in Eric's general direction. "How about you tell me anyway?"

Eric takes a breath, girding himself. "You . . . you and Kelly . . . you'd met at one of the Innovation Park happy hours. Started running together. And then I found out you were having an affair."

Adam glances at me, raising his eyebrows in an appraising way. He's surprised, obviously, but I realize I'm not. All of a sudden, certain experiences make a lot more sense. My hallucinations in the woods and in the Brazier. That must have been one of our meeting places.

Eric stares holes in the table as he continues talking in that same toneless voice. "I confronted Kelly about it, and she . . ." He raises his eyes to mine, as angry and hurt as if he's talking to the version of me who actually did these things. "You left me," he says. "For him."

I feel a perverse sense of shame, followed by a fierce urge to defend myself. "So you thought you'd just go back and fix it."

His eyes fall to the table again, his breath trembling as it goes in and out. "I had to."

The aggrieved note in his voice is what really gets me riled. "Why? Why couldn't you work things out with me like a normal person? Obviously there was something wrong in our marriage, if I was having an affair."

"I—"

"Or you could have accepted that it wasn't going to work. That we, you and me, weren't going to work." I gesture between us. "You'd think after five times, you could take a hint!"

The echo of my voice dies away. Eric looks like I've slapped him. Then he says, "That was actually the fourth time."

"What?"

"That was the fourth time. The second to last. The time after that . . . You're right—I could have done things differently. I should have gotten you to go to the doctor before we— We were trying to have a baby." His voice cracks on the word *baby*. "We had a couple setbacks—"

"Setbacks?"

"You, um, you lost the pregnancies. And you wanted to give up, and you're right, you're absolutely right, I could have been more sensitive, I shouldn't have pushed you to keep trying . . ." He's babbling, agitated, as though I'm arguing with him, or maybe he's arguing with a version of me that isn't here. "But we were so close to getting it right." His hands form fists in his lap, then loosen.

I don't remember any of this. Maybe because it's in the future, rather than the past, of a different timeline. I do remember my memory of the wine tasting off last night, a reflection of a reflection, and of course Eric's panic when we had unprotected sex. I must have conceived soon after my birthday—maybe even on my birthday—and miscarried not long after. A couple, he said. A couple setbacks. I feel sick.

Eric takes a breath like he's going to continue, but I say, "Stop." I can't take one more revelation on top of everything else. He prevented me from going to art school more than once, pressured me to get pregnant, wouldn't let me leave him. How can knowing more possibly help?

He opens his mouth again, and I say, "No. Stop. You don't need to tell me anything more." I sound so tired. "There's nothing you can say that will make me forgive you."

Eric shrinks back. "I'm sorry," he whispers, but it means nothing. He means nothing.

I turn to Adam. "And if you want my opinion, reWind shouldn't exist at all. People shouldn't be able to fuck with other people's lives like that, whether they know about it or not."

"You want me to kill him for you?" Adam says. I gawk at him in horror until he breaks into loud laughter. "I'm just kidding, don't look like that. I mean"—he shrugs—"I am going to kill him."

"What?" I say.

"What?" Diane says, from her spot.

"He's an observer," Adam explains. "They both are. With them gone—with no one left who has memories of alternate worldlines—the timelines will collapse into the one that makes the fewest changes in the status quo. Gnii can create a closed timeline curve like it's trying to, and then reWind will work again."

Which means missing dogs will stay missing, and dead people will stay dead. Unless someone else—Adam, I suppose—travels back and creates another worldline.

"You told me we were dealing with sophisticated saboteurs," Diane says, "who needed twenty-four-hour surveillance. But these people obviously have no idea what they're doing. I'm not going to prison for murdering an innocent couple."

"Diane." Adam enunciates the syllables in a way that makes it clear it's not her real name, his tone perfectly balanced between patronizing and hectoring, and the peanut-gallery part of my brain mutters, *You got away from Eric, only to end up with this guy? Girl, you need to take a break from men.* "You don't fully understand the science. But I'm telling you, this will fix our problem. Or go a long way toward fixing it."

Diane's not having it. Shaking her head, she holsters her gun. "I'm out. I quit." She moves toward the foyer.

Then several things happen at once.

Adam's on his feet and around the table before I can see how he got there. His gun, which had been aimed somewhere between Eric and me, now points at Diane. Who has re-drawn on Adam.

As far as I know, Eric's never fired a gun in his life, so I don't know why he goes for Diane's instead of trying to escape. But his movement gives me an opening. The sliding glass door is closest. I'll have to unlock it first. Don't run toward the woods; run around the house to the street. Climb the fence. Remember to scream for help—

My chair scrapes as I shove it back. I feel it without hearing it, because the sound of Adam's gun going off drowns it out.

It's not loud, barely louder than the chair's feet on the tile. A small explosion that echoes flatly against the walls in the sudden silence.

Eric slumps to the floor.

Adam's gun is small caliber, doesn't make a big hole, but a dark stain spreads quickly across the front of Eric's shirt. Adam and Diane stare down at him. There's an eerie silence, except for Eric's ragged attempts at breathing, his whimpering, and I realize it's not silent after all; the silence is inside my head. I've already hit the floor, so I crawl over to him and stack my hands on top of his chest, guided by dim memories of cop shows. I center them where the stain begins. *Firm pressure. Stop the bleeding.* It won't stop. Eric's blood coats my hands.

His eyes, narrowed with pain, find mine. His lips move.

"Don't try to talk." My voice is a croak. My hands look gloved, now, like Adam's. "You're gonna be okay." He's not. I feel sad about that, somewhere inside myself.

"Fuck!" I hear Diane yelling. "Fuck!"

Eric's mouthing something at me. His breath comes out in a rasp. "Hello . . ."

"Eric, I'm serious, shut the fuck up."

He smiles a little. "Hello . . . gnii. Wake words." His gaze shifts past me and I think, *Oh shit, this is it,* but what can I do, what the fuck can I do?

"Eric. Eric." I repeat his name like a spell that will keep him alive. His eyelashes flutter at the sound of my voice. Such lovely eyelashes, long and full; why am I thinking about eyelashes?

His mouth moves again. "Let's kill . . ."

A presence comes up behind me. I lean closer to Eric. *Don't touch me, don't take me away, I can save him.* "Let's kill some astronauts," Eric breathes. His mouth moves once more, but there's no breath behind the words.

A strong hand takes me by the shoulder, hauling me backward. I try to scramble to my feet but the hand shoves me back down to my knees, soaking them with the blood covering the floor. Adam's above me, so I have to twist my neck around painfully to look at him. His gun's still in his other hand, the one not holding me.

"Fuck," Diane says again, sounding like she's stuck in a really bad traffic jam. "I can't fucking believe this shit, I can't—"

Adam looks down at me, his face blank. "I'm really sorry about this, Kelly."

I fight the panic. Bite back the cringing, crawling words in my mouth. *Please don't kill me. I won't say anything to anyone. I'll do whatever you want.* The drive not to die is more tenacious than dignity or logic. I manage a "Fuck you," and he chuckles, half-admiring.

"It'll be quicker if you don't resist," he says. I'm having trouble keeping my breathing steady. My heart throbs in my ears, making it hard for me to think. The sensation of having a gun pointed at me, knowing it's about to go off, is like an out-of-body experience. I can't make myself believe my life is about to end. I can't breathe. Black flowers burst around the edges of my vision. My head wants to droop, but I fight to keep it raised. I have the superstitious notion that as long as I keep an eye on the gun, he can't shoot me with it.

"Turn around," Adam says, but my last act of defiance will be to make him look me in the face while he kills me. He lets go of my shoulder and I catch sight of the smartwatch on his wrist, above his glove. The watch with gnii installed on it.

He said jumps weren't working, wouldn't work until Eric and I were both dead, but he could have been wrong. Maybe Eric's backdoor would have worked. Since we entered this room, Eric could have used reWind to avoid this entire situation. I wish he had.

"I said turn around." Adam plunges his fingers into my hair and turns my head himself, forcing me to face Eric's body. Eric lies on the floor, his eyes open in a horrible, slack, dead way. He was fighting to speak at the end, but he wasn't making any sense. Joking. He must have thought he was somewhere else.

I remember the shapes his mouth made. *Go back.*

Adam releases me with a shove that tells me I'd better not move. I'm still terrified, but now I've got hold of a thread that might lead me out of here.

Go back. Eric was trying to tell me something after all. Back to when?

The way my life had gone, I couldn't see any way to fix it from where I was.

Back to the beginning, of course.

That's impossible. The only way to make a long-term jump is to use the code Eric added when he worked at gnii, and I don't have the trigger phrase that enables that code.

The realization hits me in a bright flare. Our joke, our astronaut joke. I thought he was drifting, but he was giving me the keys. *Let's kill some astronauts.* That's the trigger phrase. It has to be.

But I need a command. *Go back* is too general, despite what Eric's session reports said about not specifying a destination.

When is the beginning? When I was born? The moment Eric and I first met? When I agreed to go out with him?

Loop closure required. That was one of the error messages, gnii trying to tell its makers why it wouldn't work. Closing the loop can mean tying up loose ends, or cutting them off. I think of the business-speak my graphic design clients sometimes email at me. *Let's close the loop on this. Let's circle back.* I think of my morning runs, how I go for miles, over and over the same ground, and always end up back home.

Through the blood pulsing in my ears, I hear Diane saying to Adam, "Do it, if you're going to. Then let's clean up and get the fuck out of here." She sounds resigned.

Close the loop. It has to work. It's worth trying; it's not as if I have any other options.

Hello, gnii. Let's kill some astronauts. Close the loop. The wake words, the trigger phrase, and the command. The magic words.

I pull in a breath, close my eyes, and speak them quickly, before Adam can stop me.

41

A BRIGHT TONE FROM ADAM'S WATCH, ONE I HAVEN'T HEARD before, makes me open my eyes. He lets out a muffled exclamation and I start to turn around, so the shot catches me in the shoulder rather than the back of the head.

The floor comes up to meet me. I hear another firework blast and pain bursts in my back.

It didn't work. I can't make myself care very much. I wonder, distantly, if I'll continue to exist in some form once my body is gone. But then the room spins, a wild juddering that slams me back into the physical world with nausea and pain. It's bad when I close my eyes, worse when I open them and see that everything remains stationary: the table legs, Adam's feet in running shoes, the blood-slicked tile under my cheek, all in stillness. The motion is inside me. The pain ratchets up to intolerable levels. I hear myself groaning and whimpering in agony. Then I'm drifting away: from the pain, but also from my body. Dying, that's what it is. I'm dying.

I feel a blast of panic as I try to hold on to consciousness, to keep from sliding over the cliff. But there's no edge to grasp. No more body. Nothing

---

FEAR IS PHYSICAL. With no heart to pound, skin to sweat, or glands to secrete adrenaline, I'm no longer rooted in space or time at all. And so, after one final burst of alarm, I'm not afraid.

Yet having a consciousness without a body is the most disorienting thing I've ever experienced. I could dissipate at any moment, if moments existed here, in this place that is no place. I'm in the process of doing so, and it takes eons. Or—it's no time at all, negative time, a replaying of the same hundred millionth of a second over and over and over, wiping a little more of me away with each pass. Dispersing what was me, what was Kelly, into stardust among the rest of the universe's matter and energy until I'm caught up in the rhythm, part of a system so immense that any single entity is a speck inside a speck inside a speck. I perceive scenes from my own life, the life of Kelly—who I am not, but who I have always been and never was—as part of the pattern, not in terms of good or bad or even a linear narrative. Nothing matters the way it did when I was inside it. And yet everything does, every tiny thing, every breath and leaf falling and star being born and cell going to its programmed death. The eternal balance of order and entropy. If I could only let go, let go of that last remaining fragment of myself and truly become part of it—I'd get it, I'd grasp it. It wouldn't be me, but I'd be part of it. I just need to stay

42

I'M RUNNING.

I can't see. My head pulses rhythmically (*wah-wah-wah-wah-wah*) and I feel like I've fallen into a cartoon world. The smell of cut grass tickles my nostrils. My legs tremble and my feet falter. I stumble to a stop.

Light leaks back into my vision, and a scream comes from my right.

"Kelly! What the fuck are you doing?"

I bend over, resting my hands on my knees, staring at chalked grass.

"Hey! Uh-uh, Spence, that would be a red card." The voice is authoritative, female, familiar. I raise my head. A tall, solidly built woman with a braided ponytail jogs across the field toward me. In my peripheral vision, other figures come to their own uncertain stops.

A wave of nausea makes me spit on the ground. I puke a stream of thin, darkish liquid. *Good thing I didn't eat a big lunch,* I think, and then I'm confused. When was the last time I ate? The stir-fry in Eric's and my kitchen?

"Oh, hey, Holter, you all right?" The woman's hand rests on my back, and her name falls into my mind. Ms. Díaz, my soccer coach. We all call her Ms. Tara. I'm at practice.

It's my seventeenth birthday.

In the future, or in a dark parallel universe, my husband lies dead on the kitchen floor of a suburban trilevel and I'm about to die along with him.

The command worked. I sent myself back. I closed the loop.

"Here, drink some water," Ms. Tara says. I straighten, take the bottle she hands me, and swish a mouthful from it. I'm still shaking, my body not yet convinced it's out of danger. "Better?" Ms. Tara asks, after I've taken a longer drink. I nod. "Give her some space, ladies." My teammates are clustering close. Their concern comforts me.

"You gotta stay hydrated," Ms. Tara says to the team at large. "Especially now it's getting warmer out. Okay, we were about done anyway. I'll see you tomorrow! And I want to see! Everyone! With a water bottle!"

Alicia takes Ms. Tara's place beside me, guiding me off the field with a hand on my back. Katie, with an expression somewhere between contrition and rebellion, presses in to give me an aggressive half hug. "You gotta stay hydrated," she booms in my ear in a low-pitched parody of our coach. Now I remember how Katie was always making fun of her for being a lesbian. Not that we knew for sure that she was, or that it would have mattered.

My friends bear me away in a bubble of chatter and laughter, Nicole bringing up the rear. I try to relish being part of a group again. Having friends, real friends. But most of me is still back in that house on Oriskany Way. And then I remember Eric's waiting for me.

The parking lot comes into view. I can't see him yet, but he's there in my mind's eye, stepping forward, his face blank with nerves and hope. He'll have just traveled back for the first time, made his first long-term jump. The one that starts it all, him trying to rewrite the past until he gets it right. He doesn't know yet that he can never get it right. He doesn't know what's in his future.

I have to warn him; I owe him that much. His actions were deeply fucked up, and I'm still not convinced he knew how wrong they were, but in the end he did the right thing. And now he can learn, before he makes the same mistakes again. If he'll listen.

In a bizarre twist, he feels more familiar to me than anything else going on right now. He feels almost like comfort.

"Hey, guys, I just remembered I've got another ride home."

Katie, Nicole, and Alicia all look at me. Our after-practice routine was to go to someone's house (Katie's, usually) and watch TV or make fun of people online until my dad picked me up. "Who do you have a ride home with?" Katie asks.

"This kid from history . . . we've got this class project we need to work on."

"Um, you were puking five minutes ago," Nicole says.

"I'm fine now. I think I just needed to get it out of me." I see Eric, standing by his car, watching us. "We're really behind. See you tomorrow!" I split off before my friends can ask any more questions, hurrying toward Eric with a wave. "Hi!" I say, which makes him start like I've pulled a gun on him. "You're giving me a ride," I tell him sotto voce. "Get in the car. It's okay." He blinks, nods, and moves toward the driver's door.

"Text us when you get home," Katie calls, shooting a glare at Eric. I wave my agreement and get into the passenger seat. Eric has a nice car. Clean. Latin trap blasts from the speakers when he cranks the ignition, and he hurriedly turns down the volume.

"Sorry."

"It's fine." I clasp cold, sweaty hands together in my lap. I have no idea how to begin. Eric eases out of the parking lot. I keep quiet until we've joined the flow of traffic on Main Street. Andromeda Creek's tiny; we'll be at my house in five minutes.

"So," we both say at the same time.

"You first," Eric says.

Me first. I have to step out onto the limb. What if none of this has been real at all? It's a possibility. But if I've learned one thing from all this, it's that doubt and hesitation won't get me anywhere good.

"Okay, don't freak out," I say. "I know about the time travel."

43

HE TAKES IT PRETTY WELL, AT FIRST. HE BLUSHES WITH PLEA-sure when I mention we got married. But he starts to look un-comfortable as I get into the weeds.

"So I guess I shouldn't write those reports." He takes a sip of his Coke; we're sitting in the parking lot at Burger King.

That's what he got out of my story? Don't leave a paper trail? "No, you shouldn't do any of it, because A, you end up dead, and B, manipulating someone else's life to suit your desires is wrong."

"It's not manipulation," he counters. "It's iterating until you get it right."

"Right for who? I made choices you didn't like, so you went back and erased them. Do you honestly not see how terrible that is?" He gets a mulish look on his face, so I press on before he can argue with me. "We're back at the beginning. You can break the cycle, this obsessive pattern you got into. It's like that expres-sion, right? 'When you're a hammer, everything looks like a nail.' Well, when you have a time machine, every problem looks like a reason to go back and fix it. But I'm telling you now, it's not. That's not how you solve problems."

He looks at me and I can see it, the moment he realizes he's not going to get what he wants. His perfect date he's been planning for years, his dream girlfriend, his tranquil marriage. None of it's going to happen. And it's his own fault.

I soften my tone. "I know you didn't mean to bring disaster on us. You just wanted something you didn't have before. That's understandable. But you don't need me to have a good life! You can work on yourself all on your own. For yourself, not for me or anyone else."

He's silent for so long I start to feel nervous. If he raises his voice, if he does anything even the slightest bit threatening, I'm out of here. I'll walk home, or better yet, go inside Burger King and call my dad. I reach up to play with my necklace before realizing it's not there.

I jump when he speaks, though his voice is quiet. "We don't know for sure that you fixed it. That the error won't happen again in the future. I guess we won't know until twelve years from now. And we've already deviated from the original timeline, the one where I never went back. You telling me all this will affect what happens."

"Yeah, and maybe I shouldn't have. But I wanted you to be able to make your own choices." *Like I didn't get to.* "It would be impossible to do everything exactly the same way." And, I realize, I wouldn't want to. There are definitely things I would do differently. Take some business courses, for a start.

"We don't know what else might have changed, even if the loop-closure error is resolved." He looks more hopeful about this than otherwise, and I remember there's probably a lot he would change too. Now he'll get the chance. "We should make a contingency plan."

"For what, your old boss showing up and trying to kill us?"

"For whatever might happen. We'll need to keep up with the development of gnii, or anything like it."

"Sure." I eat a cold French fry out of the paper bag, make a face, and stare out the window at cars going through the drive-through.

"Kelly."

I don't look at him.

"I understand why you're angry. I mean, listening to you talk about how different your life turned out when you were with me. I understand how you'd feel manipulated."

I still don't look at him.

"I didn't mean to . . . That's not what I wanted to do at all. I just wanted to be close to you."

"You don't even know me."

"But I want to."

I turn my head, studying him. He glances away but then meets my gaze steadily. I get ready to say that we don't always get everything we want; in fact, very few people get even a small part of what they want. But then I remember that this Eric hasn't committed the abuses the other one did. Not yet. It wouldn't be fair for me to treat him as if he has.

Underneath that thought is the cold voice of reason, telling me not to leave him without hope, because men without hope are liable to do desperate things.

"Let's live our lives and see what happens," I say.

He looks at me a moment longer, as if he's memorizing my face. Then he says, "Okay. I'll type up what I can remember tonight." He smiles. "I wonder if the company can sue me for violating a nondisclosure agreement from another timeline."

"If they can't, obviously they have no problem going with plan B." I sit back in my seat, massaging my forehead.

"Are you okay?"

In my state, I'm touched deeply enough by the concern in his voice that tears come to my eyes. "Are you?"

He waves a hand, a pushing-aside gesture. It reminds me of him as my husband. How he'd take on difficulties for me, shield me from them. More often than I wanted, but it came from a place of love.

"I'll take you home," he says. He puts his hand on the key in the ignition but doesn't turn it. A wistful expression crosses his face. "Our date . . . I had it all planned out like you said. I was going to take you to *Les Mis*. Fancy restaurant. Everything perfect."

"Really knock my socks off?"

"Yeah, well, I knew I'd have to."

"Listen, Eric . . . you're a nice guy." His face shuts down. "I mean, you're a good person. I like you."

"But not that way."

I let out a sigh. "We've both lived through this age; we know how hard it is to figure out who you are. And I think you really need to. I know I do. So let's do that. Okay?"

He pauses, like he's trying to think of something to say that will bring me around. For a half second, I almost want him to. Then he says, "If that's what you want." As he starts the car and pulls out of the parking lot, he looks solemn but not miserable, which I hope means he's taken in everything I've said and will consider it deeply. We ride through town in silence, both of us wrapped in our own thoughts.

It's still too early for my dad to be home, but my mother's car is in the driveway. "I'll see you at school," I say. "And I'll text you about the thing. Operation Don't Let Eric Get Killed Again."

"Operation Sidestep." His mouth pulls up on one side.

"That's catchy, I like it."

He glances at me, surprised, and his ironic little half smile turns into a real one. I let myself smile back. He's so young; both of us are. In the past twelve years of memory, I've seen more of his face than of my own. I've watched him transition into adulthood, and he's watched me. But this version of him doesn't remember it. This version will have to grow up on his own.

I lean over and kiss his cheek, an impulse I regret as soon as I lean away and see the hope on his face. "Okay," I say. "Bye."

He waits to back out of the driveway until I get inside. As I step into the kitchen, my mother calls from her and my dad's room, "Kelly? Is that you?"

"It's me." My voice doesn't sound quite like mine: it's more high-pitched, clearer than the one I'm used to. Newer.

But it's me.

My mother comes into the kitchen. "Who was that that dropped you off?"

I forgot she can see the street from her room. And I forgot about parents, the need to manage and circumvent them.

"This guy Eric from school. You remember, we did the history paper together."

Her eyebrows lift. "Oh. So he's giving you rides home now?"

The old inclination rises in me to deflect, to put up walls and keep her out. But behind her challenge I can sense her simple wish to connect, and I'm more aware now of what I'd lost with her. What I'd never really had, not since I was young and we both learned I wasn't as much like her as I looked. Closeness. Trust. Our relationship has been defined by resistance, by our subtle and not-so-subtle opposition to each other. Maybe we can do better this time. I think about the bomb in her chest. I'll have to remind her to get her mammograms. So many things to remember now.

I lean against the counter. "He . . . likes me."

Her face softens. "Do you like him?"

I start to say no, but what comes out of my mouth is "I'm still kind of figuring that out."

"Well, don't take too long. It doesn't pay to be too picky, you know. That's how you end up without a date to prom."

The dig is not subtle. *Got it: I should settle for anyone who looks at me twice.* I don't say it—those words belong to an older, tireder me—but now I remember why talking to my mother raises my blood pressure.

Then she smiles and hugs me, and I soften a little. "Go get cleaned up, birthday girl," she says. "I'm making spaghetti. And we have a cake."

Alone in my childhood bedroom, the weirdness of all this breaks over me. I can hardly fathom what's happened in the last day, from my perspective, let alone my entire adult life. I could drive myself mad trying to make sense of it. Better, for now, to let it wash over me and see if any conclusions reveal themselves.

I text Katie to let her know I'm home, turning off my phone afterward to duck her inevitable questions. I take a shower in this old-new body that hasn't made any irreversible mistakes yet. I've been given the gift and the burden of choice. Not of complete foresight, however: I won't retrace the path of any of my former lives. I know that much.

Dressed, I lie on my bed, watching the early evening light slant through my window. My mother's kitchen noises are comfortingly familiar. My thoughts turn to Eric and the shared purpose that links us together. I feel a sense of responsibility for him, of obligation, and maybe something more, but I'm not sure it's enough to sustain any kind of relationship.

In art school, I learned that failure is not an end but a beginning. You have to give yourself permission to stumble on the way to figuring things out, because that's the only way to push boundaries. It's the same with technology: failure is a step on the path to innovation. Of course, underlying that tenet is the expectation that eventually you succeed, or else fade into obscurity, which has always been my biggest fear. And now I know why the prospect of being ordinary scared me so much: not because it's unpleasant, but because it's so easy. I learned that in art school too: that especially if you come into success, the temptation will be to keep reworking the formula that launched you, rather than compete with your earlier self to get better. The worst thing you can do is get into a pattern where you're just repeating yourself.

Gnii offers—will offer—the benefit of failure without the consequences: infinite chances to get things right, or some nebulous and ever-changing definition of *right*. I told not-Adam I didn't think gnii should exist, and I still don't, even after it saved my life and Eric's. Isn't that part of the urgency and beauty of life, that you get only one? If you can go back and do it over as many times as you want, then it's like listening to the same playlist over and over until your favorite songs, the ones that raised goose bumps on your arms at first listen, become nothing more than background noise.

I don't know if Eric will agree with me, or how much we'll be able to do to prevent gnii from coming into being. You can't stop progress. The foresight I have now is an illusion, but I feel as though things will end up in a better place this time, and not just because they ended so badly before. I don't have any more control than I did previously, but this time I won't let fear drive or limit me. I have to try, even if I fail, because nothing is certain, ever, for anyone.

I can live with that.

44

Twelve years later

I'VE BEEN AT THE GALLERY FOR HOURS, MAKING SURE EVERY-
thing is ready, control-freaking despite all the preparation of the
last several weeks. I'm exhausted before the first attendee steps
through the door, but it's worth it: I want everything to be perfect. This is my night.

I get a second wind as friends start coming in. They con-
gratulate me on my first solo show, and some of them even
remember to wish me a happy birthday. "Twenty-nine, right?
Saturn return!" cries a woman I vaguely remember from art
school, one of several of us who moved to New York to try our
luck. It was a bold choice that paid off in my case, less so in hers:
she teaches yoga now.

When she hugs me I get a whiff of rosemary essential oil. "So
many fundamental shifts are happening in our lives right now,"
she says, earnest as a fortune-teller. "Even the positive ones can
be overwhelming. I've got a little business, I can hook you up
with crystals, wellness cleanses, extracts . . . I'll give you friend
prices!" She hands me a card and I squirrel it into the pocket of

my dress—I made sure to wear a dress with pockets—to throw away later.

It's started to rain, and as the rooms fill up they begin to smell faintly of wet wool. People laugh, drink, eat; some even look at the art. My friend Alicia from high school comes with her wife. My phone buzzes repeatedly as people from home, and from my life after I left Michigan, text me their congratulations. My parents can't be here since Mom's finishing her last round of chemo—I plan to fly home for a visit next month—but Dad messaged earlier. Happy birthday Bug we'll be thinking of you on your big night Mom says tell you she's proud of you. My favorite text—from Nick's phone, though it isn't from Nick—consists of a long string of emojis and hi aunt K this is Malik!! My dad said to say good luck so Good luck and happy birthday love Malik.

I feel buoyed with love and good wishes. I hold a glass of wine but sip from it infrequently; it's there mostly so I have something in my hands. I don't want my senses dulled. This— the crowd, the buzz about me in the art world, future reviews and features and sales—is not what my work is about. It's not the fruit of my labor: my work is the fruit of my labor. But that doesn't mean I don't enjoy it.

I can't point to one single factor that's led to my success, though certain events have had outsize influence. My decision to move to New York, obviously. Before that, the fellowship that allowed me to get my MFA, funded by a consortium of tech-startup founders who are also avid collectors. I've found a sat-isfying irony in the fact that apps paid for my degree. In my former lives, the lack of positive feedback dragged me down, but this time each small accomplishment has created forward momentum that motivates me to work harder, to push myself and achieve more. Progress is addictive, in art as in all other areas.

The profiles and previews that have come out about me are mostly positive and thoughtful. I'm an artist to watch, which brings more attention and money, which in turn offer a measure of security. For now, at least, I have the freedom to make work instead of patching together flexible paying gigs as I'd been doing for the past few years. There were times when I thought about moving back to Chicago, where life is slightly cheaper and more gentle. But I stayed and it's paid off, at least for the moment. I know how precarious success can be, but even a little makes me happy. And I know, in my heart, that the work deserves the attention.

I've been thinking about this series for years, but I started working on it only eighteen months ago. It stands in stark contrast to my prior work, which is mostly abstract, but I think some of the impetus behind it has been in every painting I've ever made. I only waited to make the concept explicit.

The series consists of self-portraits, photo-realistic, painted with a double-exposure effect so there are always two of me. One version faces the viewer, while the other focuses on her surroundings. In some of the canvases my surroundings are well-defined. A formal living room, furniture standing at right angles, where one of me stands at the window with my back to the viewer while the other, a ghost, peeks from behind a drape. A street with the sun beating down, my face distorted in fear while a shadow creeps over me from behind. In other paintings the surroundings are only a suggestion. In the largest, I'm hardly there at all amid painstakingly layered patterns of lines and color.

Of course, my work draws on my experiences in my former

lives and in that strange in-between space I visited when I jumped back. But it's not a dry well, now that I've drawn from it. There might be enough there to last the rest of my working life. That's what makes me happiest of all.

The door opens and Linnea and Bobby sweep in, each of them embracing me in turn. "Traffic from the airport was kuh-razy," Linnea says, apologizing for being so late. "Our Lyft driver took us on a tour of Queens trying to get around it. Damn, I wish I could have a glass of wine."

"You can have one. Right?" I'm fuzzy on the guidelines about what you can eat and drink during pregnancy, since I don't have any reason to know them. And don't anticipate having one anytime soon, if ever.

"Not in public, unless I want to get dragged for drinking while I'm pregnant." She strokes her protruding belly uncon-sciously. "I'm starting to get used to sacrificing in the name of motherhood." She speaks cheerfully, but she's already had to give up more than alcohol, postponing her own opening because of severe morning sickness during her first trimester.

Bobby's arm encircles her waist as he leans down to kiss her temple. "I'll get you some water, baby," he says, and the casual consideration makes my heart squeeze. I'm single at the mo-ment; it's hard to find someone who's willing to put up with my long hours in the studio, once the first flush of attraction wears off. And I don't date artists anymore. The few with whom I've had relationships seemed to expect that my career, my work, would take second place to theirs. None of them said it outright, but they communicated it through their actions, their lack of support and interest, their general air of entitlement. I'd like to believe I don't have the same attitude, that I would support someone else's success as enthusiastically as I pursue my own, but it wouldn't be true. My mother hints that I'm too selfish to find love. Maybe that's true, although *selfish* isn't the word I'd use. *Driven*, maybe, and a lot of people still aren't prepared to accept that from a woman. But it's who I am, and so far it's been a trade I'm willing to make.

A couple approaches, people who know both me and Linnea, and it's hugs and squeals all around at the sight of her pregnant belly. My dealer draws me aside to schmooze a collector, plucking my empty glass from my hand and replacing it with a full one. After that conversation I head to the bathroom, a trip I complete without incident despite a slight feeling of trepidation as I open the door. I'm conscious that this is an anniversary of sorts.

I release myself back into the gallery and continue circulating, all the time keeping an eye on the door. I'm watching it because of another message I got earlier. I'd like to greet the person who sent it right away: he'll be out of his element here.

I told Eric he didn't have to come to my opening, though he was welcome. More than welcome. I haven't seen him in months, but we have a private chat going where we keep up with each other's lives, among other things. Last time I was home I swung through Detroit, where he lives, and we had dinner. It was nice.

I want to come, he responded with his trademark intensity, which doesn't bother me now that I know the obsession behind it is gone. You've been talking about your work, I'd like to see it. And you.

Maybe the obsession's not completely gone.

Finally I see him, stowing his umbrella in the stand by the door. He gives a faint smile when he sees me waving, and he ducks his head as he makes his way through the crowd. His hair's longer than last time I saw him. I meet him halfway, and we exchange a calibrated hug. He wishes me a happy birthday, but to my relief he hasn't brought a gift. "You look great," I say. He does. He definitely hasn't been skipping the gym.

"So do you." He looks around. "Pretty impressive crowd."

I shrug. "It's mostly friends." Which isn't true, but around Eric I still feel the urge to minimize my ambitions and achievements. I don't know why: he's been nothing but supportive. "Olivia couldn't make it?"

"She had to study for her boards." Eric's girlfriend is in her second year of medical school. I've never met her, though they've been dating for more than a year, and every time I talk to him I half expect to hear they've broken up. I hope he's not as wishy-washy when he's actually in her presence.

"But she's good?"

"Oh, yeah, she's great," he says vaguely, still looking around. "So, what do I do, walk around and stare at the paintings until I feel something?" One side of his mouth pulls up so I know he's joking. Sort of. But I'm glad Eric's comfortable enough with me that he won't pretend to gush.

"If you want. Let me show you this one, though." I usher him over to stand in front of *Untitled 4 | InBetween*. Something shifts in his face as he takes it in. The light and shadow, the fractals that combine to suggest a person that's not a person.

"You . . ." He looks shaken, and I can't tell whether my work has touched or upset him. "You painted it. The . . ." He waves his hand around, gesturing something that can't be communicated in words.

"I call it the inbetween."

He nods, still staring at the painting. He reaches a hand

toward it, then pulls back. "It's . . . I mean, I'm not sure it's accurate, visually"— I roll my eyes, inwardly—"but it brings back the . . . the feeling."

"That's what I wanted to do. It took me months to get it right." And now some collector will hang it in their guest bathroom. C'est la vie.

Unless . . . "You can have it." It's a thoughtless thing for me to say. Apart from giving up the money, the painting might already be spoken for. But Eric's one of the few people in the world who can truly understand it; one of the few who have the first-hand experience to know whether I've accomplished my goal.

Eric pales noticeably. "Thank you, but I don't really have a place for it." I don't think he's talking about the size of his apartment.

He steps away, though still within the painting's sight lines, and I get the impression he wants to get some distance while still being able to keep an eye on it. "I've been keeping up with our project."

A tiny flare of adrenaline lights in my stomach, and I wonder if there's another reason Eric wanted to be here, with me, on this particular night. "Anything new?"

"Not really. Gnii exists, they're working on revolutionary projects, blah blah blah."

"What does Peter say?"

Eric shakes his head. "He never talks about work. And I haven't asked him anything directly."

"We're never going to find anything out if you won't use your connections."

"I don't want to jeopardize his job."

"Eric. This is your life here. And not just yours." I'm surprised at him, being so cavalier. "He didn't bite when you asked if they were hiring?"

"I'm overqualified for QA, and apparently I'm not good enough to even get an interview as an engineer." He smiles ruefully. "You should've gone back further, so I could get my grades up and get into Stanford."

He's joking. I hope. I never expected either of us to arrange our lives around this project, but this version of Eric's life has followed an arc as different from the others as mine. He still attended Michigan State, but he did a lot better, and now he's a software developer at one of the startups occupying the renovated Book Tower.

"Have you noticed . . . anything?"

"Anomalies, you mean? Nope." But he looks thoughtful.

"If something happens . . ." We don't know if anything will actually change, or what form that change would take. I suppose we won't know until almost two weeks from now, at the moment from which I jumped back. I've imagined him being plunged into a new life, or remembering his own death, or just being inundated with memories from other timelines. Any of those scenarios would be traumatic. "You'll tell me, right?"

"Of course."

"I wouldn't want you to have to go through it alone."

Something flickers in his eyes as he looks into mine. "Thanks."

He holds my gaze until I give him a friendly, distancing smile and find a reason to look away. I hope that flicker was only gratitude. I know Eric would travel to the ends of the earth to help me, but there's still a fundamental lack of trust even after twelve years: his betrayal went that deep. I wonder if he'd still possess me if he could.

A part of me wants him to go through the same abrupt shift I did, so he can see for himself how upsetting it is.

"Oh," he says, reaching into his pocket for his phone, "I almost forgot." Which means he's been waiting to show me whatever it is all night. He brings up a photo, angling the screen toward me. "Look who I found."

"Holy shit." I gasp, taking the phone from him. "This can't be him." In the picture, a dog peers curiously up at the camera, as though it might be food. His tail is blurred, his ears perked, and he could be Bear's twin.

"Does he look like the dog we had?"

"Exactly." It gives me an uncomfortable feeling, thinking of the close attention Eric's given to my description of our life together, a life lived in a timeline he doesn't remember. He's been good about respecting my boundaries this time around, but the unease remains.

"He was in the shelter in Davis City. I've been cruising by there, sometimes, when I visit my parents." Eric glances down, as if the departure from logic embarrasses him.

"Did you adopt him?"

"Yeah. It was kind of weird when I met him. I mean, some of those dogs are friendly, but as soon as he saw me he started whining and pressing up against the bars of the crate like . . ."

"Like you were his long-lost person."

"Yeah. The people at the shelter said he'd never done that with anyone before. And there was a connection on my side too." Which means Eric definitely, without a doubt, knew with every fiber of his being that this was his dog. That makes me feel better, like maybe not everything is about me.

"He always did like you best." I hand the phone back.

Eric laughs a little. "I think he's got a new favorite human. Check this out." He swipes to a video and plays it for me. It's almost a minute of Olivia playing with Possibly Bear, who's plainly smitten. Olivia, I notice, is stunning despite the fact that she's wearing joggers and a T-shirt. All luminous skin and glossy chestnut hair. "She even named him."

"Oh!" For some reason, it surprises me that they'd give him a new name. "What do you call him?"

"Gaius."

"As in Caesar?"

"No, it's from a show we both watched when we were kids. Spaceships, cyborgs, you wouldn't've heard of it." He waves a hand, dismissing something formative enough that his dog's name came from it, and it strikes me that this is one piece of information about himself he never shared with me in our last life. Probably one of many.

"Did you tell her what his name used to be?"

Eric hesitates, as though he knows I'm not going to like what he says next. "I've never said anything to her about all that. It's been such a long time, you know? And I don't even remember most of it firsthand. It's almost like . . ." He trails off awkwardly, looking over my shoulder into the thinning crowd.

Almost like it never happened. I'd bet my career that's what he was about to say.

My instinct, as always, is to smooth things over. "Sure. I get it." But I feel a new separation between us, with this distance he's attempting to get from our common experience. It's something that needs to be there, but it's still bittersweet.

And I can't help but add, "I just hope you won't forget everything." By that I mean the lesson he's supposed to have learned about not trying to control other people's lives, but as soon as the words are out I realize how he could misinterpret them.

His face softens. "No." I see surprise in his expression, but no sharpening, none of that alarming intensity. Okay. Let him think I remember our time together fondly. I can give him that much.

"I think some of us are going to get dinner after this," I say. "You want to come?"

I don't expect him to say yes, and he doesn't. He makes his excuses—long day, family friends to see in Brooklyn tomorrow, souvenir shopping for his cousin's kids—and I accept them. I thank him for coming, for making the effort. We walk to the door and he collects his umbrella. "Give Gaius a tummy rub for me," I say. He nods.

We embrace one last time, and when he steps back he says, "You know I wish you all good things."

"Me too," I say, and it's true. I want happiness for him, which includes the understanding that even when you can't have what you want—what you think you want—there's always another path.

He smiles, and turns, and walks out into the rain.

Acknowledgments

Heartfelt and immense gratitude to the following folks, as well as others too numerous to name:

My editor, Jen Monroe, who is a dream to work with and (fortunately!) never hesitates to tell me when something isn't quite working, along with everyone else at Berkley and Penguin Random House who made this book better and shinier: Eileen G. Chetti for deft and thorough copyedits, Ashley Tucker for book design, Andreea Robescu and Emily Osborne for my perfectly dark and disorienting cover, and the rest of the production team.

The marketing and publicity team at Berkley: Lauren Burnstein, Tara O'Connor, Jessica Mangicaro, and the rest, who make a tough job look easy with grace, enthusiasm, and boatloads of talent. Thanks so much as well to reviewers and bookish social media mavens of every platform who have helped push *The Other Me* into the hands of readers.

My agent, Joanna MacKenzie, who is always up for brainstorming about my characters' dark secrets, and the entire team at Nelson Literary Agency: Angie Hodapp and Maria Heater for timely inspiration, Sam Cronin and Brian Nelson on the all-important contracts and financial side, Tallahj Curry and Omar Medina for keeping things running, and of course Kristin Nelson, who's made me feel so welcome.

My early readers: Rachel Skelsey-Beard; my mom, Debbie Overweg (who probably wasn't expecting the sex scenes); and Mei Davis, as well as my critique group (Felicia Lee, Arleen Wolf, Julia Nelson, Shamrock McShane, Joe Richard, and Charles Boisseau), who motivated me through multiple drafts.

Layne Fargo, one of the first people to champion this book, whose generous help and encouragement made me believe I could actually get published. My other fellow writers who've read and boosted *The Other Me*: your support means everything.

My author support groups: Shakespeare's Sisters (especially B.C. Krygowski and Lauren Beltz), the Berkletes, and the 2021 Debuts group on Facebook. Your advice, cheerleading, and commiseration have been invaluable, and I'm stoked to meet y'all in person when we can go to bars again.

My readers. Thank you for letting my made-up people live in your heads.

My former teachers: Kelly Flynn, who gave me the space to fuck up and find my voice as a writer, and the late Delores Di Giacomo, who told me my writing was beautiful. (And that I had an "evil streak." I still don't know what that was about, but it made me feel seen.)

Stephenie Presseller and Melissa and Joe Basilone: for your friendship and hospitality, and for helping me make fun bad choices in Chicago.

My parents: Bart Zachrich and Debbie Overweg; my bonus dad, the late Steve Overweg; and my in-laws, Samantha Yeh and the late Patrick Jeng. Besides offering love and moral support, all of you helped get me to a place where I have enough privilege to spend a significant amount of time making up stories.

Finally and forever: my family. Sean, who has cheered me on every step of the way even though my books don't have spaceships in them. Claudia, who's still waiting for a story about a dog who saves the world (and who will yell at me if I leave out Inara, who provides endless examples of quirky dog behavior). I love you so much.